ACCLAIM

"Brimming with magic, mystery, beauty, and heart, BETWIXT will enchant you from the first page and weave itself into your very bones. Its lyricism and thought-provoking themes on family, purpose, and responsibility will remain with you long after you read the last page and make you want to read every title the brilliantly talented Kimberly Dunham writes."

—Chelsea Bobulski, author of THE WOOD and REMEMBER ME

"A beautiful walk through the woods, steeped in magic, folklore, and forbidden romance! With prose as beautiful as the foggy mountains the story is backdropped against, BETWIXT will leave you enchanted long after the last page is finished."

—AJ Skelly, author of AN ALLIANCE OF ASH AND JADE and THE RAT KING

"This heartfelt portal fantasy tackles loss, identity, belonging, survival, and first loves. With artful language, Dunham breathes life into nature and the wilds of Alaska, crafting a place you won't want to leave."

—J.P. Lee, author of SHIFT

"Heartfelt and alluring. Betwixt enticed me with a steadily unfurling mystery delivered through vivid writing. I fell headfirst into this fantasy, and the pages simply melted away. Dunham's next book will be an insta-buy for me!"

—Elizabeth Lowham, award-winning author of CASTERS AND CROWNS

BETWIXT

BETWIXT

Quill & Flame
EmberLight

KIMBERLY DUNHAM

Betwixt

To the lonely, the quirky, the awkward. To those pushed outside of belonging.

You matter, and you belong.

PRONUNCIATION GUIDE

Draíocht: Dree-uct

Síorghlas: Sheer-glass

Ealdor: El-door

Síocháin leat: Shee-uh-khawn let

Sylvaen: Sil-vain

Agus tú féin: Ogg-us too hayne

Síocháin libh: Shee-uh-khawn liv

Deartháir mór: Dreh-haar moore

Tine Phreabach: Tinnuh fra-bakh

Dia dhuit ar maidin: Jee-uh gwitch air ma-jin

For a while they stood there, like men on the edge of a sleep where nightmare lurks, holding it off, though they know that they can only come to morning through the shadows.
—J.R.R. Tolkien, *The Two Towers*

CHAPTER 1
WASTELAND

T HE SKY WAS A perfect azure. Below, an ocean of cotton puff clouds drifted by. If Mom had been on the plane with me, I might have cared about the view. No doubt, I would have been ecstatic over the idea of moving to Alaska. But in her absence, all I felt was numb.

I flipped open my sketchbook and smoothed the page. Even with the plane's ventilation system humming in the background, it was easy to forget I was trapped in a glorified bus hanging 35,000 feet in the air. While I worked, I replayed one of the last conversations I'd had with Mom.

"I wish a lot of things could have been different for us."

"Different how?"

She didn't answer at first. "Just...different."

I finished outlining the basic layout of my new drawing. I couldn't remember a time Mom hadn't been guarded about the past. I knew she grew up in Alaska; I should have too. But despite being born there, I had no memories of the place. No stories. Nothing. The lack of information never bothered me though. All parents had their secrets, didn't they?

Soon, I lost myself in the details of my drawing. With every pencil stroke, the string of highway grew bolder. The endless evergreens gained definition. Tree shadows stretched across the page until I felt consumed by them. A few months ago, I had driven through that exact stretch of highway with Mom in southern Oregon. It felt like years had passed since then.

The woman sitting beside me, a brunette in a turquoise raincoat, leaned across the seat for the millionth time to ask me if I was okay. For the millionth time, I lied and told her I was fine. She offered a sympathetic smile. The woman's name was Leslie Foster, and she was some acquaintance of Mom's from years back. I didn't know the details of that either. But even though I had no memories of meeting them, Leslie and her husband Peter were officially my legal guardians. Living with them meant returning to Ketchikan, Alaska, the place of my birth.

Ketchikan was a tourist town nestled along the Inside Passage, the coastal route stretching from Puget Sound to Skagway, Alaska. According to Leslie, it rained a lot in Ketchikan—liquid sunshine, the locals called it. I would have to get used to that. Since Mom took me from there before I was two, everything I knew about the place came from internet searches and the brief time I'd spent with Leslie.

I looked up from my drawing as the plane began its final descent. The shell-pink clouds outside turned to steel. Jagged islands shot up out of the water. Mist swirled over an army of green-clad mountains. And then, the buildings and waterway of Ketchikan began to appear like geometric ghosts rising out of the fog.

"I hate landings," Leslie murmured, clutching the armrest.

I almost smiled. Unlike Mom, Leslie had no problem saying exactly what she was thinking. I took one last look at my drawing before closing my sketchbook and tucking it in my bag.

The plane skimmed the runway with a lurch. My back flattened against my seat as the plane's thrust reversers roared through the cabin. Across the aisle, a baby bawled until, at last, the plane's rocketing decelerated to a crawl.

"C'mon, sweetheart," Leslie said, rising from her seat along with the other passengers. "Let's go find our bags. And my husband."

Just a few minutes later, Leslie and I were waiting at the baggage claim when a broad-shouldered man in plaid caught sight of us and sauntered forward. Leslie waved enthusiastically, but I turned away. It felt like a good time to study the patterned industrial carpet lining the walkway.

"Peter, honey, this is Wren." She greeted her husband with a kiss, then moved to the side so Peter could get a better view. "Look at her. So grown up, so beautiful. She had those same big green eyes as a baby. Remember?"

Peter shifted like he was uncomfortable for me. I appreciated that more than he knew.

"You probably don't remember us, Wren," he said.

I managed a tight smile. Admittedly, it's hard to remember things that happen before age two.

Peter and Leslie helped collect our things from the baggage carousel. It felt weird to think that these strangers had been there to witness my first steps. Mom might have mentioned them to me a time or two. Maybe. She was living with them when I was born. Later, Leslie told me, she helped take care of me while Mom worked on getting her GED. Since Mom wasn't around to verify the facts, I would have to take Leslie's word for it.

"We haven't eaten yet," Leslie murmured to Peter as she hurried toward the airport exit. "Not much appetite."

Peter glanced back at me. "You like fish, right?"

I shrugged. The only fish I'd ever tasted had come from a can.

"We'll work on that," Peter said with a smile.

The wind tore at my hair the moment the airport doors slid open. Leslie turned to offer me her rain jacket, but I declined. I was already taking up space in her home and interrupting her entire life. But by the time we boarded the ferry that would take us from the airport on Gravina Island to Ketchikan, I regretted my decision. My jeans and T-shirt had been more than adequate in Fresno that morning, but the highs in Ketchikan that day were in the low 50s.

The ferry was mostly empty except for a handful of tourists huddled together on one end of the deck. Raindrops plunked down on my arms. Seabirds churned above the water, occasionally diving for fish. Peter pointed out a pod of orcas a few yards off the port side of the ferry. I shivered and pretended to care.

Peter and Leslie approached a black Infiniti parked near the ferry terminal. I took one look at the car and hesitated. Leslie's car looked like something Mom would earn a sideways glance for if she parked her clunky old Honda too close. I checked the bottom of my shoes for gum before climbing inside.

"Might as well show her around on the way," Leslie said, strapping on her seatbelt.

Peter adjusted the heat. "Are you just looking for an excuse to play tour guide again?"

"C'mon, babe. She'll need to know her way around."

Peter looked like he wanted to argue. I held back a sigh of my own. Leslie seemed to be forgetting that I wasn't there on vacation.

The wiper blades beat rhythmically, sweeping water droplets off the windshield. I had always wanted to return to Alaska and see the place where I was born, but not like this. Not without my mom.

We followed the Tongass Highway south and turned onto Mission Street, where a quaint welcome arch boasted "Alaska's First City" and "Salmon Capital of the World." Ketchikan was an assortment of brightly colored coastal buildings—marigolds, eggshell blues, scarlets, purples, and reddish browns—nestled in the crook of the mountains. The colors were captivating, but I felt myself drawn more toward the natural elements: the forest, the water, and the moody gray sky.

Leslie pointed to a cluster of stone-colored buildings peeking through the trees. "That'll be your new school."

"Edgewood High School," Peter added.

Edgewood. The name was fitting. Imposing evergreens stood in rank all around the campus, ready to reclaim the land.

The school disappeared as the road we were taking wound up into the mountains. A wooden forest service sign marked the boundary of the Tongass National Forest. And before long, Ketchikan's vibrant colors were swallowed by the forest. I gazed up at the trees—cedars, hemlocks, and Sitka spruce all soaring into the mist—and felt my chest pinch strangely. I had no idea how deep forests could be, or how beautiful.

Leslie continued sharing facts about the area, but my attention was waning. The forest fascinated me and drew me in. Soon, I lost myself in the trees, in their proud crowns and craggy branches draped and trailing with moss. The scene before me stood in direct opposition to everything I remembered about Fresno.

It was late August when I left the Central Valley, that hellish time of year when temperatures soared into the upper nineties. The sky that morning had looked like bleach-faded denim, exactly like it had the last time Mom picked me up from school.

In a matter of moments, I was back in California, and I could feel the late summer air parching my throat:

The sun was glaring overhead. Heat waves rippled off the pavement, and the strip of grass running alongside the school office had long since given up its will to live. I leaned my head against the stucco behind me and sighed. I'd spent every weekday since school started in that same spot, doing homework while I waited for Mom. I could have dealt with the bus, but Mom insisted on driving me herself. Shielding my eyes, I tried to imagine that the far-off Sierra Nevadas were enormous snow cones. But if I had a snow cone, it would already be neon blue sugar water dribbling onto my shoes.

The glint of a descending airplane caught my attention; I could barely make out the navy-and-white logo for Alaska Airlines. It reminded me that I didn't belong in Fresno. I didn't belong in Arizona, Nevada, Washington, Oregon, or any of the other places Mom and I had wandered through, either. Mom and our beat-up Honda Civic were my two constants, the closest things I had to home. Alaska, however, was in my blood.

I could almost picture it if I shut my eyes: mountains crawling with evergreens, turquoise fjords, ocean mist hanging in the air.

Air. That was a commodity we were sorely lacking in. Fresno's air was stale, dry, and streaked with wildfire smoke and exhaust fumes. On any given day, the sky ranged from yellow gray to murky brown. Sometimes, it made me afraid to breathe.

Finally, Mom's car appeared, slowing for the turn into the driveway. I shoved my English essay in my bag and stood up, noting the faint hum of Mom's pathetic speakers trying to produce something that sounded like music. If the windows were down on a day that hot, it was a bad sign.

"AC not working again?" I grumbled, tossing my backpack inside.

Mom gave an apologetic smile. As I predicted, it was hot in the car—giant convection oven on wheels hot. Within moments, my shirt was plastered to my back. Funny how small inconveniences were such a big deal when nothing in life was going particularly wrong. Or right.

"Sorry, baby girl. It went out this afternoon."

Mom was in her favorite shirt, the forest-green one that highlighted her eyes. Her auburn hair was tied loose, her ponytail draped over one shoulder. Somehow, she managed to look serene and put together even with sweat dampening her temples and wildfire smoke flooding her lungs. I had not inherited her effortless poise.

Irritated, I cranked my window lower and tried to swallow my next complaint. Mom worked hard to keep us alive—currently, two minimum-wage jobs—and she was doing it alone. She tried to pick up extra shifts, but it was never enough. Last week, our landlord taped a warning on our door threatening eviction for late rent. Mom got the payment in on time, but we didn't have much left over. And a broken AC wasn't an emergency, I reminded myself. It was only a nuisance. Mom's stereo worked, kind of, so at least we had that going for us.

"Draw anything today?" Mom asked, her tone falsely bright.

I glanced at her as she turned onto the main road. She kept her eyes glued to the windshield, but I could see the dusk-purple shadows under her eyes. I wondered if it was the heat keeping her up at night or if it was her anxious thoughts.

Mom eased to a stop at a traffic light. I cracked open my sketchbook and flipped to my most recent drawing to show her. The sketch was my fantasy landscape: a forested hillside interspersed with waterfalls and writhing mist. Mom stared at the picture with a strange look. She stared so long that the car behind us tapped its horn, then she jerked her eyes back to the windshield, and the car lurched forward.

"It's perfect," she said. "You're getting better all the time. Better than me even."

"Yeah, right."

"I'm serious."

Mom's smile remained fixed on her lips as she accelerated onto the freeway and nudged between a Subaru and a GMC. Hers was a proud, self-possessed smile, another characteristic I hadn't inherited from her. I closed my sketchbook and hugged it to my chest.

I didn't tell her about the brochure my art teacher had handed me for a university art program in Southern California. College was out of the question without a full-ride scholarship. But I didn't want to make my mom feel bad about finances; she already had enough to stress over.

"You're quiet," she said, turning down the music. "Was school okay?"

"Yeah. Fine." I wanted to change the subject before she started asking questions. She didn't need to know about the art program or about me skipping history class to avoid a group project. "What's for dinner?"

Mom hesitated. "We might have to be creative."

Creative. Another bad sign.

"How about sandwiches?" I forced myself to sound upbeat.

Mom gave me a tired look. "We're out of bread."

I had been meaning to tell Mom that the balance on my lunch account at school was running low, but it didn't seem like the best time. She looked as frustrated as I felt. The gas gauge was nearly empty, traffic was going nowhere, and we were still miles from our exit.

"So, who did you eat lunch with?" Mom asked suddenly.

I glanced sideways at her. Was she serious?

"I want to make sure you're making friends," she explained.

"Really, Mom?"

I had exactly two friends: my sketchbook and the Dewey Decimal System.

"Yes, really." Mom glanced at me. "We've moved a lot. I know it's been hard to hold on to any lasting relationships, but it's not good for you to stay isolated forever."

I wasn't isolated. I simply didn't need a whole girl posse to make a trip to the bathroom.

I had been begging Mom to let me do an independent study program since fifth grade. I'd made the argument so many times I had it memorized: I could blow through my assignments at my own pace, take care of household chores, and have meals prepped and ready for Mom when she got home from work. On weekends, I could take the city bus to pick up groceries. Doing things that way would keep me from having to switch schools every time we moved, and I could graduate early. It was the perfect scenario. Unfortunately, Mom was under the delusion that it was healthy for me to attend a traditional school and interact with people my age.

"You need people around you," Mom insisted. "People to talk to and do life with."

"People like the pair of idiots I saw today fencing with pool noodles?"

Mom cracked a smile. She and I both knew I didn't hate people; I was quiet. Awkward. Invisible. Besides, our living situation was an ever-changing mixture of short-term leases, hotels, and occasionally our car. I couldn't exactly invite anybody over after school.

"You might enjoy pool noodle fencing if you tried it," she said.

"Thanks. I'll stick to archery." I unscrewed the lid of my water bottle and took an irritated gulp. "You're forgetting that I was born with the charisma of a dead sea snail."

"Charisma isn't hereditary. It's a skill."

I rolled my eyes. Mom had to be literal about everything.

"Okay, well, I was born without the ability to exercise and develop that skill."

Mom shook her head. She could be like that sometimes—stubborn enough to make me want to claw my eyes out. Once she had an idea in her head, she stuck to it with a scary kind of determination. She was a bit like me in that way.

I was still brooding when I noticed a gold Alaska license plate in the next lane over. I thought again of the turquoise fjords, the mountains, the clear summer air. But unlike the non-functioning AC and the empty kitchen cupboards, this one felt like a good sign.

"Hey, Mom," I began, draining the last lukewarm trickle from my water bottle. "What if you tried finding a job in Alaska?"

Mom shot me a startled look. "What?"

"Hear me out." I capped my water bottle and tossed it in the back seat. "We could sell the car and use the cash for plane tickets. I bet we both could find summer work and housing. It's cooler there, plus, I'm willing to bet the air doesn't smell like a cattle ranch."

"No." She smiled. "It smells like fish."

"Yes, but they're Alaskan fish."

"I wish we could, sweetheart, but we can't."

"Why?"

"We just can't."

Traffic started moving again. I knew I had to choose my next words with care. Fresno was far from breathtaking, but it was affordable. Almost. And Mom worked hard for the life we had. I didn't want to minimize her effort.

"Is it because it's more expensive there?" I asked.

Mom's dark-green eyes flashed to mine. "Because we live here now."

I sighed and turned back to the window. Mom was always evasive with this stuff. I had been her daughter for seventeen years, and I still didn't know why we left Alaska, why we didn't seem to have any relatives or close connections, or why we were always driving across the country in search of jobs with terrible pay and cheap apartments to live in.

Mom turned to me with a smile that was one part forced, one part sad. "We'll be okay, baby girl. We'll make it."

I swallowed my argument. Mom and I had each other, didn't we?

Outside, the sun blazed orange in the late-summer sky. I knew it meant that somewhere beyond my line of sight, there was a forest on fire. But it felt more like another bad sign.

CHAPTER 2
WAKING UP

P ETER GLANCED AT ME in the rearview mirror. I straightened, remembering I was supposed to be listening to Leslie.

Leslie was going on about how British Columbia was only a six-hour ferry ride away. Only. Six hours from Fresno, and I could have been almost to Las Vegas in one direction or the Oregon border in another. I knew that because Mom and I had traveled those highways more times than I wanted to count.

We slowed for a turn marked by a cluster of eclectic mailboxes, some of which were painted to look like salmon. Fortunately, the one marked "Foster" was plain black and devoid of all fishy embellishments. Another turn, and we found ourselves traveling along a winding driveway. Evergreens loomed above us like the arch of some grand cathedral, and forest growth crept along the edges of the drive. It was as though I'd never even seen the color green before.

The view out my window made me wonder why Mom never took me to a single forest. Ever. She said it was easier to find work where more people were, but I often suspected there was some other reason for keeping us confined to the I-5 corridor. Memories, maybe. Surely, it couldn't be the trees.

"Here we are," Leslie announced.

Peter stopped the car in front of the garage. Before us stood a two-story house made of natural wood that reminded me of a log cabin. It had big windows and a dark metal roof, making it blend into the scenery, but I barely got a look at it before I heard Peter and Leslie rummaging around in the trunk.

Gathering my things, I slid out of the car and into the Sitka-and-salt-brine air. Goosebumps rolled over my arms. The yard around the house was well-kept, but back a few feet from the lawn, evergreen huckleberry, deer fern, redwood sorrel, and false azalea grew wild and tumbled out from beneath the trees. In a word, it was lush.

Awake.

I jolted. The voice was a low rumble, an earthquake inside my head. I would have dismissed it as nothing except that my knees locked inexplicably, then my arms. Bewildered, I stared down at my frozen limbs. A strange prickling sensation washed through me, starting at my feet and moving through my body. After a moment, it felt like even the roots of my hair were charged with electricity. Was I having some kind of hallucination? Low blood sugar? An allergic reaction to the trees?

Stranger still, I found that I was hyper-aware of the forest. A million evergreens began to nod at me—to beckon. Ferns rustled their agreement. Insects scurried along ancient paths lined with fungi and forest debris. Awareness, it seemed, radiated in every patch of moss, every twig, every vine. I had to fight the impulse to drop my things and go drown myself in the forest.

"Wren? Are you coming?" Leslie called from the front doorstep.

I tore my eyes from the forest and forced my focus on Leslie. She stood watching me from the porch step, her arms full of luggage.

"Yeah." I shook myself and the spruce needles from my throat. "Sorry."

Leslie's expression was worried. I was surprised to find that Peter had already unlocked the front door and was pushing luggage inside. Had I been dreaming? With a final glance at the forest, I made my way up the steps and slipped silently into the house.

Peter and Leslie's house wasn't overlarge, but it wasn't cozy either. Creamy walls, high ceilings, fawn-colored accents, and neutral artwork made everything feel glaring and desert-like in contrast to the dark foliage outside. I stepped past the entryway, wooden floors creaking under my feet. The space looked like it was staged for one of those home décor magazines stacked near registers at the grocery store.

Leslie dropped off my bags at the base of the stairs and started rearranging her ponytail. She glanced at Peter, who was staring—or glaring, rather—at something through the sliding glass.

"Hon? Are you all right?"

Grunting, Peter gestured with his elbow. "You'd never know I mowed that lawn yesterday."

I looked past Peter. The lawn and surrounding foliage looked as though they hadn't been tended in the last month. It was odd, considering how meticulous everything had looked a few minutes earlier.

"Weird," Leslie said. "Maybe it's climate change?"

I was fairly certain climate change was killing the planet, not making it greener.

Peter passed a hand over his eyes. "I'll have to get back out there this weekend."

"You sure you didn't miss a spot in front of the window?"

"Looks the same in the front too."

Leslie's frown deepened, but instead of continuing the conversation, she turned to me. "How about I show you around?"

I shrugged, too tired to bother hiding my lack of enthusiasm. Leslie smiled and gestured for me to follow. Clutching my duffel strap, I tailed her through the house as she went about opening and closing doors, fluffing pillows, and straightening towels needlessly.

Upstairs, there were two nearly identical bedrooms with white walls, beige carpet, and textured curtains. The only perceivable difference was that one of the rooms had an attached bathroom. I decided that one must be Peter and Leslie's.

"It's a little sparse in here," Leslie said, setting my bags down on a carpet imprinted with vacuum tracks.

I set down my backpack near the door. My room was as much of a vanilla wasteland as downstairs. It had a dresser, a nightstand, and a big bed topped with puffy white bedding. It was so clean I was terrified to touch anything.

"You have a nice view over the backyard," Leslie said, motioning to the window.

I nodded mutely. Looking out on a sea of mist and velvet green was a definite improvement over concrete alleyways and overflowing dumpsters.

"You're free to make the room yours. But try not to put too many holes in the walls, okay?" Leslie perched on the bed. "What sorts of things are you into, sweetheart?"

I knew Leslie was waiting for an answer, but no words came. My eyes jerked toward the window, where the tops of the trees were stirring the mist. Longing squeezed my chest and made it difficult to breathe. With an effort, I dragged myself back into the present. Maybe the novelty of being surrounded by so much beige was getting to me, or maybe I was suffering from the effects of grief and sleep deprivation.

My eyes fell on the sketchbook peeping out of my bag. "Art, I guess. I like to draw and paint."

"Like your mama." Leslie smiled. "Wren, I can't get over how much you look like her. Your chin, your mouth, your eyes—"

I stared at the floor, trying to quell the sick feeling in my stomach. Leslie had to know her words hit me like a knife thrust. I already knew I looked like Mom; every glance in the mirror was an aching reminder. And even though my hair was a shade darker than Mom's, it had the same reddish tint in the sun.

"I know the circumstances aren't ideal, but we're happy to have you living with us," Leslie said. "I hope you know I mean that."

I smelled the lie even before Leslie finished speaking. Did she honestly enjoy having a grief-stricken teenager moping around her home, taking up space and draining financial resources? "Thanks," I tried.

Leslie chewed her lip like she wasn't sure how to talk to me. I wished she'd stop trying. "You must be tired," she said.

"A little." She had no idea. The quiet at night always made space for the ache to creep in. I couldn't sleep, so I usually switched on a light and pulled out my sketchbook.

Leslie rose to leave, touching my shoulder as she went. I waited for the door to latch before retrieving the one framed photo I had of Mom from my luggage. In the photo, she was holding a tiny, hairless version of me. It was probably taken by Leslie right after I was born.

"I guess this is home now, Mom," I whispered.

But it wasn't home. Home was something I'd lost forever. Some*one*. The warm vanilla bedroom grew suddenly stifling. I set the picture frame on the dresser and went to the window to unlatch it. The wind whisked through the room and pulled at my loose hair. But even the maritime air wasn't enough to clear away the memories from the day I lost my mom: the crowded hallway, my teacher's somber approach, the look of pity on her face, the slow walk to the school office.

"Wren, there's something I need to tell you, and it's going to be hard. Your mother—" My teacher had paused to collect a breath. "She was in a car accident around ten this morning."

Panic hit like a blast of cannon fire. I asked a question I couldn't remember, a question my teacher struggled to answer. When the meaning of her words finally hit, something wrenched out of place in my middle. Shadows crept up the walls and grew all around me. Disbelief crowded my brain. My legs folded, and then the rest of me followed. After that, the ache started, and that ache was forever.

Come.

I glanced up, back in Alaska, momentarily disoriented by the ever-green-spiced air washing over me, the wind ruffling the curtains and electrifying my skin. It was that voice again, the one I thought earlier I had imagined.

Come into the forest.

Invisible fingers seemed to reach out and grab me. My knees went taut as I felt myself being pulled toward the open window. I grabbed hold of the window frame to keep from collapsing or ramming straight through the screen. I reached up and slammed the window shut. The grip on me relented at once, but my body kept trembling. No way was this a normal part of grieving.

I needed sleep. And food. Possibly medication.

I turned away from the window, determined to maintain a sense of sanity and normalcy by unpacking a few of my belongings. But even as I began rooting around inside my duffel, I could still see the restless evergreens. And I could hear the voice coming to me again, far away and deep. A whisper so loud, so quiet, it seemed liable to break the glass between me and the forest.

This is where you belong.

CHAPTER 3
OUTLANDER

I ROLLED OVER, KNOTTING the blankets with my endless tossing. Mom used to go outside when she couldn't find sleep. But between the voice in my head and the compulsive thoughts about the forest, I didn't dare.

Even when I shut my eyes, the forest remained. But instead of darkness, flickers of sunlight shone through the trees. A symphony of birdsong rose high in the golden air. Fiddleheads shot up from the ground and began to uncurl. Swollen leaf buds hung along the branches of vine maples and elderberry shrubs. The forest was awakening from its long winter slumber.

I passed through the trees, noting the scents of earth and decaying wood rising to meet me. When I stumbled across the boy, he was so real I didn't notice I was dreaming.

Beyond a cluster of hemlocks, a line of eight teenage boys stood together, all green-eyed and similarly outfitted: snug-fitting tunics with jerkins and homespun trousers in earthy tones, soft boots, leather chest guards, longbows, and bracers.

Everywhere, new leaves shook off the winter chill, turning their golden-green faces toward the sun. But the boy—the tall one with midnight-dark hair and straight-backed posture—remained unaffected by the beauty around him. I could tell by his tense, lifted shoulders that he was on edge.

An adult paced in front of the line of boys, examining each of them with critical sage-colored eyes and a stern expression. Unable to keep still, the boy drummed his fingers at his sides.

By the Tree, I wish this were over.

The boy's thoughts flowed into mine, clear enough he could have spoken aloud. Curious, I crept closer.

The adult pacing before the boys was the cohort leader, I realized, falling deeper into the boy's mind. He had given the boys the task of shaping a life-sized *Sphyrapicus ruber*—a red-breasted sapsucker. The task was simple, but not to the boy. When it came to shaping living creatures, his attempts were crude at best.

The boy's pulse sped up as he watched the other boys cast their shapes. Soon, the forest was filled with translucent woodpeckers with folded wings, long bodies, and round heads. As the boy's turn drew nearer, his thoughts turned frantic. He knew that having a thorough understanding of the object one was trying to shape was essential in creating a stable form. Bearing that in mind, he tried to recall everything he knew about the bird.

Members of the Picidae family, ruby-colored head and breast. White-bellied and black-winged. They prefer to nest in deciduous tree cavities, and their tongues are equipped with rigid hairs to collect the sap upon which they subsist.

When his turn came, the boy moved into position. He stood erect, feet spread, hands clasped behind his back per his people's custom. His posture was confident; with effort he controlled his trembling. Did the others sense his unease?

Focusing on his task, the boy raised his hands. Finding a wisp of *draíocht*—a magical byproduct respirated by the Elder Tree—was his primary goal. A warmth spread over his palms as his energy collided with the unseen substance and brought it to life.

Shaping objects started with a twisting, writhing sensation in the center of his torso. It was a feeling that was both gratifying and insubstantial at once. For a moment, the boy felt powerful. He shut his eyes, took hold of the draíocht with his mind, and pulled it snug. He tested the connection to make sure the draíocht was secure, mentally calculating his next move. *Members of the Picidae family,* he reminded himself. He fixed an image of the bird in his head, focusing on the details. He saw every feather, every barbule interlocking to fend off both wind and water.

Suddenly, without meaning it to, his mind wandered. The sensation inside him became something new, a steady thrum. A pulse. Instead of the bird, he saw an image of the Elder Tree, but not as it was. The Tree became something different: a four-chambered heart, restless and eager, pumping life and breath and magic into the grateful forest. He issued a silent command, telling the magic which form to take.

The boy immediately sensed something had gone awry. The forest was still behind him: the birds, the trees, his cohort. He kept his eyes closed, but he could feel the weight of the shape in his hand. He started to breathe out his relief. Then, the sound of suppressed laughter filled the silence behind him.

"The Flower Shaper strikes again," one of the boys nearest him murmured.

This, of course, drew laughter from the rest of his cohort. The boy looked down to find a shape-cast lump lying in his palm. The object was roughly the size of a sapsucker, but that was where the similarity ended.

A wave of heat crept over the boy's neck. It had been like this nearly every day since he first joined a cohort: he started shaping the required object well, and then his thoughts scattered. His mind would sweep him off to some green place full of growing things. The last time it happened, he made it rain pink blossoms all over the archery range. A brawler's fracture, a dislocated shoulder, and his new nickname, Flower Shaper, were all he had won in the fight that broke out afterward.

With a quick motion, the boy severed the magical connection to his palm and presented the shape for inspection. It looked like a human heart, but it was twisted and tree-like in quality, with a snarl of veins—or roots—dangling down his arm.

"It's got a tail this time," the boy murmured, disentangling himself from the tendrils.

Sitka, the cohort leader, scooped up the creation and examined it with visible disgust. The boy was humiliated. Seeing Sitka's face, the other boys began to jeer. Stonecrop snickered. Ash laughed outright. And Burdock folded his arms while making a stupid face.

"Poor lad," Burdock said, his tone patronizing. "Ought to join a girls' cohort."

Irritation twinged in the boy's middle. "At least the girls manage to shoot their arrows straight." The boy meant for his jab to sting. Burdock's archery skills were infamous for being the worst in their cohort—possibly in all Síorghlas. Unfortunately, Burdock just shrugged and walked away.

When it came to plant magic, the boy could best the rest of his cohort every time. Roots and leaves he understood; people he did not. In his experience, people were cold, merciless, and selfish. They allowed none to get in the way of their goals. And so, the boy resolved to do the same. He had clear goals himself. He also had a sound mind and an unobstructed vision of how to accomplish all that he desired. But his painful shaping and the constant bullying that accompanied it were two obstacles he could not yet overcome.

"Can't even shape as well as my sapling sister," Hawthorn said to Burdock.

Burdock smirked. "Why do you think that is, I wonder?"

The boy fought the urge to smash their faces in. He did *not* want to be made a fool by the other boys' taunts. Not again.

Hawthorn pretended to consider Burdock's question for a moment. "Either he's gone soft in the head, or—"

"Quiet!" Sitka bellowed. "Any more from you lot, and I'll have you scrubbing moss from the council chambers' underbelly again."

The cohort went quiet. The ealdor council chambers, like the other structures in Síorghlas, stood suspended in giant spruce trees growing in the center of the gorge. Scaling the trees to clean the underside of any platform without breaking one's neck was a feat. The boy picked up his things. He would let go of his anger if only to avoid unnecessary moss removal.

"It is interesting, is it not?" At the sharp voice, the boy froze in the act of shouldering his bow. Stonecrop had waited until Sitka's back was turned before moving in to harass him. "That the one who cannot conjure the simplest shapes is of...*questionable* lineage?"

The boy said nothing. Stonecrop was the son of one of Síorghlas's esteemed ealdors, and he had no problem flaunting it. Worse, he knew exactly how to strike the boy to make him cower.

"You might've been claimed if you were anything but an illegitimate son," Stonecrop went on casually.

The boy kept his eyes fixed on the ground, eyes that were the same color except perhaps a bit bluer than all the rest. He was shaking. Stonecrop's words were an attack on his very identity. The boy had to remember his training: do not flinch, do not react, do not show weakness.

"You know, don't you?" Stonecrop grew bolder. "By our laws, you should not exist?"

The boy reminded himself to breathe. He was one part fear, two parts rage. But he must not allow others to control his narrative; he had to control it himself.

"My father told me that the ealdor council makes no allowances," Stonecrop said arrogantly. "Illicit acts are punishable by death, banishment, or worse. That's why your mother was no better than a—"

"Do *not* speak of my mother," the boy interrupted.

The boy had only the vaguest impression of his mother from before she died. Some said her death was due to an illness; others called it self-destruction. The boy didn't know what to believe. But if Stonecrop kept prodding, the boy was going to lose his careful control.

"Well, then," Stonecrop said at last. "I suppose you already know what you are. Half-breed."

Before the boy could think, his fist collided with Stonecrop's face. Stonecrop stumbled into Hawthorn, hand clapped over his nose. Hawthorn shoved Stonecrop off, laughing at his misfortune. Stonecrop's pale green eyes were wide, his blood seeping between his fingers. Until that moment, it seemed, Stonecrop hadn't known he could bleed.

"Enough!" Sitka rounded on the boys. "I ought to thrash both of you—fighting like a pair of wolverines. This kind of behavior is unheard-of among my cohorts."

Sitka's wrathful gaze fell on the boy; the ealdor's son was bleeding. The boy wanted to disappear into the forest foliage, but he didn't think even the forest would shield him.

"I misspoke," Sitka said. "This kind of behavior *was* unheard of among my cohorts until *you* came along with your anger and your fragile pride." He stabbed a finger at the chest of the boy with midnight hair. "Until you can accept that you are part of the problem, there will be no end to the bloodied and battered bodies you have to account for."

The boy kept quiet, but his insides filled with a smoldering fury. Hadn't Sitka seen how Stonecrop had goaded him, how he had practically begged the boy to break his face? Ah, but Stonecrop was immune to consequences; he was an ealdor's son.

"Forgive me, Sitka," the boy murmured, trying to make his halfheart-ed bow look apologetic. "I will try to do better."

"You *will* do better," Sitka insisted.

"Aye. I will."

Then, Sitka's face took on a loathsome expression. The boy recognized it at once. It was the same pity that spared his life when those attending his sick mother learned the boy had no father.

"Consider this a warning." Sitka crushed the shape-cast heart to pow-der. The fragments poured through his fingers like glittering sand. "You will take the first and second watches for the rest of the month."

The boy accepted his punishment without comment. The string of crimson trickling from Stonecrop's nostrils was worth a month of lost sleep. Despite his pathetic pallor and the handkerchief pressed to his nose, Stonecrop was still an ealdor's son. But at least he wasn't immortal.

Sitka turned away after that. The boy meant to wander off alone, but someone grabbed him by the shoulder. The boy flinched, fearing a retaliatory blow, but he received instead a single word from Stonecrop, uttered like a curse.

"Outlander."

Outlander. The insult stung him like nettle.

The boy wanted to strike Stonecrop again—this time so his teeth would rattle—but Sitka was watching. So, he turned on his heel and fled into the forest, aimless like a feather adrift in the wind.

When I awoke, shafts of sunlight glided in through the window. I looked around, bleary-eyed and struggling to reconcile my surroundings with the foliage-rich setting of my dream, the medieval clothes, the eyes in various shades of green. The bland color of the walls, the overstuffed pillows, and the scent of freshly laundered sheets served as a reminder: like the boy in my dream, I was somewhere I didn't belong.

The light from the window fell on my bed and illuminated the drawing I'd been working on late into the night—a portrait of Mom. Her eyes stared back at me, warm and bright and glowing with life. Pain hit like a blast of winter cold. The familiar ache clambered up my throat, threatening to shred me in two. I shoved the sketchbook aside, wadded up my pillow, and used my blankets to muffle my sobs.

Losing Mom didn't only hurt; it felt incomplete. She was supposed to pick me up from school that day like normal. We were supposed to drive home and scrounge for another meal. That night, she should have fallen asleep on the couch while I sketched pictures of all the places we dreamed of going together. Later, she was supposed to see me graduate and go to college—and one day, we would go to Alaska together.

If I could, I would trade all the comfort and abundance of living in Alaska with the Fosters for one more sweltering summer day with Mom.

She wasn't supposed to die.

"Wren?" Leslie's voice called through the door, accompanied by a muted knock. "Sorry to bother you. Are you up?"

I tried to steady my voice before speaking. "I'm awake."

"Do you mind if I come in?"

Of course, I minded. Leslie had no idea what I was going through, and I didn't have the energy to make her understand. But I made a halfhearted attempt to dry my eyes and look normal. Off in the distance, a foghorn blared.

"That's fine," I croaked.

Leslie cracked the door open. "Breakfast is ready—oh, you're still in bed."

"Sorry. I'll be down in a minute."

I tried not to make eye contact. Hopefully, Leslie wouldn't notice my puffy, red-rimmed eyes. Her sympathy couldn't fix anything; it would only make things harder.

"Perfect," Leslie said brightly. "I'll let you get ready."

She backed out and shut the door. I didn't want to go downstairs, but if I didn't make an appearance, she would return to investigate.

Leslie didn't need to know how close I was to breaking.

CHAPTER 4
SHADOWS AND MIST

THE SKY BROODED OVERHEAD. Rain slapped the windshield in bursts, making conversation with Leslie difficult. I didn't mind. The rigid line of Leslie's shoulders told me that she was more nervous than me about my first day of school. I'd been uprooted from schools often enough I accepted it as a fact of life. The awkward stares and chaotic shuffle to find all my classes wouldn't be fun, but it wouldn't last long. Still, something about starting at Edgewood felt different.

Leslie adjusted the thermostat, testing the vent flow with her fingers. "So, Wren. How do you like Alaska so far?"

I twisted my backpack strap, not sure how to answer. I hadn't been in Alaska long enough for it to make any kind of impression on me. It was wet, cold, and a bit fishy. Thankfully, it didn't smell like a cattle ranch.

"It's fine, I guess."

My eyes wandered to the window and seemed to get stuck there. The forest looked inviting as ever with its feathered edges and mantle of velvet green. Fortunately, the incident with the voice in my head hadn't repeated itself. I dismissed it as temporary insanity. But still, the forest intrigued me.

"Hey, does anyone ever go out there?" I pointed out the window.

"In the forest? Not that I know of."

"Do you?"

"Not here." Leslie tugged the rubber band out of her hair and fluffed her roots. "Too dangerous. Don't forget you're in Alaska. The bears outnumber people here, and occasionally, we even see wolves. Anyone could get lost or injured or fall into a muskeg."

Dangerous or not, the forest was breathtaking. Moss fell from the trees like tendrils of living lace. Green things twisted and grew in unpredictable angles. Ruffled yellow mushrooms popped up through the leaf litter. To me, it looked more like a sanctuary than a death trap.

"Did you have any friends back at home?" Leslie asked, breaking the silence that had fallen between us. "A boyfriend, maybe?"

"Not really."

Even if I'd had friends and considered California my home, why would I want to talk about it? I'd just left everything behind.

"Ah, well. I'm sure you'll make lots of friends in time. Lots of kids your age live in town." She glanced at me. "Plenty of boys too."

Leslie's tone was way too suggestive to be casual. Annoyed, I twisted the drawstring on my jacket. If she thought I'd come to Alaska so she could play fairy godmother and find me a nice Alaskan boy to date, she was wrong. My life was complicated enough without my guardian doubling as a personal dating service.

Leslie finally fell silent. I watched the forest streak by, grateful for the quiet. Maybe both of us were worn out by the emotional strain of existing around other humans.

"I'm sorry," Leslie said suddenly. "I keep looking at it like we've known each other your entire life, but maybe it isn't that way for you."

"It isn't."

"I'll have to remember that."

The earnestness in Leslie's voice surprised me. Other than Mom and my art teacher in Fresno, I didn't think most adults listened to me any more than my peers did.

"Peter and I weren't as involved as we wanted to be while you were growing up. There's a college savings account for you, and we sent birthday cards from time to time. The cards always ended up being returned." She paused. "Not that I blame your mom for that. I know you two had to keep moving."

My irritation morphed into something quieter. It had bothered me that Leslie and Peter had only involved themselves in my life after Mom died. The college savings account surprised me, but the bit about the birthday cards hit even harder. I hadn't considered that the Fosters might want to know me but couldn't.

"I barely knew you existed," I admitted. "I thought it was the same for you."

"Not at all."

Leslie's response sent my thoughts spiraling. Mom and I literally knew no one. We never got close to anyone or made any lasting relationships. That's why Mom listed Leslie, supposedly an acquaintance from years back, as an emergency contact on my school documents, but she rarely talked about her.

"It's weird. My mom came from here, but she hardly told me anything about it."

Leslie turned down her music. "I don't understand it either, Wren. Your mom wasn't one to volunteer information. I don't know much, but I'll tell you what I can."

As Leslie spoke, I could almost see the images play out before me. The forest was blanketed in white. Leslie had parked her car and was on her way into a store when she saw Mom. Mom huddled under the trees at the edge of the parking lot, lost and nearly invisible. Leslie bent down to talk to her and make sure she was okay. Mom raised her head, startled and distrusting. She didn't understand that Leslie was simply offering to buy her something warm to drink.

She was cold and dirty, and her clothes were strange—like a costume. By talking with her, Leslie could tell she had no idea how to fend for herself in town.

"Peter and I agreed to set her up on the couch for the night and take her to the shelter in the morning." Leslie's eyes skimmed the crosswalk ahead of us. "We gave her dinner and a change of clothes, but when she didn't know how to use the shower, I knew something was seriously wrong."

"She didn't know how to use the shower?"

"She said she'd never seen one before. Same with the oven and the vacuum cleaner."

I shifted my backpack with my feet. Mom had to be one of the most consistently put-together people on the planet. How could she not know about basic appliances and bathroom fixtures?

Leslie continued her story. "She didn't give much explanation for her situation—only that she had to leave her home suddenly. She didn't have any kind of identification, and she hesitated to give out personal information. We didn't want her to struggle alone, so we let her stay with us while she figured things out. Then you came along. You lived with her in our guest bedroom for your first year or so. After that, she packed up and boarded a plane to start a new life. We tried to get her to stay, but she was convinced she needed some distance from this place."

I watched the raindrops beading on the glass. It struck me that Leslie was the one telling me this and not Mom. Leslie and Peter had supported her in a way that was hard to imagine. They were generous and kind, and she had been totally dependent on them. The fact that they'd been trying to send me birthday cards for years told me that they weren't the strangers I thought they were.

"What about my dad?" I asked. "Did she ever say anything about him?"

My heart pumped hard while I waited for Leslie's answer. Mom had always been tight-lipped about her past; her relationship with my father had been no exception. She'd given the impression that my dad was just some guy. Now, I wasn't sure what to think.

"I'm sorry, Wren. Your mom didn't like to talk about him—not even with me. If anyone knew who he was, I'm sure he would have been contacted after her death."

Leslie's honesty stung as much as it helped. If she could be so straightforward with me, why couldn't Mom? I'd spent my whole life knowing nothing and hardly being bothered by it. Now, I was starting to think I should be bothered.

It made no sense that Mom left Alaska. Even if she had to leave her home, what was wrong with staying near Peter and Leslie? And why had she felt the need to downplay their roles in our lives? Did she enjoy having no connections and living like a fugitive?

I didn't want to admit it to myself, but I was slowly coming to a realization. Instead of the Fosters, it was my mom who was the stranger.

"Are you okay?" Leslie asked.

"Yeah. I'm fine."

Fine wasn't an accurate description of my emotional state. It felt like the air was folding up around me. Mom hadn't simply omitted a few things—she'd kept everything from me. I wasn't even sure who she was anymore.

Leslie pulled into the school parking lot and tried to smile, but her eyes were troubled. I knew she could tell I wasn't okay. But I was hardly paying attention to the conversation anymore. My eyes were locked on the forest. Mist clung to the mountains like tatters of wool. The longer I stared, the more I could swear I saw a ghostly form slipping through the trees. But I knew the only things haunting me were the unfamiliar shadows of Mom's past.

CHAPTER 5
INVISIBLE

"I T WASN'T ANYTHING LIKE this back when I went here," Leslie mumbled.

Leslie's Infiniti inched forward in line. She'd already been circling the perimeter of Edgewood's parking lot like a vulture in search of prey for twenty minutes.

"Peter can probably help you find a decent car once you have your license. Then you can drive yourself if you like."

It was clear by the strain in Leslie's voice that she wanted as little to do with the drop-off line as possible, but she was too worried about me to let me take the bus. Mom had been the same way.

Mom. The liar.

"Maybe I should park and get you checked in," Leslie said, her voice bordering on panic.

The idea of Leslie walking me to the office was worse than doing it alone. Among other problems, she was still trying to figure out drop-off line etiquette. I undid my seatbelt and reached for the door handle.

"That's okay," I said, snatching my backpack. "I've done this before. Thanks for the ride."

I slipped out the door before Leslie could argue. A haze of woodsmoke hung in the air as I stepped up to the curb, which was already swarming with adolescent humans.

"Nice car," someone yelled.

I ignored the comment and stalked toward the office building. Already, rainwater dampened my shoes. All the other students were wearing flannel shirts, fleece or shell jackets, jeans, and neoprene boots. They understood how to dress for the weather, unlike me.

I spotted a small building marked as the office and slipped through the door. The air was pungent with the scents of Juicy Fruit and old heater, surrounding me as I walked to the counter where the receptionist sat beneath a taxidermized elk head.

"Hi." My mouth dissolved into sandpaper as I stepped up to the counter. "I, uh—" Then my eyes strayed to the elk's head. It had a stare that was as unnerving as it was empty.

"Do you need something?" the receptionist demanded, chewing her gum aggressively. She stared at me like I had interrupted her favorite show. A peek at her monitor informed me that she had been perusing social media.

I shot the elk's head another wary glance. Did the receptionist put it there to intimidate new students? "I think I'm supposed to check in here. My name's Wren Ashwood."

The receptionist continued her rhythmic chewing. For a long time, her eyes remained as blank as the dead elk hovering above her. Since she wasn't speaking, I figured I'd help her along.

"Ashwood," I said again. "With an A."

"I heard you."

"Okay."

She sighed like she was bored even thinking about me. "Oh, I remember. You're new."

I couldn't think of any other reason I'd be checking in twenty minutes before the bell.

The receptionist started shuffling papers around in a half-distracted manner. I opted to avoid the elk head's gaze while I waited. The school office looked like an outdated trailer home masquerading as a hunting lodge. Checkered curtains framed the window. A ceramic bear on the table held a fish in its mouth and a sign that read *Good Things Come to Those Who Bait*. The wood-paneled walls were dull with age and featured photos of every graduating class since the early seventies. The clothes and hairstyles evolved along with the photo quality, but the presence of Xtratuf boots remained consistent.

The receptionist snapped her gum, causing me to jump. I turned to find her waving a stack of papers at me and looking extremely put out while doing so. Why did she bother showing up when she hated her job? I took the papers to stop her from flapping.

"So, I'm all checked in?"

"Schedule is on top." She snapped her gum again for emphasis.

I figured that was as close to a yes as I was going to get. I turned and slipped out the door.

Outside, the rain had turned to mist. The wind swept up the scents of the forest and brought them close. Salt brine and evergreens. I kept close to the side of the office to avoid being trampled. Edgewood's campus was as rugged as its wilderness backdrop—except with more concrete. The walkway was slick, plastered with leaves and forest debris. Evergreens fanned over the roof of a short structure attached to the gym. The main building was a largish two-story structure unquestionably newer than the rest. There were a few other buildings, long and squat, huddled together like they were in council with one another. Between the buildings, I caught a glimpse of a run-down basketball court, a track, and a meadow dotted with lupine and scarlet paintbrush.

I sidestepped a herd of chatty girls and paused at the corner of a building to look over my schedule and other papers. There was a campus map along with an assortment of reminders and advertisements for sports and clubs. A flier printed in the school colors—red and gold—grabbed my attention. Archery club. I thought back to a time when the sunset air was bright with late summer gold. Mom and I didn't have much, but one possession she prized was her bow. She stood beside me with her feet positioned apart, arrow at full draw, and her hair blowing around her like a flame. She had taken me to an empty lot and set up some targets and was instructing me on how to shoot.

"Release the string all at once. Don't let it roll off your fingers. Your arrow will fly straight if you just"—her finger twitched on the string, and the arrow shot forward—"let go."

Her arrow struck dead center.

The memory triggered a familiar heat behind my eyes. I blinked back tears and shoved the flier to the bottom of the stack. I didn't want to cry at school, but it was hard not to. The pain of losing Mom was tangled up with the disorienting realization that I hadn't even known her. Every memory felt like a lie.

You are lost. You are searching for answers.

The voice rooted my steps. My skin prickled like someone had rubbed it with ice.

Find them.

The warning bell startled me back into my senses. A few other students shuffled past. I pushed the papers into my bag and edged toward the main building behind them, scared of my own mind.

Once I was inside, I made my way down the hall. Students flitted around like birds on a power line, slamming lockers and shouting. Their excessive noise and activity reminded me of all the reasons I hated public high school. I reached for the classroom door and paused. My hands were trembling. I didn't know if the voice I kept hearing was internal or something else, but it made a compelling suggestion. If I wanted answers, I needed to find them.

I shook myself to clear the cobwebs from my brain. Class was about to start, and I was frozen to the door handle. I breathed deep for courage and went inside.

"You must be the new student."

I jerked my gaze to the front of the classroom. A stocky man in a striped polo peered at me over wire-rimmed glasses. I stared back at him, clutching my backpack like a life preserver as a group of rowdy strangers sauntered past. Why did people *walk* so loud? The teacher glanced at a notebook lying open on the podium.

"Wren, right?" He looked at me for confirmation. I nodded. He bent down and wrote something in his notebook. "Welcome to Edgewood."

"Welcome to hell," one of the boys echoed.

"Quiet!" the teacher barked.

The class erupted into snickers. It felt like everyone was staring at me like I was a heap of roadkill, but only one or two curious gazes met mine when I looked up. The teacher shuffled a few things around before handing me a textbook and a syllabus.

"You can take a seat next to Stephanie."

He waved a hand to an empty seat in the third row. A girl with a knotted yellow bandanna in her dark curly hair raised her eyes briefly.

I slipped away from the podium and made my way to my seat. There was a flurry of movement as the class pulled out their textbooks, whispered to their friends, and tried to hide phones under their desks. A few students were engaged in a frantic struggle to complete homework. A girl raised her hand and launched into a debate with the teacher over their last assignment. The teacher only gave her partial attention. He was busy glaring at his monitor like the thing had issued him a personal insult. I suspected his PowerPoint presentation had gone awry. I pulled out my notebook and started doodling. If there was one thing I could count on, it was my ability to remain invisible.

"Hey, new girl."

I looked up. A blonde girl across the aisle was addressing me. She had startling jade eyes and a pleading expression on her face.

"It's Wren," I managed.

"Nice. Hey, do you have a pencil I can borrow?" She waved a half-blank homework sheet at me in response to my entirely blank expression.

"Oh—sure."

I reached into my backpack, wondering what kind of person begs a pencil from the new kid on their first day. I drew out a pencil and handed it to her. The girl gave me an odd look.

"That's a pen."

"It's a mechanical pencil."

The girl looked skeptical. "It doesn't have an eraser."

"That's because I don't usually need erasers."

The girl looked hurt by my response. I didn't know why. I didn't have an infinite assortment of school supplies to hand out to whoever asked for them.

"Sorry," she muttered. "I'll ask someone else."

The girl turned to beg a pencil off her neighbor across the aisle. I hunched over my drawing, trying not to be bothered. Sometimes, it felt like I was out of context no matter what I did—like the world itself was constructed the wrong way to contain me in it.

That is because you don't know who you are.

I took a sharp breath. The air around me tittered like a laugh. Outside, the evergreens waved and danced. The rain was only a sensation of movement beyond the glass. I tried to shut out the voice again, but then I realized something: it was right.

I knew next to nothing about Mom's childhood or adolescence. I didn't know anything about her adult life before she had me either. I didn't even know her parents' names, whether she had siblings—anything. The more I thought about it, the stranger it seemed.

The classroom door creaked open. I raised my eyes to the front of the classroom. A late student walked in, but the teacher didn't seem to notice; he was still engaged in a battle of man versus machine. He seemed to think clicking rapidly would magically unfreeze his computer and make his slide presentation work. I didn't mind. My thoughts about Mom tangled around me like a blackberry thicket, making it hard to concentrate on a lecture.

Mom must have had a home once in order to lose it. What Leslie said made me think she'd come from some sort of isolated community off the grid. Her unfamiliarity with basic convenience items told me she'd had limited contact with the outside world. But why didn't she tell me about any of those things?

You must find out the truth for yourself.

My pulse stuttered. I could find out about Mom if I wanted to. Being in Ketchikan put me close to the place she had come from. It made it convenient for me to search for answers knowing there had to be records of her somewhere. Mom was gone—she couldn't stop me from searching for the truth hidden behind all her lies and omissions. But what if she had a reason for wanting to hide?

The teacher finally got his PowerPoint working and called students to order, but class was the furthest thing from my mind. Mom lied to me, and I had the power to find out why. The only thing that was holding me back was fear. I had no guarantee that I would be able to live with whatever I learned.

While I was still puzzling out my thoughts about Mom, the air stirred with a scent like evergreens. I looked up, half expecting to see a vision of her ghost. Instead, I locked eyes with a boy sliding into an empty seat across the aisle. His hair was dark and windblown, and he had possibly the most vibrant golden-green eyes I'd ever seen. He had a look of mild surprise on his face, but it vanished behind a quick smile. After that, he turned away.

I made it halfway through the day without another negative interaction. Most of my classmates ignored me, which worked fine for me. At lunchtime, I found a quiet spot on one of the concrete steps outside and sat down with my sketchbook. Mom's unfinished portrait stared back at me from the page. I wanted to finish it but found there was something about it I couldn't quite get right.

A group of boys stood nearby, talking loudly. One of them was the green-eyed boy from earlier. I ignored them and focused on my sandwich until I heard someone say my name.

I looked up without meaning to. A boy with bronze skin and an embarrassed smile met my eyes. Someone from the group nudged him.

"Matt. Just go talk to her."

I hunched over my sketchbook like a deranged hermit crab and pretended to be engrossed. I didn't want to deal with people today; I wanted to sit alone and think.

"Hi there." The boy's brown eyes were warm and friendly. "I'm Matt."

"Wren," I managed, clutching my sandwich for protection.

Matt pushed a hand through his black hair, tousling it. He looked like he didn't know what to say. He glanced at the other boys for help, but they were pretending not to notice us.

"Hey, is that a self-portrait?" He flicked his chin.

I glanced down at my sketchbook. "Oh. Uh—"

I trailed off as Matt leaned in for a closer look. A formline raven pendant dangled from a chain around his neck, swinging like a pendulum.

"Looks like you."

He raised his eyes to mine. He was closer now—a little too close. I could hear some of the boys snicker. I might not have minded Matt's attention under other circumstances, but it was too much, too fast. I barely felt like I could interact normally with other people. The pencil ordeal had been embarrassing enough; I wasn't ready to face another encounter like it.

"I should, um—" I gestured at my lunch. "Sandwich."

I took a bite. Matt was visibly confused. Some part of me knew I wasn't acting normal, but another part of me didn't care.

"Oh, sorry," he said. "I didn't mean to keep you from eating."

"It's okay."

He sat down next to me and tried to smile. His smile was kind, but it did nothing to dispel the tension knotting in my stomach.

"So, who is she?"

For a moment, I didn't know who Matt was talking about. He made a motion as if he meant to draw my sketchbook closer. I reacted without thinking, slamming the cover closed on my sketchbook. As I did, a burst of heat leapt up through my core and shot from my palms. Matt jerked backward, barely pulling his hand back in time.

"Oh, gosh." I shot to my feet. "I'm sorry—I'm *so* sorry. I don't know what happened." I looked at my hands. Nothing about them looked out of the ordinary. Had I imagined the flash?

"Your reflexes are insane," Matt said with a shaky laugh.

I pulled the book to my chest, embarrassed and not sure where to look. The other boys stared at me like I was some kind of ravening wild animal—all except for the one with green eyes. He said something to the others, and they all scattered like a flock of mildly dazed seagulls. Soon, I was left with only Matt.

"I'm not finished," I babbled, "and I'm superstitious."

Matt rubbed his neck. "I didn't realize that."

"Anyway, I should get to, um—" I paused, trying to remember my next class. "Art."

Matt tried to smile again. "No worries. See you later."

Oh, I was definitely worried. On top of everything having to do with Mom, I was hearing voices and seeing things. I wandered to the nearest girls' bathroom in a haze of uncertainty. Right before I touched the sketchbook, there had been a streak of silver light. It made me think of the boy from my dream, conjuring silvery objects out of thin air. But I didn't have magic. No one did.

Still, I couldn't deny what was happening to me. The reality I knew was starting to erode. Even the voice in my head agreed that Mom wasn't the person I thought she was. She kept secrets from me. She might have omitted the truth for the simple reason that she was shielding me from something dark, or she might have done it because she was ashamed. It didn't matter. If I didn't try to find out about her past, the truth about her might vanish like the morning mist.

Dark or not, I had to find the truth for myself. I needed answers.

CHAPTER 6
FRAGMENTS

EDGEWOOD'S LIBRARIAN WAS DEFINITELY a vampire. She had a flawless complexion, thick lashes, and blood-red nails and lips. She was so engrossed in her book that I didn't even think she was breathing. I avoided her by ducking around a display on Indigenous peoples and Ketchikan's commercial fishery.

I skipped the cafeteria at lunchtime on my second day and went straight to the library. I planned to start small on my quest to find out something about Mom. Because she came from Ketchikan, there was a chance she had attended Edgewood at some point. If so, there had to be some kind of record of her. I selected a nature guide from the shelf I was staring at for drawing inspiration, before scurrying off in search of an unoccupied computer.

I logged into the school's database and searched until I found digitized copies of Edgewood's old yearbooks. I was scrolling through the offerings when I realized something—I didn't actually know how old my mom was. A tiny tremor worked its way through my hands. For some reason, I couldn't recall a single instance in which she had celebrated her birthday. This was going to make figuring out Mom's years in high school a bit more challenging.

Unwilling to give up, I did some mental math to estimate a broad date range for the years Mom might have attended school and jotted them down on a corner of my sketchbook. I started my search but didn't make it far before the bell rang, signaling the end of lunch. Frustrated, I logged out and scooped up my things, then headed for the checkout. I'd resume my search as soon as I could find a spare minute.

I laid my book on the counter at the checkout, but the librarian didn't budge. She was gripping a worn paperback in her talon-like hands, looking for all the world like she was about to rip it apart.

"Hi, um—" I cleared my throat.

The librarian jumped, letting out a little shriek and dropping her book. I glanced down at the book. Its cover displayed a bare-chested man in a kilt with a scantily-clad woman clasped in his arms. Flushing, the librarian scooped up her book and tossed it into a pile of nonfiction returns. She smiled and began shuffling books in a jerky, compulsive manner. I couldn't tell if she was more worried about my sudden appearance or that a student had witnessed her questionable reading material.

"Can I help you?"

"I have a book to check out." I nudged it toward her, pretending not to notice the battered romance novel hiding in plain sight.

"Oh." The librarian smiled. She lifted her chin, smoothing a wisp of dark hair behind her ear. An assortment of metal bracelets jangled on her wrist. "Of course. Name?"

"Wren Ashwood."

The librarian's fingers were already flitting over the keyboard. "Did you find what you were looking for?"

I thought about lying to avoid conversation before it dawned on me: she or other people on staff might have known Mom when she attended Edgewood.

"No, actually—" I paused to get my story straight. "I was looking for information about someone who used to go to school here, but I didn't find much. It's for a research project."

The librarian opened up the book and scanned the sticker inside, humming the first line of a song with a distinct vibrato. Judging by her choice of reading material, her mind was off gallivanting through the heather in eighteenth-century Scotland, wrapped up in a pair of beefy arms. I didn't think she'd be much help. Still, it was worth a try.

"It's a research project on a former student."

The librarian looked doubtful. Apparently, Edgewood didn't put out many graduates who were likely to become the topic of research papers one day. I tried to look confident.

"What sort of information are you looking for?" she asked.

"Anything. Yearbook photos, articles in the school paper, tardy slips—"

I winced. I was sounding a little *too* desperate.

"Did you try the yearbooks?"

I nodded. "Any chance I could access academic records?"

"I'm afraid not."

I held back a groan. Finding out about Mom was going to be harder than I thought.

"Is there anything else I can help you with?" the librarian asked.

I opened my mouth to say there wasn't, but a quiet rumble infiltrated my thoughts.

Ask about the forest.

I didn't have time to even register the unwelcome voice invading my thoughts. Its words spun images across my mind—sweeping evergreen fronds, rough-hewn bark, soft moss, and gray-green lichen. Above and around me, evergreens loomed close, walling me in and closing over the sky. I should have felt terrified, but instead, I felt strangely at ease. Secure.

"What about the forest?" I said aloud, half wistful as the images faded from my vision.

"The forest?"

"It's for another project."

A dash of skepticism returned to the librarian's expression, but she erased it with an indulgent smile. I was just another awkward high school student who didn't understand how conversations worked. She closed my book and pushed it toward me, tapping the cover with a red finger-nail.

"This is an excellent place to start," she said. "I'm told these nature guides are comprehensive."

I pulled the book toward me. Plant identification wasn't what I was looking for; the nature guide was strictly source material for my art. Something like desperation swelled up inside me.

"It's the forest itself I'm curious about," I insisted.

Once the words were out of my mouth, I realized they were true. There was something about the towering evergreens cloaked in mist that filled me with a strange sense of longing.

After what felt like several minutes, the librarian still hadn't said a word. She stood staring at me with an expression that was utterly blank.

"Um—" I tried, halting my thought.

The librarian reached down to pluck an invisible pearl of lint from her sleeve. "Yes?"

"I wanted to learn more about the forest. Has anything"—I paused again, searching for the right word—"weird ever happened there?"

The glazed look on the librarian's face cleared in an instant. "Well, let's see now." She frowned, her bracelets tinkling as she splayed thin, pale hands on her desk. "A girl went missing some two, three years ago this April."

"Who was she?"

"I don't remember her name," the librarian admitted.

I drummed my fingers on the counter, impatient for more. It wasn't what I really wanted—information about my mom—but at least I was getting *somewhere*.

"People around here know the forest isn't a safe place to go," the librarian went on. "There are a lot of wild parties—college kids getting drunk, doing drugs, getting up to all sorts of mischief. I've heard there's trash everywhere. Probably tourists. Makes my blood boil."

I watched her anxiously, waiting for the punchline. I'd never been inside the forest, but the trees I saw bore such pristine beauty it made my heart ache. It didn't look as though it had ever been disturbed by humans.

"Did they ever find the girl?" I pressed.

"What?"

One glance told me the librarian had zoned out again. Her pale hands were already inching toward her book, her eyes glazed over.

"The girl who went missing," I said. "Was she found?"

"Someone went missing?"

I stared at the librarian, but the look on her face made it clear she was in earnest. Was she okay?

"You were telling me about a girl—"

Before I could finish, the librarian drew her book toward her, flipped it open, and began reading like I wasn't even there. My mouth fell open. Somehow, her reaction scared me more than the elk head lady in the office ever could. I shut my mouth and backed away from the counter, numb with shock.

My movement must have caught the librarian's eye because she looked at me, jolting as though startled all over again by my presence—as though I had been invisible to her.

"Can I help you?"

I hesitated. Maybe the woman had some sort of condition I was unaware of. I shook my head.

The librarian flashed a friendly smile from behind the counter where she was trying in vain to conceal her paperback. "Better get to class," she said cheerfully.

Like I was the only one with responsibilities I was neglecting.

"Enjoy your book," I muttered, half hoping she'd hear me.

The librarian didn't respond. I slipped out of the library and found my way back to the main building, feeling like little more than a passing shadow. Were all the staff members at Edgewood this unhinged, or was it me?

CHAPTER 7
HERBLORE

I SPENT EVERY DAY at lunch poring through old yearbooks. But despite my diligence, I wasn't making much progress. I examined and re-examined all the yearbooks. I meticulously scoured the names in every class, trying to keep a sharp eye out in case Mom went by a different name in high school. I even tried zooming in on the pictures in case Mom went by another name *and* looked completely different back then. When that failed, I expanded the date range to the point that it was absurd—there was no way Mom was in her late fifties when she died. I spent so much time looking for answers about my mom that I was neglecting my homework, and my grades plummeted as a result.

I took my seat in biology one day and pulled out my sketchbook, tucking it halfway under my notes like I always did. A row of bean seedlings had been laid out on the table before me, the specimens from a recent germination project. Around me, the classroom buzzed with activity. Students were roaming the aisles to turn in homework and get back to their seats. Two boys were having a heated discussion about a football game. And the girl at my table thought she was being sly with her phone. I ignored all the chaos until the bell rang.

The teacher quieted the class and began her lecture. I pushed my pencil around and tried to make it look like I was taking notes. Really, I was making plans to refine my search.

I jotted down a few notes on the back of Mom's portrait—things I should have known about her but didn't. The list was long. I was starting to think I should expand my search beyond the school on the off chance that Mom had gone somewhere other than Edgewood for high school. Maybe I could find a birth announcement in the newspaper scans at the local library or something.

A draft caught the leaves of the bean seedlings and made them shiver. I paused, lifting my gaze to the window. The clouds outside parted to reveal bright air and pale-blue skies. My eyes traced the ridges where forest-clad mountains met the sky. I meant to return to my notes, but I couldn't will myself to look away. The smudge of dark-green forest outside the window called out to me and drew me in.

My pulse twitched and trembled as a nameless emotion swept over me. I needed to stand under those enormous spruces. I needed to touch the living wood, to breathe the forest air and walk in the dusk-like shade beneath the trees.

Before I knew it, the tables disappeared. A forest grew, and a path through the trees opened up before me. I slipped though the gap, running invisible fingers over the moss clinging to gigantic tree trunks. The scent of growing things filled my nostrils. I drew it in with relish. It only took me a moment to realize where I was—back in the forest, dreaming again about the boy with the midnight hair.

The boy dashed through ferns and evergreens and salal, his manner lithe and his footsteps soundless. A pair of marbled murrelets chirped from their hiding place overhead, and sword ferns sprang thick from mossy snags near his feet. The boy was barely aware of where he was going—only that his feet were carrying him toward the eastern gate and out of Síorghlas with all the haste and surety of a young stag. Eventually, the other boys would catch up with him. If he wanted to avoid another fight, he had to keep moving.

Breathless, the boy finally slowed to a walk. Spruce, hemlocks, and cedars grew close around him, marking the boundary separating Síorghlas from the rest of the forest. The boy paused beside a cluster of birches to catch his breath and to decide his next move. He couldn't go back to his cohort. He wouldn't. It didn't matter how much he excelled at his studies, or how great an effort he made at casting shapes; his people would never accept him as he was.

The boy clenched both fists and stared up at an irregular patch of blue sky hemmed in by evergreens. More than anything, he wished he could be someone else. Someone who could command respect. Someone with power and influence. He wished he could be the Wind Shaper.

Both oral history and the ancient texts spoke of the gift of the Tree with a solemn air. It was well known that the Tree chose a bearer before birth and that the gift might lay dormant before manifesting under the direst of circumstances. The role existed for the care, cultivation, and careful governing of the forest, of course, but most scholars agreed that whoever the Tree chose was allowed uninhibited access to both energy and draíocht. The Wind Shaper even held the power to control wind and storms affecting the forest. In short, the gift was power.

But there was no Wind Shaper; the last had gone on to the bright place two decades earlier, and none had appeared since. The boy imagined what it might be like if he could make it rain when he wanted to. He could clear away the snow by redirecting the sea wind. He could make the thunder crash and the river waters heave. And he could bring the rain to water the forest, then he could sweep away the clouds to make way for the sun, coaxing the springtime blossoms into bloom. He would have all the power of the forest, but rather than seeking revenge on his enemies when they came crawling to him out of fear, he would choose the path of peace.

The boy stood still and quiet, soundlessly pleading with the Tree. He knew the Tree could sense his motives. It knew whether a person was pure of heart and whether they were unselfish. It could tell whether one would choose to honor the gift for the good of their forest home. And it would know that by the boy's just governance, his people would finally acknowledge his blood was of no less value than the purest of his people.

Suddenly, the sound of raised voices leaped into earshot. The boy's heart tumbled inside his chest. How long had he lingered there, muttering like an idiot? His silent pleadings to the Tree remained unanswered. He gathered his wits about him and stole away in search of a better hiding place until the other boys lost interest and gave up the chase.

The boy ran on through the trees, barely pausing to take stock of his surroundings. Before he knew it, he collided with something solid. The something he ran into gave a startled cry, and both it and him went tumbling into a patch of wood sorrel.

The boy lay there for a moment, panting, sprawled across whoever it was he had knocked down. Before he could figure out who it was, a hand reached out and flung him away.

"Get off!"

He only had the vaguest impression of wild copper hair and angry eyes as he flew backward into the thicket. The boy was hardly surprised; he was all knees and legs and elbows. He had hoped he would have filled out by age seventeen, but he hadn't. While the others grew strong and broad in the shoulders, he remained tall and lank, trim as a twig.

Groaning, the boy looked up. The wild hair and furious green eyes had transformed into a girl.

"I am dreadfully sorry," he stammered, getting up and offering his hand. "Let me help—"

Scowling, the girl slapped his hand away and got up. "You've helped enough, thanks." As the girl stood, the knife at her side glinted in the light. It was not an ealdor's knife, but it was the kind only the ealdor's nearest kin carried. The boy's jaw went slack.

"Um—"

The boy rubbed his hands on the legs of his trousers, not sure what to say next. The dark but luminous green eyes glaring up at him didn't belong to just any girl. Every boy in his cohort—in the whole forest, no doubt—knew to whom they belonged. All the boys talked about her. All of them stared at her from afar, but no one was stupid enough to try anything. The girl was the daughter of one of Síorghlas' ealdors, exactly the kind of girl he had no business knocking down in the middle of the forest.

And besides the protection of her mother, the ealdor's daughter herself was cold as ice. Never in a thousand ages would she have spared the boy a second glance. Until now. And the look she was giving him was anything but friendly. The boy felt like he had stumbled across the den of a hungry bear. He decided the best approach was to back away slowly.

"*Síocháin leat.*" He recited the traditional greeting with a bow before beginning his retreat. "The fault is mine. I ought to have been watching my way."

"At least you're not as stupid as you look."

The boy paused, not sure whether to feel whipped or indignant. He stood back, gazing at the ealdor's daughter, drinking her in: her heart-shaped face, her evergreen eyes, and her shapely form. And aside from casting him into the bushes like a thing unwanted, she moved with all the grace and serenity of a doe.

The ealdor's daughter straightened her tunic and flipped her hair, indignant. "What are you staring at?"

"Forgive me." He swallowed and tried to look away. "I do not believe we've met."

"Perhaps not," she agreed, plucking a bit of tree bark from her hair. "But I know of you. You are that orphan boy with a reputation for atrocious shaping and a knack for getting into fights."

"I believe you are mistaking me for someone else."

"I assure you I am not."

The sound of uncomfortable laughter filled his ears—his own. The ealdor's daughter picked up her shining hair and began to plait.

"Whatever are you doing out here alone?" she asked. "Shouldn't you be with your cohort?"

The boy bristled. Pretty or not, he would not admit to an ealdor's daughter that he was running away. If word reached Sitka, he'd be cleaning the undersides of every structure in Síorghlas for the rest of his life.

"I could ask you the same," the boy said coolly. "Are you keeping watch on all the other cohorts so you can report their misdeeds to your mother?"

The ealdor's daughter stared at him with a flat look, neither amused nor injured by his insult. She looked numb. The boy instantly regretted his words.

"I shouldn't have said that," he murmured, half apologetically, half fearing for his hide.

"Oh, you needn't fear me, lad. My mother takes reports only from those she views as trustworthy and deserving of her time."

The boy winced at the girl's harsh tone regarding her mother. Though ealdors were elected, the office they held was an institution raised by the Tree itself. And the Tree, of course, was the ultimate authority, the very heart of the forest. No one questioned or criticized the ealdors without fearing consequences.

"I am sorry," the boy said, feeling as though he were backing away from a thicket of devil's club. "Truly—"

"Never mind that." The ealdor's daughter waved his words away, the look on her face determined. "Would it shock you if I admitted the truth?"

Aye, the boy thought. *That it might.*

He waited in dubious silence as the ealdor's daughter reached into her satchel and drew out a leather-bound book. With a sarcastic flourish, she presented it to the boy. Something about her agitated movements made it obvious she was used to not being taken seriously.

"I am attempting to create reference material for my upcoming herblore examination," the ealdor's daughter said.

That was it then—the ealdor's daughter meant to cheat. Intrigued, the boy took the book from her hands, careful not to touch her, and turned to the first page. The parchment was a swirl of color and exquisitely detailed plant illustrations, all labeled in a neat, flowing script.

"You are an artist." Awestruck, the boy turned the page with great care. "And a skilled one at that."

The ealdor's daughter dipped her head in humble acknowledgment. "My mother thinks it's all foolishness, of course. Not that she pays much attention to where I am or what I'm doing—unless it makes her look bad, of course."

The boy glanced up in surprise. "Foolishness?"

"Aye. Scribbling pictures is for children, she says. It does nothing to boost one's status as ealdor kin."

"I see."

Perhaps being an ealdor's child wasn't quite as glamorous as Stonecrop pretended it to be. And that sudden knowledge made the boy uncertain. Perhaps the ealdors and their kin were less out of reach than he thought.

"We are expected to learn the plants by memory for our examination," the boy said, cautiously stepping closer.

"Yes, well not all of us can live up to the expectations thrust upon us. And as you know, my mother is an ealdor—"

"—so, you can't afford to fail."

The ealdor's daughter looked down. Privileged as she was, the girl was taking a bold risk. All students were expected to learn flora by touch, by scent, by the way the light filtered through the foliage. If the ealdor's daughter was caught cheating, it could mean an additional year of study at best and a lifelong reputation for dishonesty and noncompliance at worst. The boy wondered how far behind the ealdor's daughter was in her studies, how difficult it must be to admit she was falling behind when everyone knew who her mother was.

From birth, the girl must have had expectations thrust on her; how lonely her existence must be because of it. No doubt her parents were forever occupied with council duties, and, of course, everyone else in Síorghlas was afraid of her because of her mother. Though the boy had little in common with her, he knew what it was like to dwell in perpetual solitude. And he knew what it was like to be desperate for escape. He looked toward the path he'd been taking—the one he'd hoped to follow out of Síorghlas moments earlier.

"Your idea is a good one," the boy said, closing the book. "But I may have one better." The girl gazed up at him doubtfully. "I may not be skilled at shaping, but herblore is something I understand. If you like, I could help you with your studies."

The ealdor's daughter looked thunderstruck. "You'd do that for—me?"

"Aye." He handed her the sketchbook. "And I hope you keep scribbling pictures. You're very good at it."

The girl's lips curved into a smile. She accepted the book, hugging it to her like it was the one thing in the world keeping her afloat in a sea of solitude and unmet expectations.

"I would be grateful for your help," the ealdor's daughter said, her voice sounding oddly choked. "Though I'm not sure my mother would approve."

"Good thing she only takes reports from those she deems trustworthy and deserving of her time."

The ealdor's daughter laughed. An answering grin spread over the boy's face—he could feel it. She was cautiously opening up like a flower in early spring still vulnerable to winter's frost. To him. And he knew too well what it was like to be vulnerable. He wouldn't betray her trust.

Her dark-green eyes swept over the boy. "You're not quite what I expected, you know."

Still grinning, the boy pushed his hair out of his eyes and tried to stand up taller. Something about the way she was looking at him made him suddenly bold.

"Neither are you."

The ealdor's daughter said nothing. But although she held her chin high, there was a dash of color creeping over her cheeks, staining them a lovely shade of rose.

"We can meet here tomorrow at noon—if you're available, of course," the boy said.

"I am." She paused to cast a guilty look over her shoulder. "But just now I ought to be going—before my mother's guard finds me out."

"Of course."

"Tomorrow then."

"Tomorrow." The boy bowed in farewell. "May the stars light your path—"

Instead of reciting the traditional response, the ealdor's daughter broke protocol by stepping forward to touch his hand. "They always do, don't they?"

At her touch, a thrill rushed through the boy stronger than the stirring of his shape-gift, sharpening his senses and setting his stomach afire. He felt himself fighting the urge to smile again.

"Aye," he said. "I suppose they'd have to."

With a flash of bright hair, the ealdor's daughter turned and disappeared into the trees. As the boy watched her leave, something stirred inside him. Perhaps it was mere attraction, or perhaps it was the unfamiliar mingling of hope and doubt. But the doubt was louder than the hope.

She was, after all, an ealdor's daughter.

My pencil lead snapped.

I found myself still sitting in biology, where the teacher was in the middle of her lecture. Even the girl beside me still had her phone under her desk and was furiously typing something. What was her name—Andrea or something? I didn't care. Since no one had noticed me zoning out, I searched for a new pencil to resume my notetaking. But I couldn't get the dream about the boy out of my head.

Who *was* the boy?

I reached out to finger the tiny leaves and delicate stem of the bean seedling before me. If I tried, I could almost convince myself that the dreams I was having were nothing more than some kind of wild coping mechanism, but like last time, the images were *so* vivid. I could still smell the mingled scents of earth and decaying wood. I could feel the breeze as it pushed its way through the trees. Sword ferns burst from the ground, moss crept along every surface. There were mushrooms with golden caps, fragrant wax flowers, unruly brambles. And what was the name of the city in the forest? Sheer-something?

Síorghlas.

A chill started at my neck and crinkled over my shoulders.

"Miss Ashwood, did you catch that?"

Ms. Li's voice wrenched me fully into the present. I jumped. The intermittent chorus of coughs and yawns broke apart. Pencils stopped scratching. Even the fly in the window momentarily paused her droning as a painful silence filled up the room.

"Yeah. Um"—I slipped my sketchbook beneath my horticulture notebook—"oxygen is vital for microbe—respiration."

"For *root* and microbe respiration," Ms. Li corrected.

I glanced down at my nonexistent notes. "Right. That."

"While you're in my class, I expect you to stay on task and pay attention. I'm not giving this lecture for my own benefit." She gave me a severe look. "Consider this a warning."

Quiet laughter bubbled throughout the classroom. Andrea, or whatever her name was, pressed her fist to her mouth like she was trying not to join in. The look on her face made me want to grab her half-hidden phone and throw it at her face.

Ignoring my more violent impulses, I ducked my head and started on my class notes. Ms. Li went on with her lecture, but I barely heard it. I was still pondering my dream. I shook myself. Wondering about the boy wouldn't help me get any closer to the answers I was looking for. I needed to focus.

I'd had misgivings about Mom's past even before she died, but I'd ignored them. Leslie confirmed my suspicions about Mom. She helped by recognizing my need for truth and telling me what she could of Mom's story, but her knowledge was limited. And so far, my search through old yearbooks at the library was a bust. There had to be another way to find what I was looking for.

There is only one way.

I jammed my jaw shut and tried to shut out the voice, but its words were like a siren's song echoing through my mind; I couldn't unhear them. My fingers went to the bean seedling again like I was searching for comfort and grounding in something living. I absently ran my index finger from root to crown. My toes tingled—then my limbs, then my middle. A gentle, stirring feeling started in my feet and moved to my gut, then onward into my fingers. I was having some kind of episode. There *was* no voice. My mind and body were intact. There was only the classroom, me, and my exhausted mind. And Mom's secrets.

I traced the length of the seedling with my fingers like lines on a palm. What if they were connected somehow—the dreams, the voice, and Mom's secrets? The strange light that had burst from my hands. It could mean something that my dreams involved an isolated people group like the one Mom had come from. It could mean something that the light I'd shot from my hands resembled the magic in my dreams. Or it could all be coincidence—the need for me to find connections and look for answers where there were none.

"What is that?"

The girl at my table shot out of her seat, her chair clattering onto the tile. Ms. Li gaped at her, and before anyone could do anything, let alone figure out what the girl was freaking about, the class exploded with panic. Chairs screeched, students cried out and began scrambling onto their seats. No one paid attention to the teacher issuing orders like a drill instructor, they were too busy pointing. At me.

"How is she doing that?" someone cried.

"Is that a plant?"

"It's *moving*."

I glanced down—and hurled myself out of my chair. Shaking, I grabbed the table behind me to keep from falling. The seedling I'd been stroking had transformed. Tendrils of vine curled over the table, sending trembling, serpentine vines covered in purple blossoms all the way to the floor.

"What did she do?" someone asked in a shrill whisper.

I had no idea. Apparently, Ms. Li had other ideas. She came raging at me like a thundercloud.

"What is this, some kind of prank?"

"A—prank?" I asked incredulously.

"Whatever you want to call it." She gestured to the monster plant sprawled before me. "I want to know what this is."

"A bean plant?"

"Your sarcasm isn't doing you any favors right now."

"I'm being serious. I have no idea what happened."

"Really?" Ms. Li gave me a severe look. "You're telling me you didn't do this?"

I tried to speak, but the answer stayed locked up inside my throat. Catching sight of my face, the teacher softened. I either looked terrified or like I was about to explode. Collecting herself, she pressed her fingers to her temples and took a deep breath.

"Okay, everyone. Let's calm down. Return to your seats."

The class complied, albeit reluctantly. Meanwhile, Ms. Li came toward me, lowering her voice so only I could hear.

"Wren? Do you know what happened?"

I stared at my hands, speechless and shaking and wondering what on earth was wrong with me. I could feel Ms. Li's eyes boring into me. I could sense the class staring at me with a hungry sort of dissatisfaction. I could hear their whispers. More than anything, I wanted them all to go away and leave me alone, but my ability to turn myself invisible at will, it seemed, had abandoned me.

Ms. Li exhaled a long, tremulous breath. She sounded like an exasperated parent trying hard not to yell at their perpetually misbehaving child.

"I'm trying to help you, but I need you to communicate with me. I need answers."

The silence pressed in close. It felt like the whole class was holding its collective breath, waiting to hear my answer.

"I don't have any," I said weakly.

"Are you sure?"

Ms. Li narrowed her eyes like she didn't believe me. I wanted to scream in frustration. Why would I lie about something like that? Why would anyone?

"Do you think someone else might have switched out your plant while you were distracted?" the teacher asked.

I wanted to laugh. Who could have pulled something like that off with the whole class looking on?

"Wren?" Ms. Li pressed.

"No," I said hoarsely.

"That seedling became a mature plant in a matter of minutes," she said. "Was it a practical joke?"

"I'm not really the joking type."

Ms. Li leaned forward, resting her palm on the table. "Wren, I'm concerned about you. Your grades are suffering, you rarely pay attention in class, and now this. I want to get to the bottom of this so we can work through it together."

"I'm telling the truth," I said. "I don't know what happened."

With a sigh, Ms. Li pushed herself up off the table. "Why don't you see me after class?"

I focused on her writing scrawled across the whiteboard to keep from lashing out like I wanted to. I couldn't believe I was being punished for something I had no control over.

The bell rang a minute later. I stayed in my seat as the other students filed out of the classroom, giving me a wide berth as they passed.

"Wait here," Ms. Li said, throwing a suspicious look at the vine encircling my table. "I've got to phone the office."

She muttered something else about having to cancel an important meeting before picking up her phone and stepping into the hall. I bit back the smart remark I wanted to throw at her. I knew what she was doing—trying to make me feel guilty for inconveniencing her. But when I thought about it, her reaction made sense. Like me, she was coping. She had seen something impossible, and she wanted an explanation, a confession. It was easier to accept me doing something malicious than to think that I had no control over what happened.

Still rattled, I gazed at the row of seedlings. Some of the sprouts were so small they didn't have true leaves, making mine appear that much more out of place.

"I know what that's like," I whispered, reaching out an empathetic hand to touch one of the leaves.

To my surprise, the plant shivered again. Purple flower petals faded and fluttered down as tiny green bean pods appeared and began swelling at an impossible rate. I jerked my hand back.

"No way."

I shook my hand out and stared, remembering how Peter kept complaining about his overgrown yard. I thought about the thriving row of plant cuttings lining my bedroom window, and the way they had rooted overnight. I recalled with alarm the way my toes tingled every time I left the sidewalk at school to cut across the grass.

Could I manipulate plant growth?

Suddenly, the classroom felt stifling. The air seemed to bend around me, walling me in and smothering me. With Ms. Li out of sight, I knew I couldn't stay cooped up any longer. Without pausing to consider repercussions, I jumped up, picked up my plant, shoved it into my backpack, and slipped invisibly out the classroom door.

CHAPTER 8
FREAK

SOMETHING SLAMMED INTO THE bathroom door like a battering ram. I thought I'd locked it, but it flew open, groaning on its hinges. Suddenly, I wasn't alone with my plant friend anymore. Vines snaked around me, twining up my legs, over the bathroom floor, and into the stalls. It was probably tumbling into the toilets, but I'd been too scared to verify that theory. I stared wildly at the girl who'd entered, wondering how on earth to explain the wild mess of vines I was sitting in.

"Whoa! Are you okay?" she asked.

Was I okay when I couldn't make it through a school day without hearing voices, seeing visions, assaulting innocent boys, and exploding plants? I had no idea anymore.

Silently, I willed the stranger to back out the way she'd come and never look at me again. Instead, she darted to snatch a tissue from the box on the counter. I hadn't realized I'd been crying until she crouched down and handed it to me.

"Thanks."

"What happened?" she asked.

I indicated the whole bathroom with a wave. "I got in a fight with a plant and lost, obviously."

"I can tell."

I finally managed to look up. The girl was holding a violin case wrapped in band stickers. She cleared a few vines away, laid down the violin, and slapped a tattered paperback on top. She was petite with olive-toned skin, sea-gray eyes swept with eyeliner, choppy maroon hair, and a lip ring.

"Do you need anything? Weedkiller, or garden shears, or..." She trailed off.

"I'm fine." I shoved the vines aside and stood up.

The girl said nothing. I made my way to the counter, avoiding the vines mingling with crumpled paper towel balls that had missed the trash bin earlier. Why did I feel so dead tired?

Folding her arms, the girl came to stand behind me. I turned and caught a glimpse of the text on her shirt: *socially, legally, and mentally unequipped to deal with the human race.*

Now that was a sentiment I felt to my core.

"Really?" the girl asked. "I kick open the bathroom door and find you crying and drowning in a pile of hostile plants, and you tell me you're fine?"

"It was a freak thing," I said, not knowing how else to explain the incident.

"Emphasis on the 'freak.'"

"Thanks."

The girl watched as I picked up a paper towel and began using it to sweep vines off the mirror and out of the sink. I had no idea what to do with the mess—cram it in a trash can? Burn it? To my surprise, the girl quit impersonating a punk rock statue and started to help by unwinding the vines that were caught in the paper towel dispenser. I was grateful for the help, but I still wanted to be alone.

"Hey, um," she said, breaking the silence. "I didn't mean *you* were a freak. I'm just bad at talking with people."

I understood that more than she knew. "It's fine."

"Cool." She used her combat boot to nudge a few leafy stragglers toward the garbage bin. "So, does that Infiniti ride as nice as it looks?"

It took me a moment to place "Infiniti" as Leslie's car.

"I guess," I said, finding it awkward that she'd noticed what car I came to school in. "Are you into cars?"

"I hate cars." The odd girl laughed. She threw a few more bean strands into the trash and straightened. Kicking several vines out of her way, she turned and disappeared into one of the bathroom stalls. "You're not in Kansas anymore, are you, Toto?" she asked.

"What?"

"I mean you're not used to life in a small town." There were scraping noises as she cleared the stall of all its viny inhabitants. "Everybody's in your business whether you like it or not because this is Alaska, and this school is approximately the size of a toaster. You sneeze in biology, and the whole student body knows by lunch. You come to school alone in a beater car, and everyone knows your parents made you pay for it yourself. You bring your own sandwich for lunch and sit by yourself every single day, and people start to speculate food allergies, indigestion, restrictive diet, finicky eater, soulless demon—you get the picture."

I knew without asking that the sandwich-eating demon without a soul was me, but I wasn't bothered by the description.

"And if you're going to magically manipulate plants and cry during lunch, maybe find a better hiding place. There are a couple of single-occupancy bathrooms over by the office. They haven't been cleaned in decades, and they may or may not be haunted by a melodramatic female ghost in glasses and a Hogwarts robe, but no one will ever bother you in there—trust me."

"Thanks. I'll keep that in mind."

The beaten book balancing precariously on her violin case distracted me from being properly appreciative. It was a Jane Austen treasury with Colin Firth on the cover and tiny hand-drawn hearts floating around his head. Above the title, someone had scrawled, "This book belongs to the future Mrs. Darcy."

I glanced up as the girl reappeared, stuffing a few more vine tangles into the trash on her way to the sink. Judging by her appearance, I wouldn't have pegged her as an Austen fan.

"I'm Emery, by the way," she said, attacking the soap dispenser to the left of the sink.

"Wren."

The bell rang, reminding me that lunch was over, and my stomach growled, reminding me that there was an untouched sandwich languishing in my locker. I sighed. A quick survey of the space told me our job was finished. The trash bins were overflowing with foliage, but at least the rest of the bathroom was clear.

"Thanks for your help," I said, preparing to leave.

"No problem," Emery said. "So, who drives that Infiniti anyway? Your rich grandmother?"

"My guardian."

Emery's eyebrows scrunched together. "Your *guardian*?"

"Yeah." Not wanting to discuss my family dynamics—or lack thereof—with a stranger, I turned to slip out the door. "I should go."

I still had a lot to think about—and a lot of confused emotions to work though. To begin with, I now knew that I had some sort of bizarre ability to control plant growth, and I hadn't decided yet whether to think it was cool or horrifying. I wanted to find someplace quiet to sift through my memories and figure out if it had any connection to my mom. I thought I could slip outside and find someplace to hide out until Leslie came, but Emery snatched up her violin case and hurried after me.

"Hang on," she said. "You can't get rid of me that easily."

Exasperated laughter bubbled out of me. "I'm trying get to class."

"Then why are you headed for the exit?"

I barely resisted the urge to lunge for her violin case, smack her with it, and run. "Look, I appreciate your help back there, but you don't have to keep following me around."

"I do if I want to figure out what happened."

"I don't know what happened, okay?" I started walking faster.

Emery's diminutive form bobbed alongside me, struggling to keep up. She had to be at least four inches shorter than me, and I was on the low end of average height. Did this tiny human seriously kick the bathroom door in?

"That's fine," she said. "Maybe we can put our heads together and figure it out. I'm good at that sort of thing."

I stifled a groan. Emery had been kind enough to help me clean up my mess in the bathroom, but the last thing I needed was an irritating amateur sleuth trailing me to try and figure out what was wrong with me. Sensing my hesitation, Emery glanced down the empty hall. All the responsible students were settling into class right now, and I was possibly a wanted criminal for escaping punishment after the plant-growing incident.

"Trust me," Emery insisted. "You need my help."

"I do?"

"You're in over your head with this stuff," she said. "You keep looking around like you're avoiding someone, and you clearly don't know how to skip class properly." Before I could argue, she grabbed hold of my wrist and began herding me down the hall. "Act confident. Don't hedge. I'm your walking hall pass."

"I don't think hall passes work like that."

"No arguments," she ordered.

I let out a huge sigh. Either I had gained a sidekick, or I had become one.

"Let's start with back story," Emery charged on. "Where are you from?"

I kept an eye out for teachers or other school faculty as we made our way through the main building. Emery was right: I wasn't practiced in the art of skipping class, but even I knew stealth was required. Emery, however, had other ideas. The farther we walked, the more her volume increased. She'd already told me all about the killer snickerdoodles at her favorite cafe and bakery in Ketchikan, using full-arm gestures to emphasize how massive and glorious they were. With a sigh, I drew up my hood. Emery was about as subtle as a flamingo visiting an ant farm.

"I've moved a lot," I said.

"Really? Why?"

"I wish I knew."

"Interesting. Is someone in your family part of the Witness Protection Program?" Emery let go of my wrist to fling the doors open. "Or are you a changeling?"

"Not that I know of."

"Any chance you've been bitten by a spider?"

"Please stop."

Emery ignored me. I could hear her puffing and struggling to keep up with my normal stride as she trailed me through the courtyard. She went on to suggest a number of other plot lines she'd ripped from books and movies until I stopped responding. I was half ready to turn around and give myself up to the biology teacher when Emery gave the most absurd theory yet.

"How about this: your parents are wanted criminals? Or—plot twist"—she snapped her fingers and pointed finger guns at me—"*you're the criminal*—"

"Emery. This is getting weird."

"Not any weirder than you making plants explode all over the bathroom."

She wasn't wrong.

Emery grabbed my wrist again, pushing me through the parking lot toward her car. "I'm trying to help you out, but you're being surprisingly unhelpful."

"Sorry."

"No, you're not."

"Fine," I ground out. "I came here because my mom died in a car accident two months ago, but that isn't the worst of it. After she died, I found out she kept her entire life—her past, her family, everything—a secret from me. I know she grew up here, but that's it. I've tried looking her up, but I don't even know her birth date. She wasn't the person I thought she was, and it's freaking me out."

Emery paused at the back end of a dented Jetta with a smashed taillight, looking thoughtful for once. Either she was surprised by my sudden verbal flood, or my story had sobered her.

"That's what you're doing every day at lunch, isn't it?" she said. "Looking for her?"

"Yeah."

She was silent a moment, then said, "Well, why don't we start there?"

"Start where?"

"Start looking for clues about what's going on with you by finding out more about your mom's past." When I gave her a blank stare, she went on. "If you have some freak ability—sorry—it might be hereditary. If not, you haven't lost anything because you're still finding out the truth about your mom."

I took a moment to consider Emery's proposition. On the one hand, I was bothered. I already wasn't overly enthusiastic about having her asking questions and following me around. I hadn't asked for Emery's help to begin with, and sharing what little I knew about Mom with her felt like sacrilege. Emery didn't know Mom; she had no personal investment in finding out where she came from and who she was. Emery's only satisfaction would come from solving the case. On the other hand, I had to admit that allowing Emery to team up with me meant covering more ground, and hopefully, finding out the truth sooner.

"I guess that makes sense," I relented.

Emery's eyes lit up like she was a little kid and I'd given her a vat of sugar to ingest. She twisted around to pat the trunk of the car she'd been leaning against as she made her way to the driver's side.

"This is Albert," she announced. "My boyfriend."

"The car?"

"Don't call him that."

"Sorry."

Emery climbed inside, tossed her violin in the back, and reached across the seat to crank open the passenger window. "Get in, loser."

I opened the door and slid inside, deciding it was best not to ask about Emery's relationship with her car. Sheets of classical music were strewn across the floorboards, and there were fast food wrappers, a pair of brand-name gym shoes, makeup packaging, and a wadded-up hoodie to contend with. I could deal with the trash, but it was a struggle to stay where I was with stickers like "Old Fart," "Kiss my Bass," and "I Brake for Tacos" plastered on the passenger door.

My stomach growled at the thought of food, tacos or otherwise. Unfortunately, I'd skipped lunch, and my sandwich was sitting alone and abandoned in my locker.

Emery hummed a tune while she jabbed her keys in the ignition. A metal song came rattling out of her overworked speakers. She slipped on some sunglasses, backed out, and hit the accelerator. Within moments, she was sliding out of the school parking lot, pounding her steering wheel and center column like it was all part of her drum kit. Was the feeling of regret supposed to hit the minute we left campus, or was this a little premature?

"This is great," Emery said, shouting to be heard over her blown subwoofer. "I never perform as well without an audience."

"Glad I could help," I said sarcastically.

"No idea what your name is, by the way. How about I call you Lillian?"

"How about no."

Emery ignored me and kept singing. When we came to a traffic light, she leaned across me to shout lyrics out my open window at a pair of construction workers in orange vests. The construction workers shook their heads at Emery and laughed. Apparently, this wasn't the first time Emery had tried to woo them with her theatrics.

When the light turned green, Emery made sure to squeal her tires extra loud. It might have been cool if it weren't for the fact that the song on her stereo changed, and it was now playing an iconic pop melody from the 90s. As soon as Emery noticed it, she scrambled for her phone and jabbed the skip button.

"Not sure how that got on here," she mumbled. "It was probably my punk little brother. He loads songs on here to mess with me."

"At least he understands your musical taste."

Emery made a choking noise. "Not *mine*."

"Right. I'm sure your little brother is a huge Backstreet Boys fan."

"Maybe he is. You don't know." She cast a shifty-eyed glance in my direction.

I almost cracked a smile. Judging by her defensive posture and panicky tone, Emery wasn't as confident as she let on. I nodded to her Jane Austen treasury sitting on her dashboard.

"Does Mr. Darcy know?" I asked.

"Mr. Darcy *gets* me."

"Mr. Darcy might get you, but he finds your taste in music barely tolerable."

Emery shrugged. "Every relationship takes compromise."

"Mr. Darcy doesn't compromise. His good opinion once lost is lost forever. Or at least until he dies."

"Mr. Darcy is immortal," she said, carefully enunciating every syllable. Something told me she didn't like my irreverent tone toward her favorite work of fiction.

"Mr. Darcy is a fictional character."

Emery slammed on her brakes hard enough to hurl me into the wind-shield—and she would have if it weren't for my seatbelt. "Get out of my car."

Despite Emery's threats, she started driving again, and within minutes, she had parallel parked on a side street. Stopping the engine, Emery tore off her seat belt, threw open the door, and dashed toward the wooden walkway. I followed behind at a distance as she threw her arms in the air and twirled in circles, singing show tunes. She had a good singing voice, but her dance moves were left wanting; she ended up nearly windmilling into an older couple posing for a picture.

"You sure you need caffeine?" I murmured, following her inside a little cafe strung with patio lights.

"Always."

We walked up to the counter, and Emery peered into the glass bakery case. Her whole face lit up when she saw what was inside.

"Last snickerdoodle of the day, and it's mine," she said. "I call it fate."

I didn't answer; I was too busy staring at the apple, cheddar, and turkey panini sitting unclaimed at the edge of the counter. The bread looked so crusty, so perfectly golden—

Emery nudged me. "Get something."

I hesitated, stomach grumbling loudly. "I don't have any cash."

"Oh, don't worry. I've got you. My dad gives my little brother and me tons of cash. It's his way of making it look like he cares about his kids."

A few minutes, two drinks, a sandwich, and a cookie later, we sat down at a mosaic-top table in the corner, surrounded by local artwork and eclectic décor. The paintings on the wall were vivid displays of Ketchikan's docks and iconic buildings, but the Tongass was barely a sweep of green in the backdrop. For being on the edge of the largest national forest in the United States, I found the lack of forest depictions disappointing.

I was halfway through my sandwich when my phone vibrated. Annoyed, I relinquished my sandwich long enough to slide my phone out and check the screen. Leslie was heading to the school to pick me up. I typed out a quick message telling her I got out early and was at a coffee shop with a classmate but that I would be home by dinner. She responded almost immediately asking me to call.

My thumb hovered over the screen, but I couldn't think of anything to say. Skimming over my missed messages, I realized she had sent at least three messages in the last half hour alone. My teachers might have told her about the plant-exploding incident, but more likely, they wanted to know why I was missing my classes. Knowing Leslie, she was probably worried that I skipped to do drugs in the back of someone's truck while they spun donuts in the Walmart parking lot.

"You could probably kill with that look," Emery observed.

"I get like that when I'm hungry." I stowed my phone and picked up my sandwich, promising myself I'd call Leslie after I finished.

"So, who was that text from?" Emery asked, taking a sip of her mocha. "Your guardian?"

"Yeah." I finished my sandwich and wiped my fingers on a napkin. "She's not all bad, but she hovers."

"Unstable family members are the best." Emery tore off a bit of her cookie and stuffed it in her mouth. "I have several I'd be happy to part with if you ever need more."

"Thanks." I didn't bother reminding Emery that Leslie wasn't family; instead, I wrapped my hands around my mug and contemplated the perfectly poured foam rosette. "What's your family like?" I asked.

Emery made a face. Over her shoulder, the mist threaded its way through the evergreens. I didn't actually care about Emery's family. I wanted to steer the conversation away from my current living situation, and I still wasn't convinced I wanted Emery getting involved.

"My dad's a lawyer," Emery said with obvious disgust. "Right now, he's on city council—Chris Innes—never vote for him. Anyway, we live with the life-size Barbie my dad's married to, enough cars and trucks to feed a small, impoverished nation for at least a decade, a demonic cat who hates me, and my little brother, Parker. Park's fourteen and already has relationship problems because he's my dad's offspring. He's technically my half-brother, but he's the only one in the family I'd go to jail for. My dad and Ange though—might as well be another species."

"Wow." I took a sip of my drink, then wrenched away from it. The drink was scalding hot.

"It's a shame we can't pick the people we depend on for survival," Emery said.

"I hear you." I picked up my cup again and blew across the surface. "Yesterday, Leslie asked how I'd feel about therapy."

Emery almost choked on her drink—either because it was the approximate temperature of molten steel or because she was trying not to laugh. She wiped her mouth with the back of her hand, eyes sparkling. "At least she's trying to show you she cares," she offered.

"I guess."

Emery tapped the tabletop. "Let's get back to the matter at hand. What can you tell me about your mom?"

"She came from Ketchikan."

"You already mentioned that. What else?"

"Um...she had reddish-brown hair, green eyes—like me, basically. She hated technology. She loved to draw. She was always working, but she had a tough time holding down a job. That was why we were always moving."

"Interesting." Emery dug a notebook from her backpack and started taking notes. "Did she ever *say* that was why you guys moved a lot?"

"Well, no. She just always found a reason to get back on the road."

"Sounds to me like she was running from something," Emery mused. "Something that happened here."

I started to take another sip of my drink, then stopped. The voice entered my head again, earthy and deep.

You are near to the truth.

Unwillingly, I lifted my eyes to the window. The trees waved their hands at me, silent and beckoning.

Come.

"You okay?" Emery asked, leaning forward. "Lillian?"

With an effort, I tore my gaze from the window. "It's Wren."

"You look more like a Hazel. Maybe an Edith."

"You don't get to rename people." I tried my drink again, my mind still half on the forest. "Have you ever noticed anything—I don't know—*abnormal* about the forest here?"

"The forest? What do you mean?"

I hesitated. Emery already thought I was a freak. I *knew* I was a freak, but I did not appreciate being reminded of it.

"Spill, woman," Emery said.

The words tumbled out before I had a chance to call them back. "I have this feeling about it. Like it's aware. And it's—watching me."

Emery gave me a weird look. "You sure you don't need that therapy Leslie suggested?"

I swirled my drink around in my cup, suddenly wishing I hadn't spoken. "Forget it."

Sighing, Emery laid down her cup and picked up her cookie. "Now that you mention it, there was something weird that happened a few years back. A girl from our school went missing out there. Her car turned up at the edge of the forest, but there were no signs of a struggle. She just disappeared. Rescue crews turned up nothing. Rumors circulated about *Tornit* and aliens and hexes. Mostly, people figured it was a freak incident, but it gave everyone a weird feeling." Her expression turned thoughtful. "Her name was Amber something. Martinez, maybe?"

I slid to the edge of my seat. What Emery was telling me felt important, but like when the librarian mentioned what must be the same incident, I couldn't say why.

"And they never found her?" I asked.

"Not as far as I know."

"But people went into the forest before she disappeared, right?"

Emery shrugged. "From what I've heard, it's a bunch of old guys drinking and skeet shooting. Not my idea of a good time."

I scowled into my mug. Maybe I hadn't seen the part of the forest Emery was talking about. I hadn't been inside, but I hadn't noticed any tire marks, shotgun shells, or broken clay pigeons. Oddly, her story did line up with the librarian's.

"Wouldn't they want an open range for shooting?"

"You'd think." Emery broke off another piece of her snickerdoodle and popped it in her mouth. "These cookies are phenomenal. So buttery. Want one?" She held out a piece to me, but I declined. Shrugging, Emery crammed another bite in her mouth.

"What about you?" I asked. "Have you ever gone out there?"

But Emery acted as if she didn't hear me. Her eyes were fixed on some obscure point across the cafe, and she was busy grinding the remnants of her prized cookie to powder.

"Emery?"

She blinked twice. "What?"

"I asked you a question, but you sort of dozed off."

"You did?"

"Are you sure you're all right?"

Emery didn't answer. Her eyes dropped to the mound of crumbs on her plate. A crease formed between her brows like she couldn't understand how her fingers came to be coated in cinnamon sugar.

"Yeah, sorry. I have a headache." She dabbed her fingers on a napkin, pushed her plate aside, and stood up. "C'mon. I better take you home before your unstable guardian does something weird."

CHAPTER 9
FOXES AND WOLVES

"Wait," I said. "You don't think she even went to Edgewood?"

"That's what I'm saying."

Emery leaned back and put her feet up in a neighboring chair. With her newly dyed electric-blue hair, her winged eyeliner, and her shirt that read "I hate you because you make me hate you," she was a cheerful storm cloud.

"You can try requesting attendance records in the office, but they might not give them to you because of FERPA. That stands for Family Educational Rights and Privacy Act," Emery said proudly. "I googled that."

I didn't want to admit it, but Emery was probably right. She and I had claimed a computer at the school library to look through useless yearbook photos. Again. It was as if I were caught in a time loop. Every day, I sifted through the same photos, and every day, I found nothing that could indicate Mom had ever set foot on Edgewood's campus.

"But I'm her kid."

"You can still try," Emery said with a shrug. "They might consider your interest legitimate, but I have a feeling you're looking at a dead end."

I banged my head on the keyboard and groaned. And then I remembered—Mom hadn't even known what a shower was when Leslie met her. She probably *hadn't* gone to Edgewood.

To her credit, Emery didn't laugh when I told her about my revelation. Two days had passed since our little school-skipping adventure. Leslie hadn't been thrilled about my life choices when I got home from the cafe, but Emery proved her worth by smooth-talking Leslie. She reminded Leslie that I was a girl who had just lost her mom, after all. I'd been having a hard day and needed a friend to step in and comfort me. I made sure Leslie couldn't see my face when I rolled my eyes. Leslie bought the story and even invited Emery to stay for dinner. Clearly, Emery had inherited her silver tongue from her politician father.

"What now?" I asked, ignoring the computer keys grinding into my face. "More internet research?"

"I spent a few hours looking up your mom last night and filling out a couple of forms under your name. I basically came up with nothing."

"You do know that's illegal, right?"

"I'm willing to commit forgery for you. That's the kind of friend I am."

"Wait. What about hospital records?" I thought about my birth certificate, stating I'd been born in Ketchikan. Conveniently, Mom's birthday wasn't on it.

"Won't work," Emery said. "HIPAA remains in effect for fifty years after a person's death. It stands for the Health Insurance Portability—"

"I know what HIPAA is."

"Since we're not finding anything online or at the school, I think we should try the public library. We might find her birth announcement in the local paper, and that'll tell us her date of birth. Maybe we'll even come across the names of her parents." Emery stood, slid on her backpack, and picked up her violin. "But that'll have to wait for another day. I've got band practice in eight minutes."

I sighed into the keyboard. "Fine. See you."

Emery gave a little wave and walked off.

I meant to get up and walk to class, but I found myself totally unable to move. My brain was congested with what-ifs. What if Emery and I came up with nothing? What if Mom's past was buried for good, and I really had lost her forever?

I squeezed my eyes shut against the panic and tried to breathe, tried to remind myself that I didn't have to figure everything out all at once. I hadn't exhausted every resource yet. Emery was willing to help me in my search for information about Mom, and if Peter and Leslie knew how desperate I was for any trace of her, they might help too. And if all else failed, I could use my college money to go to school to become a private investigator.

I knew what Mom would say. *Go to school to pursue what you're passionate about,* she'd tell me. *Get out there and try things. Make mistakes. Make friends. And learn to forgive yourself.* I smiled, then sighed. It didn't matter what Mom said, because she'd lied to me. Slowly, the room around me faded, and the next thing I knew, I was back in the forest.

The boy sat on a low-hanging evergreen bough with the ealdor's daughter sitting close beside him. Even though I couldn't see his face, I could tell that some time had passed. The boy was taller and broader in the shoulders. His hair was longer too. The ealdor's daughter, however, remained unchanged. She was wearing a midnight blue tunic, and her hair was done up in a loose braid with a few star-like wildflowers tucked throughout.

"—and that's how you'll pass your herblore examination," the boy said, closing the book on his lap and turning to the ealdor's daughter.

The ealdor's daughter was silent for a moment. Beneath the setting sun, her hair blazed with red-gold fire, and the scent of her was like wildflowers. The boy leaned in. He noticed that the ealdor's daughter didn't withdraw her hand when he casually bumped it with his own. He had placed his hand strategically, hoping their knuckles would brush whenever either of them leaned in to speak.

"I don't understand at all," the ealdor's daughter said with mock wistfulness. "I'm afraid you'll have to explain it all over again."

"All?"

"You didn't realize you were tutoring a dunce, did you?" Something about her tone told the boy she wasn't as much of a dunce as she pretended to be. He felt a shameless smile playing at the corner of his mouth.

"Tutoring a fox, more like," he said.

"Fox?" The ealdor's daughter pretended to look shocked. "Listen to the lad. The very cheek."

Eyes smoldering, she repositioned herself to slide down from the branch they were perched on. Quick as a flash, the boy jumped down and reached out to place a steadying hand on her waist.

"I've no more cheek than you, lass," he said, guiding her carefully to the ground.

"Perhaps."

The ealdor's daughter let herself fall against the boy. She stayed there a moment longer than necessary before extricating herself. The boy felt his heart beating hard. He knew he was smiling like an idiot, but he couldn't help it. Something—he didn't know what—was blossoming between him and the ealdor's daughter. He didn't know whether to fear it or be in awe.

"Well then." The girl suddenly stretched on her toes to plant a kiss on his cheek. "Until tomorrow."

The boy stared speechless after the girl's retreating form. The touch of her lips, of her shape-gift, still burned on his skin. He would never be the

Wind Shaper as he wished, but it seemed the boy possessed another kind of power. He could make people like him—powerful people. People like the ealdor's daughter.

Shaking himself, the boy climbed back onto the evergreen bough and drew out one of his own books. While the ealdor's daughter had been studying herblore, the boy had been learning the workings of Síorghlas. He worked hard to understand the rotations of the guards, the distribution of food and clothing, and the justice system. Where others maintained the status quo, the boy looked for weaknesses and formulated solutions. Once, he had brought his propositions before the ealdors and had even managed to capture their attention. He even fancied he might like to *be* an ealdor one day.

But one matter continued to haunt him—

"Evening, scumbag."

The boy froze. He was well accustomed to Stonecrop's nightly greeting, but he never enjoyed it.

"You sit there all day and fritter away your time, reading a lot of nonsense." Stonecrop stared at him with bulging eyes, wiping his nose with his sleeve. "Non-*sense*."

"I am sure you're right." The boy turned the page in his book. There was no use explaining anything like political ambitions to the likes of Stonecrop.

Stonecrop stumbled into the light of a shape-cast lantern and leered up into the tree. Suddenly, Stonecrop lashed out with a blow at his boot. The boy picked up his feet just in time. He might be unskilled at other things, but at least he was quick, body *and* mind.

There was something odd in Stonecrop's bearing that evening. His eyes were gleaming and bloodshot, and his steps swayed in an ungainly manner. No doubt he had been sampling one of Columbine's juniper berry concoctions and gotten carried away.

"What's that pretty lass see in you, huh?" Stonecrop leaned on a lower branch, breathing heavily. "She's always hanging around with you these days. Quite chummy-like."

The boy did not answer. Officially, he and the ealdor's daughter were only friends. He couldn't hope for more until he found himself a seat on the ealdor council. But there was no use explaining that to Stonecrop either.

Annoyed, Stonecrop suddenly grabbed at the boy's book. This time, the boy was too slow to keep Stonecrop from hurling it into the dirt. Stonecrop guffawed while the boy climbed down from his cedar bough to retrieve his book.

"I always thought your books were rubbish," Stonecrop announced.

"That's because you don't read."

"I read"—Stonecrop hiccupped—"loads."

The boy picked up his book and dusted off the cover. "You are inebriated."

"We're getting off topic."

"You mean you had a point?"

"I've seen the way you look at her." Stonecrop stepped closer to the boy. "The way you sit close. The way you touch her and make it look like an accident. Bet she likes the attention."

"Shut up."

Stonecrop laughed. The boy could feel his neck burning. He searched the forest for something to focus on, something to ground himself. He had to stay calm; he had to control the narrative. But Stonecrop wasn't finished.

"She would never take you seriously anyway. She couldn't." Stonecrop wiped the spittle from his mouth and cackled absurdly. "She is an ealdor's daughter and an attractive lass. And you are—whatever you are."

The boy was well aware the ealdor's daughter outranked him in every way, but it stung to have a drunken Stonecrop remind him.

Stonecrop was standing close enough that the boy could smell his breath befouled with alcohol. "When that pretty lass kisses you, does she know she's kissing the filthy mouth of a half-breed?"

The boy's breath hissed out through his teeth. The ealdor's daughter hadn't kissed him like that. He wanted her to, but he knew better than to encourage something that would incite her mother's ire—not when the ealdor's favor was essential in helping him achieve his goals.

"Why don't you fight me in a proper duel?" Stonecrop took another swing at his book and missed. "Ah, right. You can't."

The boy tried to shut Stonecrop out, to listen instead to the quiet sounds of the forest. But the feeling of panic rose up inside him until it consumed him. No one could prove his father had been an Outlander. No one could argue with him having a shape-gift. And yet, any doubt about his pure ancestry could prevent him from achieving ealdorship—and from claiming the ealdor's daughter for his own.

"Are you listening to me?" Stonecrop laughed. "Outlander?"

Something inside him snapped. Before he realized what he was doing, Stonecrop was flat on the ground. The boy watched him for a moment, shoulders heaving. He had only meant to shut Stonecrop up. He turned away, thinking that would be the end of Stonecrop's drunken flailing, but he was wrong.

Stonecrop's leg shot up reflexively, aiming a kick to the boy's gut. The boy spun away. Groaning, Stonecrop rolled over and scrambled to his feet. Within moments, the boy was backed against a spruce, taking a hit to the jaw and another to the stomach. Even in Stonecrop's addled state, he was a worthy opponent.

"Does that lass know what you are?" Stonecrop shoved the boy back into the spruce. The boy could taste the blood filling his mouth. "An orphan? A misfit? A tragedy?" He grinned like a wolf. "A mistake?"

Seething, the boy raised his eyes. Gathering his wits about him, he disarmed Stonecrop with a quick knee to the groin, enjoying the way the older, larger boy curled in on himself and retched. As the boy stood over Stonecrop's pathetic form, a coldness came over him, a bloodthirst. Baring his teeth, the boy took one swing and then another.

Outlander.

The sound of his punches became rhythmic, hypnotizing. Stonecrop's allegations meant the boy would never be an ealdor. Never have respect. Never be accepted by his people. Never make the ealdor's daughter *his.*

Stonecrop held up his hands, weeping for mercy, but the boy had none.

"Stop!" a voice cried out. "What are you doing?"

The boy ignored the cry. Some part of him knew the voice, but he had no power to restrain himself. He was beyond himself.

"Stop it!" the ealdor's daughter shouted. "You will kill him!"

Some part of the boy heard her and understood. Straining every muscle, he froze. Stonecrop made a soft groaning sound, but he did not move.

The ealdor's daughter knelt, eyes wide in disbelief. "What have you done?"

The boy looked down at his swollen, bloodied hands and started shaking. He couldn't answer.

The ealdor's daughter shuddered. "I thought—"

The boy raised his eyes to the ealdor's daughter. She swallowed and tried again. "I thought you were better than this."

"I am not sure I am."

"No." The ealdor's daughter wrapped her arms around him and drew him close, heedless of the blood. "You are."

The boy couldn't lift his hands to return her embrace. His eyes were glued to Stonecrop's inert form. Around them, the ground was wet; by daylight, the boy knew it would be a crimson dreamscape. Inside, the boy was screaming *I did this.*

"You lost yourself." The ealdor's daughter stroked his hair as she spoke, her voice thick with emotion. "You gave into fear."

Lost himself? More like he'd never found himself to begin with.

"We shall figure this out," the ealdor's daughter assured him. "We'll make it right."

The boy shut his eyes and tried to breathe, but the pain in his chest was too much. There was no making this right. All the things Stonecrop said disturbed him for one reason—they were true. No matter what Stonecrop had said or done, he didn't deserve this.

The boy covered his face and began to sob.

CHAPTER 10
MISSING PIECE

MY FEET POUNDED THE concrete in a frantic rhythm. I had to get out of the library—out of the school. Voices were haunting me. I had a personal force field. I could control plant growth. And now, the outcast boy in the forest I kept having dreams about had turned into a murderous lunatic. It was the sight of the blood that triggered me. I could still hear my teacher at Fresno High talking soft, her voice muffled by the door as she relayed information about Mom's accident to the other staff.

"They're saying she fell asleep at the wheel and veered into traffic on northbound SR-41 near Jensen. There was a big rig involved, and—it was bad."

The salt wind whipped my hair as I ran. I didn't see Mom's body after the accident. I didn't need to. My imagination conjured images for me for weeks afterward.

The blood is the reason.

I stopped cold, nose to limb with the forest boundary. Why was I punishing myself? My brain was already overwrought with the grief of losing Mom. I was obsessing over her reasons and torturing my mind into instability. It wasn't my fault Mom had hidden the truth about her past for my entire life. What I needed was for Mom to have been honest with me. But she died without telling me the truth, so I had to figure it out for myself.

I hold the key to truth. Give me your trust. Come.

"Who are you?" I asked aloud.

There was no answer. The trees were astir with whispers, their dark feathered tops undulating like millions of beckoning fingers. Somehow, I had the sense that it was what had been speaking to me.

"That makes no sense," I murmured.

But neither did anything else. Suddenly, I was curious. What if the forest was talking to me? What if it really did contain the answers I was looking for? My hands reached out of their own accord to drag aside the juniper. The foliage shook in the wind and seemed to part way for me. I was almost there.

"You really think you should be going in there right now?"

I jerked and stumbled backwards. The boy with green eyes stood a few yards off with a motorcycle helmet in his hand.

"It's broad daylight, yeah? You're going to give us all away. I can't follow you around killing every rogue patch of wildflowers you accidentally grow this side of the third barrier."

I hadn't noticed the boy's accent before. It lilted and swayed in a subtly melodic way. Was he from Europe—Ireland, maybe?

"What are you talking about?"

He gestured in the direction I'd come from. There was a trail of bright green grass and wildflowers in the otherwise dead grass, leading back to the school. At the look on my face, the boy took a cautious step forward. His footsteps were silent, graceful, even. The gait of a hunter.

"Don't look so worried," he said gently. "I've seen worse than anything you've done. Not much worse, but a little."

I tucked my hair behind my ear and tried not to look like my eyes were flooding. "I don't know what's wrong with me."

"About the same thing that's wrong with any of us, I imagine."

"I'm serious." I gathered my breath. "First, I found out that my mom was lying, then there was the lightning, the plant, the dreams, and now this. It's too much."

The boy gave me the ghost of a smile. He had no idea what I was babbling about. I felt my composure start to slip. I turned away to stifle a sob.

"Hey, it's okay." I could hear the boy shift closer. "You'll do fine here. Just try to keep calm. Take breaks when you need them. Try blending."

Blending?

"I can help," the boy continued, "but I can't do much if you lose control and kill someone."

"Kill someone?"

The boy gave me a half-amused, half-exasperated look. "Relax. I'm on your team. No need to pretend with me."

"I'm not pretending anything."

"No. Of course not." There was a sarcastic edge to his tone, making it clear he didn't believe me but was willing to play along. "Try to keep things under control, all right? The last thing we need is some scandal putting the good people of Ketchikan on edge."

Sighing, I pulled the damp ends of my hair under my hood. "No offense, but everything you said is both cryptic and unhelpful."

He backed up, giving me a two-fingered salute. "You'll get the hang of things here. If you need anything, come find me. I'll be around."

The boy's careless attitude annoyed me. I didn't think he had any idea what I was going through, and he didn't care either.

"Really?" I shouted after him. "Because I'm still trying to wrap my head around blending."

The boy paused his retreat and turned back, giving me a slightly baffled look. "You know—blending. You don't want to be seen, yeah? When you concentrate on that feeling, you distract people away from yourself. People who aren't me. I'm immune, obviously."

"Obviously."

He frowned. "Who are you, anyway? I've seen you around at school, but I don't think we've met."

"Wren. And you are?"

"Alder," he said, his fingers twitching frenetically at his side. "You said your name is Wren? Bit unusual, that."

I stared at the mud squelching beneath my boots, too frustrated to answer. Everything about our conversation had been a joke to him. And my name wasn't that unusual.

"I need you to tell me something." Alder stepped nearer, his voice dropping almost to a whisper. "Are you Sylvaen?"

"Am I *what*?"

"Can I see your hand for a moment?"

I gave him a bewildered look. He made a frustrated sound and grabbed my hand. Energy blazed beneath my skin, flowing through my limbs and rooting me to the earth. I gasped and jerked my hand back.

Alder pushed his hair back from his forehead and twisted around to look at the trees. He swore under his breath and immediately apologized for it. I would have found his apology funny if it weren't for the tingling numbness eating up my hand.

"It's like I thought," he said. "You're Sylvaen."

I shook out my hand, watching for a glint of mischief in Alder's eyes. There was none.

"And—that's a bad thing?"

"It is if you don't even know about blending." His expression was grave. "Listen, you might be in danger. They won't like the idea of someone with a shape-gift being born outside the forest. You may be seen as a threat. If you want to stay safe—and possibly alive—you'll want to stop making wildflowers grow. And throwing shape-cast shields. And making trips into the forest."

"You say that like it's easy!" I exploded. "Like I have any control over what's happening."

Alder didn't answer immediately. He clenched his jaw and glanced back at the forest. It looked as though he were locked in some internal debate. Meanwhile, the forest around us was dead quiet. I could have sworn even the evergreens bent closer to listen.

"I can help you," Alder said, his eyes doing a quick sweep of the forest. "There is a way to control your gift. It'll take time though—and practice."

I watched Alder carefully—his serious eyes and rigid posture. His hair was rumpled and damp, sticking up at odd angles. A moment earlier, he hadn't cared about me or my problems—only that I was making more work for him. Now he was acting twitchy and paranoid.

"I'm getting the impression helping me puts you in some kind of danger," I said.

"Don't worry about me."

The way he swallowed made me think someone should probably worry about him—someone other than me. I had enough problems of my own.

"Let's start by building your resistance to the forest's call." Alder indicated the trees with a toss of his head. "The forest won't hurt you, but you'll need to learn to fight it, or it'll pull you right back. You can start by listening to the rhythm it makes. Count the measures. Use it to regulate your breathing. Counterintuitive, I know, but it's effective."

I gave him a weird look.

"Trust me," he said.

Still wary, I shut my eyes. At first, all I heard were normal forest sounds. Rainwater drips. Birds rustling. Tiny creatures scuttling in the underbrush. Then I noticed the rumbling. The noise was deep, steady, and earthy—a cross between a lead vocalist and a bass beat that set the tempo for the rest of the players. The forest was a churning, growling thing, as restless as the ocean all around us.

"It's like music," I said wonderingly.

"Aye. Music that's on a frequency all of its own. You and I can hear the trees absorbing nutrients, growing, communicating with one another and with us because we're Sylvaen. It's the rhythm of the forest's life force. This side of the third barrier, the sound acts like a magnet for Sylvaen— "

"—and repels anyone else," I said, thinking of the librarian and Emery. I still didn't know what Alder meant by "Sylvaen," but I opened my eyes to find him watching me, his eyes doing a quick sweep over my face and limbs like he was checking for signs of damage.

"You all right now?"

"Yes. Thank you."

"No problem." His gaze wandered away from me and up to the trees. "You look less pale than you did a minute ago."

"I feel better."

The pull I felt toward the forest was still present, but less potent than before. It had changed from an irresistible force to a world brimming with mystery and possibility. The magical world belonging to the boy in my dreams was real, and that meant that the boy in my dreams was real—but who was the boy? Was he connected somehow to Mom's past? Was he Alder? No. The boy in my dreams didn't seem like someone willing to take risks to help someone else; he was the kind of boy who wanted to hide.

I glanced sideways at Alder. His defensive stance and compulsive backward glances screamed anxiety. He had something to hide, but his reasons differed from the boy in my dream in that they were unselfish. I wondered what kind of trouble he would be in if he were caught helping me. The fact that he was sticking his neck out for me told me he was a good person despite his ill-timed humor earlier.

Alder caught me staring at him and cleared his throat. "The last bell rang a while ago now. Mind if I walk you to the pickup area?"

"That's fine." Though I couldn't imagine why he would want to.

Alder turned and walked with me toward the school parking lot. I pondered silently as I fell into step with his stride. If me being Sylvaen—whatever that was—so easily explained the strange things that were happening to me, then maybe it could help explain something about Mom's past too. Either my father was Sylvaen or my mom was, but I'd never seen Mom throw light shields at people or make plants grow. Once, she'd even managed to kill a cactus.

"You still seem"—Alder took a moment to decide on a word—"tense."

I peered up at Alder. His eyes were every bit as disconcerting as they had been the first time I'd seen him. Only this time, there was kindness there too. "It's a lot to take in," I said.

"I can imagine." He rounded the corner of the office a half step ahead of me, his helmet tucked under one arm. "Try to relax. Distract yourself. Do something fun."

Not all of us were great at fun, but Alder didn't need to know that.

"There's a beach party next weekend," Alder said. "You could come if you wanted. It's an open invitation to the class."

The idea of a beach party hardly appealed to me, especially one with a bunch of people from school I avoided daily. I stalled for an excuse. "I'll think about it." It was a bald-faced lie. But the fact that Alder had invited me personally felt kind of—pleasant.

Alder and I arrived in a nearly empty parking lot. Most of the other cars and buses had gone already, but a familiar black Infiniti idled at the edge of the pickup lane. Leslie waited anxiously next to her driver's side door, which she'd left open to any interested car thieves. She uttered a choking cry that sounded a bit like a seal's bark.

"Where have you *been*? I've been here for over an hour. Your teacher called and said you missed class again. The office didn't know where you went. And after that incident in class that happened a few days ago—"

"Incident?" Alder asked.

"I might have exploded a plant in class," I hissed.

"You're going to be a handful, aren't you?"

"You sure you don't want to rescind your offer to help me? It's not too late."

His lips curved into a smile. "I'm sure."

Leslie paused a few paces away, dabbing her eyes with her sleeve. "Next time, can you please call or text or—" She stopped talking when her eyes landed on Alder. In an instant, her whole being lit up. I pretended not to notice. Alder didn't need to know how weirdly enamored Leslie was with the idea of me dating a nice Alaskan boy. Unfortunately for Alder, he looked like a prime specimen.

"I should go," I said, worried about the appraising look Leslie was giving Alder.

Alder nodded. "Try not to explode plants."

"See you."

Alder took off like a gust of wind. Leslie took a moment to collect herself before making her way to the driver's side. I couldn't tell if she was mad at me about missing the pickup line or giddy that I'd been talking with a boy. I climbed into the car and stowed my bag between my shoes, hoping Leslie wouldn't be mad about the mud I was leaving all over her floor mat.

I reached for my seatbelt, watching Alder as he sprinted across the parking lot. His posture was confident, his back arrow straight. Fluidly, he donned his helmet and climbed onto a neon-green sport bike. I both hated and admired him for how awesome he looked. His decision to help a misfit like me made even less sense when I thought of how many friends he had. Regardless of his reasons, Alder was Sylvaen—like me. But he was also Sylvaen in a way that I wasn't. He had information—information that could lead to answers about Mom's past. Or at least about my father.

Leslie released the parking brake, her eyes fixed on the athletic figure speeding out of the driveway on his sport bike. "Who was that boy?"

I rolled my eyes at the window so Leslie couldn't see. If she thought she was being subtle, she was wrong. "Alder something. I've never talked to him before today."

"He was cute."

Sure. He was also exactly the second male she'd seen me make eye contact with since arriving in Ketchikan.

"Were you walking with him to discuss an assignment?" she asked.

"We were planning our honeymoon in Cancun."

Leslie gave me a confused look and turned on her music. I was grateful for the lack of conversation that followed. I didn't need personalized matchmaking services, I needed to find out more about the Sylvaen. And the only person I could think of who could help me do that was Alder.

CHAPTER 11
CONSPIRACY

T HE WATERS OF THE Inside Passage were steely gray, hemmed in by evergreens and crawling mist. Clouds gathered around the edges of the sky, swinging low over Annette Island. A seaplane with "Northern Lights Excursions" painted in block letters landed with a gentle whoosh. And while the scent of October woodsmoke lingered in the air, Leslie's Infiniti sat idling in the parking lot at Rotary Beach, drawing more attention than I would have liked. Unfortunately, my ability to remain invisible didn't extend to inanimate objects like Leslie's wannabe sports car.

I didn't want to be at Rotary Beach. Even Emery was surprised when I told her I was going. Peter and Leslie knew me well enough to be surprised too. But no one was more surprised than me. I hated putting myself in awkward social situations more than most people hated seeing me in them. Unfortunately, the beach party was the best chance I had of getting to talk to Alder—assuming he would even show up.

"Have Emery bring you home by ten," Leslie said for the millionth time.

"I will."

"And don't go anywhere except the beach, Emery's house, or home."

"I won't."

Leslie looked relieved. "And if anyone offers you alcohol—"

"I'm not going to drink, Leslie."

"Good. And Wren?"

"Yeah?"

"You know what to do if you run across a bear?"

I lost all patience at that. Leslie thought I had the maturity of a four-year-old high on Halloween candy. "Stop, drop, and roll?"

Leslie looked horrified. I held up the can of bear spray Peter had given me earlier and gave it a gentle shake.

"Kidding."

Leslie shook her head and muttered something about me being worse than Peter. I thought Peter was a pretty okay human, so I took Leslie's remark as a compliment.

I climbed out of the Infiniti, stowing the bear spray. The ocean air was cool and crisp, albeit a bit damp. I slipped on a beanie and looked over my surroundings. A cement causeway jutted out into Revillagigedo Channel, creating a small body of water with a glassy surface. The water accurately reflected the mountains, the deep tree shadows, the mackerel sky. But it was the forest on either side that captivated me. The endless trees looked like tufted brushes painting the sky. I could hear the forest speaking inside my head, its voice a memory of root and earth, beckoning me to enter.

Matt walked by, carrying a load of fishing equipment from the back of his truck to the beach. He caught my eye and offered a friendly smile.

"You made it," he said, sounding surprised.

I nodded and tried to give him at least a pleasant expression. Matt returned my almost-smile with a thumbs up and hurried after an adult—probably his dad. I didn't blame him for avoiding me after the sketchbook incident.

I drew my backpack straps over my shoulders. A group was already clambering around the tide pools, bending low to examine marine life clinging to the rocks. I might have considered joining, but I didn't want to risk making the kelp grow or shooting someone with a beam of silver light. I cringed at the mental image and wondered if I shouldn't have come to Rotary Beach after all. Before I could reflect further on my life choices, Leslie bid me goodbye and drove off.

"Edith!" Emery yelled from halfway across the parking lot. "Lose the hat. You look like an angsty sunflower."

I walked over to Emery's car and climbed inside. She was listening to music and applying a fresh coat of black to her nails. Her hair color had its own theme—cotton candy. Somehow, she managed to look edgy and chaotic even with pink, purple, and turquoise in her hair.

"You do know my name, right?" I asked.

"Of course, Ingrid. What took you so long?"

"Leslie was making sure I don't get mauled by bears."

She tossed her nail polish in the center console. "Again?"

"Third time this week."

"So, here's the plan," Emery said, pushing her car door open and climbing out. "We stay a few minutes, eat their food, steal a bag of marshmallows, and run."

"Run where?"

"Away." She made a walking motion with her fingers like she thought I needed a visual demonstration to understand.

The beach was a short walk from the parking lot. I kept a hand on my beanie to keep it from flying off as we trudged past the weathered picnic tables and playground equipment.

"I still don't get why you dragged me out here," Emery complained. "A beach party really doesn't feel like your scene."

"I like the beach," I said defensively.

"Maybe. But you hate people."

She had me there.

Everyone was already sectioned off into groups when we arrived at the fire. Emery strode purposefully into the uneven circle of driftwood logs and ratty camp chairs. Within minutes, she had her hands on two roasting sticks and a half-empty package of hot dogs. I was impressed.

"Make yourself useful," Emery said, thrusting a roasting stick into my hands. "Since you dragged me here against my will."

Dragged her. Emery had been *thrilled* to have an excuse to go to the beach party.

Across the circle, two boys started fencing with their roasting sticks. One of the adults confiscated the sticks, worried someone would poke an eye out. Emery suggested that the boys be allowed to continue their fencing match. By the calculating look on her face, I knew she had her eye on the marshmallows and was hoping to eliminate the competition.

Waterbirds wheeled and cried over the sunset-gilded channel. I pretended to roast hot dogs with Emery, but really, I was keeping an eye out for Alder. Unfortunately, it looked like he was a no-show. Disappointed, I turned back to the pirouetting flames. I was beginning to think coming to the beach had been a waste.

Emery nudged me with her elbow. "You look like someone stole your favorite drawing pencil."

"I'm fine."

"Is that why you've been stealing glances at the parking lot every thirty seconds?"

I shoved a bite of hot dog in my mouth so I wouldn't have to answer.

A couple minutes later, Matt's group returned with their fishing gear in tow. There was a huge commotion over the haul of fish they brought in. I shuddered when someone started gutting fish. A moment later, someone else was slapping jewel-pink fillets on the fire grate. The fillets sizzled, and the air filled with oily smoke. Nauseated, I hid my nose in my jacket sleeve. The evening was not going the way I'd hoped.

"Alaskans," I muttered.

Emery eyed me. "What's your problem?"

I grunted in reply. Emery looked confused.

"What was that—an elk's mating call?"

I nearly tumbled off the log. The voice that spoke was decidedly male. Alder stood a little to my right, hair messy and golden-green eyes full of amusement. I had no idea how long he'd been standing there.

"I was going for moose, actually," I said, trying not to sound defensive or like he'd scared the living crap out of me.

"I think you nailed it."

"Thanks." I smiled inwardly. I'd all but given up hope that Alder would show, but he was here now, and with him, my answers. Now I needed to find a way to engage him in conversation and bring up the Sylvaen casually. People with tree magic living in plain sight, no big deal.

Alder held up a box of graham crackers and a marshmallow bag like a peace offering. "Mind if I sit here?"

I watched his face for a moment to see if he was serious. He had friends; why did he want to sit with Emery and me? Also, wasn't he worried about being caught helping me? I answered in a thin voice. "Sure?"

Emery poked her head around me. "Where's the chocolate?"

"In my pocket," Alder said.

Emery looked satisfied. "You can sit."

Alder settled beside me on the driftwood log and reached for a roasting stick. Emery caught my eye. She grinned, using her entire head to point at Alder in the most obvious way possible. I scowled in response. Emery figured out that it was Alder I'd been watching for earlier, which meant she likely had completely the wrong idea about why I'd done so. Perfect. Now I had to figure out how to get rid of her without making her *feel* like I was trying to get rid of her.

"Are you okay in there?" Alder asked, craning his neck like he was trying to see me better.

"It's her makeshift respirator," Emery explained. "She's allergic to fish."

"No." I lowered my sleeve cautiously. "I just never eat scaly water meat that tastes like trash."

Alder ripped open the bag of marshmallows. "You do realize you moved to the Salmon Capital of the World?"

"I'm trying very hard to forget that."

Alder started to laugh, but was interrupted by playful screams rising above the sound of the waves. One of the boys was chasing some girls with what looked to be an empty crab shell strung with long tentacles of seaweed.

"Look, Wren." Emery pointed toward the screaming girls. "They're even more terrified of dead sea creatures than you are."

I ignored Emery's comment. The girls' delighted shrieks swelled as they ran, their feet pounding the wet sand.

"I don't think *terrified* is the right word for it," Alder said, returning his attention to the marshmallow he was roasting.

"I would be." Emery's grin turned wolfish. "But only if there were a hot lifeguard nearby."

"You should try it, Em." I tossed a scrap of driftwood into the fire. "Colin Firth might be out there with his shirt soaking wet, waiting to save you from a crab carcass."

"If only," Emery sighed.

"Emery, you don't strike me as someone who would want help in that situation," Alder said, pointing with a graham cracker. "You'd be the one doing the threatening."

"You're thinking of Wren. Never get between that woman and a sandwich."

"Only a hot sandwich," I corrected, drawing a smirk from Alder.

"Sandwiches aren't sexy though," Emery said.

"But they are bready."

"Which is the same thing," Alder put in.

Emery gave us both a disparaging look. Before she could say anything snarky, her phone buzzed. She checked her phone, scrolled through her messages, and made an aggravated sound.

"Freaking dad." She jammed her phone back into her pocket and stood up. "I have to go pick up Park. Right *now*. He just got dumped, and he's standing alone outside the movie theater like some lost puppy. Dad's Tesla is in the shop, and he forgot how to drive any of his other *three* cars." She rolled her eyes so hard I was afraid they might get stuck. "And my evil stepmother probably has split ends or something."

"Wait, so…" I got to my feet. "We're leaving?"

Emery's phone started ringing. "One sec. It's the Trophy Wife."

So much for finding out more about the forest.

Emery pressed her phone to her ear, snatched up the bag of marshmallows Alder had brought, and ran off before anyone could stop her. Alder locked eyes with me and gave me a mystified look.

"I understood none of that," he confessed.

"Same."

My mind raced with ways to broach the topic of the Sylvaen. Before I could decide on a proper icebreaker, a group of guys yelled to Alder from across the beach. Alder unceremoniously stuffed the remnants of his s'more in his mouth and got up. Sighing, I picked up my backpack and followed Emery toward the parking lot. Rotary Beach was a lost cause.

Emery was halfway across the parking lot, throwing her marshmallow bag around and yelling expletives into her phone. Even though the phone was pressed tight to her ear, I could hear Angela, Emery's stepmother, defying physics by audibly screeching about Parker having to wait out in the rain. Emery shut her eyes and swore again.

Not only was it *not raining,* but also Angela was the only person in Ketchikan who was afraid of damp weather when it happened. Emery often claimed that her dad had his wife built to order and forgot to include a brain.

Emery came back, huffing and muttering under her breath. "I have to head straight to the theater," she said, kicking at the rocks near her feet. "It's an 'emergency.'"

She glanced at something beyond me. Her eyes took on that eerie, conspiratorial look she'd had when plotting about marshmallows. I followed her gaze and nearly swore myself. Alder stood beside me, holding his motorcycle helmet chest-high like he was about to enter a jousting match. Curse his creepy silent footsteps. I hadn't realized he'd left his boy squad and followed me.

"Hey, Ainsley," Emery said, her tone anything but casual. "You mind giving Ashwood a ride home? I have to run."

I smelled a setup. On the bright side, at least Emery could remember surnames when she wanted to. "You're ditching me?" I demanded.

"I'm doing you a favor." Emery shot a meaningful look in Alder's direction as she slid into the driver's seat. "You're welcome."

"If I get mauled by a bear, I'll tell Leslie it's your fault."

Emery laughed, popped a marshmallow in her mouth, and started her engine. "See you at school."

I watched Emery peel out of the parking lot, silently cursing myself, Emery, and the moment I decided to come to Rotary Beach. Mostly, I cursed Emery.

"So—you're really worried about bears?" Alder asked.

I turned, more than a little reluctant to meet his eyes. What if he thought this whole charade was my idea?

"Not really. My guardian is worried for me."

Alder nodded like Leslie's paranoia made perfect sense to him. "Well, this *is* Alaska." He let his gaze wander up into the darkening sky overhead. "It isn't like walking down a beach in California."

A beach. In Fresno.

"What, will I be eaten by a moose or something?" I deadpanned.

"Moose are herbivores. They're also not in this part of Alaska. You might meet a bear though. Or a wolf."

"I know Krav Maga." *Know* was a stretch. I'd had a couple of lessons from a neighbor. She stopped inviting me to class when she realized Mom couldn't pay.

Alder's lips twitched. "You're planning to use Krav Maga on a bear?"

"Only if I feel threatened."

"I think your guardian might have the right idea being worried about you."

Yeah, well my guardian also thought I was an idiot who didn't know how to talk to boys *or* react rationally when I met a bear, but she was wrong. I knew *exactly* how to handle an encounter with a bear thanks to Mom, and I didn't know how to talk to *anyone*.

"So, Emery said you need a ride?" Alder asked, piercing me with his unnerving gaze.

My face started to burn. Emery was going to get one nasty text message when I got home. Possibly several.

"That's all right," I said, scooting away from him. "I can call my guardian. I don't want to make you leave early."

"I don't mind."

"You only have one helmet," I pointed out.

"Matt has one you could borrow. His da's got a pair of dirt bikes on his trailer." He swung his head toward the other side of the parking lot.

"But what about the Sylvaen—wouldn't this qualify as helping me?"

"Don't worry about that." His eyes took in my retreating posture. "But I should ask if you *want* a ride home. I'm happy to do it, but no pressure."

I hesitated. I wanted to talk to Alder—had even planned to—but accepting a ride home from him felt like falling into Emery's trap. Still, an opportunity like this wasn't likely to present itself again. If I wanted a chance to talk, I needed to take it while I had it.

"Okay, sure," I said. "If Matt's all right with me using his helmet." After I nearly took off his hand.

Alder's face lit up in a grin. "Let's find out, yeah?"

CHAPTER 12
ALDER

THE SKY WAS CHANGING colors, and the streetlights were flickering as we made our way along rows of parked cars. Alder paused by his neon green sport bike waiting at the edge of the parking lot, its badge proudly displaying "Kawasaki Ninja" on its fuel tank.

"Have you been on one of these before?" he asked.

I shook my head. Alder zipped his hoodie and gave me a crash course on riding motorcycles. He told me about leaning with the bike around corners and avoiding burns from the exhaust pipe.

In the shock of Emery's scheming, I'd forgotten that Alder's helmet wasn't a prop. Even though he looked cool riding it, a sport bike seemed an odd choice in a place with 140-160 inches of annual rainfall and the occasional bear sighting. Also, any attempts at conversation would be futile with helmets on. So much for getting a chance to talk.

"You look worried," Alder said.

"I'm not."

"Okay."

I wasn't *exactly* worried, but I had concerns. What was I supposed to hold on to—*him*?

"I think that pretty much covers it," Alder said. "Ready to try it out?"

I gave Alder directions to my house, and then he had to help me snug the strap under my chin. The scents of motor oil and engine parts overwhelmed my senses, but at least the helmet went on comfortably.

When Alder was satisfied with the fit, he put on his own helmet and swung fluidly onto the bike.

I climbed into position behind Alder, trying not to overthink the situation as I put my arms around his middle. He started the engine, and I felt the bike shudder beneath us. Since he wasn't freaking out, I assumed the hugging part must have been expected or at least understood.

A moment later, we were accelerating onto the South Tongass Highway, flying around the bends in the road, and rushing in and out of tree shadows. Autumn gold clung to the edges of the sky. The wind sent leaves scudding across the pavement and made me feel as though we were all movement, all speed. Immortal. Suddenly, Alder's impractical transportation choice made sense to me. Grinning, I leaned forward and let the forever dusk take me. But all too soon, the moment was over.

We rounded a corner, and the trees thinned, the houses growing closer. I was disappointed to recognize an assortment of familiar sights because it meant the ride was over: the house with the bright purple door, a yard with a collection of wood carvings, the neighbor's rusty truck, and the cluster of salmonified mailboxes. Peter and Leslie's evergreen-lined driveway was still more magic than mundane—but only for the evergreens crowding close overhead and casting the drive into deep shadow.

We stopped inside the circle of yellowish light coming from the front porch, where Alder stopped the engine and held the bike steady for me to dismount. All around us, the wind rushed in like an exhale. The air was full of mist and the heady scent of woodsmoke.

Alder slid off his own helmet and glanced at me. "How was it?"

"Amazing."

He smiled. His hair, normally careless in a boyish sort of way, was matted down from his helmet. He ran a hand through it, restoring it to its former unkempt glory. There was a restlessness about him, a nervous energy that manifested in him drumming his fingers against his jeans as he glanced around the yard.

"Mind if I walk you to your door?" he asked.

I laughed. "Still worried about those bears?"

"Yeah. I'm worried what you'll do to them."

Vibrant red clung to the leaves of the big leaf maples branching out above us. I walked with Alder to the door, wondering all the while how I was going to explain the motorcycle helmet to Peter and Leslie. Worse, how would I explain the tall, lithe boy walking me to my front door instead of Emery? I was busy mulling over what to say when I heard the voice again.

Come.

I gazed out at the trees. The wind made a soft noise. The mist whispered secrets. There was a feeling of expectation in the air. Of inevitability.

"You're turning into quiet Wren." Alder's voice drew me back. "Listening to the forest?"

"It's hard not to."

"You'll get it." He gave me an encouraging smile. "Promise."

I nodded, and together we made our way toward the front door. My phone buzzed with a text from Emery as we rounded the corner of the garage:

am i crazy, or was alder ainsley sitting awfully close to you tonight?

I dismissed the notification fast. At least I had phone service.

answer me, woman.

I tried to type a response, but my phone vibrated again.

he's kind of cute if you're into twigs.

I thrust the phone back into my pocket. Emery *would* interpret Alder's attention that way. She knew nothing of Alder's connection to the strange magic I seemed to possess. But regardless of Emery's misguided ideas, Alder had the answers I was looking for.

"Hey, Alder," I said, pausing at the front door. "I wanted to ask you—"

The door flew open behind me with such force I could feel its wind. I whipped around to find Leslie standing in the doorway with a shotgun in her hands. I gasped and staggered backward, nearly falling into Alder.

"Wren! We didn't expect you back yet." Leslie pressed a hand to her chest and laughed, tipping the gun downward. "I thought I heard something out front."

"So, you thought you'd shoot it?"

"Well..." Leslie's smile went from sheepish to blinding when she noticed Alder. "Wren, who's this?"

"Alder."

Leslie tucked her gun back and put out a hand to shake Alder's. Alder smiled and gave her hand a firm shake. Going by the look on Leslie's face, I could tell she was charmed. The idea that Alder had taken me home instead of Emery didn't bother Leslie in the least.

"So, Wren. Are you and Alder friends?" Leslie asked.

I clenched my jaw. All I wanted was to talk to Alder alone for a minute, thank him for the ride home, and get rid of him before Leslie started booking wedding venues.

"No."

"Okay." Leslie smiled strangely at me. "Well, since you're home early, would you two like to come in and have some popcorn and hot chocolate? Peter was just making some."

Alder spoke up before I could say anything. "I would love some popcorn and hot chocolate, but Wren might not want me to come inside since we're not friends."

"That's not what I meant," I protested.

"It was heavily implied."

Smiling broadly, Leslie held the door open in invitation. "Come in, you two."

Leslie gave Alder another beaming smile once we were inside and darted off to stow her shotgun. Alder and I took off our shoes in the entryway and stared at each other like a pair of petrified idiots. From the kitchen, I could hear the dull clatter of pots and dishes coupled with the low murmurs of Peter and Leslie's conversation. I didn't trust Leslie not to take advantage of the situation. I decided to act.

"Alder." I grabbed his wrist, ignoring the energy crackling beneath my fingers. "I need to talk to you. Now."

Alder looked startled. "Okay."

Before we could get anywhere, Peter rounded the corner and thrust out a hand to greet Alder. I dropped Alder's wrist like it was fire and pretended to busy myself hanging up my jacket. Was it me, or was the universe conspiring against me to keep me from talking to Alder?

Alder and Peter immediately struck up an animated conversation about sport bikes and 4-stroke engines. By the time they got to back-torque-limiting slipper clutches with an assist mechanism, I was done. Alder was either exceptionally skilled at schmoozing adults, or he was genuinely a likable person. Unlike me. I slunk off to my bedroom in defeat. I would try again with Alder at school on Monday.

I had pulled out my history textbook and put on my Power Rangers socks when a soft knock sounded at my door. I got up to answer it.

"Hey." Alder glanced down at my socks. "Aren't you coming back down?"

"I have homework." I waved my history notes in the air for emphasis.

"Oh." Alder looked like he was deciding whether to argue or retreat. "Mind if I come in?"

"Knock yourself out."

Alder wandered a little way inside. His eyes took in my bedroom decor—string lights, plants, miscellaneous sketches, a sparse shelf of books alphabetized by author's last name. I'd never seen him look quite so uncomfortable before.

"Did I do something that bothered you?" Alder asked.

"No."

"Really? Because I'm getting the impression that you don't want me here."

I heaved a sigh, cast my history notes aside, and picked up my sketchbook. "I guess—" I hesitated, trying to decide how much to say. "I didn't want you to think I set things up with Emery at the beach, that was her thing. And then there's Leslie with her snacks. They've got it in their heads that you and I should be dating or something. It's completely stupid."

"Completely."

"Anyway, I want you to know it wasn't my idea to get you to take me home or lure you into my house with snacks. It was Leslie's."

Alder smiled a little. "People are always threatening me with food. I'm used to it."

"Still…" I turned to my open bedroom window. The breeze rustled my curtain and made goosebumps rise along my arms. "I don't want to make you feel like you have to do something you don't want to." I flipped open my sketchbook and started drawing. It took me a moment to realize Alder had gone dead quiet. When I looked up, he was staring at me with an expression that was perplexedly thunderstruck. Finally, he spoke.

"Wren. It's not like I'm here against my will."

"You think that now, but Peter's hot chocolate has been known to put people into chocolate-induced comas. Trust me."

Alder came over and sat down next to me. "I guess I'm about to find out."

Right on cue, Leslie appeared with two massive mugs of hot chocolate heaped with ruffles of whipped cream and chocolate curls. Alder's eyes popped open wide.

Leslie smiled, thrusting a mug into Alder's startled hands. "I hope you like coconut."

"I hope you like arranged marriages," I muttered.

Alder paused in the act of bringing his mug to his lips. He gave me a grin, but there was a hint of worry in his eyes. Good. Maybe he would take Leslie as a serious threat and steer clear of her scheming.

"Popcorn will be up in a minute," Leslie said, breezing out the door.

Alder took a tentative sip of his hot chocolate, then sank into it with a quiet groan. I sketched while he had his moment with the hot chocolate. He clearly wasn't taking my warning about hot chocolate-induced comas seriously.

"You drew that?" Alder asked suddenly.

He leaned over to get a closer look at my sketch. It was a drawing of a vine-covered archway leading into the forest. Alder laid his hot chocolate aside.

"May I?" he asked.

"Go ahead."

Half unwilling, I handed Alder my sketchbook. He smoothed the page and let his eyes roam over the details, drinking in every shadow and highlight. Even in artificial light, his eyes were like sunlight on spring leaves.

"Wow, Ashwood." His eyes lifted to mine. "You're amazing."

I blushed. It was less about the compliment and more about the fact that Alder had caught me staring at his eyes. "Thanks."

Leslie came by with a bowl of popcorn. She grinned hugely when she saw Alder sitting close and flipping through my sketchbook. I scowled at her to let her know I wasn't going down that easily.

Soon, Alder and I were laughing and talking as I showed him more of my drawings. He leaned in, drawing his knee up to his chest. Something about his dynamic pose and tall frame made me itch to sketch him. He was willowy and graceful, beautiful in a boyish sort of way—anyone with an artistic eye would notice.

"Are you looking at me or through me?" Alder asked suddenly. He bobbed his head around like a pigeon, trying to see if I would follow his gaze. My whole face sizzled.

"Sorry. I zoned out there for a minute."

Alder stopped his pigeoning. "Was there something you wanted to talk to me about?"

I was relieved by the subject change. "I want to know more about the Sylvaen."

"Okay." Alder snatched up a handful of popcorn and tossed it in his mouth. "What specifically?"

"I want to know who they are, and"—I hesitated—"why you think they'll view me as a threat."

Alder took a moment to swallow before answering. "If you weren't born in the forest like the rest of us, you aren't bound by our laws, and you haven't gotten the proper training. You use magic without having any control over your gift. They'll see you as a rogue, someone who might use your gift to gain leverage and harm us and the forest."

I wanted to laugh. "Why would I do that?"

Alder gave half a shrug. "Some people will do anything for power."

"All I want is to find out the truth about my mom." I drew my knees up to my chest and stared out the window, willing the pain and the emptiness to subside before continuing. "She died in a car accident. That's why I came here to live."

Alder's eyes dashed to the photo on my dresser. "You look a lot like her."

"Everyone says that."

"It's true." He paused. "Do you think she was Sylvaen?"

"I don't know. Leslie told me some stuff that made me realize my mom had her share of secrets, so maybe. I thought if I talked to you, you could help get me closer to finding some answers."

As Alder held my gaze, his eyes softened. He breathed deep and seemed to consider for a moment. "I can try, but I'll have to be careful. If the Sylvaen find out about you, they'll try to capture you. Some might even want to kill you."

The shock of Alder's words tumbled through me. It was already insane to think that people with forest magic really existed. It was even more insane to think that I had magic and that the Sylvaen could kill me because of it. But the absurdity of our conversation didn't matter as much as finding answers.

"Are you serious?"

"It's possible," Alder said. "They might dismiss you as some Outlander girl with pretty green eyes, or they might not. Just don't let them know you have a shape-gift, and *don't* go into the forest."

I tried to follow what Alder was saying, but his use of the word *pretty* to describe something about me threw off my concentration. Maybe it was because I'd been admiring his bodily proportions like some haggard old creep with a wandering eye. Emery and Leslie would be thrilled.

"Maybe you can tell me a little bit about it," I said, struggling to collect my thoughts. "Since I can't go inside."

"What would you like to know?"

"Do you live there?"

"I live with a host family here in town at the moment. My family is in Síorghlas though; that's our city in the forest."

Síorghlas, the glimmering city in the treetops from my dreams. Instantly, my mind filled with images of the boy in the forest and his surroundings. Had the forest sent me images of the Sylvaen while I was sleeping and daydreaming? And if so, were those made-up images or concrete events that actually happened?

"Sheer-glass?" I asked, stumbling over the unfamiliar word.

Alder smiled. "Good pronunciation, that."

"Thanks." I smiled back. "What's it like?"

Alder thought about it for a moment. "Green."

"O—kay. Can you be more descriptive?"

"Maybe emerald?"

"Wow." I tossed a popcorn kernel at his nose. "At least tell me about the Sylvaen. And don't tell me they're green."

"We're regular people, really. We have our own way of life. We have our magic. And we don't want people to change us."

"That's it?"

"More or less."

Maybe I was Sylvaen after all.

Alder rested his mug on his thigh and sighed. "Most of us live in Síorghlas, though there are a few smaller settlements and some outposts for sentries who guard our borders. There could be other Sylvaen in the world, but if so, we haven't encountered them. We forage, hunt, and garden—but we have no currency, no electricity, no indoor plumbing. We're led by a council of ealdors who sort of keep an eye on everything and look for peaceful ways to deal with conflict. Mainly, we work together to keep the forest healthy. It's hard to explain, but it works."

I turned to the window again. "Sounds idyllic."

"It could be." Alder sounded almost wistful. "Some people think we've shut ourselves off too much from the outside world, that we've become hostile toward it. We've forgotten that welcoming strangers and outsiders is a huge part of who we are, and that the forest is off-balance because of it."

The wind wafted into the bedroom, and with it, the briny scents of kelp and saltwater mingled with earth and forest. I thought about the sickening images of the boy beating the other senseless. Was it the hatred that boy experienced that led him to such violence?

"The Sylvaen don't like people who don't fit in," I said aloud.

"That's one way to put it."

I couldn't help the sinking sensation that enveloped my chest. The Sylvaen didn't sound all that different from people outside. And for some reason, that disappointed me. I picked up my hot chocolate mug again and took a sip, my mind still flitting around the boy with the midnight hair—on his unusual speech patterns, unfamiliar clothes, and foreign customs. I thought about the city threaded in among the trees, of the magic that sparkled silver in the hands of its users.

"You have a silver tree, right?" I asked. "The Elder Tree?"

Alder looked surprised. "Did someone tell you about it?"

"I dreamed about it."

"You what?"

"I keep having these dreams," I repeated. "They pick up pretty much where the others leave off. There's this boy in them. I can't ever see his face, but I can hear his thoughts."

"The Elder Tree has been known to give the Sylvaen dreams when it's trying to communicate something important," Alder said. "But you've never been in close contact with it, so that doesn't seem likely."

"You think the dreams are its way of messing with me?"

"Hard to say. The only way to know for sure would be if you went into the forest and found you were still having them. But that's not possible because you can't go inside without compromising your safety."

I watched my curtains dance in the nighttime breeze and felt myself slipping back into that quiet place where I could hear the forest's voice, where I could feel the pull of it dragging my attention away from the present and into the trees. I wasn't convinced the dreams were arbitrary.

"I guess not."

CHAPTER 13
THE FOREST'S SPELL

S OMEONE CLEARED THEIR THROAT loudly, startling Alder and me. We looked up to find Peter standing in my doorway wearing plaid pajamas and a serious expression.

"Time to wrap up," Peter said. "It's getting late."

It wasn't even ten yet. In fact, Peter and Leslie were usually up late on Fridays watching movies in the living room. I suspected the pajamas were a passive-aggressive way of reminding Alder who was in charge and who was being watched.

Alder was quick to take the hint. He pushed himself to his feet, muttering something about losing track of time.

"I'll bet," Peter said.

Alder walked briskly down the stairs with me trailing behind. He paused in the entryway to slip on his shoes. I waited, wondering if there was a cryptic way to ask him how he intended to help me with the Sylvaen. But I could see Peter and Leslie creeping around in the shadows. Watching.

"I'll see you Monday, then." Alder stood from tying his shoes. "And try to leave those bears alone, yeah?"

"I'll leave the bears alone tonight," I promised.

"Good."

Peter coughed softly from the corner where he was lurking. I opened the door, eager to let Alder out and be rid of Peter and Leslie's insinuations.

The fragrance of rain on evergreens whisked past as Alder slipped out onto the porch. Peter came to stand beside me in the doorway like some kind of flannel-clad gargoyle. Leslie hissed something at Peter, which he ignored.

"Thanks for the hot chocolate," Alder said to Peter.

"Yep." Peter looked out across the yard. "Fog's thick tonight."

"Be careful, Alder," Leslie agreed.

"I will, thanks." Alder turned to cross the porch, then paused to glance back with a shy sort of smile. "Goodnight, Wren."

Before I could reply, a jet of silver light shot across the yard. A breath of wind stirred the evergreens. The trees ruffled like a million black feathers sweeping the sky. I couldn't think. I couldn't do anything but stare at the light glimmering like frost and let it drag my conscious thought deep into the trees.

"Wren?" Leslie sounded worried. "Are you okay?"

She is here.

"Wren?" Leslie asked again.

Vaguely, I was aware of Alder standing there. I felt his attention on me, but I couldn't tear my eyes away. There along the tree line stood a figure edged in silver.

Do you see her? Do you not feel how your heart stirs within you?

The figure's gaze locked on mine and held on. She stayed where she was, never moving, never speaking. I lost all my breath. It had to be some kind of mistake, a hallucination, or something else because what I was seeing was impossible.

Mom.

Longing gripped me like a fist around my throat. Desperation. She was there, *alive*, standing in front of me with eyes that felt like looking at a reflection of my own. I choked out a sob and lurched forward.

Alder was there in an instant. "What are you doing?"

I felt the rhythm of his shape-gift as he caught me by the arm. His grip was gentle but firm, drawing me to a halt.

"Please. You have to let me go." I jerked my arm.

"Into the forest?" Alder's voice was incredulous. "I can't. You know that."

Come, Wren. Come into the forest.

I tried to pry Alder's fingers loose from my forearm. When that failed, I paused to gather my wits. Alder was taller than me and definitely stronger. Before I could elbow him in the ribs or go for his thumbs, he folded me into some kind of complicated grappling hold.

"Wren, what's going on?" Peter asked, his voice rising in alarm.

Alder ignored Peter. "The forest is getting to you, Wren."

I gritted my teeth and tried to jerk free. Alder's grip remained firm, his palm and fingers a jolt of heat wrapped around my forearm.

"You're not yourself," he grunted. "Please—stop for a second. Breathe. You're not safe going in there."

She is waiting.

The figure turned and slipped back into the trees. I let out a frustrated cry and shoved Alder. He stumbled a bit but held on.

"You don't understand," I ground out. "It's her. My mom—she's alive. I have to get to her."

"What on earth—" Leslie looked at Peter.

Peter's voice rose above Alder's, Leslie's, and the forest's. "I want someone to explain to me what's going on *right now*."

"Wren, listen." Alder turned his back on Peter and looked me in the eyes. The pulse of our mingled shape-gifts was so intense my teeth started to ache. "You're not thinking clearly. The minute you cross that tree line, you're passing the third barrier and telling everyone who you are. Your life will be forfeit."

"Hang on, you two." Peter held up his hands as if to show a pair of wild animals that he meant them no harm. "Let's all calm down."

I didn't want to believe Alder. I couldn't. How could the forest create something so exactly like Mom? Doubt clouded my thoughts. I shook my head to clear it. Specks like embers swirled before my eyes. All of this was overwhelming. Too much to believe.

"Wren?" Alder slackened his grip. "Are you okay?"

My legs gave way. Of course, I wasn't okay; I was out of my mind. Delusional. That was the only explanation for anything that was happening.

Vaguely, I was aware of Peter standing over me, of Leslie pacing in an agitated manner. She looked like she was hesitating over whether to call the cops or go for the shotgun again.

"Wren, what did you think you saw?" Peter asked, bending to meet my gaze.

Peter's question struck a nerve. Why was I doubting myself? I knew exactly what I had seen. I wasn't crazy. "I didn't *think* anything," I said, pushing myself to my feet. "I saw my mother."

Peter's expression was blank. "Your mother?"

"Yes. My *dead* mother."

Leslie looked at Alder with tears in her eyes. Peter, at least, had the decency to look uncomfortable.

"It's the forest, Wren," Alder soothed.

I whirled toward Alder. "Don't you dare tell me she's in my head! I know what I saw. She was *right there.*"

Peter glanced helplessly at Alder. It was clear he didn't know what to do with a raving teenage girl who started fights with boys over whether or not she was seeing her deceased mother in the forest.

"Wren, sweetheart." Leslie came to stand next to Peter. "I think it's time to go inside."

Trust your instincts, Wren. Trust.

"I can't, Leslie."

Peter took a step toward me, then hesitated. "Wren, you need to come inside. It's cold out, and Alder thinks you're in danger."

"She is," Alder agreed.

Leslie's eyes grew round with worry. "What kind of danger?"

"She has the forest in her blood," Alder said. "She can do things—make plants grow, create objects out of ideas from her head. There are people like her out there, but they won't appreciate the fact that she wasn't born and raised in the forest. They'll see who she is and what she can do, and they will capture her—possibly kill her—simply for existing."

Leslie shivered, gathering the collar of her bathrobe against her throat to fend off the night's chill. Peter, on the other hand, looked skeptical. He turned to Alder.

"You expect us to believe Wren has—"

"Magic," Alder said. "Yes."

Peter gave a disbelieving smile, but Leslie put a hand on his shoulder. "Peter, hon. Remember how strange things kept happening with Laurel—the trees that would appear in our yard overnight, the lights under her door at night, the strange noises? The same sort of things are happening with Wren. I think maybe Alder's telling the truth."

I wondered what sort of bizarre magic things I'd been doing unconsciously that Leslie had picked up on. Was I shaping in my sleep? Making the plants in my window grow?

With a weary look, Peter turned back to Alder. "All right. Who are these people?"

"Sylvaen," Alder said.

"And you know this because—?"

"Because I'm one of them."

And Alder did look Sylvaen. He stood tall, regarding Peter with a lifted chin and an otherworldly air. I half expected silver lighting to shoot from his palms.

"Hang on." Peter held up a hand. "There are people out there who are hiding and running around doing magic, and you're claiming to be one of them?"

"That's right," Alder said.

"And"—Peter stole a glance at me—"they're going to hurt Wren?"

"If they catch her, they might."

Peter made a sound that was somewhere between a sigh and a groan. "If all this is true, why haven't I ever seen any freaks doing magic tricks out in the forest?"

A smirk formed in the corner of Alder's mouth. "You really think we're stupid enough to let you see us?"

"Fine." Peter appeared unconvinced. "Regardless of who's telling the truth and who's delusional, nobody's going into the forest tonight. Wren, you need to get inside. Alder, thanks for keeping her here, I guess."

Peter glanced at me. I glared back. My insides twisted hopelessly into a million tangles—anger, doubt, desperation. But the forest knew me; it understood my need. If I didn't act now, I might never get the chance to find out the things Mom had kept hidden from me. But did I have the courage?

"She's pale," Leslie said, worry coloring her tone.

"Cold too." Alder touched my cheek with the back of his hand. "She looks like she's about to pass out. Let's get her inside."

I jerked away from Alder. "I'm not going anywhere."

"Wren—" Alder started.

I can give you what you seek. I can give you truth.

I sucked in a breath and turned toward the forest. Cool forest air rushed into my lungs, reinvigorating me. I was tired of being lied to and patronized. I was tired of people feeling like they owed me pity. What I wanted was to find my own way, to be okay without anyone's help. And that started with finding out the truth about Mom's past.

Leslie glanced at Peter. "Maybe we should call somebody."

"In the morning," Peter agreed.

A glimmer of silver beneath the trees was the confirmation I needed. I *wasn't* crazy. Leslie's startled cry echoed behind me. Alder's hand grazed my arm. But I left it all behind and bolted straight into the dark. Alive or dead, Mom was out there. If I didn't go now, I might never have another chance to find out who she really was.

I was ready for the truth.

CHAPTER 14
IN A WEB

THE FOREST WAS ALIVE with nighttime whispers. Moss slicked the ground beneath my feet and tumbled from evergreen boughs like swaths of green fabric. Leslie's voice rang out in the distance, but the forest's call was more immediate, more real.

Every nerve in my body sparked with vitality. I was aware of the restless evergreens, the mist and moonlight overhead, the patches of star-and-cobalt sky. I wove in and out of the underbrush, following the light. It grew nearer with every step. My chest pinched with hope. Mom wasn't far.

I took another step, and my boot snapped a twig. The moonlight dimmed. I gasped, realizing for the first time how dark the forest was.

"Are you lost, little bird?"

I stood still, breathing hard and straining to see in the dark. "Alder?"

"Not quite." There was a smile in the man's voice as he drew nearer. "You look frightened. Are you unwell?"

I didn't answer. The steam from my breathing caught an errant moonbeam. An impatient sigh issued from the shadows, and a hovering ball of silver light appeared. The man commanding it was tall and broad-shouldered, wearing a mask and a dark-colored cloak. Most importantly, the man was not Alder.

"A bit shy, are we?" he asked.

I backed into a tree trunk. The man pulled down his mask. He cast off his hood and studied me with bright green eyes. He was younger than I expected, but his light cast harsh shadows over his face and exaggerated his sharp-cut jaw.

"Why are you in the forest?"

I swallowed and tried not to stammer. "I was looking for someone."

"The third barrier ought to have kept you out. I suppose I'll have to deal with you now." He mussed his hair. "But how to do it?"

"I can just leave."

The man studied me a moment longer. I glanced down. A cruel-looking knife glinted at his side. Young or not, the man looked dangerous.

"Ah, I know you," he said. "You're that curious creature I've seen dawdling along our borders. I've been expecting your return."

I could barely make out the outline of a path beyond the man's hovering light. If I could avoid falling into a muskeg in the dark, I could get away. What I needed was an opening.

"My apologies. I suppose we've not been formally acquainted." The man swept into a bow. "I am called Rowan. And you are?"

"Not really interested in making friends, thanks."

Rowan's jaw twitched. He placed his hand on the tree trunk behind me and leaned in. "Your sharp wit will do you no favors here."

I forced my gaze to stay locked on him instead of wandering off in the direction I wanted to go. Rowan looked like he knew his way around the forest. If I wanted to outrun him, I would have to rely on speed and surprise.

He glanced to the side. "Ah, Alder. I'm glad you've come to join us. This little bird and I were getting acquainted. Do you know—you've chosen a most peculiar subject for practicing heroics. Her eyes are Sylvaen, but she has the manner of an Outlander."

Alder appeared like a panther sliding out of the shadows. The look on his face was grim. "You certainly have some interesting ideas, Row," Alder said. "How about you give her some space?"

"I cannot blame your weakness, I suppose. She is the most interesting thing I've encountered on my night patrols in quite some time. Odd though, considering I've never seen her in Síorghlas."

"I admire your confidence, considering how rarely you've been to Síorghlas of late."

Rowan lowered his arm and faced Alder. "If she is what I expect, her very existence is a violation of Sylvaen law. The ealdors will want to know."

Alder produced a glowing orb and rolled it around on his palm. "Are you the ealdors' lackey now?"

"Not all of us have the luxury of stumbling across their favor by accident. They may overlook your little transgressions, but the rest of us must suffer the full extent."

"You make it sound as if it's something I want."

"You make it sound as if you're miserable in your little gilded cage." Rowan smirked at Alder's dark expression. "Do what pleases you, brother. It makes no difference to me. But know that I am willing to take any advantage I may by whatever means necessary."

Brother? I wondered if I had misheard Rowan. Then I recognized the similarities between them: their noses and chins, their dark hair, and their angular features.

Rowan raised a fist in the air and whistled. A company of masked and hooded sentries materialized out of the trees. Alder raised his hands and greeted them with a shower of silver projectiles. A dozen spheres raced toward the sentries, spinning around one another until all I could see was a blur of silver light. The sentries cried out as they dodged the attack, but it wasn't long before several retaliatory strikes went streaking in Alder's direction. Alder blocked and countered so fast it looked like starlight was being hurled from his palms.

Seeing my chance, I tried to slip away. One of the sentries caught me around the middle. I swung at him and tried to jerk free, but he held me fast. The sentry had the advantage of weight and muscle. I could never beat him using brute force. I would have to break him down.

"You are being absurd," he said in a bland tone. "You are an unskilled fighter and clearly outnumbered."

"But not outsmarted." Remembering my Krav Maga, I grabbed the sentry's thumb and forced it backward. The sentry let out a startled cry and released me. I used the opportunity to gather a quick breath before starting toward the trees. The sentry caught my wrist and dragged me back.

"The lass puts up a good fight, Amaranth," a nearby sentry laughed. "You will need to do better if you want to best her."

The young man named Amaranth grunted, blocking a blow that would've broken his nose if I'd managed to land it. A snarl replaced his impassive look. Grabbing my forearm, he twisted it behind my back. Red-hot pain seared through me, and I let out an involuntary scream.

"You will inflict much less pain on yourself if you keep calm," Amaranth said.

"On you, maybe."

"Do not test me, Outlander."

I took a mental inventory of my assets. Amaranth's boot rested an inch from mine. The leather looked soft, not like the steel-toed mammoths Peter wore to work. I raised my foot and brought my heel down hard on Amaranth's foot. Amaranth growled and cursed. His grip on my arm slackened enough for me to twist around and kick him in the groin.

The sentry let out a roar and slapped me hard. Everything turned bright white around me. I slumped to the ground. The sentry towered over me. I was amazed he was still standing despite his pained wheezing, and I was still more amazed when he managed to flip me onto my stomach. I could taste the tang of blood on my tongue, and I could feel the pressure increase on my jaw as he shoved my face into the dirt.

"I will finish you," Amaranth said in a voice that was deadly calm.

Faintly, I could hear Alder yelling, his voice strange and dissonant. He started toward me, but he had little time for reprieve—a falcon made of silver light angled toward him. His free hand shot out, fingers splayed, palm upturned. The forest filled with shapes of translucent silver—birds, beasts, weapons. The silvery objects dove toward the sentries, forcing them to take cover.

My head felt strange and light with Amaranth's boot crushing it. I kept still, waiting for my skull to burst. Then, I heard Rowan's voice ringing out sharp and clear.

"Enough, Amaranth. Bring her to me."

The pressing weight on the back of my head eased. I coughed up dirt and gasped for air. My body still pulsed with adrenaline.

"Outlander scum," Amaranth spat.

I raised myself on shaky arms and looked for Alder. He was still engaged elsewhere. What he lacked in bulk, he compensated for in speed. His slender frame was a blur of motion as he wove in and out of the sentries' range.

Another sentry picked me up and shoved me at Rowan. Rowan caught me with a firm hand. He took hold of my chin, tilting my face toward the light.

"Don't touch me," I warned.

Rowan chuckled. "You are in no position to make demands."

"I'll make them anyway. Back off."

Rowan's features took on a predatory look. "I think it is time you were taught some respect."

Panic chilled my limbs and blood. I tried to think. Alder was fully engaged in a battle against the other sentries; he couldn't help me. And the path leading out of the clearing was behind me now. I was mentally calculating my chances of trying the boot trick with Rowan when I felt cold fingers on the back of my neck. He brushed my hair aside.

"I can see why my brother is protecting you. You have fire inside. It almost makes the thought of your tainted blood"—his voice lowered to a purr—"bearable."

Fury replaced the fear inside me. An image flashed across my vision of me twisting a silver blade to Rowan's throat, and then the thought ignited. Heat pulsed through my veins as something awakened inside me. A primeval instinct. My fingers closed on something cold and bright, deliciously solid: a knife made of starfire. In one swift movement, I broke free of Rowan's grasp and shoved him backward. His back hit a tree trunk. I closed the distance between us, pressing the knife tip to his throat.

"This is your last warning, Rowan. Keep your disgusting hands off me."

"You haven't any idea what you're attempting—"

I pressed the knife tip harder, silencing him. A bead of red trickled onto the blade. "Maybe not. But I'll do what's needed to protect myself."

His mocking expression turned uneasy. We both knew he could easily overpower me, but I could just as easily cut his throat before he got the chance.

"Hey, Rowan." Rowan and I both turned. Alder stood there with a silver ball hovering in the air above his palm. The sentries behind him lay scattered around the forest in various states of defeat. "I've told you before—you shouldn't pick fights with girls. They always outsmart you."

Rowan pushed past me while I was distracted. The knife I was holding shattered when it hit the forest floor, leaving me weaponless. Fortunately, Rowan had a new target—his brother. He reached for the knife at his side, but before he could use it, Alder struck with a series of silver flashes. Rowan growled and parried the attack with a blast of magic. Alder thrust his palm outward. Twelve tiny silver blades glanced off Alder's swiftly conjured light shield and fell harmlessly aside. Rowan panted. Alder tossed his hair out of his eyes and widened his stance, ready for more.

"Admit it, Row," Alder said. A silver flash erupted from his open hand and shot toward Rowan. "I've always been better at shaping."

Rowan easily deflected the attack. He cast a shape like a silver spear and drove it toward Alder. Alder gazed steadily forward, twitching his fingers at the last possible moment. A flurry of silver wings erupted from his palm and rammed straight into the oncoming spear. Both spear and winged creature shattered like glass and winked out of existence.

"I remember." Rowan panted. "But I too have my strengths."

Rowan assumed a ready stance. He feinted to the right, then left. Alder mirrored his movements. The brothers were wildcats circling one another, graceful but deadly. All at once, Rowan shot forward and body-slammed Alder. Somehow, Alder managed to slide out from under Rowan's bulk. He jumped to his feet and raised his hand as though he meant to cast a shape. Rowan was on him in an instant. A swift blow to the stomach, and Alder doubled over. Rowan stepped back, allowing Alder a moment to right himself. Alder took a kick to the knee and another to the stomach before managing to jab his elbow into Rowan's chin. Rowan cursed and fell backward.

"You need to get out of here, Wren," Alder said, peering into the shadows. "Now."

Rowan was on his feet again. Alder raised his fist into the air. The sentries were starting to stir when the whole forest trembled. The air turned breathless and cold. An enormous silver panther emerged like mist from Alder's hands. The panther flicked her tail, watching me through wide crystalline eyes. She leapt into the air and crashed down like a growl of thunder. I stumbled into a run, dodging to miss the sentries even though they were too busy watching the giant shape-cast wildcat to worry about me. I wasn't planning to stick around and find out how the fight turned out.

Oddly, my senses seemed to sharpen as I ran. The evergreens blurred like smoke plumes on either side of me. I skimmed alongside a thicket of blackberries, thorns slashing at my cheeks and legs. My feet made soft scuffling sounds in the moss and forest detritus. A creek trickled to my left. I could sense the snags and fallen logs to my right along with the devil's club growing along the main path. But I had little time to revel in my heightened awareness; heavy footsteps crashed behind me like a bear charging its prey.

Some visceral instinct told me that my trajectory would lead me parallel to the forest's edge for a long way before rejoining the main road. From there, I might find a place to hide and wait for daybreak. The sentries wouldn't follow me into Ketchikan in broad daylight without some kind of disguise.

Before I could avoid it, a doe dashed across my path. The doe lifted her nose, tasting the urgency in the air. I could see the whites of her eyes, the elegant curve of her head and neck. There was something in her eyes—an acknowledgment, an invitation. She turned suddenly, her tail a tawny flash as she disappeared into shadow. In a split-second decision, I changed directions and followed the doe.

As I ran, a strange sense came over me: certainty, a completeness. The forest was perfection itself. I wanted nothing more than to slip through the evergreen shadows, following deer paths that led to new discoveries, reveling in my solitude, and chasing whimsy. For a moment, my heart was full, nearly exploding with perfect delight. But all too soon, the sound of human footfalls drew me back. The doe disappeared. My pursuer was right behind me, moving with all the speed and power of a wildcat. I could almost glimpse his form through the trees as he ran alongside me. He moved with a grace of his own, but it spoke more of power and less of stealth. I couldn't afford to lose my lead.

Sensing the need to change directions, I veered to the left and vaulted up onto a fallen log. My pursuer's feet landed moments after mine. I spread my arms for balance and weaved among the saplings springing from the decaying wood. My mind began racing ahead of my body. Six more steps, and I would have to jump the gap between this and the next log laying end to end. One powerful leap would be enough to propel myself over the distance, but I needed to take aim and adjust my balance.

Five more running steps. Four, three, two—

My feet slipped.

I teetered off the edge and crashed onto the forest floor, landing hard on my side. Pain shot up my arm and down my leg, but I didn't have time to pause and assess my injuries. I pushed myself to my feet right as my pursuer landed nimbly beside me.

"I am beginning to think you cannot admit it when you've been bested," Rowan said, breathing hard.

Gasping, I found my balance and plunged deeper into the trees. Rowan kept after me, his powerful body apparently conditioned for strenuous pursuits. I could tell he was herding me in an uphill direction. My footing was less certain and clumsier than it had been. Being in the forest invigorated me, but I was beginning to tire. The injury in my ankle made it worse. Besides all that, I wasn't physically equipped for life-or-death cross-country ventures. But what I did have was intense determination.

I took a few quick turns and looped around in order to break out of the pattern Rowan was setting for me. The sound of his breathing grew increasingly rugged. His footsteps began to recede, but I didn't slow down until I tripped over an exposed tree root and landed on my face.

Get up, Wren, I screamed at myself. *Get up!*

But I couldn't get up. I couldn't pull enough oxygen into my lungs. I couldn't summon the strength needed to peel myself off the ground. Then, the moon appeared, temporarily illuminating an unfamiliar old growth forest. Tendrils of moss spilled from above, tickling the midnight air. I had wandered much deeper into the forest than I meant to. And strangely, that innate sense of direction that had guided me away from Rowan had vanished. The last few moments of running were a blur. Had I been cutting through the forest or running parallel to its edge?

I scrambled up and continued onward. I considered trying to scale the nearest mountain in hopes of obtaining a better view. I could find my way back to Peter and Leslie's house. But without the aid of daylight to guide me, I could end up more hopelessly lost than ever. Before I could decide what to do, a deep, singsong voice was in my ear.

"Got you." Rowan's hand clamped down over my lips, muffling my scream. I kicked and flailed, but his thick arms wrapped around me from behind, dragging me back into darkness. "Easy, little bird."

Clearly, Rowan was overestimating both my desire and willingness to comply. I yelled and threw my head back into his chin. Rowan uttered what sounded like a curse in another language. Furious, he grabbed me and threw me onto the ground.

"Worse than a child. If you will only be still a moment—"

I didn't wait for him to finish. I was already ten steps away when he made a frustrated sound. After a brief chase, he snatched me up again, jerking my arms and locking me in his grip. My breathing came in quick, panicked gasps. I remembered the knife at his side. With an effort, I wiggled my arm free and reached for the knife. Just as I brushed the handle, he flicked the knife out of its sheath and tossed it to the ground.

"You've more fire than I dared imagine," Rowan said. "But you are forgetting that you've entered a world that is not your own."

I tried to slap him, trip him—anything—but he kicked my legs out from under me and dropped me to my knees. He grabbed my hair and jerked my head back, forcing me to stare up at the sky.

"Is this part of that formal acquaintance you mentioned?" I asked.

Rowan didn't answer. With one hand, he dug something out of a hidden pouch or pocket at his side. The moonlight shone off a tiny vial with some sort of dark liquid sloshing around inside. Rowan wrestled the cap off the vial using one hand. In a moment, he had it pressed to my lips.

"Drink," he ordered.

"You first."

He grabbed hold of my face, forcing my jaw open. I tried to bite him but only succeeded in biting the insides of my cheeks. Sighing, Rowan drained the vial's contents into my mouth and held my mouth shut with a grip like death. "Swallow," he commanded.

I coughed and gagged and jerked my head. The liquid swished around inside my mouth, strong and bitter and burning like acid. Rowan held on, his fist iron tight over my nose and mouth. Another moment or two, and I would run out of air. Tears dribbled down my cheeks as the liquid finally seared its way down my throat. At last, Rowan released his grip.

I slid onto my knees, coughing and trembling. A tingling lightness began to fill my body; it crept from my throat to my chest, into my limbs. I shivered, simultaneously cold and sweating.

"You will be rather drowsy soon, I expect."

A sedative, then. Gritting my teeth, I grabbed Rowan's arm and pulled him down to my level. I wanted to pummel him unconscious, but I barely had the energy to lift my chin.

"Your stubborn determination is both remarkable and pathetic," Rowan said.

I drew back my arm and backhanded him across the face. Finally. He twisted his arm free and threw me off, more annoyed than injured. He then retrieved his knife from the place where he'd thrown it and examined the blade.

I stared into the forest-colored tedium and let my head roll back. I was dimly aware of the leaf litter entwining itself with my hair, but I didn't care. Grunting Rowan peeled my listless body off the ground.

"Where are you taking me?" I managed, my words slurring together.

"Síorghlas. The ealdors will want to find out who you are and where you come from—"

The world around me swooped and jolted. Everything turned inside out as Rowan tossed me over his shoulder like he was the hunter, and I was his prey.

"—before they kill you."

CHAPTER 15
OUTLANDER BLOOD

ALL THE COLORS SWAM until they formed a new picture in my mind—one of the dark-haired boy I kept dreaming about. This time, he was wearily ascending the stairs into the upper regions of Síorghlas. Alone.

The aerial city gleamed jewel-bright against the shadowed trees, but as before, its beauty had no effect on him. He had retreated too far inward to notice anything but the darkness growing inside himself. Above him, the Elder Tree loomed in the night, tall and proud. And watchful. It shone silver-white—a beacon in the dark forest, reminding the boy it knew all. The boy noted the Tree's silence toward him, its condemnation.

Wincing, the boy remembered his plea to the Elder Tree for the gift of the Wind Shaper. Now, he understood why it had denied his request. The Tree saw all—past, present, and future. It had always known who the boy was and what he would do. He didn't deserve to be in the forest. He didn't deserve to be called Sylvaen. The boy felt he was unworthy of his gift, weak as it was. Weak as *he* was.

Maybe, the boy thought darkly, he should have let Stonecrop finish *him* off that night...

The boy came into the garden at the top of the city. A few short weeks ago, the boy had plans to swear his loyalty oath to the Tree, the Council of Ealdors, and to the Sylvaen people. Now, he knew better. He had one thing to do before he left the forest: separate himself from the ealdor's daughter before he tarnished her name along with his.

Some part of the boy registered the fragrant abundance growing all around him, but the pleasure of it fell flat on his senses. He only had eyes for the ealdor's daughter, standing in her usual place where she could gaze down at the city below. The ealdor's daughter was beautiful but pale. All her bright hair hung free, and the cloak she was wearing was lined with fur. But despite her wraps, the boy knew the ealdor's daughter wasn't cold. Síorghlas's temperature was perpetually mild, moderated by the magical properties of the first barrier. There was something else plaguing the ealdor's daughter and making her shiver. Him.

Before meeting him, the ealdor's daughter's life had been simple. Dull, perhaps, but easy. Now, she was the companion of a would-be murderer—his accomplice, even. And she had everything to lose.

The ealdor's daughter straightened when she caught sight of the boy. "I was beginning to think you weren't coming."

The boy slipped to his place at her side and said nothing. He gazed unseeing at the Elder Tree, at the canyon walls strung with waterfalls, at the girl. He was loathe to do what he knew he must. The ealdor's daughter smiled at the boy like she always did, but there was a new wariness to her expression, a reflex to look away whenever he met her eyes. The boy gripped the railing before him, struggling to find the right words.

"I came only to tell you that you needn't trouble yourself with me anymore," he said at last.

"I'll trouble myself all I like."

"Why?" The boy stared past the shape-cast lights strung on evergreen boughs around and beneath them. It felt like the darkness was the boy's companion that night, his very kin. "It isn't as though I can undo what I've done."

"No."

The boy passed a hand over his eyes. It was only because of the ealdor's daughter that he had avoided detection for his wrongdoing. The ealdor's daughter had possessed the presence of mind that night to fabricate a story. Somehow, she'd managed to cast the boy as a hero and herself as a witness. Stonecrop had been attacked by a large, predatory mammal. The creature, intending to feast on his prey later, lumbered off into the forest leaving Stonecrop for dead. The boy found Stonecrop barely alive and carried him to the healers. And by sheer luck, there really had been a wolf pack patrolling the borders of Síorghlas that very week, confirming the ealdor's daughter's false narrative.

No one questioned the boy with midnight hair. The ealdors and healers blamed Stonecrop's condition on the stars' alignment, the alcohol he had consumed, the negligence of Sitka, his cohort leader. Thankfully, Stonecrop survived, though his recovery was slow. And even when he could speak again, he claimed not to remember what happened that night.

"Perhaps you've been given a second chance," the ealdor's daughter said, drawing the boy's attention back to her. "A chance to do better."

The boy stared off into the obsidian night. He was too busy drowning in a sea of convoluted thoughts and self-loathing to reply. The only chance he'd been given was a lie, a lie spoken by someone who had more power than him simply because of her birth. No one questioned *her* lineage. No one doubted *she* was fully Sylvaen. The boy would never have that luxury.

"You should do better yourself," the boy said. "Keep better company. By nature, I am dangerous. Volatile. An Outlander."

The ealdor's daughter shook her head. "The Elder Tree gave you a gift. It doesn't matter whose blood runs through your veins."

"It may not matter to you. It will to the ealdors."

The ealdor's daughter fell silent. Like the boy, she knew he would never be able to join the ealdor council if he couldn't prove pure lineage. It had only been a delusion he'd been feeding when he dreamed of joining the council.

"The ealdors cannot determine your fate," the ealdor's daughter said hotly.

"The ealdors determine everyone's fate."

"True." The ealdor's daughter twisted to face him. "So, we must make certain they alter your fate for the better."

The boy was skeptical. "How do you propose we do that?"

"We investigate." The ealdor's daughter began pacing, ticking off points on her fingers. "We search the library: census records, collections of written correspondence, historical documents. We sift through every last book and parchment until we find record of who your father was."

"And if we don't find any?"

The ealdor's daughter stopped pacing and raised her chin. Her sweet floral fragrance wafted toward the boy. With her straight-backed posture, her elegantly woven cloak, and her proud expression, she looked more the ealdor's daughter than ever she did before. "Then we take your fate into our own hands," she said.

The boy felt his eyes widen. What the ealdor's daughter was suggesting was forgery, a crime the ealdors would not deal with kindly. Or humanely. "Listen to yourself," the boy gasped.

But it was the boy who sounded unconvinced. The ealdor's daughter was offering him a lifeline. Without it, the boy might never amount to more than a simple gardener or a scribe's apprentice. He might never have a life of his own, a home, a respectable occupation, or—he glanced shyly at the ealdor's daughter—a wife. A family. He'd never had that kind of belonging before. He took a breath. If he accepted the ealdor's daughter's help, there could be misery for them both—or there could be glory. He hesitated a moment before speaking.

"Why are you doing this for me?"

The ealdor's daughter raised her eyes to his. She picked up the boy's hand and pressed it in hers. Together, their shape-gifts combined to make an irregular rhythm.

"I want to help you become who you're meant to be," she told him.

"Why?"

"Because I know you."

"Not a real answer, that."

"Then hear this." The ealdor's daughter gripped the boy's hand harder. "I know that the young man standing before me is a gentle soul who keeps better company with plants than with his own kind. He is quiet, diligent, eager to perform, but he does not allow others to trample him. His life has dealt him a hard hand. And yet, he is not calloused. His desire is to find his place among his people and to help the world around him flourish."

The boy felt his pulse throbbing in his neck. "Utter nonsense."

"You don't believe me?"

The ealdor's daughter often communicated directly, but she had never spoken like this before. The look in her eyes meant she was determined to be understood. To show she understood him. To be believed. The boy couldn't accept it.

"No."

The ealdor's daughter's mouth curled into a smile. She reached out and touched his cheek. Her touch was a thrill, her closeness intoxicating. The boy shivered. His place, he screamed at himself. He *must* remember his place.

"I can't—" he began.

"Can't what?"

The ealdor's daughter's gaze was unrelenting. Helpless, the boy let his eyes fall to her lips. Síorghlas was below, all sparkling lights and silver radiance, but not even that compared to the ealdor's daughter standing before him with eyes the color of the evergreens. The boy looked away, fighting to keep himself in check. She was still an ealdor's daughter, and he was nothing. No one. And no amount of dreaming would change that.

"I love you," the ealdor's daughter whispered fiercely.

The boy's breath flooded out of him. "You what?"

Before he could think, the ealdor's daughter leaned forward. Her lips found his in the dark.

Uttering a noise between a laugh and a sigh, the boy wound his arms around the ealdor's daughter and brought her still closer. All he could think was how absurd it was that the ealdor's daughter cared for him. Loved him. *Him.*

The ealdor's daughter tangled her fingers with his. He could feel his heart's rhythm speeding up, drumming inside his chest, threatening to explode. Could the ealdor's daughter feel it too? Did she know how afraid he was—or how eager? Boldly, the ealdor's daughter kissed him again. And the boy let that kiss sweep him away.

CHAPTER 16
COMPLICATED

I WOKE AND FOUND myself lying in the dark. Above me, the trees were shadows against the low-hanging clouds. The rush of a waterfall filled my ears, and my body ached like I'd tumbled down a mountainside covered in bricks and boulders. As my eyes adjusted to the dark, I could see a mountain rising before me and disappearing into the mist.

"Get up."

I winced as someone grabbed me roughly by the arm and dragged me to my feet. My hands were bound. It took me a moment to puzzle out the night's events, but then I remembered the voice in the dark, the silver blade, the vial I had been forced to drink from. Had the sentries carried me all night? And where was Alder?

The sun made its slow ascent in the eastern sky. We went a little way before coming to a silver bridge with no railing. The bridge spanned a gash in the earth and disappeared straight into a waterfall. The sentries formed a single-file line and started across, dragging me between them. I tried to memorize how they navigated the slick surface of the bridge in case I managed to escape.

"Careful, Outlander," Amaranth sneered behind me. "If you fall, none of us will go after you."

At our approach, the waterfall split like a liquid curtain, ushering us into a dark cavern. Two of the sentries cast shapes to light the way forward. Their lights revealed that we were walking a ledge no wider than the bridge had been. Fortunately, the footing was less treacherous. The path we were on led us through an opening in the wall and away from the ledge. We passed into a chamber made of hewn stone. The walls were decorated with engravings: a tree with twisting roots and interwoven branches, a man's face made of leaves, a pattern with three spiraling arms.

We took another turn and then burst into the open. The air was bright, permeated with the fragrance of evergreens. Something about the scent made my heart churn and swell, but I couldn't say why. The sentries came to a sudden stop. A gate stood before us glimmering silver.

"What is your business in Síorghlas?" a voice demanded.

Two guards stood before the gate with bows held at the ready. The points of their arrows glinted dangerously. Rowan strode forward, drew off his hood and mask.

"We come to present a suspicious individual to the ealdors for questioning," Rowan said, bowing.

One of the sentries prodded me in the back with the tip of her bow. I stumbled forward, a girl dressed in jeans and a hoodie in a crowd of medieval-looking sentries wearing cloaks and armed with bows and hunting knives. The guards looked at me and exchanged a glance.

"Outlanders may not proceed past the first barrier without permission," one of the guards announced. "You will have to obtain clearance from the ealdors."

"But the ealdors are in council for the next three days."

The guard touched his bowstring. "If you take issue with the law—"

"I take no issue with the law," Rowan said quickly.

"Good." The guard puffed out his chest. "It is decided then. The lass will be incarcerated until the ealdors can arrange a formal audience."

I glanced back at the tunnel. It didn't seem likely that I would make it back to the bridge and across it without receiving an arrow in the back. My prospects for escape were diminishing fast.

Rowan offered a stiff bow, although he didn't look happy about it. "So be it."

At that, the guards lowered their bows. Another guard appeared to open the gate for us. We walked through the opening. Síorghlas was nestled in a ravine, hemmed in on three sides by sheer rock walls. The moss-and-stone walls surrounding us trickled with a million tiny waterfalls spilling into turquoise waters below. Fern clusters adorned the ravine's steep sides, and here and there, tiny white flowers dotted the moss. It was even more awe-inspiring in real life than it had been in my dreams.

Síorghlas's architecture was every bit as impressive as its surroundings. The city grew layer upon layer like tiers of a wedding cake. Giant Sitka spruce trees had been manipulated into a complicated assortment of bridges, platforms, and arches suspended in the air. There were thatch-roofed cottages and hanging gardens, stairways and amphitheaters and archery ranges, clotheslines and brightly colored banners and windows gleaming like prisms in the early morning sun.

A silver tree grew in the center of the ravine, smaller than the rest. But despite its size, the tree eclipsed the innumerable Sitka with its delicate grace and its light. Veins of color—pink, blue, and gold—ran along its trunk. I could feel magic pulsing from it like an electric current and knew at once that it was the Elder Tree.

One of the sentries grabbed the leather cords binding my wrist and used them to drag me forward. I felt like an unwilling dog on a leash. Rowan's company split up and went in different directions. Amaranth and a sentry named Sorrel led me along a rough-hewn plank bridge and across a springy lawn of moss. Soon, I found myself being shoved through a door at the base of a spruce tree. I tried to gain my bearings, but I only caught a glimpse of the dark, narrow insides of the tree before Amaranth started shoving me up a flight of stairs.

There was a door at the top leading into a spacious room with curved walls, a rounded window, and a modest bed. A rudimentary desk sat in the corner with a wooden chair drawn up to it. I took in a stone pitcher and basin lying atop, but the room had no other adornment. As far as I could tell, there weren't a lot of items that could aid me in escaping, although the window held some promise.

The sentry named Sorrel took hold of my arm and sliced my bonds free. I rubbed the raw, chafed skin and muttered my thanks. The sentry looked surprised. He sheathed his knife and stepped back. Apparently, he wasn't used to common courtesy.

"Do not unbind the Outlander," Amaranth snapped. "She is danger-ous."

Dangerous? I smiled. Maybe that groin-kick landed harder than I thought.

"I am only allowing her the use of her hands," Sorrel explained. "She ought to be able to do some things for herself."

"She ought not to be allowed to live."

Amaranth's words sobered me. The sentries I'd been traveling with cared very little whether I lived or died. Rowan made it clear that he was only delivering me to the ealdors because he thought it would gain him some kind of advantage. I had no allies, no protection, no idea how to navigate a strange culture with its even stranger customs. If the people I had encountered so far—who were willing to drug and kidnap me for their personal gain—were representative of the Sylvaen, I didn't want anything to do with them.

Amaranth gave me one last look of loathing before leaving. I heard the door lock behind him, followed by the echo of footsteps on the stairs. I didn't waste any time once the sentries disappeared. The building had one window, and I needed to check it for weaknesses before I did anything else.

After a not-so-brief examination of the window, I was forced to admit defeat. The window offered no opportunity for escape. I could push it open a couple of inches but not enough to slip through. Not only that, but the tower I was being held in was suspended hundreds of feet above the forest floor. It was unique from the other buildings in Síorghlas in that it had no external platforms, balconies, or stairways. There were no easy handholds for me to climb down with either. I wouldn't be escaping that way unless I was very confident in my tree-climbing abilities or felt like plummeting to my death.

I spent an hour or two checking for trap doors or secret tunnels. Next, I tried using every method of opening a locked door I had ever seen on movies or the internet. My progress was inhibited by the fact that the Sylvaen didn't have any kind of traditional locking mechanism like I was used to. Whatever kept me inside was located on the other side of the door. Even if the Sylvaen had used modern locks, I lacked the tools or expertise needed to open them. The only exit I could escape from was the stairway, and I didn't know how to access it.

I sat down heavily on the edge of the bed. The tree groaned in the wind, the room swaying like a lone ship adrift in an evergreen sea. I thought about Peter and Leslie. I thought about Emery. I thought about Alder taking on eight sentries in an insane attempt to help me escape. Where was he now? Where was the figure of Mom I'd seen in the forest—the one that started this whole mess? Was anyone contacting the police about my disappearance, or did the third barrier prevent them from even knowing where I went?

Maybe Alder was right. The forest had never called me for any legitimate reason; it was just messing with my head.

I must have fallen asleep, because I woke to find a Sylvaen woman scrubbing at my face with a white linen cloth. She had on a long green dress with a purple shawl, and her hair was braided to one side. The woman met my eyes briefly but kept working on my face—treating my wounds. When she finished her work, she gestured to a food tray sitting on the edge of the desk and departed. I scowled at the tray. I didn't want food; I wanted to escape the strangely comfortable prison the Sylvaen were holding me in. But the food tantalized me with its buttery smells.

My stomach grumbled loudly, reminding me it had been hours since I'd last eaten. I gave into my hunger and got up to investigate.

A bowl of mushrooms in a cream sauce sat on the tray, alongside steamed greens. There were also berries and seed bread drizzled with honey, soft white cheese, gamey meat, and some kind of root vegetable mash seasoned with fresh herbs. I was too hungry to care if the food was poisoned. I made quick work of the bread and meat and chased it down with a purple-colored beverage that looked and smelled like berries. By the time I finished, I decided that if there was anything worth living in Síorghlas for, it was the food.

I felt better after eating, but another check along the edges of the door didn't reveal anything new. The door was still bolted from the outside, and I was still stuck in a holding cell until the ealdors decided to come get me out of it. I was about to give up and resign myself to whatever fate the Sylvaen chose for me when a new thought occurred to me: the Sylvaen woman who brought me food had come in that door and returned through it unaccompanied by sentries. I jumped to my feet and noticed the rug beneath them. If I could find a good place to ambush the Sylvaen woman from, I could use the rug as a makeshift weapon to stall her and race out the door. It was far from an elegant plan, but it could work if I acted quickly. I would work out the rest of the details like slipping past the guards at the city gate once I was free from the tower.

I left my food tray where it was visible on the corner of my bed. Then, I scooped up the rug and crouched with it behind the door. The hardest part would be waiting for her arrival.

After several minutes of crouching, my muscles started to throb. I still hadn't recovered from my trip through the forest the night before. I shifted and stretched my cramped legs, but I still felt uneasy. Painfully restless. I tried to distract myself from the discomfort by thinking about what I would say to Peter and Leslie when I returned to their house.

"Hey, sorry I freaked out and ran into the forest after my dead mother. I was kidnapped, drugged, and taken into a foreign city by Alder's demented brother. But I'm okay now."

The faint rustle of fabric interrupted my thoughts. I glanced up with a start. The air stirred like someone had just walked into the room, but the door hadn't opened. I twisted around to make sure I was alone. What I saw made me lurch to my feet.

"Mom?"

Mom stood in front of me, her form outlined in a gentle silver light. I choked on a sob. The fine lines around her eyes and the dark shadows beneath them had vanished. She wore a tunic embroidered with leaves and knotting patterns and tailor-made trousers. For the first time, I recognized her for exactly who she was. *What* she was.

"You're—" My words faltered as I struggled to piece them together. "You're one of them. You're Sylvaen. Why didn't you tell me? Why didn't you say anything?"

Mom gazed at me but didn't answer. My hands trembled. Her chest rose and fell in a noiseless sigh. Although her lips didn't move, I could imagine her reply. "It's complicated, sweetheart."

After everything that had happened, she was still keeping secrets from me.

"You know what's complicated? Having my mom die and finding out afterward she's been lying to me all my life. Hearing voices in my head. Finding out I have magic. Seeing images of my dead mother in the forest. Getting captured and brought into a place where I'm told I'm not even allowed to exist. That's complicated."

Mom gazed steadily at me, her lips moving in silent utterance of my name. I was too angry to stop.

"I hope you're happy knowing that your unwillingness to confront the truth put me in the worst situation possible. You left me alone and unprepared because you were too afraid to handle it yourself."

Mom took a step toward me and held out her hand, her eyes sparkling silver with unshed tears. I hesitated, my cheeks steaming with angry tears. I knew Mom's life had been hard. She had to figure out how to raise a kid completely alone. She had to learn how to live in a world she was totally unfamiliar with. But she could have at least been honest with me. I stepped back and shook my head. I wasn't ready to forgive her—not for this.

Mom stepped back too. And then, she shattered like glass.

CHAPTER 17
THE EALDOR COUNCIL

Anxiety knotted my stomach. The evergreen boughs overhead mimicked my restlessness in the way they bent and twirled and rustled their branches. I liked to think they were sympathizing with me.

I stood unbound, sandwiched between two masked and hooded sentries on a wooden platform in the trees. The sentries kept careful watch in case I tried to escape; little did they know I was still too sore to try more than crawling unsupported.

Sorrel, the kind sentry from Rowan's cohort, had informed me about my pre-trial hearing. I hadn't expected to find a crowd of Sylvaen gathered to stare at me like I was some kind of living museum display. Skittish stares met me in every direction. An ocean of faces seemed to follow my every twitch and sniffle, their voices murmuring like the low roar of Síorghlas's many waterfalls. One face in particular stood out to me from the edges of the crowd—one who met mine without immediately turning away. The face belonged to an older woman who was plump and silver haired. She had stooped shoulders and intelligent green eyes—eyes that seemed to read my fears and consider them. She held my gaze for a moment longer, her expression neither welcoming nor hostile. And then, like the others, she turned away.

I turned away from the crowd and examined the woven branches bending over the platform like a lattice roof. Morning light filtered in through the openings and made patterns of shifting light and shadow across the smooth wooden floor. Here and there, patches of moss grew with tiny ferns and white flowers. It was hard to appreciate the beauty of it for one awful reason: I had a meeting with the Sylvaen ealdors.

Trembling, I watched thirteen solemn figures approach single file from the direction of the rising sun. They moved with such rigidity and such grace it made my scalp prickle. Their robes were long, and sweeping, and deep purple-red. I imagined their clothes as rivulets of blood. I checked my posture. If I wanted to survive, I had to show the ealdors a kind of humble self-assurance I didn't possess. If I didn't, my meeting with the ealdors might turn sour faster than anticipated.

While the other ealdors seated themselves, one broke off and moved to the middle of the platform. He held his chin high, exhibiting all the power and authority one might expect from a leader. Raising his hands, he quieted the crowd.

"Friends, as your head ealdor, I welcome you today in joining our council for an emergency meeting. We are honored by the presence of three of our choicest pupils—"

Behind the ealdors, three young Sylvaen quietly took up their posts. I did a double take when the tall boy with dark hair turned out to be Alder in a form-fitting green tunic, trousers, a belt etched with interlocking knots, and a golden-brown cloak fastened at the shoulder with a tree-shaped brooch. His shoes, too, had been exchanged for tall leather boots. But despite his put-together appearance, Alder looked haggard. His eyes met mine and did a quick survey of my person before turning away again. On his right stood a blond boy I recognized as a junior from Edgewood, and on his left stood a tall, lean young woman with a frosty pallor.

"—Alder, Heath, and Briar have each shown incredible leadership ability since saplinghood," the head ealdor went on. "Their presence brings with it the freshness of youth and the promise of a secure future for our people and our way of life."

Briar. I stared at the proud-looking girl with fair hair standing next to Alder. Hadn't Rowan mentioned her during his tirade?

I didn't have much time to think. The speaker was busy naming each of the ealdors present and thanking them for their service to the council. When he came to himself, the man simply bowed and thanked the people for allowing him to serve them. He had a powerful voice but an unassuming appearance. He was tall and thin with pale features and thick dark hair. His temples were touched with silver, and yet, his unlined face made it difficult to determine whether he was closer to boyhood or old age.

"As many of you know, Hornbeam, our oldest and most esteemed senior council member, has fallen ill and has declared himself unfit for duty," the ealdor said. "Our healers are working from dawn to dusk to cure his malady. In Hornbeam's stead, we have elected Lupine to take up the seat of ealdorship."

A tall, stately woman stood and bowed, smiling as she gazed out over the crowd. Her eyes were seafoam, her skin a rich russet. Her dark hair was woven into an elaborate braid that coiled around her head and draped over one shoulder.

"Our members have gathered to address a matter of great import. Recently, a concern has arisen that the third barrier's effects have begun to wane. We have received reports of Outlander sightings in our part of the forest. Rumors among the people have begun to circulate."

The crowd began to murmur.

"It is my intent to address these concerns," the speaker assured them. "The Outlander you see standing before you today"—he gestured vaguely in my direction—"was captured and brought into our city not four days ago. It is reported that she has breached the third barrier of her own volition. The ealdor held up a hand to quell the murmurs. "We will not at this time conduct a formal trial. We have much information to learn and little time to do it. Alas, other pressing matters impose on our time this morning." A few sparse chuckles rang out from the other ealdors. The speaker smiled and went on. "Once we have established her identity and motive, we may move forward with discussing her fate, be it release, imprisonment, servitude, termination, or perhaps some solution which has thus far eluded me."

The ealdor punctuated his sentence with a casual wave of his hand. I was little more than another problem for the ealdors to attend to.

"Without further ado—" The speaker turned to me at last—and froze. I wanted to laugh. Had he never seen an Outlander before? Had he been expecting to find a girl arrayed in full Sylvaen garb? Quietly, he cleared his throat. "Forgive me. We are not accustomed to seeing Outlanders in our realm. May I ask your name?"

"Wren Ashwood."

"Curious name, that," he mused. "Now, Wren Ashwood"—the ealdor started to pace like the prosecuting attorney on a court drama—"the Sylvaen border is protected by magical enhancements. Only our own kind may enter. Outlanders are usually repelled by the distracting force of the third barrier. So how is it that you found your way into our realm?"

I silently cursed the Sylvaen holding me captive for not giving me any clues about my hearing ahead of time. I didn't know anything about the Sylvaen or their ealdors. Any of my words could be used to trap me, and I would have no idea until it was too late.

"I thought I saw someone at the edge of the trees," I said carefully. "I thought maybe she needed my help."

That was close enough to the truth to keep me from displaying any obvious tells. I hoped.

"Who did you see?" the ealdor asked.

"I—I can't say for sure."

The ealdor stopped his pacing and stared at me, scrutinizing every aspect of my face like he was searching for evidence of a lie. I held his gaze, forcing myself to maintain eye contact. That was good, wasn't it? Or would staring the man down be seen as a threat? Satisfied, the ealdor turned away.

"What was it about this individual that made you think she needed your help?" he asked. "Was there a visible injury?"

"Not exactly."

"I'd appreciate a more direct answer, Outlander."

I thought about telling the ealdor right then about seeing Mom in the forest, but something held me back. If Mom was Sylvaen, and if she left Síorghlas for a reason, I had no way of knowing whether that reason put me in any kind of danger by association. I decided to take a different direction. Squaring my shoulders, I looked the ealdor in the eye.

"It was more a feeling I had than anything else," I said. "I don't have a more direct answer to give."

The ealdor's eyes narrowed. "How old are you, Wren Ashwood?"

"Seventeen."

"And you attend studies? At the public school?"

"Yes."

"Alder," the ealdor said without taking his eyes off me, "would you please step forward?"

Bowing his head, Alder moved through the semi-circle of chairs and made his way to the center of the dais. "*Síocháin leat,* Head Ealdor Valerian."

"*Agus leat féin.*" The ealdor dipped his head in reply. "I believe you study at the same institution as this Outlander. Tell me, have you on any occasion become acquainted with her?"

A muscle tightened in Alder's jaw. "I have."

"And do you believe her capable of malicious intent, especially in regard to the safety of our people?"

"Definitely not."

"Very well." Valerian began pacing again. "I do wish to ask two final questions, Alder, if you will indulge me."

"Of course." Alder bowed again.

"Do you know whether this Outlander was aware of our presence here before she entered the forest?"

"I do not believe so," Alder said.

"And you are convinced that the third barrier is weakening, and that her trespassing into our realm was mere innocence and error?"

Alder hesitated. "I am no expert on these matters, but I think that a probable explanation."

Valerian dipped his head. "Thank you, Alder. I see no reason to question you further. The Outlander, it seems, has done nothing deserving of death."

Alder still didn't look at me, but even from a short distance, I could see that the tension in his shoulders and jaw had eased some. I felt my body mirroring his posture. The ealdors didn't see me as an immediate threat. For now.

"Head Ealdor Valerian!" I turned to see a man shouldering his way through the crowd. "I have an urgent message regarding the proceedings."

The Sylvaen parted to make a path for him. The man hurried up the stairs, knelt before the ealdors, and passed a tightly bound roll of parchment to Valerian.

Bowing, Valerian accepted the roll and broke the seal. His lips moved silently as he scanned the letter's contents. Finally, he looked up.

"The letter is from the commander of one of our sentry cohorts," he announced. "The one who captured the Outlander."

My heart seized. *Rowan.*

"The commander claims that not only is the lass of Sylvaen descent, but she is also in possession of a shape-gift and has indebted herself to the forest so that she cannot leave."

The assembly dissolved into chaos. Six ealdors surged from their seats, their red robes flowing like so much blood. Gold specks swirled before my eyes, entangling themselves in the shifting light and shadow. Just like that, whatever safety net Alder helped cast over me shattered.

Some ealdors thought I should be held indefinitely as a prisoner while others insisted that the Sylvaen never kept prisoners and that doing so was a denial of their nature as peacemakers and keepers of the forest. Valerian attempted to quiet the chaos, but the shouting continued; some in the crowd were even calling for my immediate execution. I was a stranger, they said. I had seen too much, and I might take word to the Outlanders about the Sylvaen.

"Enough!" Valerian's voice rasped above the din. "Public proceedings are paused until further notice. The ealdors will deliberate this matter in private. The lass will remain under constant supervision until we've reached a decision. In the meantime, no one will attempt to harm her unless they want to answer to the council. You are all dismissed."

At Valerian's pronouncement, the silver-haired woman I'd made eye contact with earlier rose fluidly from her place among the crowd. She traversed a short stairway to where the ealdors were seated. Seeing her, Valerian bowed low. The woman ignored the courtesy and started speaking quietly. Valerian's expression darkened, his gaze settling on me.

"I am no one's instructor," he said loud enough for me to hear.

"Except for Alder?"

"Aye, Alder is an exception."

"You owe this much," the woman insisted. "Find a way. Make it right."

Valerian straightened, smoothing his robes. He thanked the woman coolly for her input. "I'll attend to you both shortly, then," he said.

"Very good."

The woman picked up her long green and turquoise robes, locked eyes with me, and strode forward. The guards on either side of me bowed to the woman. She acknowledged them each with a slight bow, then turned to me.

"*Síocháin leat*—Peace be with you. I am called Aster."

"Hi," I said uncertainly. I wasn't going to bow if that's what she expected. The woman smiled and took me gently by the arm.

"Come with me, Wren," she said. "You needn't be afraid."

I caught sight of Alder as he strode to Valerian's side. His gaze flicked to me—only for a moment. I turned away from him. I would have to tread carefully and trust my instincts if I wanted to survive, but that was nothing new.

Surviving was what I had been doing ever since Mom died.

CHAPTER 18
TRAITOR

ASTER LED ME ALONG a winding path to a door in a tree painted bright red and ushered me inside. She hung her cloak on a hook by the door, then put out a hand to take my jacket.

Aster's turquoise tunic was a welcoming contrast to the bloody maroon of the ealdor's robes. In it, she looked less like a portent of doom and more like the Keebler elf's grandma.

She waved me toward an array of cushions on her floor and hurried off to the kitchen. While she rummaged around, I took a brief survey of the main room. Dust motes swam in the daylight streaming in from a south-facing window. The room itself was narrow and round with a spiraling staircase in the middle ascending into the rooms above. A curving hallway and a modest kitchen broke off from the main area. Colorful rugs and knick-knacks had been displayed on nearly every surface, and there was an overwhelming herbaceous scent coming from the corner window facing the east. Plants hung from the ceiling and tumbled out of jars and bottles. A few were even clustered on the table, catching spare rays from the morning sun.

"Head Ealdor Valerian and I have decided it best to communicate with you in private," Aster called from her kitchen. "We thought you would be safer this way—protected from harm. Some in the crowd are of a more hostile disposition toward Outlanders."

I had noticed the hostile part, but I had missed the bit where the head ealdor wanted any part of this conversation. As far as I could tell, Aster had strong-armed him into it. I still didn't understand how. "Valerian wants to protect me?"

Aster bustled across her kitchen alcove, putting a kettle on what looked like a small wood stove. "Valerian desires fair treatment for all, Sylvaen or otherwise."

A clatter punctuated the end of Aster's sentence. I peeked further into the kitchen to make sure she was okay. Grumbling and muttering, she picked up the tray that had fallen on the floor and set it on her prep surface. Then, with her back to me, she stood on her toes to reach into a cupboard. In a moment, she had procured four mismatched cups for tea.

"What do you know about the Sylvaen?" Aster asked. She laid the teacups next to a wooden tray on the table. Then, frowning, she re-arranged them.

"Not a lot. I only just found out I was Sylvaen myself."

Aster looked disappointed. Mumbling to herself, she lined the tray with a bit of fabric and laid out some cookies on it. I watched as she placed four tiny, iced cakes on the tray next to the cookies, then she spent the next minute fussing with their placement. Watching her made it hard not to fidget.

"Is there anything I can do to help?" I asked.

"Thank you, Wren. I—"

I waited. Aster didn't seem to remember she had been speaking. She dusted her hands on a napkin and tried again with the cakes. This time, whatever minute adjustment she made satisfied her. She stood back and admired her handiwork.

"You must understand something about Valerian—" she began. The sound of a knock at the door startled her so hard she nearly upended the tray. "Ah. That'll be the door." Aster checked to make sure her cookies were unharmed, then she smoothed her wispy hair and went to unlatch the door.

"Síocháin libh," Aster said in greeting. "It is grand to see you both so soon."

Valerian and Alder bowed in unison. The pair looked like Christmas in their respective red and green attire. Stooping to enter, Valerian went on to exchange trite pleasantries with Aster, though the mood between them was decidedly cool. Still, Valerian bowed repeatedly and showed Aster the utmost respect by letting her direct the conversation. Socially, I expected Head Ealdor Valerian to outrank a commoner like Aster. Maybe the Sylvaen took extra pains to honor the elderly.

While Aster and Valerian talked, Alder's eyes met mine and held them. I started to smile, but he gave a subtle shake of his head and turned away. I wondered what that meant. Were we pretending not to know each other?

Finally, Valerian turned to me. "I am pleased to make your acquaintance, Wren." There was something in his sincere smile that startled me, though I couldn't say what. "Even though I would have preferred it to be under, shall we say, less strenuous circumstances."

I struggled to arrange my face into something pleasant. "Yeah. Same."

"Please have a seat." Aster herded us toward a multitude of cushions on the floor before disappearing into the kitchen.

"Alder here is my protégé," Valerian said, folding his lean frame into a sitting position. "I take it you've met?"

I couldn't help risking a glance at Alder. He was standing a little behind Valerian, raking a hand through his hair and staring intently at a knot in the middle of Aster's rugged wood floor.

"Once or twice," I said.

"At school, yes?"

I nodded. Valerian laid his hands in his lap. He looked out of place among Aster's colorful cushions and tapestries. He was pale and stately, but he had an air about him that was almost approachable. Maybe I was seeing his diplomatic skills shining through.

Aster returned and brought in her much-fussed-over tea tray. Frowning, she set down the tray and adjusted the placement of her iced cakes again. Alder leaned forward eagerly, his eyes shining when he spotted the cakes. He had a similar reaction when Leslie brought him hot chocolate. I had to suppress a smile. Alder had a bit of a sweet tooth.

"I confess, I hardly understand what you young people want with those Outlander institutions when you can just as easily complete your education here in Síorghlas," Aster said.

Alder reached for a cake. "You say that because you've never been to the Outlands, Aster."

"I've never felt the need," Aster said blandly.

Valerian's eyes twinkled with amusement as Aster served his tea. "It is a unique cultural experience, Aster."

Something about his smile continued to unnerve me.

"We've got plenty of culture here," Aster said.

Aster went to my cup next, then Alder's. I tasted my tea, a chamomile and spearmint, flavored with a bit of honey. It was the blend Mom would make after a stressful day at work. But there was some additional flavor I couldn't name. A flower, maybe? Or a fruit? After two sips, I could feel my limbs growing hot. My mind felt strangely alert. It felt like I'd woken from a fantastic night's sleep.

"Ah, Wren. I can see your eyes are brighter," Aster said. "Dried fruit from the Elder Tree contains a certain virtue." She gestured to the teacup in my hands. I took another sip, enjoying the way it stole away my weariness and invigorated my limbs.

"There's lots of appeal to visiting the Outlands." Alder went on. "They have a vast assortment of literature, music, history, traditions, food—all kinds of things. And did you know, Aster? It is the habit of some to place meat, cheese, *and* vegetables between two slices of bread. They call it a *sandwich.*"

"How uncivilized," Aster mumbled into her cup.

I quirked an eyebrow at Alder. He shot me a wicked grin before turning away.

Setting his cup aside, Valerian leaned forward. "Enough idle talk; time is pressing. To begin with, Wren, I am dreadfully sorry about today's proceedings. The hostility was shocking, though hardly unexpected. We are a peaceable people. We do not give ourselves to outbursts and barbarianism. But you see, your arrival is a painful reminder of our recent past. One of our young men formed an attachment with an Outlander, and it ended poorly for all involved."

Alder flinched, but Valerian didn't seem to notice.

"I believe you meant no harm when you breached our border. But—pardon my forthrightness—your existence, coupled with an active shape-gift, is in direct violation of Sylvaen law."

I wrapped both hands around my cup. Ah, yes, the old crime of existence. I'd been hearing I was in violation of it ever since the day Alder stopped me from crossing the forest's border. I'd felt hints of it far longer.

Aster turned to Valerian. "Valerian. How is it that Wren possesses a shape-gift when all excommunicated Sylvaen are stripped of their powers?"

Valerian took a sip of his tea, his eyes trained on my face. "Therein lies the problem. We know it only takes one parent with magical abilities at the time of conception to pass on a shape-gift."

"Yes, I know." Aster waved his words away. "What is your meaning?"

Alder's legs bounced to a silent rhythm, painting him as the picture of perfect restlessness. He was—nervous. For me.

"For Sylvaen to engage in intimate relations with Outlanders is unthinkable, punishable by death."

"Okay. But why?" I asked.

"Because they might conceive a child." Valerian set down his teacup. "Many believe mixed blood weakens our gifts and breaks down the boundaries between us and those of a different nature."

I sniffed. "Have they not heard of birth control?"

Alder spit a mouthful of tea back into his cup.

"We try to instill self-control and a strong sense of morals in our youth," Valerian said.

"So, it's about health risks and morals?" I asked, not quite sure I followed Valerian's logic.

"It is about *more* than health risks and morals." Valerian folded his long hands. "Our way of life is dependent on individuals living in harmony with one another, the forest, and our laws. We cannot afford for our young people to become enamored with Outlandish ways. All gifted Sylvaen must give energy to the forest. If we do not, our treaty with The Elder tree is broken, the protection over the forest is compromised, and we lose our home and way of life. Not only that, but we cannot risk having half-breed Sylvaen with unchecked abilities scattered beyond our borders. I cannot say what even *one* Sylvaen might do without our laws to restrain them."

"Maybe she would end up drugged and bound, dragged across the forest, and locked in a guard tower?"

"The means of your arrival was not of my choosing," Valerian said. "But caution is necessary. You understand, do you not?"

Frustrated, I gazed into my teacup, swirling its contents. "Honestly? No. I'm not half-Sylvaen because I want to be. I never would have come here or bothered you if Rowan hadn't dragged me here. And regardless of your laws and morals, I don't think it's fair or reasonable to execute people for existing."

"It is not my intent to execute you," Valerian said. "My desire is to preserve your life. But you are more open-minded than we are. Many see your way of life as incompatible with ours. And the more you try to change our ways and convince us that you know better—" Valerian stopped speaking. A crease formed between his brows. He leaned forward, putting a fist to his mouth. "Forgive me, but you do so remind me of your mother. The resemblance—your mannerisms, your features, your expressions—it is startling."

My heart kicked me in the ribs. Mom. The reason I was here. The reason for all of this.

"You knew her?"

"She was an acquaintance of mine once, I suppose." Valerian withdrew his hand from his mouth. "How does she fare?"

I looked at my hands, struggling to process the information. If Valerian knew Mom, he might have some of the answers I was looking for. "She's—dead."

At my words, the room went silent. Aster bowed her head and muttered a few words in another tongue. Alder rolled his teacup in his palms, watching me with a look that was hard to read. Meanwhile, Valerian stared at me with a disbelieving expression. It shocked me to think these strangers from Mom's past might be moved over the loss of her. The isolated life Mom and I lived made it hard to imagine her ever having relationships or connections before I was born.

Clearing his throat, Valerian sat up straighter. "I was not expecting such news."

Mom's presence in the room was almost palpable at that moment. I wondered if the others were aware of it. It felt as though any moment, she might appear around a corner with her serene smile and an explanation. It was all simply a big misunderstanding, she was still here, and she was still someone I could trust. The image made me ache inside. I was suddenly desperate for more information about her past.

"Can you tell me why she left Síorghlas?" I asked Valerian.

"Indeed." Valerian lifted his gaze to the herb bundles drying beside Aster's window. "Quite simply, she was a traitor to her people."

Mom was a traitor?

Valerian went on. "It is my understanding that after swearing her oath of loyalty to the Sylvaen, your mother attached herself to an unknown Outlander, took him as her lover, and departed."

I frowned, keeping my eyes trained on the embroidered orange cushion Valerian laid his hand on. The person Valerian described didn't sound like Mom at all. She sounded impulsive and careless. Then again, I never knew my mom back then. Maybe she had been keeping secrets from me all my life for the simple fact that she was ashamed of her past.

"The Elder Tree has a particular order, you see," Aster explained. "A young person, such as Alder here, takes part in his Becoming—his time of wandering—allowing him to interact with Outlanders on a personal level. Our hope is that he will see futility there and recognize the value in our way of life."

Valerian dipped his head in agreement. "When Alder comes of age, he will choose whether to take up his birthright and pledge loyalty to his people or dwell among Outlanders as an Outlander. To leave permanently, he would have to surrender his shape-gift. If he were to refuse, the forest might drive him mad with its call."

"Aye," Aster said. "Not only is the laying down of one's shape-gift beneficial to the individual, but it is also part of our agreement with the Elder Tree."

Frowning, I fingered the rim of my teacup. "So, you're saying you don't think my mom surrendered her gift?"

Valerian considered the question before answering. "Indeed. It is our belief your mother violated the Elder Tree's given order, which, according to the council, is treason."

"That's impossible," I said. "My mom didn't have a shape-gift."

"No, and you didn't either," Valerian said. "A person's shape-gift will lie dormant in the absence of *draíocht*—the magic gifted to us by the forest—and awaken when it senses magic nearby. But even when your gift is inactive, its presence will impart a long-distance longing for the forest and for the Elder Tree. That longing would only be satisfied with your return."

Finally, I understood why Mom refused to take me back to Alaska when I pleaded with her. She knew I had a dormant shape-gift. The moment I climbed out of Leslie's car and breathed in the evergreens for the first time, my gift awakened. In that instant, I became who I was, and my fate was set in motion. There was no going back to sleep. But still, why didn't she tell me?

"But Valerian," Aster said, "Wren's mother *did* lay down her shape-gift. I witnessed it myself. But at the time, I was unaware of her, er—condition."

Condition being pregnancy. With me.

Valerian took a careful sip of tea. "Aye. If any of us had known, we would have been obligated to act much differently. We would have abided by the law, as is our duty."

Alder's mouth slipped open. It took me a moment to understand Valerian's meaning: if the ealdors had known mom was pregnant with an Outlander baby, they would have killed her—killed us both.

My heart thrummed painfully against my ribs. I looked from Aster to Valerian and back again. Aster's expression was grave, but Valerian's was unreadable. Suddenly, I couldn't keep still. I slammed my cup down hard enough to slosh tea over the side and jumped to my feet. The three Sylvaen looked up at me in surprise.

"I can't stay here," I gasped.

Aster laid her cup aside and pushed herself upright with a groan. "Wren, calm yourself."

"How can I do that? You're using me to finish what you started with my mom."

"We're not going to harm you in any way." Gently, Aster took my arm. "Please sit down. We will discuss this."

I shook my arm free and backed away. "This whole thing was inevitable. I was always going to die at Sylvaen hands for being the wrong person born the wrong way in the wrong place. My mom *knew* this would happen, and yet, she did nothing to prepare me for this. Nothing."

Alder looked like he was going to be sick. Maybe he was starting to realize I was actually going to die.

"The past is unimportant. What matters is you are here now." Valerian rose to his feet, gathering his ealdor's robes neatly around him. "It is true that you are in some danger, but we wish to prevent you dying, Wren. Your mother believed all life had value regardless of its form. Although I disagree with many of her decisions, I've always held a high opinion of her ideals and wish to honor her by preserving your life."

I took a moment to calm my panicked breathing. "How so?"

Valerian smiled oddly again. "We must change your stars, and we must do so by treading carefully."

Aster began wiping up my tea mess. I wondered how she could stay so calm when the entire world felt like it was crumpling like tin foil.

"She's right," Alder said, sliding to the edge of his cushion. "Diplomacy won't work here; Rowan saw to that. You witnessed the crowd's response. Wren's only chance for survival is escape."

"Peace, Alder." Valerian's voice was firm but gentle. "Do not let the compassion in your heart turn to recklessness. Our laws must be upheld. If we aid Wren's escape, we are complicit in a crime and guilty of treason."

"Valerian," Alder said. "They called for her execution."

"Valerian and I will do our part to ensure Wren's safety," Aster said, gathering up the sodden dish towel and carrying it to her kitchen. "Much of what took place during the proceedings was actually in Wren's favor."

Alder looked unconvinced. "But how do we persuade the more radicalized among us that she isn't a threat?"

"She must prove herself," Valerian said. "Unless a decision is unanimous among the ealdors, execution is unlawful. I will work to secure a trial period, and it is during that time that she may yet tip the balances in her favor. The more challenging task will be convincing the ealdors to release her. She may never be permitted to leave Síorghlas."

Aster returned from the kitchen. "Could you live here indefinitely if needed, Wren?"

I gazed down at my teacup in quiet contemplation. The idea of never returning to Ketchikan made my stomach twist unexpectedly. What about Peter and Leslie? What about Emery? And what about graduating high school?

But I wasn't close with Peter and Leslie, and Emery was barely more than an acquaintance. Besides, what did I have to look forward to after graduating high school? A part-time job? Maybe college? The art program in Southern California felt like nothing more than a distant dream—an impossible one. My entire life consisted of plans for survival and nothing else.

"I guess I'd have to," I said.

"Excellent," Valerian said, clapping his long hands together. "What I suggest then is for you to assimilate with the Sylvaen and to do so quickly."

Alder jerked his head up in surprise. "Assimilate?"

"Aye, lad." Valerian looked at me. "If Wren wants the people to believe she isn't a threat, she must become one of us. She will deny her Outlander ideals and past. She will learn our ways, familiarize herself with our culture, and contribute to our society. She must demonstrate that she is willing to work hard and, in time, truly become one of us."

Alder rubbed his chin. He looked like he wasn't sure what to make of Valerian's proposition. In truth, I wasn't either. I never intended to be captured, imprisoned, and forced to take on a new identity in the name of survival.

"Now then." Valerian clapped Alder on the shoulder, startling him out of his pensive mood. "I envision no better time to begin Wren's assimilation process than right now. I would like her to see our fair city, educate herself, observe our way of life. But at present, I have a great deal of record-keeping and civil complaints to attend to. So, I would like you to escort Wren for an afternoon in my stead."

Alder snapped to attention. "Of course."

"Good lad."

Valerian brushed quickly past me on his way out the door. Although he didn't say it, I had the distinct impression that Valerian couldn't get away from me fast enough.

CHAPTER 19
UNDER WING

"**I**'M NOT SURE WHAT to think of Valerian's plan," I confessed to Alder.

Alder gave me a sympathetic look. "Aster will help you in her way, but she's easily distracted. And Valerian is, well, Valerian. He's a politician. I'm sure he doesn't want to lose the favor of the people."

"So, trust them, but don't trust them?"

"Aye, and I can help you too. If we play our cards right, your assimilation could work."

I didn't want to assimilate; I wanted to find out what I could about Mom and get out of Síorghlas. Unfortunately, I was running short on escape plans.

"Do you know anyone in Síorghlas who might know something about my mom?" I asked hopefully.

"Not off the top of my head," Alder said. "And if she was a traitor, people might be reluctant to say anything. You might try searching records at the library when you can—I can help with that too." Alder smiled brightly. He was entirely too eager about this helping-me-with-my-assimilation thing.

"Thanks."

"We'll find out the truth in time," Alder promised. "For now, we should start with the grand tour."

I stifled a groan. Síorghlas was a multi-tiered tree house maze. "Was Valerian's tour idea a scheme to get me so lost and disoriented that I could never leave?"

Alder chuckled. He picked up my hand and placed it on his forearm. "It's okay, Wren. You're not doing this alone."

I frowned. "Sorry—did I miss the part where you asked me to prom?"

"Sylvaen custom." Alder patted my hand. "Keeps the bad fairies away."

"Did you just make that up?"

"Not entirely."

I felt my lips cave toward a smile. Touring Síorghlas with Alder might not be all bad. It might give me the chance I needed to explore probable escape routes. Maybe I could even pick up some clues about Mom.

Alder led me up and down Síorghlas's stairs too many times to count. Wherever we went, foliage consistently lined the steep face of the rock wall beside us: moss and ferns, bunchberry, and evergreen saplings. Alder pretended not to notice me panting and fighting for my life after all the stairs. He pointed out the gardens, the library, the berry patches, the trees he used to climb with his siblings, and the market stall that carried the best summer berries. His enthusiasm reminded me of Leslie when I first arrived in Ketchikan.

"This is the infirmary." Alder waved to a door surrounded by flowerpots and hanging plants. "Most births and deaths happen here or at home. We pay taxes to the U.S. government and go to hospitals when needed, but we prefer our herbal remedies and magic-induced healing."

Sylvaen dwellings grew sparser near the top of the city. Steep rock walls hemmed in Síorghlas on either side. I considered rock climbing as an escape option, but I had no climbing gear and zero experience. The ravine leading away from the city held some promise except that it would be impossible to navigate without a boat in the wide spots. I didn't know if the Sylvaen *had* boats, let alone how to work one.

We wandered into a steep and narrow alleyway overhung with trailing mosses and vines. Alder paused and drew me aside to allow a man leading a goat passage up the winding stairs. The air there smelled more strongly of spiced wood and cookfire. Doors hung in the walls accompanied by potted plants. Big earthenware jars stood here and there with rigging to collect rainwater. I tried to orient myself as we turned down another passage, but my mind struggled to internalize all the complexity of Síorghlas's layout.

"You look Sylvaen," Alder said suddenly.

"It's the clothes." I touched my braid self-consciously. "Or the hair."

Aster had insisted I dress the part of a normal Sylvaen girl before we left. I was now similarly outfitted to Alder, only my tunic was the vibrant gold of an autumn sunset and had a feminine cut and a dark green bodice. Aster completed my disguise by fastening a silver pin embossed with a fireweed stalk on my cloak.

"No, it's you," Alder said. "I didn't notice how much before."

I turned to find his gemstone-green eyes fixed on me. The look on his face made my chest pinch. I let go of his arm.

"So, how do Sylvaen get food and clothes and other items they need?" I asked, suddenly desperate for a way to get Alder's eyes off me. "Is it all produced by magic?"

"Not all. I'll show you."

We went a little way before coming into view of an open-air market. The space was crammed with people, booths displaying wares, and brightly colored banners. There were hunting knives, speckled eggs, dried fish, and hand-carved bows. Someone played a jaunty tune on a fiddle. Children were everywhere, running underfoot and playing a game that looked like tag with a leapfrog element. I wondered what it was like to grow up like that—to live carefree and confident without worrying about basic things like survival.

Further into the market, a man lounged in a hammock strung beneath two gnarled limbs, playing music on a flutelike instrument. Before him, shapes in the form of tiny people danced around an even tinier silver fire. A few yards away, a little girl stood and watched. She was mesmerized by the music and the tiny dancers. Her mother put an arm around her shoulder and drew her close. I felt a hard lump form in my throat. I would give anything to have Mom there standing next to me while I struggled to navigate Sylvaen customs and protocol.

A moment later, I felt a touch on my arm. "Stay close, okay?"

Alder's voice came out all soft and whispery. He smelled good too—like evergreens and boy shampoo. Flustered, I shoved my romantic delusions aside and focused on navigating the crowds.

"We have a bartering system like the Tlingit and Haida," Alder said, guiding me with the slightest touch on my arm. "We have our own laws, customs, and ways of governing ourselves, but some of what we practice today has Indigenous influence. A lot of us even have Indigenous ancestry."

We passed a booth displaying colorful fabrics embroidered with leaves, trees, and interlocking knot patterns. The patterns coupled with the Irish-sounding Sylvaen accent puzzled me.

"I would have guessed you had Celtic ancestry," I said.

"We do. And some of us also have Tlingit ancestry. We've been allies and have intermarried with one another for a very long time."

We paused at a market stall displaying inkwells and brass pens tipped with turquoise feathers the color of an Alaskan fjord. While Alder traded for something, I admired the iridescent hues of a geode set out on display.

"How long ago did the Sylvaen come here?" I asked Alder as we wandered away from the booth.

"We don't know exactly, but it was before the Outlanders came. Our Celtic ancestors would have crossed Canada and the Northern United States before landing here."

"What made them choose Alaska?"

"A good question, that. Our ancestors came carrying the seed that would grow into our Elder Tree. According to legend, it's a direct descendant of a far older Tree. They needed to germinate the seed and plant it before its light and magic faded, but they had to do it in exactly the right spot."

"And that was here?"

Alder nodded. "The Tlingit and Haida welcomed our ancestors and found they had a lot in common. Both groups had a strong sense of community and tried to live harmoniously with the world around them. So, the Sylvaen stayed, planted the seed, and constructed Síorghlas and the magic barriers that protect it. Indigenous people, with or without Sylvaen ancestry, can cross the barriers without being affected by the magic. Unlike Outlanders."

I watched the crowd with their bobbing heads and endless meanderings. They all seemed content to live like they did—isolated and law-abiding and disdainful of people like me. "The Sylvaen really don't like Outlanders, do they?"

Alder shrugged. He guided me past a mushroom cart, explaining how some Sylvaen felt that being around Outlanders eroded Sylvaen culture. They worried Sylvaen youth would adopt Outlander ways and forget their own.

"The Elder Tree initiated an agreement with our ancestors," Alder went on. "We call it the Elder Covenant. It wants our partnership in caring for the forest. We give our energy to the forest and keep things running smoothly. In turn, the forest provides us with things like passage, food, shelter, and magic.

"But not everyone agrees about all the things the Covenant contains. Some say we're meant to disentangle ourselves from the outside world entirely, but others think the Tree encourages hospitality and only wants us to keep from losing our Sylvaen identity. Either way, the Covenant states that if we don't do our part, the magic fades."

I thought about Valerian and his concern about weakened magic. "Is that what happens if Valerian's fears are realized and everyone chooses to leave Síorghlas after their Becoming—the magic fades?"

"Hardly anyone chooses to leave. The ealdors ensure teaching about the Elder Covenant starts around the time we can crawl."

"The Becoming hardly sounds a choice then."

"I hadn't thought of it that way." A strange look passed over Alder's features. He looked at me for a moment before lowering his head. "You're right. There's injustice here, like how we treat Outlanders, but I don't know what to do about it. I'm powerless—a coward."

Alder was wrong; he wasn't powerless. I had seen his magic in the forest. He could pull me in for a bear hug as easily as he could tear me apart. He had been holding back with Rowan—but he also didn't let Rowan have his way.

"You're not a coward, Alder. Think about how you stood up to Rowan."

Alder smiled ruefully, his gaze turning distant. "I didn't exactly win that fight, now, did I?"

"Maybe winning isn't the same as overpowering," I said. "You could have chosen not to get involved. You could have destroyed Rowan, but you didn't. You defended me *and* you held back from seriously harming your brother. I think that shows you're a pretty good person."

Alder turned to me, his lips parting slightly. "You think that?"

"I do."

This time when Alder smiled, it was genuine. I hadn't noticed the metallic flecks in his eyes, the wave in his hair, the slight upturn of his nose. Or the fact that when he smiled, I wanted to keep staring and not look away. I might have kept staring too if it hadn't been for the creaky voice that spoke.

"The wind in the Elder Tree blows ever strong, but it breaks not its boughs."

Alder and I turned in unison. An elderly man with a walking stick bowed to Alder with a fist clamped over his heart. Alder went from looking content to wildly uncomfortable in an instant. He returned the formal-looking bow with a pained look. Satisfied, the old man hobbled away. I watched his retreat, then turned back to Alder.

"You're not Sylvaen royalty, are you?"

Alder smiled like he found the question funny. "The Sylvaen don't have royalty."

"Are you training to be an ealdor?"

Alder's smile disappeared. "Ah, no. Nothing like that. I'm allowed to attend council meetings. It's um—strictly a ceremonial position." He ducked under a low-hanging arch made of golden fabrics and woven vines. "Are you hungry?"

I *was* hungry, but I was more interested in finding out why Alder was rubbing his palms on the legs of his trousers like he was suddenly nervous.

"You were standing with the ealdors at my hearing," I said, walking faster to keep up with Alder's long-legged stride. "You were at Aster's too—you came with Valerian."

"I'm his mentee." He paused by a market booth selling bread and other baked goods. A long line of patrons stood before it, waiting their turn. "This place has amazing pastries. You want one?"

I narrowed my eyes. Alder had a height advantage, but I had a look that, according to Emery, was bordering on murderous. Alder instantly became fascinated by a random waterfall across the canyon.

"I want to know why you're being evasive," I said.

"I'm not being evasive." Alder's voice climbed higher than usual. "I'm starving."

He probably *was* starving. Judging by his slim physique, the guy had the metabolism of a hummingbird. But he was also being evasive.

"Valerian's head ealdor," I said, folding my arms. "He's way too busy with all his ealdor stuff to bother helping people like me. So, why are *you* his mentee?"

"Fine." Alder folded his arms, mirroring my posture. "You want the long answer or the short one?"

I glanced toward the booth. "It's a long line."

Alder took in a long-suffering breath. "Normally, Sylvaen educate formally to eighth grade. After that, our families choose private tutoring, participation in the Becoming, an apprenticeship in the trades, or some combination. My family isn't high on the echelon of Síorghlas's societal ladder, so private tutoring wasn't an option for me. But as you may have noticed, I have a strong gift. Valerian saw my talent and offered to take me under wing. That's it."

That *wasn't* it. It was part of the truth, maybe, but Alder was still withholding something. Something important. And I was dead sick of people keeping secrets.

CHAPTER 20
OBLIGATION

ALDER AND I HAD barely finished eating and were on our way again when a pair of small girls with matching strawberry curls darted out of nowhere and shot straight across our path. I grabbed Alder's arm without thinking. Children weren't normally frightening to me, but these two were flanked by an assortment of shape-cast animals: wolves, a stag, two porcupines, mice, a bear standing on its hind legs. The pair moved so fast I couldn't tell who was chasing whom. Alder watched them with an amused expression, but when the animals started crawling up people's legs, he decided to intervene.

"Cress!" he yelled. "Clover! I thought you two lost the privilege of shaping in public."

The girls skidded to a halt and looked around. Then, spotting Alder, one of the girls leaped into motion. Eyes shining, curls bouncing, she vaulted herself straight at him and landed in his arms. Alder tossed the little girl in the air and caught her. She exploded into a fit of giggles.

"*Deartháir mór!*" she cried joyously.

"Older brother," Alder translated, with a glance at my hand holding his arm in a death grip. "You okay?"

I let go of his arm, making a mental note that Alder had not one but three siblings. I wondered what it was like to have any.

"Have you brought us any presents?" the girl asked Alder.

"No. And I would ask if you were good whilst I was away, Cress"—he looked pointedly at the assortment of softly glowing animals nipping and chasing their tails—"but I think I already know the answer."

The girl wrapped her chubby arms around her brother's neck and kissed his cheek. "I've been very good! Clover too. We painted the front door for Ma this afternoon. Bright red with dots like a ladybug. Ma has yet to see it, but I know she'll be pleased."

Alder opened his mouth, then shut it. I had a feeling that Cress's mother would, in fact, not be thrilled with the new paint job on her front door.

The second girl looked at me then and stabbed a chubby finger in my direction. "Who is that?"

Cress frowned. "It is not polite to point, Clover."

Ignoring her sister, Clover continued to point. "Is she your girlfriend, Alder?"

Alder turned red. "Ah, no Clover. This is Wren. She is, um—"

"His captive," I supplied.

Clover's eyes went wide. Alder gave me a disparaging look before informing his sister that he was my captive and not the other way around. While he was still speaking, I felt something snuffing in my hair. Turning slowly, I discovered a shape-cast elk watching me through wide, quicksilver eyes as it chomped on the end of my braid. Horrified, I tugged my hair out of its mouth.

"Her hair is like copper," Cress observed.

Also, my hair may or may not have been full of shape-cast elk slime. I didn't know if animals made of shapes possessed salivary glands, and I was afraid to find out.

"Aye," Alder said. "She has sunset in her hair, that's her magic."

In spite of the eight-hundred-pound elk nuzzling my hair, I managed to smile.

"I've lost a tooth, Alder!" Clover blurted.

The little girl clapped her hands behind her back like a tiny sentry and bared her teeth, showing the gap where her lower central incisor ought to have been. With Cress still in his arms, Alder bent down next to Clover with sudden interest. The three of them shared an animated conversation about fairies—both good and bad—who stole little girls' teeth and used them to create big, hairy monsters. Soon, Alder was sporting a shape-cast silver beard and a wide-brimmed hat. He and the girls started blowing shape-cast bubbles across his palm. Giggling madly, the girls jumped to catch the bubbles as they ascended into the air. They were so caught up in their games that they didn't notice when a woman, plump and pretty, came bustling into the square with another small child on her hip.

"What in the Elder Tree is all this commotion?" she demanded.

Alder stood up fast, his hat and beard disappearing in an instant. Cress, still clinging to Alder, buried her face in his shirt, and Clover crept behind his leg. The shape-cast animals vanished along with the bubbles and my new elk friend. I had to resist the urge to hide behind Alder too.

"The girls were keeping me out of mischief," Alder said, setting Cress down.

The woman, I assumed to be Alder's mother, looked me over. Strawberry curls ringed her face, and she had tied a band of apple-green fabric in her hair to match her eyes.

"This is Wren." Alder grabbed me by the shoulders and turned me to face his mother like he was presenting me for inspection. This time, I had to resist the urge to turn around and smack him. I already hated meeting new people, but today was especially brutal. I still hadn't fully recovered from my hearing.

"She is having her first look at Síorghlas," Alder said. "Valerian has her undergoing cultural assimilation and requested that I escort her for a few hours."

Alder's mother tried to bow to me, but the boy in her arms squirmed and fussed, babbling nonsense. She shushed him, bouncing him a little too exuberantly in her agitated state. "Cedar, do cease your squirming."

The little boy kept squirming in defiance of his mother's plea. I amended my earlier mental count; Alder had four siblings.

"It's—nice to meet you," I stammered. My face reddened. I couldn't remember the traditional Sylvaen greeting, and I wasn't comfortable bowing. But I wasn't sure it was expected of me anyway this early in my assimilation.

"*Síocháin leat*, Wren. I am called Foxglove." Her rich Sylvaen accent flowed like music. "You are very welcome in Síorghlas."

Welcome and Síorghlas didn't seem to belong in the same sentence in my opinion. "Thank you." I tried not to be obvious about the fact that I was looking for some kind of escape route—anything to get me out of meeting another stiff, pretentious Sylvaen.

"You know my son Alder?" Foxglove asked.

"A little."

"Aye. He speaks well of you, though your acquaintance hasn't been long." Foxglove glanced at her son. "But he usually is a good judge of character."

Foxglove may have been right about Alder's judgement when it came to other people, but he was needlessly hard on himself. I couldn't help but remember him calling himself a coward.

"Now, what's this I hear about your venture through the forest?" Foxglove asked. "It seems you had a run-in with one of our sentry cohorts?" Foxglove's eyes bore into mine. I felt myself shrinking back beneath her gaze. Her question felt like a trap. Rowan, the leader of that cohort, was her son.

"Oh, that," I said. "It was a little rough, but I survived. I'm sure Alder could tell you about it sometime."

Foxglove looked dissatisfied. Where was my ability to blend when I needed it? Fortunately, she had the decency not to press me further.

"I heard Rowan and his cohort were sent back to the border immediately after they returned," Foxglove said to Alder. "Do you know why?"

"The ealdors are worried about a weakness in the third barrier," Alder said.

"Valerian would be better off employing *himself* at the border if it's a weakness he's concerned about."

"Valerian doesn't care much for performing tasks he finds menial." Alder's tone was more diplomatic than his words implied.

"Aye, that I know." Foxglove settled the little boy more securely on her hip. "Valerian's skills lie in getting other people to do his undesirable work for him." Foxglove shifted again. I noted the pointed look she gave Alder, which he either tactfully ignored or didn't notice. By "undesirable work," Foxglove apparently meant escorting me around Síorghlas.

"The ealdors really do think the barrier is weakening, Ma," Alder said. "This isn't the first time they've said so. They keep it quiet, of course, but I've heard them."

"You should let the ealdors determine that, Alder. Don't interfere."

Alder smiled. "I try not to, but you know me."

Foxglove lifted her eyes skyward and heaved a sigh. "Well, anyway. It doesn't matter much so long as Rowan is being kept busy and out of trouble. Come, little lasses." She gathered the girls to her with a hen-like gesture. "Da and Hemlock will be starting on supper by now, and I want your help with tomorrow's bread."

I glanced at Foxglove, alarmed. How many children had this woman given birth to?

"Oh, and Alder?" Foxglove said. "Remember to fetch your sister's longbow from Sage. He ought to have it repaired by now." She reached out with her free hand to touch Alder's cheek. "We will see you at supper, lad. You won't be too late, I hope?"

"Not too late," Alder said.

Satisfied, Foxglove turned back to me. "It was lovely meeting you, Wren."

"Likewise," I lied.

Foxglove hurried off, skirts swishing. Cress and Clover followed close at her heels. I was still reeling over the number of siblings Alder had. Wasn't birth sort of traumatic for all involved? Also, which of Alder's tiny sisters had a longbow and why? The pair couldn't have been older than six.

"Went all right, that," Alder said.

"Did it?"

We went a little way and came to stairs leading downward. Already, the sky was bruised purple with twilight in the west, revealing the first few specks of starlight glimmering across the expanse.

"You look tired." Alder paused on the landing. "Not in a bad way."

I wasn't only tired, I was angry. Since coming into the forest, nothing had gone my way. I'd been drugged, captured, and imprisoned in a foreign city. I'd been put on trial and told that I had to fight for my right to survival. Valerian sent me off with Alder to go explore Síorghlas and exchange pleasantries with people who had no real interest in getting to know me. All I really wanted was to return to Peter's and Leslie's house so that I could regroup and resume my search for clues about Mom.

"Thanks for noticing," I said flatly, starting down the next flight of stairs. The city, the sky, the first evening stars all shone with a starlike silver glow, but I hardly cared. I wanted to get away.

"Ashwood, wait." Alder's footsteps hurried to catch up. "Did I do something to upset you?"

"I'm sick of being interrogated by strangers."

"You mean my ma," Alder said, drawing even with me.

Alder looked like he was caught somewhere between amusement and penitence. I let out a pent-up sigh. He didn't get it, how could he? He'd grown up in the company of all these stiff customs and traditions. It was all second nature to him. We passed a dozen or so doorways and softly glowing windows. Strings of freshly laundered linens drifted in the breeze overhead. Alder ducked beneath someone's white bedsheet and turned down a side alley, gesturing for me to follow.

"I'm sorry, Wren," Alder said as we slipped between two residential buildings. "I wasn't expecting to run across my family today. Next time, I'll avoid putting you on the spot."

I muttered my thanks and turned away. I didn't want to be angry with Alder, but I didn't know how not to be.

Alder seemed to sense my mood, because he didn't try to engage in conversation. Instead, he led me on quietly through the outskirts of the city. I had no idea where we were going, but I trusted Alder's sense of direction and familiarity with Síorghlas. Shape-cast lanterns lit the path sparingly, bobbing like buoys in the twilight air. An archway made of living wood rose up before us, seemingly leading to nowhere. Alder caught my gaze again as if to make sure I was paying attention. We passed through, and in a moment, the heavy evergreen boughs parted way for us. Together, we stepped out onto a secluded overlook, an intricately-formed balcony growing out of the tree it was suspended in. At the view spread out before us, I caught my breath.

"What *is* this?" I asked, my voice tinted with wonder.

Before us and on either side, the dark shapes of evergreens framed a panoramic view of the mountains. Above, the sky was endless, a liquid onyx canvas splattered with stars, and below, Síorghlas was all mist and evergreens and starlit radiance. Ketchikan was down there—I could see the glowing gold of its lights. Somehow, the lights of the city didn't detract from the rugged beauty of the mountainside; if anything, they enhanced it.

"This is my favorite spot," Alder said with a shrug. "It's where I come when I need a break."

I walked up to the railing and rested my arms on it. "I can see why. It's beautiful."

He leaned his tall, boyish form against the railing beside me. "Aye, that it is. Thought it would appeal to your artist's eye."

It did. But it also helped loosen the knot cinched around my heart. Alder was attuned to me well enough to recognize when I might need a break, and he was also aware of what things I enjoyed. I glanced curiously at him, but he was staring at the scenery. I hadn't so much as thought about drawing since the night of my capture. Suddenly, the landscape stretching out before me was begging to be captured in graphite. If only I had my sketchbook.

"You look like you're thinking something," Alder mused.

I turned to him. His eyes were on me again, aglow with moonlight. With his high-collared tunic, tall boots, and his cloak slung over one shoulder, he looked like the main character from some fantasy movie or video game. That strange, feverish, mushy-headed feeling overcame me again. I clenched my jaw against the onslaught.

"Are you surprised?" I said finally.

Alder smiled. "No. But I haven't got a map to help me navigate inside your head."

I fingered the embroidery on my sleeve. Alder was kind. Loyal. Dependable. I wasn't invisible to him like I was to nearly everyone else, and I'd let the novelty of it lure me into trusting him. I meant to keep it all inside, but instead, I felt the words spilling out of my mouth before I could stop them.

"I'm sorry, Alder. This place is beautiful, and I appreciate you bringing me here. But I can't enjoy it right now. I'm still struggling to process the fact that magic is real, that all of this is real. That I'm half-Sylvaen and here in Síorghlas against my will. That the only thing I want right now is to find out something about my mom's past, and I can't even accomplish that right now. And—I'm having a hard time feeling like I can trust you."

Alder's smile faded. "I see."

"Look." I locked my hands into fists. "I know you don't owe me any explanations, but some things happened this afternoon that were weird. Before I came here—before my mom died, she was the only person in the world I could trust. And then I found out she was keeping all these secrets."

Alder took a deep breath. "You're wrong. I do owe you an explanation."

I waited. Alder ran his fingers through his hair, making the flatter parts of it stand on end. For some reason, he wouldn't look at me.

"I'm bound," he said suddenly.

"You're what?"

"A binding is a legal obligation to marry someone," Alder clarified. "It was some scheme by the ealdors three years ago. I wasn't even legally old enough for a binding at the time, not that the ealdors care much."

My mouth slipped open. Alder had a marriage arranged for him. What made it complicated was that I was fairly sure he had feelings for me. "That's um—wow." I settled my hip against the railing and tried to sound indifferent. "Who's the lucky girl?"

"Her name's Briar. And she's anything but lucky."

I remembered the girl with an expression like winter incarnate standing beside Alder at my hearing. She was pretty, but Alder didn't sound smitten, he sounded bitter.

"You like her, right?"

"I liked her once, I guess." Alder leaned his elbows on the railing and sighed. "But it's hard to like someone who spends all her time degrading you and wishing you were someone else."

"Oh." I pasted on what I hoped was a normal expression. "Can't you break it off?"

"Briar can. She's the daughter of an ealdor. But she won't have it annulled. She can't stand me or my family, but she goes along with it because her parents tell her to. They think it'll improve her rank and social status."

I frowned. Alder was still hedging around a secret. How could he improve the social rank of an ealdor's daughter—was his shape-gift really that strong?

"Rowan seemed to think you had some influence with the ealdors," I reminded him.

"Yes, well Rowan's an idiot." Alder continued his obstinate stare into the trees. Deep purple clouds swirled in the western sky, piling up on each other and obscuring the moonlight. "And that's another thing I should have apologized earlier. What Rowan threatened you with was disgusting and inexcusable. I'm so sorry you had to deal with it."

"It's not your fault. Rowan thinks I'm dangerous."

Alder's lips quirked. "Oh, aye. You're very dangerous."

"I'm a little dangerous."

"A little."

I glanced sidelong to find Alder watching me, his chin resting on his arms. A tiny smile remained fixed on his lips. I returned his smile without meaning to. Something about Alder disarmed me—invited me in. Despite his binding, I wanted to get closer. But I didn't dare. I hardened my resolve and turned away.

"Rowan is right." I plucked a fern from the railing and ran it through my fingers. "Not everybody in Síorghlas loved the idea of me walking away from that council meeting alive. Valerian knows that, and he's keeping his distance. But you're here. And by spending time with me, you're making it clear to everyone whose side you're on."

"I *am* on your side, dork."

I glanced up. The boy standing beside me with magical powers and medieval clothes was completely at odds with the boy from Ketchikan with his motorcycle and hooded sweatshirts. And yet, the two sides of him were inseparable.

"Maybe you shouldn't be."

Alder rolled his eyes. "Are you trying to get rid of me again?"

"No." I twirled my fern. "But I'm worried. Rowan knew you lied about the barrier to protect me. He warned you that if the ealdors found out, you'd be guilty of treason."

"I thought we'd already established that my brother's head is full of rot."

"And I thought we already established that you don't owe me anything."

"Who said anything about owing?" Alder pushed himself away from the railing. "I thought we were friends now. Or at least that we'd moved past being *not friends*."

"Friends or not, I don't need your help. I'm more than capable of surviving on my own. I've been doing it my whole life."

Alder took another step closer. "This isn't about you being helpless, Wren. It's about you being ill-equipped to take on a situation that is more complex and dangerous than you can imagine. It's about having someone to watch your back, fill in your blind spots, and make sure you stay alive."

My heart thumped. Alder cared about me even though he wasn't supposed to. The more he and I spent time together, the more we understood each other. Things between us had shifted from strangers to acquaintances to friends to something that put us both in a precarious position. The realization that he had feelings for me and I for him brought me little comfort.

"I'm here because I made a stupid choice." I lifted my chin, undaunted by Alder's height advantage. "I never asked you to risk your welfare and possibly your life for me."

"I know what's at stake. And you never had to ask."

I let out an aggravated breath. "What about your family? If you help me, they might—"

"My family is going to be fine." Alder touched my elbow. "It's you I'm worried about."

If Alder kept looking at me like that—with eyes that were bright and warm and filled with peridot fire—I was going to cave. Quietly and half against my will, I shifted away from him. It would be best if he tried worrying about me a little less.

CHAPTER 21
SHAPES AND STARS

T HE MOONLIGHT SHONE SILVER through the window, signaling the beginning of another dream. The boy was there, lying in bed awake, trembling. He wasn't alone.

Despite the winter chill, a sheen of sweat shone on the boy's brow, arms, and chest. The throbbing in his neck was evidence that his heart would not calm. He reminded himself that the sentries surrounding him with their arrows nocked had only been a dream. The sentries were apparitions, their arrows a metaphor of his shame.

Still shaking, the boy sat up. Six months had passed since he presented the ealdor council with a letter proving his lineage and securing a provisional seat for himself. His nightmares, he knew, were only the disquiet of his own restless mind, but he was not deceived. The peace he now possessed was fragile for two reasons: his attack on Stonecrop, and the ealdor's daughter lying on the bed beside him. He gazed at her hair fanned out over the pillow. The sound of her even breathing meant she was still asleep, blissfully unaware that the boy's night terrors were growing increasingly frequent. With the image of the sentries still fresh in his mind, the boy climbed out from under the woolen blanket and began searching for his things.

"Wherever are you going?" the ealdor's daughter asked in a sleepy voice.

The boy froze. "I did not mean to wake you," he said, slipping his tunic over his head.

"You know I am not a sound sleeper."

He paused a moment, considering the ealdor's daughter's moon-struck eyes. He knew a lot of things about the ealdor's daughter he shouldn't—the curve of her neck, the warmth of her skin, the soft give of her lips. The ealdor's daughter was the source of his ever-present guilt. She was the daughter of an ealdor—a true daughter of the forest—while he was the son of no one. Even The Elder Tree had abandoned him.

"I am leaving," he said firmly, bending to lace his boots. "And I'll not be returning."

The ealdor's daughter watched as he fastened his cloak with a tree-shaped pin, the official seal of the ealdors. The boy longed to return to her side, to soothe the worried crease between her brows. But he knew the kind of attachment they'd formed was forbidden. He'd taken the ealdor's daughter for his own, body and soul, without earning her hand in marriage. If her mother ever found out, there would be consequences; at best, the ealdor would make sure the boy never attained a seat on the council, and at worst, she would see him executed. The boy knew that if things continued as they were, their luck would run out. Eventually, he and the ealdor's daughter would be discovered. He couldn't live with the anxiety.

"I—I don't understand," the ealdor's daughter said.

The boy stood to face her. "Suppose the ealdors found out about us. Suppose your mother—"

"My *mother* hardly recalls my existence."

"That may be." The boy picked up his bow. "But your mother has the power to keep me from retaining my seat on the council."

"Is that all you care about?"

The boy hesitated. By the look on the ealdor's daughter's face, he could tell she was angry. "Your mother also has the power to keep me from earning your hand," he said gently. "And she will exercise that power until I can gain some notability."

"Aye. My mother would agree to nothing between us short of you becoming a full-fledged ealdor."

The boy laid down his bow and went to her, picking up her hands. "Then that is what I shall do."

"It could take years. Do you understand that? Years without so much a glance between us. I can't—" The ealdor's daughter bit her lip to hold back a sob. "I thought we were happy as we were."

"We *are* happy." He pressed his lips to each of her fingers in turn. "All I ask is for us to be safe as well as happy. We've taken too many risks. If the ealdors find out about Stonecrop or about my relationship with you, our stars could take a turn."

"Our stars are what we make them."

The ealdor's daughter pulled her hands away. Suddenly, the boy was angry. Did the ealdor's daughter not see that some things in life were beyond a person's control? That one could try their hardest and still end up miserable?

"Suppose you conceived a child," he said.

"I won't." The ealdor's daughter turned to glare at him. "I've taken all the necessary precautions."

"Aye." He sat down on the edge of the bed. "I know that. But anything could go wrong." As it so often did in his experience.

"We could leave," the ealdor's daughter said, shaking the auburn hair out of her eyes. "We could live without fear by starting a new life somewhere else." There was an odd sort of blaze in the ealdor's daughter's eyes, a determination the boy had never seen before. He found the look troubling.

"If we want to change our stars, we'll do it here in Síorghlas," he insisted.

The ealdor's daughter released his hand, drawing her arms around herself. "I'm afraid—afraid of our stars changing *us*."

"What do you mean?"

"My mother—" the ealdor's daughter's voice broke. "She always chose Síorghlas over me. She was afraid to lose what she and my father worked for."

The boy winced. Even though the ealdor's daughter spoke out of her own hurt, her words felt like an accusation. She thought that once the boy tasted power, he would change. That he would become no better than her ealdor mother. The thought saddened him. How could she not trust him after everything they'd been through?

"That will never happen." He reached out to gather the ealdor's daughter in his arms. "I swear it on the Elder Tree."

The ealdor's daughter nodded through her tears. "You are a good man."

"I am not a good man. But I will do everything I can to become one. For you—" Brushing aside her coppery hair, the boy took her face in his hand and swept a kiss against her temple. "Beautiful Laurel."

I woke up shivering. The blanket Aster had given me to sleep under was a bright patchwork of reds, yellows, and autumn golds. But despite the differences between the sunlit world I was living in and the moonlit one in my dream, the images still felt haunting and vivid. The girl, the ealdor's daughter who kept showing up in my dreams, wasn't a faceless stranger. I knew her.

Mom.

I shivered again. If the girl in my dreams, *the ealdor's daughter*, was really Mom, then her disappearance from Síorghlas was that much more puzzling. Didn't she have a privileged existence? And who was the boy—my father? I dismissed the thought; my father was an Outlander. Maybe the boy had some other significance to Mom's story.

I felt sick and dizzy. Seeing Mom alive and young had been disorienting. But that must've been how she looked when she lived in Síorghlas. Even now with my eyes open, I could see her. She was there, dressed all in green with the sunlight shining in her hair. How often had she walked through Síorghlas as I had the night before, surrounded by growing things and twisting walkways lit with silver light? How often had she watched the sunset or felt the rush of an evergreen breeze mingled with ocean air and magic? And then, I thought about the boy. Did Mom's connection with him have something to do with her leaving Síorghlas?

The sound of footsteps echoed in the hall. Aster was up. Quickly, I slid out from under my blankets, made up the bedding, and began searching for my daytime clothes. From our brief encounters, I'd learned that Aster was fussy and particular. I didn't think she'd react positively to me still lying in bed. If I wanted to make it to the library or start making inquiries about Mom, I would have to get on Aster's good side.

"Ah, grand," Aster said, clapping her hands together. "I was afraid I'd need to wake you. You were out late with Alder."

"Sorry."

Aster waved my apology away. "I don't blame you, lass; I blame Alder. Respectable lad he may be, but he must learn what is and isn't an appropriate hour to be escorting a lass through Síorghlas."

I blushed. "We ran into his family."

"Aye, and no doubt he took you to look at the stars afterward." Aster laughed at my expression. "I know the habit of Sylvaen lads when they've got a pretty young lass on their arm."

I was speechless—speechless and hot all over. Aster knew about Alder's binding, didn't she? Besides, Alder hadn't taken me to look at the stars. He had taken me to look at the mountains surrounding Síorghlas. The stars just happened to be there too.

"I've got a bath drawn for you behind the curtain and breakfast in the main room," Aster said, breaking me out of my thoughts.

"Thanks—I appreciate it."

She dipped her head in acknowledgment. "After today, I'll have you start drawing your own baths and helping with household chores. I can be hospitable for a time, but I am no one's maid."

After breakfast, Aster showed me how to draw water from the pump outside and haul it. I ended up washing dishes while Aster moved furniture around and worked on clearing a wide space in the middle of her main room. I thought maybe she was planning on having me help her with some kind of crazy deep clean of her entire living space, but she apparently had other ideas. She came into the kitchen and drew up a stool to sit on while I finished sweeping.

"How are you at shaping?" she asked.

"Decent."

"Grand." Aster nodded to herself. "But we'll want to take you beyond decent, and we'll want to do so rapidly. Do you object to some instruction?"

"Not at all."

Aster rose with a groan from her seat and motioned for me to follow her into the main room. Laying the broom aside, I dusted off my trousers and hurried after her. With the furniture and cushions cleared to the sides of the room, Aster positioned me away from the front window and then took her place before me.

"First, we'll want to sort out some important matters," Aster said. "We need to pinpoint your magic type."

She explained that a person's shape-gift usually fit into a specific category. Sylvaen were encouraged to find their magic type early so that they could tailor their training. A person's magic type told which items a person would be best at shaping. Working within the lines of one's shape-gift also meant exerting the least amount of energy. Also, magic types allowed some influence over corresponding real-life objects.

"We have plants, animals, weapons, and earth types." Aster ticked each category off on her knobby fingers. "And we have healers, of course. My da was skilled with architecture and my ma with minerals. My late husband was a weapons type. You might even find fire or water—I happen to be one of only three water types alive. There are more obscure categories, of course, but let's focus on eliminating the basics."

Aster had me start by shaping several random objects—rocks, knives, a flame. I did okay, but none of my shapes stood out as particularly stable or unstable until I got to animals. Even after concentrating hard, all I was able to produce was some kind of twisted rodent thing and a dead-looking bird.

"Definitely not animals," Aster grumbled.

"What was my mom's magic type?"

"Unspecified." Aster drew a large, dusty book from one of her bookshelves and started flipping through the pages. "Let's see, then. What haven't we tried?"

"Her gift was unspecified?" I asked in surprise.

"Aye. Your mother could shape well enough, but she never mastered any particular category. That can happen on occasion. It usually means something went awry in early development. Your mother had other skills of a non-magic variety. She was particularly good at archery, if I remember correctly. And I think she could mix tinctures well enough, but she was no healer."

I gnawed my lip, hungry for more about Mom's past but not sure what to ask. The fact that Mom was skilled at archery didn't surprise me; it was something I knew about her already—one of the few remaining things that aligned with the person I knew. But to hear that her shape-gift was unspecified startled me. What could have gone wrong in her early development, and would that same factor affect me?

"Worry not," Aster said as if guessing my thoughts. "Unspecified gifts are rare, and it is very unlikely for them to pass from parent to child."

"Even though my father was an Outlander?"

Aster gave me a severe look over the top of her book. I had a feeling that mentioning my Outlander father in Síorghlas wasn't a good idea.

"Aye, lass," Aster said. "Even then. We will find your type."

While Aster skimmed the pages of her book, I found myself thinking of Alder. I didn't have to worry so much about tripping over Sylvaen conventions when I was with him. If I did something wrong, he would patiently explain the rules. If he were the one teaching me magic, he'd call me a dork and tease me about my demented animal shapes, but he would also smile and encourage me to keep trying. And then he'd show off by shaping a perfect peregrine falcon or something. The jerk.

"What is Alder's magic type?" I asked Aster.

Aster glanced up. "Alder's gift is unique."

I'd seen Alder shape all kinds of things that night in the forest—weapons, mist, water, birds, a panther. The only common theme I could think of was speed, maybe. Or agility.

"I expect the lad never told you himself?" Aster asked.

"He doesn't talk about himself much."

"No, I suppose he wouldn't." Aster frowned at her book. "Perhaps you should ask him yourself."

I opened my mouth to press her. If there was one thing I hated, it was knowing that someone was withholding information from me. Like Mom had. Aster had the answer to my question, and I didn't know why, but I was dying to know the answer. But before I could get the words out, Aster held up an index finger. "Ah. We've forgotten plants."

"But Alder—"

"Hush, lass. Time is of the essence. Shape a twig if you will. Or a bit of moss."

Frustrated, I thrust my palm into the air. The object materialized without me even thinking. I held out my hand and presented Aster with a perfect shape-cast twig, complete with leaves and a cone-like fruit. Aster smiled proudly.

"That's it, then," she said. "You're a plants type."

I didn't answer; I was too busy staring at the twig in my hand. I didn't need to study plant lore in Síorghlas to know that I was holding a twig from a red leaf alder.

"Your eye for detail is remarkable," Aster said, moving around me to examine the shape. "But your shapes are still connected to your source. That makes them unstable, and it uses up your energy quickly." She plucked the shape I was holding from my palm and gave it a gentle tug. The shape came to a stop midair, jerking like a yo-yo on a string.

"Think of shapes as those things you Outlanders call balloons," she said, forming a kind of ball in the air with her hands. "It takes energy to expand a balloon and give it form. Once you've got it as full as you like, you can either tie it off or let the air out. But you cannot stand there all day breathing into it or you'll faint. In the same way, shapes keep feeding off your energy until you break the connection it has to you—what we call its source."

At least I finally understood how Rowan and his sentries were able to best me. My shape-cast knife had been good but was incomplete. Unstable. No wonder it shattered so easily.

"As children, we learn to sever our shapes immediately. It helps maintain the integrity of the shape, but more importantly, it protects us from energy depletion."

Aster dropped the shape-cast twig back into my hand and showed me how to break its source. The technique wasn't as intuitive as I thought.

Even when I got it right, there was an odd sense of pain and pressure like someone had placed a tourniquet around my magic supply.

"Good," Aster said. "Again. And keep your shapes small. Focus on accuracy. Even small objects can be used as weapons if needed."

I assumed the proper stance Aster had shown me and shaped a fireweed stalk. Shaping took a serious toll on my energy. Aster told me that the more complex the shape was, the more it drained my energy. Shaping didn't feel draining until I severed a shape from its source. Then, it felt like I was being tied in knots. By the time we finished shaping, I was seeing stars.

"You've done well, Wren-bird." Aster patted my shoulder.

"Thanks."

"You remind me a bit of your mother."

My whole body jolted and started to tremble. "Wait. *You* knew her?"

"Not well."

"What was she like when she lived here?" I demanded. "Who were her parents? Where did she live?"

"Patience, lass. That is a good deal too many questions all at once."

"I'm sorry." But I wasn't sorry; I was impatient. I had come this far, and I still didn't know much more about Mom than I had when I first arrived in Síorghlas.

Aster crossed the room and started returning her cushions to their usual positions. "Let's see. It's been a good many years. A diligent student, she was. At least when she applied herself. But she was stubborn to a fault. Unwilling to take any kind of criticism—"

"Were you her teacher?"

Aster smoothed a cushion and stood up. "At times, and in a manner of speaking."

"Do you know why she left Síorghlas?"

"That I cannot say."

I was disappointed. "Is there anyone else who could tell me? Did she have any close friends? Any relatives?"

Aster dragged a side table in front of the window and stood back to admire the effect. "I'm afraid I am not the best person to ask."

I couldn't let Aster off so easily. She *had* to know something—something that would give me some inkling as to where to start searching for the truth about my mom. I thought of the boy from my dreams. What if he was still living in Síorghlas? Would he have some of the information I was looking for?

"She had a friend here, I think. A boy with dark hair. He would be an adult now. He and my mom spent time together. I think they were in a relationship at one point. Do you think—"

"I am sorry, Wren. I was not aware of any such boy, and I am sure that neither he nor I could give you the answers you seek."

My pulse quickened. Admittedly, I hadn't met a lot of people in Síorghlas yet, but what if I'd already encountered the boy and hadn't realized it?

"Was it Valerian?" I asked.

"Your mother had many friends and acquaintances; Valerian was part of the latter category. He admired and respected her, but the two had little interaction."

"Who else could it have been?"

"Many lads had their eye on your mother when she was young," Aster said with a shrug. "I was not aware she favored any of them especially."

"She did."

Aster turned to me. "Did she tell you this herself?"

Aster's words struck like a blow. If Mom had told me anything at all, I wouldn't be in Síorghlas. I wouldn't have been captured and dragged before the Sylvaen ealdors to discuss whether I would be allowed to continue living. And I wouldn't be stuck trying to figure out my shape-gift *and* the truth about my mom.

"Do not lose heart, Wren," Aster said kindly. "In time, I'm sure you'll learn all you like. But for now, what's most important is that you focus on the task set before you."

Right. Assimilation. The hopeless cause that was supposed to save my life. Aster turned and started rearranging a small vase of flowers on the table in front of the window. She thought the conversation was at an end. But I had one more question to ask.

"How were you acquainted with my mom?"

Aster's shoulders tensed. "I knew her mother."

"Wasn't her mother an ealdor?"

"Aye."

"I thought the ealdors kept to themselves."

"They have some friends," Aster said. "Even among common folk."

Something about Aster's responses bothered me. It reminded me of trying to squeeze answers out of Alder. I squared my shoulders. I wasn't going to be put off again. "You know something, don't you?" I took a step toward Aster. "About my mother."

Aster's shoulders heaved. She spun to face me, knocking over the flower arrangement. The clay vase hit the floor and broke. "Lass, I've told you all I can. The questions you ask come with a price. You seek information, but anyone who shares that information is put in immediate danger. Your mother was a traitor—that is all you need know."

"But—"

"Be silent." Her eyes, dark and keen, were filled with a cold fire. "And if you cannot restrain your curiosity long enough to keep from assaulting me with questions in my own home, we will find other lodging arrangements for you."

Startled, I took a step backward. "I'm sorry, Aster. I didn't realize—"

"You *will* realize it from here on." Aster's look softened, but only a little. "Your time would be better spent studying."

I nodded in silent acknowledgment.

Aster bent to pick up the flowers and broken bits of pottery. I turned on my heel and hurried out of the room. If I wanted answers, I would have to look elsewhere. Aster couldn't help me. Or she wouldn't.

CHAPTER 22
THE DANCE OF THE FLAME

"WITH FEELING, LASS," ASTER urged, raising her hands like a conductor before an orchestra.

I went through the dance steps again, dipping and twirling and crossing one ankle in front of the other where appropriate. Aster's warbling hum was supposed to compensate for our lack of music. I felt like an idiot.

"It is called *Tine Phreabach*," Aster said. "The dance of the flame. You must move with grace and intention. Think of a flame buffeted by the wind."

"Um, okay."

I tried to make my flailing more passionate. Like all the previous times, I started out all right until Aster increased the tempo of her humming and then kept interrupting it to critique my footwork.

Since our last conversation, Aster's hostility toward me had vanished. We had fallen into a kind of rhythm. I didn't ask about my mom. I helped Aster with household chores, and she guided me in my assimilation process. Which was good because I would have been totally lost otherwise—not that I was trying. Aster had me studying an ancient language, reading Sylvaen history and literature, learning to forage, *and* practicing my magic. And dancing.

"Ah," Aster said, drawing backward to avoid a collision. "Perhaps with less aggression."

I stopped dancing and let my arms fall. Aster was under the bizarre impression that the fate of all Síorghlas—or at least my continued existence—rested in my ability to perform traditional Sylvaen dances. If Aster was right, I was probably going to die.

"Aster, I don't think I can do this. I'm not good at this kind of dancing."

Aster opened her mouth like she was about to say something like *nonsense*, but she changed her mind. "You simply need more practice," she decided. "And a proper dance partner. Perhaps I can find a young man—"

Right on cue, a knock sounded at the door. Aster smiled and went to the door. I silently prayed that the person at the door would turn out to be a woman. The last thing I needed was some stranger to humiliate myself in front of.

"Alder! Excellent. Please, come in."

I shut my eyes and nearly swore. Of all the males in Síorghlas—

Alder stepped inside. "Is everything all right, Aster?"

"Aye. We need a young man. Do you know how to dance?"

"Pretty well," Alder said. And his eyes found mine in an instant. He looked like he didn't know whether to be concerned or amused at my wilted posture.

"Excellent." Aster clapped her palms together. "Wren is learning to dance, and I don't know the man's part. Would you be willing to aid us?"

I shook my head at Alder, but he only smirked and turned back to Aster. "I would, but I'm not sure Wren can handle it. She looks about done in."

"She will handle it," Aster assured him.

"But—"

"Hush, lass. If you want to live, you will dance." Aster marched off into another room. Why did her words feel less like a warning and more like a death threat?

"So." Alder unpinned his cloak and popped open the top buttons of his collar. "What are you learning? Green Steps? The Stag and Bear?"

"*Tine Phreabach*, I think."

Alder paused in the act of rolling up his sleeves to stare at Aster across the room. She stared right back at Alder, lifting her chin in a silent challenge.

"If Wren can dance that, she can dance anything," Aster said.

Alder looked like he wanted to argue. Instead, he took my hands and walked me across the room. The rush of his shape-gift propelled my heart into overdrive—or maybe it was just the feeling of his hands gripping mine.

Aster verbally guided us through the first steps of the dance. I succeeded for about a minute before I had an incident with Aster's rug and another with Alder's feet. Aster shook her head and mumbled something about ineptitude.

"Maybe we can try this outside," Alder suggested. "Do you mind, Aster?"

Aster waved a hand in the air. "Do whatever it takes. You're staying to eat, of course?"

"Aye," Alder said. "Thank you, Aster."

Aster disappeared into the kitchen. I used the opportunity to wander a little way from Alder. No harm in stalling a bit.

"What is it with you and meal invitations?" I asked Alder, scanning the trinkets on Aster's shelf.

"I have a knack for unintentionally charming older women into feeding me." He took my hand and tugged me toward the main stairs. "C'mon."

Like other Sylvaen dwelling spaces, Aster had multiple balconies, most of which had gardens growing on them. Alder led me out onto a broad balcony sheltered by an overhang of evergreen boughs and aspens dipped in gold. He knew the layout because most of the homes in Síorghlas had a similar design.

"Does this look all right?" Alder asked.

I let my gaze sweep over the gorgeous scenery and pretended to shudder. "I hate it. Let's try somewhere else."

"Would you prefer the market square?"

I thought of the busy marketplace with its swarms of people. "Not really."

Alder smirked. "That's what I thought."

He took my hand and guided me through the first movements with ease. I tried to keep my head on the steps, but it wasn't easy. His touch crackled like someone had lit a sparkler and thrust the hot end into my palm. Worse, the light filtering through the autumn leaves brought out the gold in Alder's eyes. Without meaning to, I would catch myself staring and look away fast. And then I would trip and the whole dance would fall apart.

"This is hopeless," I said.

"Maybe we can try some music."

"It might help more than Aster's singing."

Alder dug his phone out of his pocket. His Sylvaen tunic and trousers were a stark contradiction to the phone in his hand. Síorghlas had a strict ban on any sort of technology—a ban that Alder was ignoring. Either he was a rebel at heart, or he was willing to bend the rules for me. The thought made me a little giddy and, simultaneously, a little sick to my stomach. I didn't need him taking stupid risks for me.

Alder hit "play" and tucked his phone in his pocket. In a moment, a Celtic tune started with a tin whistle and a drum. Alder caught me by the hands and guided me into a spin, our boots crunching in the fallen leaves.

"Never mind Aster," Alder said, "she's a ruthless instructor."

"Ruthless to the point of making death threats, apparently." I huffed out a breath. "I don't see why I have to do all this to pretend I'm Sylvaen and prove that I have the right to exist."

Alder guided me into the next turn. "You *are* Sylvaen. Your mother passed on a shape-gift to you. And even if she hadn't, you would still have the right to exist."

"It's not like I asked for that shape-gift."

"Maybe not, but you still have it."

"I wish I didn't." I paused while Alder did a spin thing around me. "Without it, there would be no scandalized stares or whispers. No medieval clothes. No disastrous assimilation. No being on trial for existing. My life wasn't great before finding out I had magic, but it was definitely simpler."

Alder grabbed my hands again and pulled me back into the dance. "I'm also not sure you quite understand what you're saying."

"I'm not sure *you* understand what I'm dealing with."

"Not perfectly," he admitted. "But I do know your shape-gift isn't just an inconvenient thing that happened to you. It's a part of you, and it always has been, even when you didn't know about it."

"If that's true, it's a part of me that's very likely to get me killed."

"Not if I can help it." Crossing wrists, Alder turned with me in a quick circle and then pulled me in fast. I bumped into his chest with a gasp. I apologized, but Alder stopped me. "This dance is a tug of war. I pull you toward me, and you push me away."

"Um, okay." I gave Alder a hard shove. He used the momentum of my push to glide skillfully into his next steps. Then, taking my hand, he pulled me back toward him.

"We're acting out a story," he said. "All Sylvaen dances are depictions of fireside legends."

"How does this one go?"

Alder drew me into another series of complicated steps. Then, he told me a story that began with a traveler passing through a village.

The traveler was walking down the road when he spotted a pretty girl out gathering wood next to her cottage. Intrigued, the traveler stopped by her gate and asked for some water in exchange for gathering the girl's firewood. The girl had a garden and animals, but she was running her farm all alone. She was worried about how she would gather the harvest in time for winter, so the traveler offered to stay and help. The girl, whose only concern was maintaining her farm, was glad to make use of the traveler. The traveler's labor became the price for food and lodging in the girl's stable.

The more time the traveler spent with the girl, the harder he fell for her. The traveler ended up doing most of the farm chores: milking the goat, fetching the water, and fixing the leaking roof of her cottage. Meanwhile, the girl avoided him. Day after day, the traveler stayed and worked for the girl until one day when he confessed his love and intention to marry her.

"Marry her?" I laughed. "That was quick."

"The guy's a traveler. It's not like he has time to date."

"But he has time to flirt and work on a farm and get married?"

"Touché."

I gave Alder another scripted shove. "What happens next—does she run away with him into the sunset?"

"Not exactly. The girl agrees to marry him but avoids him even more than before. Soon, the traveler realizes the girl is only using him. The traveler demands honesty from the girl—either she meant her pledge and will consent to a binding, or she will send him on his way."

"And then what?" I panted as Alder chased me across the balcony. "Does the girl light something on fire?"

Alder laughed breathlessly. "Is that what you do when people collect firewood for you?"

"That's not a thing people do for me."

"Because you would become an arsonist if they tried."

"Maybe. But I want to know why it's called *Tine Phreabach*."

Alder caught up to me and pulled me partway into his arms. "It's a metaphor, weirdo. It has to do with how flames flicker back and forth instead of committing to a single direction."

"That sort of makes sense," I conceded as I broke away from Alder. "What happens next?"

"The girl hesitates. She's starting to have feelings for the traveler, but she's afraid either that the traveler only wants to marry her for her land or that he'll leave and she'll be alone again. The girl agrees to a binding, but then runs into the forest. The third part of the dance is about the traveler chasing the girl into the woods to try and win her heart."

"So, he really cares about her then?"

"He does." Alder grabbed my hand and brought me in close. I didn't know if we were acting out the part of the story he was describing or if we hadn't gotten there yet. I started to spin away again, but he held on to me. "Not this time," he said, moving my hands to his shoulders. "Like this."

We turned and swayed together with the same rapid movements, but our steps were harmonious this time. When Alder spun me this time, he did so inside the circle of his arms. I was grateful my tunic's high collar hid the pulse pounding in my neck.

"Who wins the chase?" I asked, returning my hands to Alder's shoulders.

"The traveler catches up with the girl, and—the dance ends with a kiss, traditionally."

I stumbled to a halt. "It what?"

"Ah, don't worry. I'd never kiss a girl without asking."

I didn't answer. Alder studied me, his eyes searching mine for something I couldn't name. His gaze fell to my lips, then flitted away like the aspen leaves falling around us.

I wanted that kiss. And I couldn't help but feel like Alder wanted it too. But there was one problem: Alder was bound.

"I think I'm ready for a break." I released my grip on Alder's shoulders and practically shoved him away—unscripted this time. "How about you?"

Alder gave a vague nod. He stood there rubbing the back of his neck and looking lost in thought while I planted myself on Aster's low garden wall. After several minutes, Alder came to sit beside me.

"Wren, there's something I should tell you," he said. "About your ma."

My breathing hitched. My fists clenched. My entire body snapped to rigid attention. Mom was the entire reason I was here—the half-veiled *why* behind all that was happening. Any answers Alder could give me would make all the nonsense customs and books and dances worthwhile. Why hadn't he brought this up sooner?

"What is it?" My voice trembled.

"You were right about seeing her in the forest. She's there—in spirit. I found out she's Betwixt. That's like a state of existence between two worlds, the one we know and the bright place we pass on to."

I stared at fists in my lap and tried not to cry. Mom was really there and always had been. I hadn't imagined any of it.

Alder went on. "She's invisible without you superimposing a shape-cast image over her presence," he explained. "She was here a few minutes ago, watching us dance. I would have said something, but I'm still getting acquainted with her presence. It's hard to separate the forest's noise into voices."

Voices. But Mom acted like she couldn't speak when I encountered her in the guard tower. I turned to look at Alder.

"How are you able to hear her?"

Alder flinched. "It's sort of an ability I have. A gift that keeps me attuned to the whole forest. The Elder Tree gave it to me, but there's something wrong with it. I can't hear the Tree anymore. The reason I can hear your ma is that her being is still tied to the forest. Her spirit's being held here instead of passing on."

I shuddered. The Elder Tree was less living organism and more raw power; Mom's presence being tied to it was terrifying.

As I considered Mom's plight, something new occurred to me. The old man bowed formally to Alder in the market. Rowan hurled accusations of privilege at him. Alder's status was such that it elevated him to Valerian's mentee, bought him admission to council meetings, and made Briar want to marry him despite her personal feelings. He wasn't royalty, and he wasn't an ealdor's son—he was something far more powerful.

"Hang on a second." I scooted away from Alder to get a better look at his whole person. "*You're* how the Elder Tree communicates with the Sylvaen."

"Aye." Alder swallowed in a way that made it look painful. "I'm the Wind Shaper."

CHAPTER 23
CLEMENCY

I T WAS TWILIGHT WHEN Aster and I walked through the third-tier entrance of Síorghlas's library. Like most of the buildings in Síorghlas, the library existed in the space of a giant, hollowed-out tree. I gaped at hundred-foot shelves stretching from floor to ceiling—shelves that were both tidy and uneven.

As the older woman searched for titles, I found myself rehashing my last conversation with Alder about Mom being Betwixt and his identity as the Wind Shaper. I couldn't understand why Alder was so embarrassed by his role, but I was even more curious about Mom. Why was she Betwixt? Was her status as Betwixt permanent? Had she revealed herself to me because I could do something to reverse her in-between state?

"Books do not leave our library unless one is an ealdor, so you will have to study here," Aster explained, laying another book on my stack. "You may keep your book selections in one of the reading alcoves to return to later. Please print your name, the date, and the titles you've chosen in the logbook there. And keep your books tidy."

I shifted the books in my arms. "Sure."

The library's rounded walls were lined with books and lit with gleaming shape-cast lanterns. Wide windows looked out on a forest touched with mist and a dusky glow. A spiraling staircase stretched the tree's length, and each level of the library had reading alcoves set at regular intervals, most of which were furnished with desks and chairs and cushions.

Aster whisked several works off the shelves and pushed them into my arms as we descended the stairs into the library's lower regions. "Tell me, lass—are you a diligent student?"

"Usually. But I've missed a bit of school being in Síorghlas."

"Good. The education you receive here will surpass one obtained in an Outlander institution."

I wasn't sure if the state of Alaska would agree about a Sylvaen education being superior when it came time for me to receive a diploma.

"Read all of these and take considerable notes," she said, laying a quill, a bottle of ink, and two rolls of parchment atop my stack. "When you've finished, come find me, and we'll resupply you."

I glanced down at the books, covering a range of subjects from plant lore to Sylvaen politics. Alder was right: Aster was a ruthless instructor. She had no idea I had better things to do in the library than study.

Aster picked up more books and parchments for herself on her way to an alcove with a wooden desk. She crowded all her materials into the alcove and laid her outer robe on the back of the chair before going back for more books. While we walked, she told me that everyone helped maintain Síorghlas's library. The whole community worked together to keep the shelves dusted and the books in order. Designated record-keepers furnished the library with new handwritten materials, and scribes worked to periodically replace worn copies with new ones. The system had apparently been in place for generations.

With another load of books in tow, Aster again found her alcove. She sat down with a groan and began sifting through her selections, all of which looked like law books or something equally tedious. She jotted something on the parchment beside her. Why she was reading law books I didn't know, but I was eager to slip away from her so that I could get to the real reason I'd come.

"Aster," I said. "I think I'll find my own alcove to study in. Do you mind?"

Aster glanced up. "Not at all. But do not stray far, and do not leave the library unaccompanied."

"Of course."

I offered a stiff bow, then wandered out of the alcove and into the woody spiral of endless volumes. The staircase wound both upward and downward from where I was standing. I looked for an empty alcove as I went, aware of the crawling sense of unease growing between my shoulder blades. It felt like someone was watching me, but when I turned, I saw no one. I dismissed the feeling as paranoia and kept going, scanning titles as I went. There were a few selected Outlander books, but everything else in the library was Sylvaen. The shelves were stuffed with oral legends that had been transcribed into reading materials, and next to them lay volumes of hand-copied plant and medicinal lore. But there were no titles that suggested they contained any information about a person being Betwixt.

Above the entrance to the history wing hung a handwritten copy of the Sylvaen loyalty oath. I paused to skim over the words:

"Here do I pledge myself, body, mind, and spirit, to Síorghlas; to the Sylvaen people; and to the Elder Tree which sustains the forest and keeps all things dwelling together in harmony. I promise to uphold the values of the Elder Covenant; to submit my will to the good guidance of the ealdor council; to dedicate my energy to the care and cultivation of all living things; to extend justice, mercy, and hospitality to all within my power; and to forsake all other paths until the ending of my days."

My mom had sworn that oath. She had said the words that bound her by honor and by magic to the Sylvaen, the forest, and the Elder Tree. And then, she violated it. Somehow, Mom was a traitor. Valerian said it was because she was seeing someone outside the forest, but I had a hard time reconciling that narrative with the immovable version of her I knew. Then again, I had a hard time reconciling a lot of things about my mom.

Still aware of the watchful presence at my back, I turned a corner and slipped out of the history section. I wandered a little further and found an alcove directly past census records and stooped inside. There was a stack of books sitting in the corner, but the alcove was empty otherwise. As I laid my books on the desk and pulled up a chair, I noticed a small, nondescript book lying on the floor. It looked like it had been quickly cast aside. Curious, I picked it up. The book was tattered along the edges. Its pages were yellowed with age, and it smelled like dust. I brushed off the cover and angled the book toward the light. *Compendium of Offenses, Book Eight*. My heart jumped. If Mom was a traitor, it was possible that this book or one of its other volumes contained her criminal record. Eagerly, I set the book down on the desk and cracked open the cover, wincing at the way the binding strained against the force of my opening it.

Instead of a title page or index, the book opened with a series of journal entries with dates that began over two decades ago. Looking ahead, I found that not even a quarter of the pages had been filled; either the Sylvaen didn't commit many infractions, or the record keepers had since discovered some other method of keeping records. I turned back to the first page and smoothed it, careful not to damage the delicate yellowed parchment.

The first few pages proved to be a disappointment. I learned that a boy had once stolen mushrooms from a neighbor who farmed them. A girl left her family to run off with a sentry. A long-standing feud between two families escalated into a weapons' match when someone's mother was insulted. From there, the entries grew more detailed. Someone had tried to bribe their way into ealdorship, and another person falsely accused his brother-in-law of murder because his wife died falling out of her tree while she was hanging clothes to dry. I turned the page and found the entry I was looking for written in the same format as the others. Inhaling sharply, I grabbed the book and brought it closer.

Laurel, daughter of REDACTED and REDACTED:

Charges of treason, shape-gift surrendered, self-sentenced exile.

Signed, REDACTED - March 27.

That was it—a bare facts, ink-blotted, amended entry. Shaking, I sifted through the rest of the pages in a hurry. If Mom was a traitor, why hadn't anyone recorded the details? Why were her parents' names hidden, and why had the signing ealdor's name been redacted? Finding nothing, I picked up the whole stupid book and fanned the pages—still nothing. I gritted my teeth and set to scanning the book's contents a third time, slowly. It wasn't until I was almost to the end of the book that a name jumped out at me:

Rowan.

The entry was dated around three years ago. Startled, I brought the book into the light.

Rowan, son of Ash and Foxglove:

Convicted on Charges of Treason/Unlawful Fraternization with Out-landers

During the fifth summer of his Becoming, Rowan began departing Síorghlas for extended periods. These intervals were regular and without explanation. His cohort leader brought the case before the ealdors, express-ing concern.

When questioned, Rowan refused to provide a sufficient explanation of his whereabouts. Later, he was discovered to be climbing into a vehicle with a female Outlander near the third barrier.

*A company of three ealdors and a sentry cohort confronted Rowan. They reminded him of the consequences of his actions. He was told that he would be imprisoned until a confession was made. Rowan refused to comply and was taken into custody. At the ealdors' prompting, he eventually confessed. He admitted to engaging in illicit relations with an Outlander (Martinez, Amber. *See Records of Notable Sylvaen-Outlander Interactions, Book 7, section VII, article 8b.)*

Frowning, I read the name again. *Amber Martinez.* Wasn't that the girl who had gone missing—the one both Emery and Edgewood's librarian had mentioned to me? Trembling with apprehension, I returned my attention to the entry.

Rowan was also discovered with traveling documents in his possession. From there, the ealdors deduced that he meant to leave the country. He intended to do so expediently and unlawfully, without surrendering his shape-gift. Further investigations revealed that the Outlander, Amber, was with child.

Rowan's Outlander counterpart was brought into Síorghlas on August 07 of the same year. The Outlander was sentenced to execution without trial, which was carried out the same day.

My hands were shaking so hard I almost dropped the book. Amber was dead, and so was her unborn child. The ealdors had killed both Amber and her baby for the crime of existing. Nauseated, I smoothed the page and kept reading.

When interviewed, Rowan's kin denied any knowledge of his activities or his intentions to depart Síorghlas. Rowan too insisted that all decisions were his own and should not reflect upon his kin. As a precaution, however, his parents were brought into custody for questioning and were later released.

*Although convicted of his crimes, Rowan received clemency. This was at the insistence of his younger brother, Alder. (Official record kept in ealdor council chambers. *See Trials of Great Importance, Book 12, section XLVII, article 9.)*

I stared at the entry, puzzling through the words. Alder had done something to advocate for his brother's life, but what? And why did it only partially work? Why hadn't Amber and the baby been spared along with Rowan? Reeling, I scanned the entry's last words:

The ealdors agreed, at Valerian's insistence, that Rowan must undergo a formal breaking. His sentence commenced on August 07, beneath the new moon, and was witnessed by all the ealdors. It will continue for six months or until he is able to show total loyalty to the ealdors. If the ealdors are satisfied, he will be reinstated as a sentry, sent to guard the forest near the third barrier—the place he was originally found fraternizing with his Outlander lover.

This misfortune serves as an example to all our people.

Signed Salal - August 15.

Rowan hadn't been offered clemency; he'd undergone psychological and possibly even physical torture. The ealdors took Rowan, punished him, and used him as an example. The girl he loved and his unborn child were dead. Rowan's existence was a nightmare without reprieve. And if what happened to Rowan was an example of what the Sylvaen did to people who found themselves in complicated circumstances, what did that mean for Mom? Was finding Rowan's criminal record the key to unlocking Mom's past? Would it help me understand why she was pinned between two worlds as she was?

I felt an edgy sensation, a pinprick of fear. What if someone caught me reading the book? Even Rowan's and Alder's parents had been questioned based on their association with their traitorous son. And then I thought about Aster. She was alone in her library nook, an old woman unguarded and unarmed. I stuffed the *Compendium* under a random book and placed both in my pile, stood, and faced the alcove entrance. I would get rid of the book as soon as I made sure Aster was safe.

Before I could make it out of the alcove, the sound of soft-soled boots padded on the stairs above. I hesitated until the hem of a maroon-clad robe appeared on the stairs. In a moment, Valerian, whom I hadn't seen since the day of my pre-trial hearing, stooped to enter the alcove. He paused, his face registering surprise upon seeing me.

"*Síoch
áin leat*, Wren." Recovering quickly, he swept into a bow. "What brings you to our library at such a late hour?"

I glanced at the window behind him. Outside, the sky was ink dashed with stars. Already, the moon was beginning its upward climb. I was seriously starting to regret not checking in with Aster ages ago.

"*Agus tú féin*," I answered with a dip of my head. "I came with Aster; she's in the law wing. I was using the time alone to study."

"Good use of your time, that."

I tried to act normal. It was hard with Valerian standing right there. I thought about his involvement in Rowan's case and shivered. Would he do something like that again—something awful to punish someone who had made a mistake?

"You are looking ill at ease," Valerian observed. "Is all well?"

"Just tired," I lied.

"Perhaps it is best you seek rest then."

"You're probably right." I bowed , hoping the record book I'd stuffed in my stack behind me was as invisible as I'd thought. The last thing I needed was for Valerian to have another reason to see me as deceitful and dangerous. I needed to keep on his good side if I wanted to survive.

Valerian bowed and swished his maroon robes out of the way, allowing me space to pass him on the stairway. I tried to keep my pace neutral and not fluttering with barely restrained panic as I slipped past.

"And Wren?" Valerian called after me. "I am confident census records will do the trick, especially if it is lulling to sleep you're after." Smiling at my confusion, he nodded to the stack of books I had left behind. I looked down. In my haste, I had covered the *Compendium* with a book of census records—clearly not one of Aster's assigned books.

"Oh, um—" I stammered. "I thought that Sylvaen language phrase-book was starting to look weird."

I could feel my face heat up with the lie. I didn't even know if the Sylvaen had such things as phrasebooks.

"Indeed."

I uttered a nervous laugh. "I'd better find Aster."

Valerian gazed at me without responding. Bowing a third time, I hurried back to Aster. I was as eager to check on her as I was to escape Valerian.

CHAPTER 24
HEART'S MUSIC

"**D**IA DHUIT AR MAIDIN,*" Alder said when I opened the door to him.

"Uh—good morning?"

Alder gave me his polar-ice-cap-melting smile. My stomach reacted with a twist. But I had to keep my head; I was so close to getting my answers.

"Hiya, Aster." Alder strode into the room. "I've come to collect Wren. She's due for a bit of archery."

My heart sank. I used to love archery, but I didn't have the heart for it without my mom. But even with her, it wouldn't be the same now that I knew she had secrets.

"Wren is also due a bit of studying," Aster said. "Her session last night wasn't too productive despite the hours we spent in the library." She laid her cup aside and twisted sideways in her chair to give me the stink eye.

I did my best not to look guilty. The *Compendium of Offenses* was still in my book stash back at the library. I had little doubt that Valerian knew about it. I needed to get back before any more ealdors rifled through my pile, but returning to the library to study was of secondary importance. I needed to go with Alder and not because of archery practice. I had a serious favor to ask.

Alder came over to rest his forearm on my shoulder. "She'll be all right, Aster. She just needs a bit of fresh air to clear that fiery head of hers."

Aster snorted. "She's got plenty of air in that head already."

"I will return the lass intact and unharmed. And better prepared to study." Alder placed a hand over his heart. "You have my word of honor."

Aster sighed deeply. "You'll ruin her head for studying altogether, like as not. But I suppose a few hours lost won't be the end of all things."

Alder offered me a covert high-five behind his back.

A few minutes later, Alder stepped out onto the walkway, our boots crunching in the fallen leaves. Thanks to Aster, I was armed with a glossy wooden bow and a green leather quiver and fitted with a pair of bracers embroidered with floral designs. I didn't know where the items came from or why Aster had them, but I was grateful.

The rush of a cool morning breeze greeted us, perfumed by evergreens and mist. I inwardly debated over whether to mention my idea to Alder or to wait for a better moment. Walking through Síorghlas meant that we could easily be overheard. And I wasn't convinced that what I was thinking was technically legal.

"By the way," Alder said as we came to a flight of stairs leading down. "My sister—"

"Took you long enough."

I jumped. A girl nearly as tall as Alder materialized and slipped to his side. She had wavy blonde hair tucked into a side braid that was already coming unraveled. The clothes she wore were similar to Alder's and mine except for her short boots, fingerless gloves, and a hand-knitted cowl secured with a small circular pin over her tunic. She spun around to stare at me as we walked.

"Hey, Cam," Alder said. "This is—"

"Wren, is it?" The girl had a smirk like Alder's. "Still not using erasers?"

I was momentarily struck speechless. The eraser snob?

"I'm Camas," she said. "Not sure you caught that the first time."

"I guess not."

Camas took the lead as we descended to the forest floor. Her jade-green eyes were full of the same playful liveliness as Alder's. "It's all right," she said. "I'm used to that kind of thing from Alder. He pretends not to know me at school or anywhere else."

Alder snorted. "I didn't think you wanted everyone knowing I had an evil twin."

It took me a moment to figure out that Alder was only partially joking. "Whoa. You two are twins?"

"Aye." Alder put his hand on his bow and ducked to avoid a tangle of wild berries that grew thick beside the path. "But I'm older."

"By fifteen minutes," Camas retorted.

I felt doubly sorry for their mother.

Soon, we came to a clearing lined with white-barked birches. Camas strung her bow while Alder used his shape-gift to make targets. While they worked, I pretended to re-check the strings on my bracers. Camas kept staring at me, and it made me nervous. I wished I'd stayed with Aster and taken care of that stupid book.

A minute later, Alder jumped down from a tree limb and landed dexterously beside me. "I thought I'd have a minute to explain about Camas coming and ask if it was okay before she showed up. I didn't mean to put you on the spot again."

Camas came over to stand beside Alder. I could feel her staring again, so I studied the target Alder had set up halfway down the range. Camas being there wasn't fine. She was an unforeseen complication. It would be next to impossible to ask Alder for the enormous favor I needed. It also meant that I needed to get rid of Camas somehow.

"I'd hate to be that target right now." Alder folded his arms. "The look on your face tells me you're about to rip it apart. Is that how you intimidate your sandwiches?"

Gripping my bow, I moved into position. "Quiet, sandwich. You're distracting me."

Alder uncrossed his arms and came closer. For no reason that I could think of, he began drawing a shape-cast line on the ground with his forefinger.

"You'll want to stand so your feet are in a straight line toward the center of the target." His hands curved around my shoulders. "Good. Now, you'll use three fingers to grip the string, but don't release quite yet."

"Um, Alder?"

The pressure of his hand on my back silenced me. "Keep your posture straight. That's it."

He went on to make several unnecessary adjustments to my elbow, shoulders, and hips. Camas cleared her throat loudly. I felt like doing the same. Alder didn't know I'd been comfortable with a bow since age ten.

Finally, Alder handed me an arrow. I took it and aimed at the target, anchoring my index finger beneath my jaw.

"One more thing," Alder said. "It's easy to overextend, so you'll want to—"

"Alder," Camas said. "Shut up a minute, will you?"

Alder gave his sister a look I couldn't see. But the moment's distraction was all I needed. I set my sights on the target, taking slow, measured breaths. One more breath and I relaxed on the exhale. The arrow fishtailed, then struck with a satisfying thud. Alder's head whipped toward the target. It wasn't a perfect shot, but it wasn't far off.

"Idiot." Camas walked up and backhanded Alder in the arm. "Her stance was perfect. As I'm sure you were aware."

Camas's comment made me feel a little less hostile toward her.

Alder rubbed his arm. "No, I missed that bit."

"Yes, well your observation skills are less than stellar." Her eyes sparkled as she turned to me. "Go on Wren. Before my brother decides your form needs adjusting again."

"She is looking a little out of adjustment," Alder agreed.

I decided to ignore them both.

After I emptied my quiver, Camas moved into position to take the next shot. Since she didn't appear to be leaving anytime soon, I seized the opportunity that was presenting itself to me.

"Hey, Alder." I sidled up next to him. "I need to ask you something."

"Okay. Now?"

"Yes but not here."

Alder seemed to understand. He motioned me a little way into the trees and hopefully out of earshot for Camas. She was preoccupied at the moment, but she wouldn't be for long. I didn't mind excluding her, but I didn't want her to know what I was up to either. I would only have a few minutes to talk with Alder.

"Do you have access to the council chambers?" I asked.

He looked puzzled. "I do. Why?"

I glanced back at Camas. Her first arrow struck its intended target, so she shot three more in rapid succession. I was annoyed that she hit the gold every time. Fortunately, she still had some arrows left in her quiver. I turned back to Alder.

"Do you think you could get something for me?"

"Maybe." Alder frowned. "What kind of something?"

"A record book. *Trials of Great Importance, Book 12.*"

Alder's brows shot up. "A record book? I'm not supposed to touch those."

"Yeah, I figured. But I really need it."

"Why?"

I tapped my fingers against my sides impatiently. I didn't want to tell Alder that my suspicions had less to do with my mom directly and more to do with Valerian and his brother. Another glance at Camas told me she was burning through arrows like a forest fire. "It doesn't matter why. I just need that book."

"I'm sorry, Wren. I'm going to need a better reason than that. I could get in trouble even for looking at the ealdors' record books. There's no way I could get you one without risking serious trouble."

I nodded. I was expecting as much. "It's the only lead I have on my mom so far."

"Ah." This time, it was Alder's turn to glance back at his sister. She was almost done with her arrows. He turned back to me with a sigh and a look of a man about to surrender. "I did say I'd help you with that, didn't I?"

I tried to smile. "I would be eternally in your debt and all that."

"You already are eternally in my debt. My feet still hurt from dancing with you."

"Oh, shut up."

Alder flashed a grin. At that exact moment, Camas turned around. It took her only a moment to spot us in the tree shadows, and she responded with an exaggerated look of disgust.

"Snogging already?"

Alder gave his sister an irritated look. While he took his turn at the range, Camas and I said nothing to each other. Privately, I still hoped she'd leave.

Alder had finished shooting and was collecting arrows when a tall girl with fair hair and an air of nobility stepped into the clearing. Camas and Alder saw her and immediately stiffened. The girl surveyed us one by one, her frosty green eyes barely sweeping over me before returning to the twins.

"*Síocháin leat*, Alder," she said. "Alder's sister."

Alder's shoulders tensed. "Briar."

"Well met." Briar favored me with another glance. "Although I see you've taken to consorting with Outlanders. No surprise, that, given your upbringing."

"Rather hard not to consort with them, as I am on my Becoming," Alder said blandly.

"Don't be smart, Alder. I'm talking about the half-breed. Shame your lot are so easily bewitched by her kind."

Alder pressed his lips together but said nothing. I wondered why he didn't respond to her the way he had with Rowan. What was he waiting for?

"Shame your lot have never *met* a flesh-and-blood Outlander," Camas retorted. "Afraid one of 'em will give you a bad fairy?"

Briar gave Camas a cutting look. "Try to show a little respect, please. Your brother and I were talking."

"All right, Briar," Alder said. "What's this about?"

"I came to ask you to exercise a little more caution regarding our arrangement." Briar shook out her shining hair. "I know you are besotted, but the least you can do is maintain appearances for my sake. My family and I have worked hard for a secure future. Unlike your family, who's too busy breeding and feeding like rabbits to ever advance or do anything respectable."

Alder had to restrain Camas, who lunged forward. "Don't you dare marry her, Alder," Camas shouted. "Tell her you won't!"

Alder looked pained. "I can't do that, Cam. You know I can't go against the ealdors."

"That is correct," Briar said. "And throwing your affections away on a half-breed doomed to death or imprisonment is ludicrous. It's the kind of thing your family does. It's what Rowan did. So, I suggest you stop before you're in over your head."

Camas jerked again. There were angry tears leaking out of her eyes. "You mouth-foaming clod. You have no idea what you're saying."

Briar merely smirked. "Don't I?"

Alder drew in a ragged breath. His eyes were fastened to the shadows beneath the trees. I had a feeling he wanted to react but couldn't. He was frozen. I didn't know Rowan's whole story, but I could see that bringing it up had a painful effect on Alder and his sister. I could feel my own blood start to boil, so I reacted.

"What point are you even trying to make, Briar?"

Briar startled like she had forgotten I was there. "I don't believe I was addressing you, half-breed."

"That's fine. I was addressing you." I stepped closer. "You might like to go around flexing your power, but the truth is that you're just a privileged politician's daughter with an over-inflated ego."

A snort-laugh from Camas and an anxious look from Alder told me that I was either very brave or very stupid for picking a fight with Briar.

Briar sighed. "Are we resorting to petty insults now?"

"That's kind of where we started, isn't it? You hurt my friends. You ripped apart their whole family and acted like you had a right to. I think Camas is entitled to call you a mouth-foaming clod if she wants to. And for that matter, I agree with her."

"Wren is right." Alder came to stand next to me. "You have degraded and humiliated my family for far too long, and I've let you. I won't do it anymore."

"I've humiliated you? You've a traitor for a brother, Alder. You may be the Wind-Shaper, but it is you who is elevated by my family's status and not the other way around."

"Keep your family," Alder said. "I don't want it."

Briar looked affronted. "It doesn't matter what you want. We have our arrangement. Are you an ealdor's son? An oath-bound citizen? You have no power, Alder."

"Not yet." Alder looked at me. "But I will find a way. One day."

Briar's limbs went rigid. She let out a sound that was something between a sigh and a scream. Then, throwing one last glance in my direction, she turned and disappeared into the trees.

"I don't think I've ever seen you stand up to Briar like that," Camas said, half amused, half in awe. "Well done, Alder."

Alder was indifferent to his sister's praise. He set his bow aside, took a step toward me, and pulled me into the world's most ridiculous bear hug. "I no longer have any doubt in your ability to take down bears using Krav Maga."

"I can't believe you doubted it before." I hugged him back.

"I won't ever make that mistake again."

"Alder was right about you, Wren," Camas said, unstringing her bow. "You've got the pluck of a wolverine. Helped the lad find his backbone, you did. If you ever team up together, the ealdors will have something to fear. There's fire in you two; you could accomplish a great deal if you wanted to."

Camas's comment sobered me. I pulled out of Alder's arms and put some space between us. If the ealdors thought I was trying to start a rebellion and that Alder was involved, it could be dangerous for both of us.

"I should probably get back to Aster," I said, trying to keep my tone neutral rather than foreboding.

I didn't want to dampen the triumphant mood with my dark musings, but I was starting to feel guilty about asking Alder to get me the book from the council chamber. I could get him in serious trouble, and I had no doubt he would take the fall for me. Then again, he was the Wind Shaper. Likely, the ealdors wouldn't be as harsh with them as they would anyone else.

"I'll take you," Alder said, hoisting up his bow and quiver.

We said our goodbyes to Camas and parted ways. Alder led me on an uncrowded path through the city. His happy mood persisted, but he was quieter now, as if processing all that had happened with Briar and pondering his next steps. If he meant what he said about breaking off his binding with her, he would have to figure out how to get some of the more influential ealdors on his side.

"You know about Rowan?" Alder asked in a quiet voice. "About how I ruined his life?"

His question startled me. "I was under the impression that you saved it."

"No." Alder raised his wistful gaze to the trees as we walked. "I confronted the ealdors, but I didn't do it because I cared about my brother's life. I did it because I was angry. Rowan had told me about his relationship with Amber and asked me to keep it a secret. I told him to be careful. Then, our parents were taken in for questioning. Camas and I tried to help care for our younger siblings while our parents were away, but Cam lost her temper a lot, and I was having a hard time reining in my power. All of us were at each other's throats all the time because we were terrified. Rowan's secret endangered all of us."

"It sounds like you had a right to be angry."

"Maybe." Alder found a spruce cone with the toe of his boot and kicked it over the side of the stairs we were climbing. "But when I went to the ealdors and demanded clemency, I stopped short of advocating for Amber and the baby on purpose. I wanted Rowan to pay for the damage he did to our family. I wanted him to live with his regret. I never dreamed the ealdors would break him by making him watch the execution, and I was too much of a coward to do anything about it when I found out."

I felt a strange mingling of revulsion and pity rise up inside me. "That's how they broke him?"

"Aye. And at that point, I could do nothing. That's why I hate being the Wind Shaper. People tell me the Elder Tree chose me for a reason. I'm supposed to be this pure-hearted, unselfish being, but everyone knows what I did. I haven't heard the Elder Tree's voice since that moment when I failed to advocate for Amber and the baby. When folks bow to me in the marketplace, I feel like they're laughing at me. Like they can see right through me. Like they're as disappointed with me as the Elder Tree."

I stared over the edge of the platform, trying to work through the ache I was feeling over Alder's words. Since losing Mom, I'd thought that grief belonged only to me. I'd thought that the burden of loss was mine to carry alone. I'd thought that sorrow was a place that only I knew and that no one could ever touch me there. But seeing Alder made me realize I wasn't the only one who was broken and vulnerable. Me using him to get what I needed from the council chamber wasn't great, but what Briar and the ealdors were doing to him was worse. They wanted both his power and his allegiance to themselves. They didn't care that Alder was hurting. Alder deserved better.

"I don't think the Elder Tree is disappointed in you. Maybe when it chooses someone pure-hearted to be Wind Shaper, it doesn't mean that they're perfect, it just means they have the humility to admit it when they're wrong and the determination to do better."

Alder raised his eyes to look at me. "Do you think that's true?"

"I think it must be."

"But I still can't hear the Tree. My gift is broken."

"Yes, but maybe that's for some other reason. You should stop blaming yourself for what happened with Rowan. Think about what you can do now instead."

He shook his head. "I can't, Wren. I—"

"Yes, you can." I took his hand and gripped it tight. "Listen to me. There's nothing about you that is cowardly or disappointing. You're a kind and selfless friend, a loyal son, and an amazing older brother. Whether you realize it or not, Síorghlas is lucky to have you."

Alder stared down at me. His wondering look melted into a soft one. "And you," he said.

"I don't think Síorghlas would agree with you on that."

"Then Síorghlas doesn't understand what it's missing." His eyes searched my face a moment before he spoke again. "I have another story I think you need to hear."

I gave him a nod, and he began telling me about a hunter who lived with his people in the forest.

The hunter's father had been the leader of the people, but he had fallen ill and passed into the bright place. The hunter was destined to become the new leader of his people. Still grieving his father, the hunter spent all his energy trying to prove himself as a good leader, but the universe was working against him. The harvest was bad. Game was scarce. And sickness began to ravage the people. By midwinter, their food stores were bare. The people were cold and starving and sick, and they blamed it all on the young hunter's lack of leadership.

The hunter felt like a failure, but he wasn't quite willing to give up. He sent out scouts to search the forest for game. The scouts reported a few deer remaining in the forest, but there was a new problem—a white wolf who was stalking the herd. The hunter knew he had to act before the whole herd was killed off. He gathered a few sentries and went on a quest to kill the wolf and bring back food for his people.

For weeks, the hunter tracked the wolf in the frozen forest. One of his men was injured and turned back. Another became sick with fever. Disheartened, the rest of the company trickled off, leaving the hunter to complete his quest alone.

It wasn't long before the hunter realized he couldn't outsmart the wolf. Shaking with hunger and exhaustion, he stumbled upon the wolf in a snowy clearing. The hunter aimed his bow—then lowered it. The enemy crouched over her kill wasn't a wolf, she was a human girl dressed in a white pelt. The hunter was stunned. She, like him, was only trying to survive. The hunter started to speak, but the girl lashed out with a knife and stabbed him before he could get the words out.

As the hunter lay bleeding, he tried to explain who he was and why he was there. He begged the girl's forgiveness for hunting her, but he lost consciousness before he could finish. Moved by pity, the girl dragged the hunter into her hut and tended his wounds. When the hunter came to, the girl was bandaging his wounds, checking for fever and infection. Soon, the hunter learned that the girl's parents had been killed by a bear. She had been hunting to feed her siblings as well as the few remaining members of her clan.

Over time, the hunter and the girl gained an understanding of one another. The hunter learned the girl's unique way of stalking prey. He came to appreciate her skill. And she, after listening to the hunter speak, was able to renew the hunter's hope by showing him signs that spring was returning to the forest—and with the spring, warmth and food and abundance. Soon, the hunter realized the girl *was* his spring. He found his belonging with her. So, one day, he worked up the courage to tell her how he felt...

Alder stopped speaking and stared at his hands. I fidgeted with my quiver strap.

"So, what happens next?"

Alder didn't answer right way. "He tries to bring his clan and the girl's together, but he fails. His people aren't happy to have extra mouths to feed and fewer resources for themselves. Things boil over until the two clans divide and threaten war. His own people capture the girl intending to burn her alive. He has to make a choice between his people and the girl he loves."

The girl he loves.

My heart started to pound. "And what does the hunter choose?"

"The ending is ambiguous, but I like to think the hunter's clan found a third way—that they reconsidered. They chose to extend hospitality to the girl and her clan before it was too late."

"But that's not how things work in the real world. Because people like to hate and look down on others. They think their way of life is infallible, and they can't stand the idea of anyone who doesn't fit the mold. They don't want to admit they're screwed up themselves, so they take all their misery and insecurity and self-hate, and they try to find someone more vulnerable than them to blame it on. Those people end up being my mom. Amber Martinez. Me. Wolf-girls or Outlanders—some of us don't have a place."

Alder stopped walking and laid his bow aside. "Yes, but you heard Camas. You and I could change all that."

"I can't change anything here. The system is rigged. No matter how well I perform, the ealdors will always set the bar higher. I've seen what they do to inconvenient people. They silence them."

"Not anymore." Alder moved closer. "Look. I know you said you're not planning to be here forever. You're on trial and all that, and then there's the matter of my binding. But you being here, being *with me*, is something I wish could go on forever."

The gravity in Alder's eyes was overwhelming. I had to look away. "I think you'd get sick of me long before we hit forever," I said, focusing on the bright leaves beneath my boots.

Alder bumped my shoulder with his. "I think you're wrong."

"And I think you're naively optimistic." I bumped him back.

"I think I'd like to kiss you if that's all right."

My whole body went still. The wind rustled the evergreens. Alder's eyes were on me—bright and hopeful—a galaxy of golden-green stars.

"I'm okay with that," I said.

My heart stumbled as Alder shifted so that he could face me. He put his hands on either side of my neck and leaned in. His lips met mine. Soft. Insistent. Every bit as electric as his touch. My whole being felt light and unsteady all at once.

Alder broke away with a noise of contentment, his soft hair brushing my forehead. All around us, I could feel the forest coming alive, growing greener and fuller. Alder saw me. He was unbothered by my Outlander upbringing or the fact that I was only a half-breed. He saw my hurt and fear and loneliness, and he wasn't afraid. I put my arms around him and pulled him close.

Maybe he was my spring.

CHAPTER 25
AT THE END

K ISSING ALDER HADN'T BEEN my intention. He was bound, and my position in Síorghlas was tenuous. I was supposed to be respecting the ealdors' rules and institutions, not actively working to tear them down. And I was not supposed to be inspiring rebellion in young and impressionable Sylvaen like Alder. But now that I had kissed him, I couldn't bring myself to regret it.

Alder left me at Aster's doorstep with another kiss and a promise to see me the next day. I wandered inside in a blur and spent the rest of the day reading and rereading the same two lines from a Sylvaen textbook on geography. Aster eventually gave up on me and told me to go to bed early. Then, she left for the library or some unknown errand. I didn't argue—sleeping was preferable to studying anyway. I was vaguely aware that failing to assimilate with the Sylvaen could jeopardize my ability to find out the truth about Mom, but Alder was getting that record book for me. If Valerian asked for a report and everything fell apart, I would still have the information I needed. I could escape Síorghlas and return to my life in Ketchikan. And hopefully, Alder would follow me there.

Wind and rain pummeled Aster's cottage that night. I had no idea what time it was. I lay awake pondering Mom and her Betwixt state. I didn't have any idea what to do about it. I didn't know if I *could* do anything about it. But I would be in a better position to figure it out once I left Síorghlas and the Sylvaen behind. I could even have Alder help me. His ability to hear Mom's voice from beyond could come in handy.

But the thought didn't comfort me as much as I thought it should. Like the rain outside, my thoughts remained tumultuous. The wind mirrored my restlessness. What if something went wrong with Alder getting the book? What if my assimilation failed and I couldn't get away? What if someone found out about that kiss? I slowly drifted into a troubled sleep, and when I did, I dreamed about the boy.

The boy stood behind the ealdors on the dais while the council read documents and talked over the contents in hushed tones. A thrill rushed through the boy when he thought about the ealdor's pin gleaming on his lapel. As an ealdor-candidate, he had not yet attained a seat, but he knew it was only a matter of time, a matter of patient waiting. A seat had recently opened on the ealdor council, and elections were right around the corner. Even better, the council was growing to accept and even respect the boy. When it came to matters of governance, the council sought his opinion and expressed approval of his ideas. For the first time in his life, he was beginning to find his place. The only thing he lacked were the maroon robes marking him as an ealdor.

Movement from the far side of the council chambers caught his eye. He looked up to see Laurel casting a furtive glance at the dais. The maroon-clad ealdors clustered together, blocking him from her view. The boy could tell by her knotted hands and worried expression that something was amiss. Quick as she appeared, Laurel changed her mind about intruding. She turned and rushed out the door. The boy stepped out from his place behind the ealdors. He had to find out what was wrong.

"Excuse me for one moment," he said, bowing to the council.

A few of the ealdors dipped their heads in acknowledgment before returning to their parchments. None of them had any inkling of the boy's relationship with Laurel, and for that he was grateful. It was what allowed him to remain on as a provisional member of the council. Putting on his cloak, the boy hurried outside to find Laurel.

Laurel ambushed him the moment he was outside. Before the boy could argue, she drove him away from the council chambers. They made it all the way down to the third tier before the boy had a chance to stop her. He wrapped his hands around her thin wrists and drew her to a stop. Her complexion, the boy noticed, was abnormally pale and all her lustrous hair hung loose and ragged. It was an unusual look for the ealdor's daughter.

"All right, Laurel," he said. "What's all this about?"

"We have to leave Síorghlas."

The boy didn't know how to react. "Leave Síorghlas?"

"Immediately."

"I don't think I quite follow," the boy admitted. "Why must we leave? Where will we go? How will we live?"

"Anywhere." Laurel threw a worried glance over her shoulder. "Only we must hurry."

Leaning in, the boy lowered his voice to keep from being overheard. "My love. To abandon Síorghlas would be treason. Not only that, but the election for the open council seat is next week."

"None of that matters now," Laurel said urgently.

The boy was taken aback. He and Laurel both knew that more than anything, this election *did* matter. Winning a seat on the ealdor council was exactly what the boy needed if he and Laurel had any hope of being together.

"I'm afraid I don't understand you." The boy plucked a bit of monkshood from a patch growing near the walkway and tucked it in her hair. "But I love you. So, help me understand."

Laurel shook her head, allowing all her bright hair to conceal her face. The boy gazed at her in bewilderment, not sure whether to be alarmed or amused by her behavior. She was obviously rattled, but why?

Gathering her cold hands in his, he bent down to place a kiss on each of her palms. "If I win this election as I expect, I only have to wait half a year until I can speak to your mother—"

"We don't *have* half a year!"

The boy was speechless. Laurel had never lashed out at him before. "Laurel, please—" He tried to calm his rising pulse. When it came to Laurel, he always held his quick temper in check. He knew what he was capable of, and he knew that Laurel deserved better than the person he used to be.

"If you can tell me what this is all about, we will sort it out and be on our way," he said. "I have a council session I'm supposed to be attending. The others will be looking for me by now."

"I am with child."

The boy stared at Laurel. Was this some strange, ill-timed joke? "With—?" he couldn't finish.

"I made a mistake somewhere," Laurel murmured. "I miscalculated."

The boy dropped his gaze to Laurel's middle. There were no outward signs, but he'd rarely known Laurel to lie or exaggerate. His stomach plummeted.

"You jest," he insisted. "Surely, you jest."

"I haven't bled in at least three months," Laurel said.

The boy felt as though the platform he was standing on had suddenly fallen away. Laurel was—with child?

Laurel went on. "I saw the signs. I tried to tell myself I was mad. It wasn't until I felt her quicken this morning—" Laurel made a soft choking sound. She looked like she was trying to swallow a spruce cone. "You understand, then, why it is we must leave immediately?"

The boy ran a hand over his face. "Laurel, I've almost gained ealdorship."

Laurel looked stricken. "You are a *father*."

"No." He shook his head. "A father is something I never asked to be."

Laurel tightened her grip on his hands. "Listen to me. If you don't claim her, they'll take her. They'll take *me*. Your child and I will be disgraced and even put to death. You know my mother has that right."

The boy tried in vain to shut out the images of his childhood. He knew well what it was like to be the illegitimate son. He was an outcast. He had worked hard to be free of the past, of Stonecrop's blood on his hands that night. But Laurel could fabricate no story that would cover up the existence of this child. He wanted to be rid of it. He took a calming breath.

"So, you miscalculated," he said evenly. "Do something about it."

A crease formed between Laurel's brows. "You want me to kill her?"

"You'll have to if you want to keep your home."

The boy had to be pragmatic. He had to control the narrative. He would not be burdened by this child any more than his father had been burdened by him. No miscalculation would derail his plans. Besides, being dead was a mercy if it spared the child a lifetime of ridicule. But his cold indifference was too much for Laurel.

"You are part of this!" she exploded. "You made the same choices I did."

"Aye. And now I'm making different ones."

Laurel clenched her fists. She was visibly fighting the urge to cry. "You can choose differently than your father did," she said in a broken voice. "You can have a life with me and with our child outside the forest. We can be together, finally free of fear and of unmet societal expectations."

The boy thought of their loyalty oaths. He thought of their shape-gifts binding them to the forest. Most of all, he thought of the ealdors and their far-reaching power. "We are Sylvaen, Laurel. Do you think we could ever be free?"

Laurel's eyes blazed at him. "You've made your decision, then?"

The boy hesitated. He did not want to lose Laurel, but he couldn't bear losing everything else either. He had already given up on his dream of being the Wind Shaper by no choice of his own.

"Everything I've ever striven for is in Síorghlas," he said.

"I'll go alone, then."

"Go where?"

"To the Outlanders."

"Laurel, my love—" The boy reached for her. He wanted the conversation over. He wanted Laurel to come to her senses and realize there was only one way forward. "I mean no offense, but you've had a very comfortable life here. You are well-educated and amply provided for in Síorghlas. To go to the Outlanders would be madness. You would be walking into a world you do not know. You would have nowhere to go and nothing to live on."

"It doesn't matter." Laurel snatched her hand away. "This child is a gift! Her life has value even if you don't recognize it. I'll not take it from her."

"Be reasonable!"

Before the boy could grasp her hand, Laurel turned on her heel and ran. He watched her retreating form with a numb feeling. Part of him was afraid she really meant to leave, but another part of him refused to believe it. Laurel was a sensible person. Eventually, he thought, she would come to her senses.

But she would not.

I woke up shaking. Aster's apartment was still dark and, as far as I could tell, empty. I climbed out from under my blankets and went to the window. Outside, the storm had grown still. But my thoughts hadn't. I finally had my answer. Mom left Síorghlas because she was pregnant with me. And my father wasn't an Outlander, he was Sylvaen. He was the boy I had been dreaming about.

But who *was* the boy? My father...had he ever achieved his goal of becoming an ealdor? Or had something happened to him a long time ago?

I gave up on sleep entirely and got up to make a cup of tea. Aster wouldn't mind if she came home and found me studying rather than sleeping, and I could use the distraction. I pulled out the geography book from earlier and sat down at the kitchen table, but I was interrupted by a sharp knock at the door. I frowned. Aster wouldn't knock on her own door, and Alder wouldn't have come back unless it was some kind of emergency. Cautiously, I set my tea aside and went to the door.

A sentry I recognized stiffened and inclined his head in lieu of a proper Sylvaen bow. I struggled to remember his name. He was the sentry from Rowan's cohort who had treated me kindly in the guard tower.

"*Síocháin leat*," he said. "Ealdor Valerian has requested an audience. He requested I see you to his garden at once."

I opened the door wider, remembering that his name was Sorrel. "Now?"

"Aye." Sorrel shifted his bow to his other hand. "'Tis only nine o'clock in the evening."

Nine o'clock. No wonder I couldn't sleep.

"Um, okay," I said. "Let me change and grab my cloak."

Sorrel stepped back, allowing me to shut the door. Was I imagining the unease in his demeanor, or was I mistaking it for mine? It hardly mattered. I needed to get the meeting over with so that I could move on to more important things like seeing if Alder had gotten the record from the council chambers. I stepped outside a few moments later and joined Sorrel, shutting Aster's door behind me.

The sky overhead was still heavy with storm clouds, but the shape-cast lanterns lit our way. Valerian's living quarters lay at the city's summit. There, the tree limbs grew thin and the Sylvaen dwellings even thinner. It gave me the impression that Valerian didn't want to be around other Sylvaen, but that wasn't unusual for an ealdor. Alder had told me the ealdors typically avoided the crowded paths frequented by Sylvaen commoners.

Sorrel opened the gate and swept a low-hanging bough out of the way. Valerian's garden was gated as well as secluded. It made me suspicious that he invited me when he obviously went to such great lengths to avoid entertaining visitors.

"Wren, wait."

I looked at Sorrel in surprise. He'd spoken to me before, but he'd never used my name.

Sorrel stepped closer, keeping his voice low. "Make sure you keep to the path here. I've heard rumors that Valerian's garden is not entirely as it appears. Don't touch anything if you can help it."

"Thanks. I'll keep that in mind."

Sorrel remained silent the rest of the way up the garden path. Finally, we came to an open space lined with dormant wild roses still dripping from the recent rainstorm. Valerian's willowy form sat on a bench beneath a cluster of evergreen boughs. He stood when he spotted us.

"Welcome, Wren," Valerian said, clasping his hands behind his back. "Thank you for coming on such short notice."

I bowed in response to Valerian's greeting. His expression was grim, but I didn't detect any outright hostility from him. That seemed like a positive sign.

"Sorrel." Valerian bowed. "I am indebted to you for carrying out my orders at this late hour. Is all well with your—"

"My father's needs are met at present, thank you," Sorrel interrupted.

I caught only the faintest flicker of a reaction in Valerian's eyes. "I am glad to hear it. And you'll inform me at once if anything changes?"

"Aye."

Valerian nodded. "Thank you for your services. You may go."

Sorrel bowed and made his retreat. Before I could venture far into wondering about his exchange with Valerian, he was gone. Valerian turned and walked toward a bench, his thin fingers trailing over the scrollwork.

"I've been meaning to speak with you, Wren," Valerian said. "Alas, my many duties have kept me fiercely occupied. Only now have I found a spare moment to inquire about your studies."

"Oh." I had to make a conscious effort to keep the worry out of my voice.

"Aster says you are doing excellently, but I wanted to hear it from you. The ealdors are preparing to make their decision, and I am hoping to give them a favorable report." He leaned forward on the bench. "Tell me. What have you accomplished to show us you are ready to live out your days as Sylvaen?"

"Well, um—"

Valerian's features became thoughtful as I spoke. In truth, I'd barely touched my geography textbook, I'd danced poorly, and I'd skimmed the first of eight books on plant lore. Other than that, I was barely aware of the other titles Aster had assigned to me. But I had discovered my magic type, and I had done well with shaping and archery.

"Let's talk more about your shaping." Valerian moved to examine the bark on a low-hanging tree limb. "Alder said you discovered your shape-gift without any external guidance. Have you learned yet how to control it?"

"I think so."

"And your magic type is plants?"

"Yes."

Valerian knelt to tend something in his garden bed. "How has your knowledge of plant lore aided you in the development of your gift?"

"Sure. Well..." My mind scurried back to my classes at Edgewood. "Oxygen is vital for root and microbe respiration. I try to keep that in mind when I shape, uh, plants."

Valerian's fingers paused on the autumn-pink foliage of a berry bush. "I'm not sure you understood the question."

I blushed. "I'm sorry. I've had a lot of subjects to study, so I haven't spent much time with plant lore yet."

"I see." Valerian stood up. "Your mother neglected plant lore in your education?"

"Most of the time, my mom had to work two jobs to make sure we had enough to eat." Mom neglected a lot of things in my education. The fact that we were Sylvaen was her most egregious omission. I felt like she deserved a pass when it came to plant lore. "She didn't have time to teach me about plants."

"Fair enough." Valerian dusted off his pale hands. "If you'll humor me, I'd like you to demonstrate your abilities." He gestured with a sweep of his hand to a bare area behind the bench. "During the warmer months, this part of the garden is filled with bleeding heart. But that season has ended. Everything has died back for the year. I'd like you to show me what you can do to revive it."

I was relieved. If there was one thing I could do well without practice, it was growing plants. I'd done it the first time by accident, after all. I took a moment to calm my breathing and focused my energy in my fingertips. The connection I felt with the plants was automatic. With a gentle touch, I coaxed the blooms up out of the soil. In a moment, the patch was bursting with pink blooms and lacy foliage. I severed the magical connection with a flourish and stood up to admire my handiwork.

"Good. You've demonstrated your abilities and fulfilled the required task." Valerian sat on the bench and reached over the side, amusing himself by stroking fern fronds and watching them uncurl beneath his fingers. "But you've also demonstrated to me that you lack something vital."

I frowned at the plants. Were they a little too green? Too abundant?

"You lack the nourishing nature of a Sylvaen," Valerian said simply.

"What?"

"I'll explain." He returned his gaze to the patch. "Just as you require sleep, plants need a dormancy period. They rest during the cooler months to conserve energy for the next growing season. Your ability to manipulate plants should be used to nourish and enhance them, never to force them to grow outside their natural limits. It is the habit of Outlanders to exploit the earth and treat its resources as disposable, which is what you have done."

"Oh."

Valerian waved his hands over the plants. One by one, the happy pink blooms faded and fell. The foliage turned pale and brittle. An angry question bubbled up from somewhere deep inside, and I asked harshly, "But what about the magic barriers protecting Síorghlas? Aren't you creating an artificial environment for the plants? How is that not exploitation?"

"Ah. Good question, that," Valerian said. "The protection of the first barrier regulates our temperatures and precipitation, making our little ravine an ideal environment for plants, people, and animals to coexist and thrive. But because our Wind Shaper is familiar with the needs of the forest, he maintains the seasonal balance." Valerian paused to glance at the clouds overhead threatening a downpour. "Except, of course, when he is agitated or distracted. Today, it seems, tending the forest's needs has slipped his mind."

Valerian's words hit me like a rock. "Alder controls your weather."

"Aye. Alder must control our weather," Valerian said. "The Elder Tree chose him for the task. It is his duty to protect, defend, maintain balance, and cultivate harmony among the forest and its inhabitants. His responsibility is immense, and even when he is away in the Outlands, it is something he does not take lightly. He has told you this, yes?"

"No. He barely even told me he was the Wind Shaper."

"Modest lad." Valerian smiled. "He thinks so little of himself needlessly."

I agreed. Alder's ability to master complex shapes without even trying was beyond enviable; it was impossible. "He's powerful."

"That he is," Valerian said. "He is the second-most powerful being in the forest. As long as he stays near the forest, the Elder Tree will sustain him. He has access to both its draíocht *and* its energy. He could level the entire forest if it pleased him."

Somehow, I didn't think Alder would like hearing that. He had to limit his power to avoid things like accidentally killing his brother, but he was also living under the expectation that he was pure and unselfish. Maybe that explained why he didn't stand up to Briar at first—he was terrified to use his power and get it wrong.

"Why does Alder place himself under the ealdors' authority when he has so much power?"

Valerian's response was automatic. "He is pure in heart."

"But he still makes mistakes."

"True enough. I suppose the answer lies in the Elder Tree-appointed role of the council."

"Of ealdors?"

"Aye. The Tree made provision for the Sylvaen to appoint ealdors. Then, the Elder Tree itself chooses a Wind Shaper every three or so generations to keep the forest in balance. When that happens, the ealdors work to support the Wind Shaper, preserve order, and provide necessary accountability. This is in case the Wind Shaper ever veers from the Elder

Tree's intended path. When there is no Wind Shaper, the ealdors will of course keep the forest running as smoothly as possible."

"So, your job is to keep order in the forest and hold the Wind Shaper accountable?"

"I and the other ealdors, yes."

"But who holds the ealdors accountable?"

For some reason, Valerian seemed bothered by the question. "Ealdors are held to the highest standards of conduct. We are humble folk. Servants. We must always put the people first. One false step, and we lose everything, and that is why we do not make mistakes."

"Never?"

"No. And unlike the Wind Shaper, we haven't any more power than common citizens."

Power.

I finally understood. The ealdors weren't worried about keeping Alder on the right path; they wanted to keep him under their control. He was a weapon, and if provoked, he could be a formidable enemy. And so, Alder could live like an Outlander in Ketchikan, but he had to report to Síorghlas. He could obtain clemency for his brother, but the ealdors required a hefty price. They gave Alder little tastes of freedom, but they kept his wings clipped. The realization made me angry.

"Just curious," I said. "If Alder is so powerful and you're...*not*, how do you hold him accountable?

Valerian's teeth flashed white in the pale moonlight. His smile was even eerier than usual. "Why this sudden interest in Alder's well-being?"

The question startled me. "He's my friend."

"Is that so?" Valerian advanced toward me, his pace slow and purposeful. The wind blew suddenly colder, chilling me blood and all. I struggled against the impulse to break eye contact. "Am I correct in assuming you've fallen in love with the lad?"

For a moment, my mind went entirely blank. "In—love?"

"I believe I spoke clearly the first time," Valerian said calmly.

"You did. But I—" My heart drummed like an earthquake. Why did Valerian's smile feel like a trap? "I don't know him that well."

Valerian stopped less than a foot from me and peered down. "Do you know the real reason you are here tonight, Wren?"

I shook my head. My mouth felt strangely foreign. Dead and dry.

"You are here because of this."

Valerian withdrew something from his robe and held it up. It was a book with gilded lettering on the front. The title gleamed in the light, and when I saw it, my heart sunk. *Trials of Great Importance, Book 12.*

"I think it was section XLVII, article 9 you were looking for, was it?" Smiling his odd smile, Valerian tossed the book down at my feet. "You are here because you made a request of Alder. Because you convinced him that you matter more than his duties as a young man of Síorghlas."

Horrified, I stared at the book. Stealing a forbidden book was out of character for Alder; it would have immediately drawn a connection back to me. It was all the evidence the ealdors needed to prove I was a dangerous influence and a threat.

"Let me be clear, Wren," Valerian said. "Alder is a true son of the forest. He is of pure Sylvaen lineage, he is bound, and he is Wind Shaper. And as our Wind Shaper, the lad is vital to his people and to the forest. If he were to fall for an Outlander the way his brother did, the results would be devastating for him and for his loved ones. And I would have no choice but to have that Outlander executed."

Valerian stared me down a moment longer before releasing me from his gaze. He put his hands behind his back and began pacing the garden. I stood silent, stiff with fear. But there was something more than fear coursing through my veins—fury. It licked at my insides like the forked tongue of a flame. I felt reckless, ready to wield a knife like I did with Rowan.

"You're afraid of me," I said. "Why?"

"Afraid of you?" Valerian looked surprised. "I am not afraid of you, lass. You are simply an Outlander. And Outlanders lack self-control."

"I'm not an Outlander. My father was Sylvaen."

Valerian stopped pacing. "Did your mother tell you that?"

"My mother didn't tell me anything. The Elder Tree has been giving me dreams."

"And have you any proof of this?"

My mind went to the boy in my dream. My father. He found a way to prove himself as having pure Sylvaen lineage, but no documents existed in Síorghlas that could save me. "They're *dreams*. They're in my head. How am I supposed to prove I'm having them?"

"Convenient it's dreams you're having, then." Valerian started pacing again. "Do you know, Wren? Outlanders may consider lying necessary at times, but the Sylvaen never condone dishonesty. This is yet another strike against you."

"You really think I'm lying?"

"I think you are exhibiting the character traits I'd expect from an Outlander. That is enough proof for me that your father was an Outlander. But you also remind me of your traitorous mother. She had a life of ease here from the start. When something displeased her, she set about trying to find loopholes. She would bend rules to her advantage simply because of who she was."

Maybe that was true. As an ealdor's daughter, Mom had a lot of power and privilege. I witnessed her using her status to get what she wanted on multiple occasions. She could have found an easy way out of her situation with my father and me too—only she didn't. She gave up her status as an ealdor's daughter and left her home to save us both.

"What did she do to make you hate her so much?" I asked.

"Hate her?" Valerian asked in surprise. "I never hated your mother."

"Yet you're punishing me for something she did."

Valerian studied my face a moment before answering. "No. You are merely the fruit of an unfortunate union between your mother and an Outlander. I cannot expect you to bear the full weight of responsibility for your mother's crimes. You do, however, exhibit a strong tendency to bend and break rules when you find them inconvenient, which I suspect is a trait you inherited from your mother."

"Inconvenient?" I was seething. "You're asking me to become Sylvaen when you say I'm not, and then you tell me I'm doing it wrong when I try. I can't do magic right, I haven't learned enough plant lore to make you happy, and I can't figure out your stupid dances for anything. To be honest, I'm not even sure I want to."

Sighing, Valerian moved behind the bench. "Herein lies the problem, Wren. You refuse to uphold our ideals. You want to reform us by thrusting your own values upon us. By all appearances, you would raze our civilization to the ground before you would adapt yourself to our way of life."

"That isn't true—"

"The other ealdors think it is true. I'm still waiting for you to prove them wrong."

"Hang on. I'm not trying to destroy the Sylvaen or change your ways or whatever—I only want to see people treated humanely. Even outsiders."

"Humanely?" Valerian's eyes were full of emerald fire. "We are *not* human, Wren. We are Sylvaen. Our ways transcend yours, and yet we have extended you a hand of mercy. You have responded with treachery. You have failed to keep your rebellious nature and your radical ideas to yourself, and you have attempted to beguile Alder. As such, you can no longer expect protection from the ealdors."

For a moment, the light of the Elder Tree dimmed. The storm rising up inside me vanished, and a sick feeling rose up in its place. I understood what Valerian meant: the ealdors were done playing diplomacy games.

"You're going to kill me."

"We will not tolerate threats to our people and our way of life." Valerian turned away, his robes fluttering in the chill wind. "Your trial concludes in three days. You may go."

CHAPTER 26
BROKEN PEOPLE

THE DISTANT LIGHT OF the Elder Tree illuminated the forest, but the light of it felt dim and cold. Low-hanging clouds stirred the sky. I wound my way through the maze of Valerian's garden, feeling like Alice on her last sprint out of Wonderland. I didn't have queens and cards chasing me down a spiraling tunnel, but I certainly had my share of people who wanted my head.

I was almost to the gate when my foot caught on an exposed tree root. I let loose a cry and stumbled into a bramble bush. Something sharp pierced my hand, but I didn't pause to see what it was. In a moment, I was back on my feet. I found the garden gate and forced the latch open. I was through it and on my way back to Aster's when I collided with a tall figure coming down the path. He grunted, startled.

"Well, you're in a bit of a hurry."

"Alder!" I wheezed.

"Sorrel said I'd find you here," he said, taking my hands in his. "What happened? Are you all right?"

I shook my head. "Valerian—" I gasped as a wave of pain sliced through my hand. "He found the book. Threatened to withdraw support. I can't—"

"We need to get you to a healer."

I looked down. There was blood on Alder's fingers. A gash ran across the heel of my hand, staining my dark green sleeve with rust. Before I could react, Alder drew out a knife, cut a strip from his tunic, and used it to staunch the bleeding.

"It looks worse than it is," I said. "I tripped a minute ago and fell on my hands. I'm fine."

"We should still clean it up."

"Maybe later. I need to find a way out of Síorghlas right away. Can you help me?"

"You're leaving? Now?"

"I have to. Valerian thinks I'm turning you against the ealdors."

"You're not turning me against the ealdors," Alder assured me. "What happened with Rowan made me see them in a different light, but that started long before you came here. Being with you made me realize I'm capable of being a little bolder, that's all."

"That's all? Alder, that's all they need. To them, it looks like me inspiring rebellion in you. That's been their concern all along. They'll get rid of me and punish you, and they'll do it by going after your family. And you know they will—they've done it before."

Alder took hold of my shoulders. "Not this time. I won't let them hurt you."

"They already *have* hurt me. My mom is dead because of them." I winced as a wave of pain rolled up my arm. It felt like something alive and venomous was crawling up my arm. I took a moment to breathe before continuing. "If I leave, I won't influence you anymore with my radical ideas. The ealdors will leave you and your family alone."

Alder's jaw tightened. His eyes shifted to Síorghlas sparkling all around us. "I think you're wrong. If you stay, you can help me prove that they're corrupt. They'll have to acknowledge everything they've done. And together, we can help them find that third way."

I shook my head. "This isn't one of your stories, Alder. This is real life."

"Yes, it's real and it's broken. I know that." He tried to smile. "But in the words of this amazing girl I know, we can stop living in the past and start thinking about ways we can make things better."

"It wouldn't work," I said firmly. "We would try, and we would fail. And I don't want to be the reason you lose everything you care about."

"I care about *you*."

I raised my eyes to his. I knew Síorghlas didn't want me, but I didn't think it deserved Alder either. Even so, hope stuck in my chest. "You could come with me," I said.

"I want to, Wren, but my place is here. My family is here. My whole life is here. And right now, *you're* here." He gave me an agonized look and exhaled raggedly. "I wish that part wouldn't change."

I shut my eyes against another twist of pain. I was starting to sweat. "Me being here—it doesn't work. I tried, and it's so hard. It shouldn't be this hard."

"It is this hard, Wren. Being a part of something bigger than yourself is the hardest thing in the world, whether that something is another person, a family, a clan. The people you love and belong with will hurt you worse than anyone, but you don't give up." He lifted his hand to touch my cheek. "You don't just leave."

I turned away from him. Síorghlas was a labyrinth of stairs, sparkling lights, and silver-lined shadow. It might be Alder's home, but it wasn't mine. I didn't belong in Síorghlas and never had. Even the forest—that voice I had heard in my head—was only toying with me. It was as treacherous as the Sylvaen themselves.

"I don't want to leave, really," I said. "But I don't have any reason to stay here." I thought of the brief time I'd spent living with Peter and Leslie in Ketchikan. Were they worried about me? Did they expect me to ever return?

"Any?" He sounded incredulous. "But—that kiss Wren. I thought that meant something."

The kiss I had shared with Alder had meant something. That kiss meant that I was falling for him. His kindness, his loyalty, his bravery, his messy hair, and his warm smile overwhelmed me. But telling him the truth might give him hope that I would stay in Síorghlas. If I stayed, Valerian and the other ealdors would carry out that death sentence they'd been threatening. I could save myself, Alder, and his family by leaving.

"I don't know what it meant, Alder," I whispered. Alder stared at me, thunderstruck. I made sure to avoid his eyes before continuing. "It was just a kiss."

Alder and I made our way to Aster's in a solemn mood. He didn't look at me once. The warm glow of silver lights blurred on either side of us, but I was barely aware of them. I'd hurt Alder. I'd made him think I didn't care. He wouldn't meet my eyes, wouldn't give me more than one-word answers to my questions. I would have to leave Síorghlas with things unresolved between us, and I knew I'd regret it. But before I could go anywhere, I had to get help from Aster.

By the time Alder knocked on Aster's door, I was struggling to keep myself upright. Aster wrenched the door open and demanded to know where I had been. When I didn't answer, Aster looked to Alder for an explanation. That was when my legs gave out. Aster gave a cry as I crumpled to the ground.

"By the Tree," Aster muttered. "Are you ill, child? Has someone hurt you?"

"She was in Valerian's garden," Alder answered, hauling me to my feet.

Through the mist, I could see Aster's eyes widen. She closed the door behind us and drew the curtains over her windows.

"She is pale as death," she said.

Alder eased me onto the floor and started unwrapping my makeshift bandage. At Aster's request, he pulled out his knife and handed it to her. From there, Aster took over.

Aster placed a cushion under my head, and, with a cool hand, she checked my forehead. Clucking her tongue, she pulled the ruined sleeve back to reveal an ugly gash seeping fresh blood mingled with something else—something greenish. Alder made a strange face as Aster pushed the fabric up higher. An angry rash wove its way over my skin like a tangle of blackberry vines, bubbling up in irregular blisters.

"Valerian's garden is a less-than-ideal meeting place," Aster said, rising to cross the room to a cabinet. There, she began sorting through glass and stone bottles. After a moment, she selected a bottle and uncorked it to sniff the contents.

"He crossbreeds ordinary plants and manipulates them with magic. He records his findings in some book of his—an unusual hobby for an unusual man. You must've pricked your hand on a specimen that was poisoned." Aster put the bottle back on the shelf and reached for another. "I haven't any antidote, but I will extract what poison I may and apply a tincture that should help."

Valerian's hobby was strange. But what was weirder was the speech he had given me about not manipulating plants beyond their natural limits. Did Valerian make himself an exception to that rule? Was he willing to sacrifice a couple of innocent plants to become weapons he could use in case he needed to defend his ideals?

Aster set about organizing the bottles, selecting some and gathering them in her arms. "I do not think your wound will require anything so drastic as an amputation," she said, making my heart stumble, "though I cannot guarantee you will have full use of your hand anytime soon. It is possible you will experience permanent muscle damage."

Alder stared down at his hands knotted in his lap while Aster sorted her tinctures. He looked like he didn't know what to do with himself. I tried not to think about how conflicted he must feel seeing me in pain while feeling the pain I had inflicted on him.

Aster found the last bottle she was looking for and returned to her place beside Alder. With Alder's help, she unclasped my cloak. Then, she peeled off my tunic, leaving me in the thin undershirt Sylvaen women typically wore. The marks of Valerian's poison plants extended all the way to my shoulder.

"Alder, fetch me that mortar and pestle lying on the table. And the roll of cloth in the box beside it."

Alder jumped to his feet and hurried to comply.

"I apologize in advance, Wren." Aster took up the bottle she had procured from the cabinet. "This will hurt. I haven't any numbing agent on hand, and there isn't time to procure any."

Alder returned a moment later with the requested items, but he kept his distance while Aster worked. I hissed and tried not to thrash or scream while Aster cleaned the wound. The sting of her tincture felt like a knife in my flesh.

"Now," Aster said, using her mortar and pestle to grind some dried herbs. She added honey to make a paste. "Can you tell me exactly what transpired in the garden between you and Ealdor Valerian?"

The pungent smell of herbs filled the room as Aster scraped up a bit of paste and spread it over my open wound. The paste burned at first, then the pain subsided. After a moment, I was able to speak.

Aster listened in silence as I told her the whole of my conversation with Valerian. The only detail I left out of my narrative was the part where Valerian accused me of being in love with Alder. Aster didn't need to know, and it wouldn't help anything between Alder and me for him to hear it. Not that Alder was listening anyway. He sat with his back to Aster's wall, head bowed and eyes downcast.

"That is grave news indeed." Aster unrolled a length of clean cloth to bind my wound. "I'm afraid, Wren, that you are in far more danger than we thought. Valerian will do what he must to keep the others from guessing the truth, and the best way for him to do that is to ensure that you as a witness lack credibility."

A witness for what?

"He doesn't need to worry about that," I said. "I won't be here to be a witness, credible or otherwise. I'm leaving—tonight if I can."

I glanced at Alder. His eyes were closed. His chest rose and fell in a regular pattern, but I couldn't tell if he was really asleep. When I turned back to Aster, she had her lips pressed tightly together. Her hand hovered over my wound, glowing with a cool silver light.

"So soon?" she asked.

"I think it's the only way I can stay alive."

"I see." Aster kept her eyes focused on her task as she wound the clean fabric around my hand. "Wren, there is something I must tell you—something I should have told you before..." She paused as if to swallow her apprehension. "Your mother—Laurel—was my daughter."

I stared at Aster without comprehension. How could she be my grandmother? I didn't have any family. When Mom died, I didn't have anyone except Peter and Leslie. They were the closest thing I had to family, and being in Síorghlas almost made it feel like I'd lost them too.

"My late husband and I were much too busy with political affairs to be bothered with our child," Aster went on. "Balsam wasn't on the ealdor council as I was, but he was very much involved with Síorghlas's internal affairs. Entire days would pass in which both he and I would be so caught up the affairs of the Sylvaen that we would forget we had a daughter. We relied too much on the system we helped create—the cohorts and their leaders—and we failed to acknowledge the responsibility we had as parents. Balsam died when your mother was fourteen, and I was too caught up in my own grief to help your mother with hers."

"You were an ealdor," I said slowly.

"Aye. I gave up that position not long after my daughter left Síorghlas seventeen years ago."

Mom, the ealdor's daughter from my dreams, had endured so much pain because of her mother's neglect. It was what caused her to run into my father's arms in the first place, and it was a large part of why she left Síorghlas when she found out she was pregnant with me. But somewhere along the way, that ealdor reconsidered. *Aster* reconsidered. So why had she waited until now to tell me the truth?

Aster continued. "Your mother came to me one day without pretense and made me aware of her pregnancy. I was furious with her for her indiscretion. I advised her not to carry to term, but she wouldn't hear of it. She wanted you. She said her heart was knit to yours. She was right, you know." Aster tried to smile, but her smile was bitter. "She proposed self-exile and left the forest soon after."

I had to work around the lump in my throat before I was able to respond. "And that's when she laid down her shape-gift?"

"No," Aster said. "Laurel never laid down her shape-gift. She hadn't time to go through with it. I altered the records kept in the library and made sure the narrative stayed vague and the information convoluted. The ealdors never knew why she left, who she spoke to, what she did and did not manage to accomplish before she left. I knew that if the ealdors could make a clear case against her, they would execute her on sight should they encounter her. But I never meant to protect my daughter so much as I wanted to maintain my status and reputation. It simply wouldn't do, you see, for an ealdor to have an unwed daughter with child. I would be ridiculed, questioned, and perhaps even dismissed from the ealdor council. Sending her away alleviated any guilt on my part. Save on the inside."

I touched the bandages wrapped around my hand, a fitting picture for my tightly-wound emotions. The silver light radiating from Aster's palm diminished. She allowed her hand to fall limply into her lap. Hearing the truth—that my grandmother was a hateful, callous, would-be murderer hurt worse than any wound Valerian's poisoned plants could inflict.

She took a tremulous breath. "Once, she tried to contact me after she left, but I took no notice. I failed my final test. After that, I never heard from her again." Aster stared off into oblivion, her dark green eyes filled with regret. "The ealdors received a similar test with Alder's elder brother. We failed that young man too, along with the young Outlander he loved and their unborn child." Trembling, Aster bowed her head. "I failed my daughter. I failed Rowan. I failed compassion, dignity, and humanity. For the sake of self-preservation, I made decisions that cost innocent people their lives and caused unbearable pain for so many others. And in the end, it was my cowardice that left you without a mother."

I wanted to reach out to Aster and reassure her, but I couldn't. Aster admitted she was wrong. She regretted her past wrongs. She claimed me as her own from the moment she laid eyes on me, and she brought me into her home and helped me assimilate. I understood why she hadn't told me the truth about being my grandmother. She was afraid I would hate her. And she was right.

"We are a broken people, Wren." At this, Aster seemed to close off from the rest of the world, drawing her arms around herself. Silent sobs racked her stout frame. "Or perhaps it is only me."

I didn't answer. Mom spent seventeen years longing for her home, for the forest, for acceptance from those she had left behind. She had found purpose in a life filled with so many disappointed hopes, and that purpose was me. She gave up her own future to ensure mine. And despite how often she had been starved for love herself, she made sure that pain was something I never had to experience. In the end, she died with all her ache and yearning for home and for love unfulfilled.

I didn't know how to forgive Aster for being the cause of that.

CHAPTER 27
LOST AND FOUND

I WENT TO BED to catch an hour or two of sleep before setting out. Aster wanted me to stay in her apartment a few days while my body recovered, but I didn't think sticking around until my trial was a good idea. Aster would pack supplies, and Alder would accompany me out of Síorghlas using his knowledge of the guard rotations. Apparently, having a sentry for a brother had some advantages.

I knew Alder didn't want to be the one to escort me out of the forest. He had barely agreed to it, and when he did, he was half asleep, bleary-eyed, and visibly unenthusiastic. He would have to don the sentry's uniform Aster had in her possession from a mending job she had done. Being alone with the girl that had broken his heart clearly wasn't at the top of Alder's to-do list. I didn't want to make him do it, but I didn't see any other options if I wanted to avoid getting caught by Rowan and his cohort in the forest.

I let my eyes slip shut, thinking of all that had to take place still before I could get out of Síorghlas. Besides navigating things with Alder, I would have to make it out of Síorghlas and past the gate guards without raising suspicions. Then, there would be the matter of evading any sentries patrolling the forest on my way to Ketchikan. The worst part, I knew, would be figuring out how to say goodbye to Alder with all that had happened between us. But I would worry about all that later. I let sleep take me, thinking of Aster and Mom and the things I had learned about the past.

The boy with the midnight hair stood gazing vacantly over the forest below. His ealdor's robes weren't enough to fend off the chill of winter's breath. Shivering, he glanced down at the open letter in his hand. The letter was from Laurel. *His* Laurel. But how could that be? Laurel, *his* Laurel had become a ghost.

He had wanted to set out from Síorghlas a million times to find her, but he always held himself back. If he left, the other ealdors would grow suspicious. Everyone knew Laurel had disappeared. Everyone knew there was some kind of scandal. Going after Laurel personally would implicate himself in her disappearance. Besides, the Outlands were foreign to him. He hadn't an inkling of where to begin his search or how to conduct it. And so, he'd waited in Síorghlas, pleading silently with the Elder Tree for a sign. Now, he had the letter.

It was true that the letter had not been intended for him. It was meant to be kept secret, passed from hand to hand until it reached Aster in the council chambers. Aster was ashamed and discarded the letter at once, but the boy found it and took it up. His heart stirred within him when he saw who had written it.

It had been half a year since he had seen her and much had changed in that time. He had won his election. He had earned an official seat on the council. He had even received honors for coming up with a resolution to a heated civil dispute not three days after he was appointed an ealdor. He had achieved his dream. He had tasted the sweetness of the honor and respect he'd always longed for, and yet, he barely felt anything. All he could think was how he wished Laurel could be there to celebrate with him. But she wasn't there. Instead, the memory of her face haunted him every moment.

The contents of the letter filled the boy with a strange mixture of hope and dread. Laurel was requesting an audience with her mother, a final chance to say goodbye. Knowing Laurel's mother had discarded the letter and refused to see her daughter, the boy took a pen and parchment and penned a letter in reply. He knew Aster's handwriting well and was able to imitate it skillfully. He would go to Laurel alone. He would speak gently to her and convince her to return. When the reply was complete, he hastened to make all the arrangements.

Hope stirred within the boy's chest as he trekked through the snowy forest alone. It had been two weeks since he received the letter, and one since he sent back a response. Perhaps the child Laurel was carrying had died. And if not, he would speak gently and convince her to leave the child with the Sylvaen refugees dwelling in the outpost at the forest's edge. That solution was gentle and should please her well enough. Then, he would return with Laurel to Síorghlas and make her his wife. And once all the shadows of suspicion passed away, they would have peace.

When he came to the meeting place, he pulled up short. His breathing hitched painfully in the winter air. Laurel was waiting at the edge of the trees. She leaned against the side of an Outlander's vehicle, clad in a heavy purple coat the color of winter twilight. She turned at the sound of his approach, and her eyes grew wide.

"*Síochán leat*, Laurel," he said, managing a bow.

"Isn't my mother coming?"

The boy didn't answer at first. Emotion overwhelmed him—gladness at seeing her again, and shock at seeing how changed she was. Her long, coppery hair was short and lusterless. Her complexion was pale, and there were dark circles under her eyes. Everything about her spoke of weariness, of hardship and pain.

"No, she is not," the boy said. "I came in her stead. The letter you received—"

"—was a fabrication," Laurel finished for him. "By you."

"Aye."

Laurel turned away, trembling. There was a strange timidity to her bearing, a vulnerability that hadn't been there before. Her accent too was strange—broad and flat and not at all Sylvaen. It was as though she'd lost all the music of her home.

"Why are you here?" Laurel asked, her voice flooded with pain.

"I wanted to see you."

Laurel uttered a sigh. When she looked at him, her eyes were dry.

"I see they've made you an ealdor."

"They have."

"Then you got what you always wanted."

The boy gazed at her. Six months ago, he could have agreed with surety. Now that he was gazing into Laurel's evergreen eyes, he was less certain. "Will you be returning to Síorghlas?" he asked, hoping she would say yes.

"I cannot."

The boy had known what her answer would be. From the moment he arrived, he'd seen it in the stubborn set of her jaw. He had meant to sweep her heart away again and change her mind, but he had no right words. "I hope—" he tried, voice breaking "I hope you found what you're looking for out there."

Laurel turned to him, her eyes blazing. "You mean all the things you denied me?"

He flinched. How could he convince her he loved her when he'd abandoned her in her hour of need? "Laurel, my love—"

"Do not speak to me of love. You, my mother, and the ealdors are all the same. Compassionless. Self-serving. You value your ideal way of life more than you value living it. I'm through with the lot of you."

As much as Laurel's words stung, they made him angry. "So, you go to the Outlanders for compassion?"

"Yes. To the Outlanders. Outlanders tend to be more forgiving than Sylvaen. They make allowances for...mistakes."

Mistakes. That was all he was to her now.

The boy concealed his hurt beneath a condescending look and a sudden bark of laughter—a cruel, bright sound, sharp like the edge of a blade. "Are you so naive as to believe you'll find acceptance in the Outlands? That you'll find peace, a home, people that care about you?"

Laurel's eyes brimmed with angry tears. She started to walk away, but the sound of a soft whimper made them both pause. The boy followed the sound. There was a bundle in Laurel's arms he hadn't noticed before, a mere lump wrapped up in a soft white blanket. The lump wiggled and uttered a soft cry.

"Have you never seen a child before?" Laurel asked.

The boy couldn't answer, nor could he look away. Laurel held the small thing to her breast, hushing it and bouncing it with an aching tenderness. It hurt the boy to watch.

"This is Wren." Laurel nuzzled the little thing with a kiss, and then held it out to him. "Your daughter."

The boy didn't know what to do, so he drew back. He had never felt so insignificant before, so disgusted and in awe. The baby cooed softly. He wanted to sink into the earth and vanish. But he didn't quite know why. After a moment, Laurel drew the baby back to her.

"Eight weeks old and twice as stubborn as you are," Laurel said with a smile. For a moment, she looked like herself again—young, happy, full of light. "Come with us. Please."

The boy said nothing. He had never imagined himself as a father. He didn't know how to be one properly. He had been born into an unforgiving society that looked down on boys without fathers. Since childhood, he had imagined escaping his rigid world, but he couldn't truly imagine himself living anywhere other than Síorghlas. As cruel as it had been to him at times, it was his home. And at last, it had dealt him a fair hand. How could he give that up?

"Laurel, I—" He could feel his heart breaking even as he uttered the words. "I cannot."

"You mean you *will* not."

A wave of fury washed up inside him. Of course, this ealdor's daughter would never understand. She had been pampered from the start. She had never known what it was like to face her peers each day with trembling knees—peers who insisted she was only ever less than she should be. Less than Sylvaen.

"Why did you arrange this meeting if you're so disgusted with the Sylvaen?" he demanded. "Why are you wasting your words? And why did you insist on bringing that?" He gestured accusingly at the bundle in Laurel's arms. "That—that *thing* is the very source of all that's driving us apart. It was a mistake. A miscalculation. A—"

"I'm not sure if you're speaking of the child or yourself." Laurel hugged the baby tighter and glared.

The boy stumbled like he'd been hit. Laurel was right. It was not the child he hated; it was himself.

Sighing, Laurel shifted the baby in her arms. "In answer to your question, I arranged this meeting to tell my mother that I'm going away from here. And I have no hope I'll ever return." She glanced up at the trees with a wistful expression. "I only wanted to say goodbye."

The boy raised his eyes to Laurel's once more. As his anger cooled, the last bit of hope he'd been holding on to crumbled inside him. Laurel was going away. "Where are you going?" His voice came out soft and quiet, sounding more like the boy he was and less like the man he kept intending to be.

"I don't know."

"The Sylvaen will hunt you. If they find out you're alive, that you haven't laid down your shape-gift—"

"Then you can tell them I am dead."

Never had the boy felt so utterly powerless. He wanted to make Laurel see reason. He wanted to grab her by the wrist and force her to return with him, but he dared not. Even now, he loved Laurel. Desperately. He didn't want to lose her, but he didn't want to hurt her more than he already had. The rift between them already felt like a chasm. If he forced her to do something against her will, she would never forgive him. Besides, returning to Síorghlas now would almost certainly be a death sentence for Laurel and for the child.

"I ought to report you." The boy sighed. "As an ealdor, it is my duty to abide by Sylvaen law."

"Do what you must. But if you send your watchers after me, know that you'll be hunting the wind."

"You're not doing things in the proper order. You'll go mad."

"I've been mad."

The boy was desperate. "You've already lost your home, your people, your way of life. What else must you lose to turn you back?"

Laurel defied him with her fathomless evergreen eyes. "I haven't lost my home; it's you who has lost yours. You will see that one day."

Though there were tears streaming down Laurel's face, she lifted her proud head like the ealdor's daughter she was. Even now, he could see she was struggling against the forest's call. Since birth, she had been in communion with the Elder Tree. It knew her by name, by heart, by spirit.

"Goodbye, Valerian."

As Laurel turned away, the boy caught a glimpse of something pink-faced and green-eyed nestled among the blankets. The boy's chest turned to ice. Not only had he lost Laurel, but he'd also lost something precious, something innocent. Something he should have been willing to die to defend.

He lost his child, and with her, he lost himself.

As I opened my eyes, the final pieces of the puzzle slipped into place. I knew now that Valerian was my father. I should have realized sooner because no matter how many times I saw him, his smile bothered me. And the reason it bothered me so much was because it was mine. It didn't matter though. Valerian was still on the same path he had been on before. He wanted to save himself. But I didn't hate him for it; I pitied him.

I climbed out of bed, feeling oddly calm. I knew who my father was and why I was an outcast. I knew that no matter how inconvenient it was for Valerian, I shared his flesh and blood. I was his daughter.

After dressing, I went to the main room. The windows were still dark. Aster was up banging around in her kitchen. Miraculously, Alder was still asleep in the main room with his head on a cushion. Near to him lay a pair of leather packs and two bedrolls. Knowing Aster, she had outfitted us to survive in the forest for a week or two at least.

"Sky's veiled," Aster said when she noticed me standing behind her. "You may meet snow beyond the second barrier."

I nodded, but I couldn't get the dream out of my head. I had to say the truth aloud.

"I know who my father is."

Aster turned, her hands dripping with suds and dish water. "I don't know if he'd be too glad to hear that, but I'm pleased. You deserve to know. He made me swear an oath I wouldn't breathe a word, else I would have told you."

"You should have told me anyway." I brought over a chair from the table and sat down. "But I think I understand. Nobody around here defies the ealdors."

"No, but they ought to."

"The ealdors will never change. Valerian sure hasn't."

"No, he hasn't," she agreed. "But that doesn't mean people can never change. Your mother certainly did."

"My mom died, Aster."

Aster dried her hands with a dish towel and heaved a sigh. "I've not forgotten, lass. Aye, your mother's days were dark, but they were not altogether lightless. She had you."

"Some consolation that was."

Aster went to her table and picked up a book. She brought it back a moment later and held it out to me. It was a tawny leather-bound book wrapped in a green and gold braid. "I thought you might like to have this," she said. I took the book and held it carefully. It felt familiar somehow—like the whiff of a scent that triggered a memory buried deep. Aster gestured for me to unbraid the cord securing it. "It belonged to your mother."

The book opened to an illustration of a spiny shrub. The shrub had broad leaves and greenish-white flowers arranged in a spiraling pattern around the stem. A smaller image in the margin, labeled *oplopanux horridus:* devil's club, showed shining red berries growing in elongated clusters. A description followed in Mom's neat, sloping hand, and her familiar signature lingered in the corner of the page—the oversized L curling beneath the rest in a perfect flourish.

I turned the page, remembering Mom's book from my dreams—the records she made to help her cheat on her plant lore examination. I turned to an image of clasping twistedstalk, all pointed leaves and bell-like flowers, with a tiny illustration of deep red berries off to the side.

Mom was an amazing artist. She was too busy to draw at the end, but she used to keep a sketchbook or two in the back seat of our car. When I was younger, I would spend hours poring over her drawings. The scenes she created seemed to burst from the page, imbued with color and a life of their own. Even now, every pen stroke, every highlight, every touch of shadow in the book Aster had given me felt like an old friend.

I turned the page and found a drawing of a small brown bird with an erect tail perched near a nest hidden in an understory of salal. Beneath the drawing was a poem written in Mom's tidy handwriting:

May the stars light your path,
May the wind drive your back,
May your arrow fly straight,
And may you fear no lack.
May the rain bring you plenty,
And may your hope hold fast.
May the Treelight guide you
Till you come home at last.

I brushed my fingers over the words, reading and re-reading them like I was drowning and they were oxygen. I returned my gaze to the drawing. The tiny bird nestled in the branches was the focal point, but Síorghlas was in the background. A smile touched my lips when I realized the bird was a wren. To my mom, that wren meant home. I meant home.

"You remind me much of her," Aster said. When I looked up, her eyes were gleaming. "Your looks, your spirit, the confident way in which you speak—they're hers, but they're also your own. She must have been immensely proud."

I was barely aware of the tears scalding my cheeks. If I left Síorghlas like I was planning to, I would never look out Aster's windows and see the evergreens sparkling with frost or gilded with morning light. Without speaking, Aster reached out to touch my cheek. The image of her cemented itself in my mind: an elderly woman with a bent back and my mom's eyes. *My* eyes. I still had so many questions, but those questions would never find their answers if I went away.

The truth was, I hadn't tried to assimilate because I didn't understand Sylvaen traditions. I had read a few books, practiced a little magic, and learned the steps of a useless dance, but I hadn't done anything to prove who I was—the pure-blooded daughter of a Sylvaen ealdor. And so was Mom.

I got up and began to pace. If Mom was Sylvaen, then she had as much right to be in Síorghlas as anyone else. The forest was her birthright. But the actions of the other Sylvaen—namely Aster and Valerian—forced her to leave her home. She became a person caught between two worlds—the one she was living in and the one she belonged to. When she died, her spirit returned home. The problem was that things were not right at home. Nothing in Síorghlas had changed since Mom left with me growing inside her. In fact, things were worse than they had ever been. The Sylvaen were still abusing people.

I took another turn around the kitchen. Mom was Betwixt instead of going on to the bright place as she should have. The barrier separating the forest from the outside world was starting to weaken. Alder couldn't hear the Elder Tree's voice. All those things together could only lead me to one conclusion: the Sylvaen were not doing their part in upholding the Elder Covenant. By mistreating people, they were neglecting to care for the forest and its inhabitants. And so, the Sylvaen were starting to lose their magic.

Alder woke up and came into the kitchen a little while later. His hair was a mess, and his eyes said he didn't want to be there. I couldn't blame him. After what I said to him the night before, he probably wished he'd never met me. But, like the loyal and dutiful person he was, he would see me safely out of the forest no matter what.

"Alder, lad. You're up." Aster pulled down a clean teacup and filled it for Alder. "The council is convening soon. There's little time to waste."

Alder frowned at the morning-bright window as he sipped his tea. "I thought you were going to wake us before dawn. The guard will have changed hours ago by now."

"Aye, but that all changed while you were sleeping." Aster nodded to me before returning to her cooking. "Wren will explain."

Alder made a half-hearted attempt to meet my gaze. I didn't know what to say to him at first. The ache in his expression was still there, reminding me of how deeply he cared about me. And yet, despite his pain, he was still standing there, still trying to put on a brave face and be there for me because he knew I needed it. He was the living embodiment of his words—he didn't give up when things were hard. I wrapped my hands around my teacup and took a calming breath. I needed to talk to him about my plan, but first, I needed to try to repair the hurt between us.

"Okay, so first off, I suck at this kind of thing," I said. "Please bear with me."

Alder listened attentively while I worked through everything that transpired between us outside Valerian's gate. It was uncomfortable to talk about my feelings for Alder in front of Aster, but time was limited. I needed to get to the council chambers, and I needed Alder's help. But aside from that, I wanted to fix things with Alder.

"I lied when I said I didn't mean that kiss." I said softly as Aster stepped out of the room. "I did mean it. I just thought it was easier to lie since I was going to leave Síorghlas and never see you again."

Alder didn't answer. He stared evenly at me, looking like he didn't know what to think. His eyes tracked Aster as she bustled back into the room. I had a feeling it was going to take time to truly mend things between us. For now, I was happy with him looking me in the eye and giving me more than monosyllabic responses. It felt like a solid first step.

"You're staying then?" he asked.

"That's the next part I need to talk to you about."

Alder gave me an expectant look as Aster set a bowl of creamy-looking porridge in front of him. I waited while she dished up another and handed it to me. I wasn't hungry, but eating seemed like a good idea. Things could go in any direction once I arrived at the council chambers. Aster's porridge could end up being my last meal.

"I have a plan," I told Alder. "But I should probably preface by letting you know Valerian is my father."

"Valerian is your *what*?"

"My father. Oh, and Aster's my grandmother. I think you were asleep for that part too."

Alder looked at me like I'd sprouted a pair of antlers. "I think maybe I still am."

"Have mercy, Wren." Aster patted Alder's shoulder consolingly on her way back to the stove. "The lad hasn't eaten yet. Wait till his stomach's half-full at least."

"I'm fine." Alder picked up his spoon. "Tell me that again, but slower. It's almost starting to make sense."

We spent the rest of breakfast discussing my dysfunctional family tree. After that, I told Alder what I had in mind for going to the council chambers. I couldn't tell if he liked my plan or not because he kept sneaking glances at Aster and asking if I'd had a brain transplant in the last twenty-four hours. After denying it several times, Aster finally said yes—she'd performed the surgery herself.

Alder tapped his fingers on the table restlessly. "What makes you think this will work better than fighting bears with martial arts?"

"Easy. I've fought bears with martial arts before and won."

"These bears are bigger, and they won't like it."

"The bears won't see it coming. I'll have my wolf pelt on and all that."

Alder smiled at the story reference. I wouldn't be wearing a literal wolf pelt, but I would have the sentry's uniform he had been planning to wear to get me out of Síorghlas. Undoubtedly, the uniform would have fit him better, but he had a different role to play.

"All right." He pushed his chair back and stood up. "Your plan is crazy, wolf-girl, but I'm in."

CHAPTER 28
HEWN DOWN

THE FOREST STOOD LIKE a regiment of green-clad sentries on the mountainside as Alder and I trudged through. Between me and the council chambers was an unknown number of Sylvaen sentries keeping watch to make sure no one interrupted their proceedings. The only hopes I had of getting past the guards were my instincts, my wit, and Alder. I prayed that would be enough.

The sound of approaching sentries echoed off the ravine walls. I turned to see two figures emerging from the tree shadows, black shapes against a pale sky. I paused to hide and check that my mask was tight, but Alder motioned for us to keep walking. A moment later, two sentries walked past, a man and a woman, armored and cloaked in green. One of the sentries laughed, oblivious to our presence. It wasn't long before their conversation dipped below the roar of a distant waterfall. I was relieved. It was one thing to pass as a sentry while accompanying Alder to the council chambers; it was another to have to give a report to a cohort leader who stopped and demanded one of me.

Alder and I came to a flight of stairs and took them two at a time. The council chambers were located somewhere on the fifth tier. We rounded the last bend a few minutes later and came to the council chambers. Two masked sentries guarded the doors to keep would-be intruders from interrupting the ealdors. I'd expected as much. Fortunately, I was on a diplomatic mission.

The sentries spotted Alder and bowed. They didn't offer me the same courtesy. I realized I must have put on the uniform of a lower-ranking sentry—I would have to keep that in mind.

"*Síocháin leat*," I said, doing my best to imitate a Sylvaen accent. Beside me, Alder coughed to cover up the fact that he was trying not to laugh. "There's been a disturbance in the forest. Something about the Outlander lass escaping?"

One of the sentries groaned. "Not her again."

I grinned beneath my mask.

The other sentry looked at Alder, then me. His green eyes reflected the light of a shape-cast lantern. "Shouldn't you be attending that yourself? Grove and I are on duty under orders from Oxalis. It isn't our habit to take sentries from their posts."

"I am aware," I lied. "Oxalis wants you at the forest border to lay an ambush. He wants strong sentries capable of using force if needed."

"That explains it then," Grove said.

The other sentry ignored Grove's comment. "The lass must have moved fast. We came on an hour before sunup, and we hadn't heard a word of her escape."

"Aye. The lass is treacherous."

Alder shifted like he didn't like the direction the conversation was taking. Good. He was playing his part well.

"Treacherous indeed." The sentry glanced at Grove, who was already gathering himself to depart from his post. "But why are you escorting the Wind Shaper? Isn't he capable of fending for himself?"

"He's wanted for the protection of the ealdors," I said. "We do not yet know where the lass is headed or what she's planning. She may double back and attack when she thinks we're not expecting it."

Grove snorted. "Stupid lass if she does that."

From inside the chambers, I could hear the low drone of voices. My heart sped up. I needed to get inside before Valerian began his address.

"I agree with Grove. Caution hardly seems necessary," the sentry said, his gaze turning thoughtful. "Why would the lass double back? She may be treacherous, but she is smart. And clearly bent on escaping."

"It isn't my job to ask questions of my superiors," I snapped. "The weakness at our borders means our ranks have already been spread thin. If we want to protect our forest from the Outlander threat, we must stay calm and follow orders. Unity is our best defense."

"True enough," the sentry said.

For a moment, I thought the sentry was going to relent. He moved as if to relinquish his post, then he seemed to think better of it.

"What is your name, sentry?"

I was ready for his question. "Purslane."

"Many thanks, Purslane. I have but one more question." He glanced at Alder. "Who is your cohort leader—the one who gave you your orders? I wish to tell him or her of your excellent service and strict observation of commands."

The question startled me. I didn't know the names of many Sylvaen cohort leaders.

"Rowan."

"How odd." The sentry lowered his mask. "I don't believe I gave that order."

I didn't have time to react. Grove lunged forward and tore off my mask. Alder was on him in an instant, tackling him to the ground. I was impressed; Alder wasn't a big guy. Before I could draw my knife, Rowan tossed me against the wall and pinned me there with one arm.

"You almost had me for a moment, clever lass," he said.

He slipped my knife from its sheath and tossed it aside, a few feet from where Grove and Alder were struggling. Fortunately, I'd learned a few tricks since our last scuffle. I worked my arm free and shaped a writhing thicket of blackberries. Rowan let out a yell and released me as one of the thorny canes made a grab for his arm.

Alder and Grove were still fighting. It looked as if I would have to go into the council chambers alone. I made a grab for the door. A moment before I touched it, Rowan caught my wrist and yanked me backward, making my teeth snap together. I wasn't going to let him stop me this time. Engaging every muscle, I strained toward the doors, bringing Rowan along with me. I'd drag him right into the council chambers if I had to.

"Not so fast, little bird," Rowan said through his teeth.

With a quick maneuver, he grabbed an arrow from his sheath and used it to knock my legs out from under me. My head slammed into the side of the council chambers. I didn't see stars; I saw entire galaxies.

"You've improved since our last encounter," Rowan huffed.

He got to his feet. Beyond Rowan, Alder and Grove were still wrestling on the ground. Finally, Alder got sick of fighting and tossed Grove aside with a gust of wind. Alder was right; it was time to stop messing around. I groped for Rowan's discarded arrow, gripped it, and waited for him to get closer.

"You're shaping skillfully, fighting well, wearing a disguise." Rowan kicked my knife over the edge of the platform and drew his own. "Impressive, really. It's a pity the ealdors aren't interested in giving an audience to half-breeds like you. Unless it's to kill you, of course." Rowan moved to stand over me. He tossed the knife in the air and caught it by its handle. "What do you think, little bird? Should I do it for them, or should I give them the pleasure?"

"I think you should watch your back."

Rowan turned around fast. Alder stood right behind him, grinning like an imp.

"Hey, Row. Still picking fights with girls?" Alder shook his head. "Bad idea, mate."

Rowan bared his teeth. He raised his arm to attack Alder but didn't get the chance. I took the arrow and used it to pin his cloak to the wall. His lunge toward Alder was cut short. He let out an angry yell.

Alder gave me his hand and pulled me to my feet. "I like the arrow trick. I'll remember that one."

"Thanks," I said. "So, how do we get inside?"

"That's the easy part."

He faced the council chambers and made a thrusting motion in the air with his hands. The sound of wind filled the ravine and blew the doors to the council chambers off their hinges. A huge crash followed. I could hear people screaming inside. So much for a diplomatic mission.

"Alder. You were supposed to open the door, not kill everybody inside."

"Yeah, I might have overdone it. They'll be fine, I think."

"But we won't."

Alder shrugged and motioned me inside. "After you, wolf-girl."

"What is the meaning of this, Wind Shaper?" Valerian demanded as we entered the council chambers.

Alder sucked in a breath. Behind Valerian, the council chambers were in an uproar. Attendants herded the ealdors into a pale, disorderly knot on the edge of the room. The ruined doors stood in a heap near the dais. Ealdors swarmed like angry bees behind the attendants, yelling orders and demanding explanations. Briar was among them, as was Heath, the boy I'd recognized during my pretrial hearing. Neither of them looked like they wanted to be there.

"My apologies, Head Ealdor Valerian." Alder bowed low, one knee on the ground. "It was not my intent to blow in the doors as I did, and I will be glad to offer my services in repairing them. But right now, Wren and I are here on a mission of utmost importance. It could not wait."

Valerian regarded us with a severe look. "Alder, you have a duty to Síorghlas. If find you can no longer fulfill your obligation, perhaps it is because this Outlander has darkened your mind with her twisted way of thinking."

"There is no darkness plaguing my mind," Alder replied. "I come before you in humility and peace on behalf of the Elder Tree. My only request is that you hear what Wren has to say."

"Well, Wind Shaper. It seems you leave us little choice." Valerian went to his ealdor's seat, dusted off the debris, and sat down heavily. "Go on."

I followed Alder's lead and bowed. "I didn't mean to threaten anyone. I came here because I think the forest is in danger of losing its magic."

A few scattered laughs echoed throughout the chambers. Most of the ealdors had brushed the dust off their seats and sat down, but one of them remained standing. He was an older man with short hair and a tidy white beard.

"What do you know about The Elder Tree's magic, half-breed?" the ealdor demanded.

"Peace, Salal," Valerian said to the ealdor. "Wren has studied a little, I think. She may have picked up on a thing or two we've forgotten. Or it is possible she is trying to manipulate us. We will know soon enough."

The ealdor looked like he wanted to argue but knew better. Valerian was his superior.

I cleared my throat and went on. "Let me give you some examples to back up what I'm saying. The Wind Shaper's gift is broken. The forest barriers are starting to weaken. My mother is Betwixt. I think we need to do something to reverse whatever is causing all this damage before it's too late."

Valerian looked stricken. "Your mother is Betwixt?"

Alder spoke up. "Aye. I've encountered her myself."

Valerian said nothing. Behind him, ealdors and their attendants began murmuring.

"Your mother was a traitor, Outlander," one of the ealdors said. "If she is Betwixt, it is likely punishment for the wrongs she did during her life. As for the rest of it—that's all hearsay. No one can prove that the forest barriers are weakening, and I have never heard that the Wind Shaper's gift is broken. Just now, the lad seemed strong enough."

Nervous laughter echoed through the chambers. The ealdor was right. By all appearances, it did look like Alder's gift was thriving.

"Things aren't always as they appear," I said. "I can't offer you direct proof, but I can tell you that the Elder Tree awakened my shape-gift and called me to Síorghlas. It started speaking to me and giving me dreams almost as soon as I moved into the area. I think—"

"Half a moment, lass." One of the ealdors, a kindly-looking young man with a perplexed expression, leaned forward in his ealdor's chair. "How do you know it was the Elder Tree giving you these visions?"

"Indeed." Salal, the bearded ealdor from earlier, found his seat at last. "What reason can you give us for believing any of this? To my knowledge, it is the Wind Shaper the Elder Tree communicates with. It certainly does not reach out to Outlanders."

The ealdor's comment bothered me. Why would the Elder Tree communicate with me? I wasn't the Wind Shaper. And despite my pure Sylvaen blood, I hadn't been properly raised in Síorghlas. I was simply me—a girl caught between two worlds. I didn't have any answers to give.

Because you can put things right.

The resonant voice seemed to fill the whole chamber, yet I knew its words were only for me. It felt like eons since I'd heard it last, and now, its presence felt like a warm, soothing breeze. I recognized the voice then as what it had always been: the Elder Tree.

"Because I am a Sylvaen who was born outside her home. My mother was the only home I ever knew, and then she died. When I lost her, I felt like I lost me too. That's why I'm warning you to fix things before it's too late and your magic dies."

"Wren." Lupine, the female ealdor who had been newly appointed at my pretrial hearing, placed a fist under her chin. "You call yourself Sylvaen. That is a title we reserve only for those of us who are wholly children of the forest. Is this a custom you are unaware of, or do you mean to suggest that you are of pure lineage?"

Valerian gripped the polished armrests of his ealdor's chair. His face was washed clean of any emotion. The knowledge I carried could uproot him from his position of power and destroy his whole life. He didn't want to kill me, but it wasn't above him to silence others for the sake of his own survival. I gathered an enormous breath for courage.

"I am of pure Sylvaen lineage."

Valerian turned bone white. The other ealdors began shuffling and exchanging glances.

"An outrageous claim," one of the ealdors accused.

Lupine put up a hand to silence the others. "And how do you know this, Wren?"

"The Elder Tree showed me my father."

Salal launched himself out of his seat and strode across the dais. "Who is this Sylvaen father of yours? Is he here in Síorghlas somewhere that he might claim you?" He met the eyes of all the other ealdors as though to make sure they were all paying attention. "Or is he conveniently dead like your mother?"

Valerian's emerald eyes burned threats. He knew that for that one moment, I held all the power. I could ruin the life of the man who abandoned my mom and me. I could crush him like he deserved. But what would that accomplish?

"Yes," I said. "He died a long time ago."

Smirking, Salal returned to his seat. Valerian's hands released their death grip on his armrests. There was an expression of extreme weariness on his face. Alder stared at me with a look halfway between horror and awe. Without naming Valerian as my father, I had given the ealdors reason to doubt the legitimacy of my claims. I didn't do it to shield Valerian from consequences; I did it because the boy in my dreams had so rarely been the recipient of kindness in his life.

"There's a rift between the Sylvaen and the Elder Tree," I said, addressing the ealdors once more. "That's what's causing the magic to fade. People both inside the community and out have been mistreated. They've been abused and harassed and forced from their homes for making mistakes or for coming from the wrong bloodline. But that kind of abuse was never what the Elder Tree had in mind when it established the Elder Covenant. Because it keeps happening, we're all starting to lose our magic. That loss is small now, but it will continue to grow. More people will die and become Betwixt. The forest barriers will fade altogether. The very architecture of Síorghlas will start to crumble, and there will be no communication between the Wind Shaper and the Elder Tree to fix it. The Sylvaen way of life will pass into the void."

Some of the other ealdors bent their heads as though deeply considering the things I said. Others turned to their neighbors and began to murmur. I had to press forward while I still had their attention.

"I'm confident that we can mend the rift together, and we can start by how we treat each other. We can share what we have, show hospitality, and listen to the concerns of others. There's one way forward, and that's for us to come together, find common ground, and work out our differences with mutual respect."

For one glorious second, I thought I had succeeded. Some of the ealdors began speaking to their neighbors in hushed voices, nodding and gesturing at me. Lupine, the ealdor who had asked me about my lineage, smiled. And then, one of the ealdors jumped up from his chair.

"What lies!" he shouted. "It is as Ealdor Valerian said before you arrived. You invent tales hoping they will gain you an advantage. You think you are immune to following the rules. You blow down the doors so you can disrupt our proceedings, threaten us, and demand we listen. You have not the heart nor the manner of the forest. You are an Outlander."

Another ealdor stood to join the first, a man with long fair hair. "Aye! I second that. There is no rift!"

My heart sank. They hadn't heard me at all. "Please, just listen," I said.

The white-bearded ealdor raised his voice to be heard above mine. "This Outlander would corrupt even the council with her treasonous ideals."

I held my palms up in a gesture of peace. "It's true that I didn't take my assimilation seriously. I didn't try to understand your way of life. But I'm ready to change that." I bowed to Valerian with a fist to my heart. "With your permission, Head Ealdor Valerian, I'd like to start over. If you give me a trial period of one month, I'll dedicate myself fully to becoming Sylvaen. If I succeed, I can be an example to the people of someone willing to grow and change to mend the rift."

Valerian remained still and silent. At that moment, Rowan rushed into the room, followed by Grove and a double cohort of sentries. Alder immediately stepped to my side and assumed a defensive stance, but the sentries didn't move against us. Instead, they positioned themselves between us and the ealdors, making sure to keep their bows drawn and their arrows on us.

"The only division here is that which you bring among us, Outlander," the white-bearded ealdor said. "You come to sow seeds of doubt and divide us. In all likelihood, it is your mixed blood that has defiled the magic and caused the Elder Tree to wither."

Several voices shouted in agreement.

"Don't you get it?" I cried. "The loss of Sylvaen magic isn't a wound inflicted by something external, it's a consequence."

The voices around the room grew louder. Alder grabbed my hand.

"You will pay for that lie!" someone shouted.

The white-bearded ealdor motioned to the sentries. A sentry dove into Alder and knocked him onto the ground. Another reached out and grabbed me, twisting my arm behind my back. With a jolt, I realized it was Rowan. Dragging me along, he walked to the dais and presented me like a prize.

"Your knife, sentry," the white-bearded ealdor barked.

Rowan quickly drew his knife from the sheath at his side. He seemed almost giddy to comply. But then, he stopped. A terrified look passed over his features as he looked up at the ealdor pointing at me. Maybe he had seen that ealdor before in a similar context.

"Make her kneel," the ealdor said, chin pointing at me. "Cut her throat. Make her bleed."

Alder lurched toward me, but the sentry holding him stopped him with a blow. Some of the ealdors yelled protests—Lupine, an older man with moss-colored eyes, a woman with twists of silver in her long reddish hair. Most of the council said nothing.

"We worried this would happen, did we not?" Salal shouted. "The Outlander has turned the Wind Shaper against us. She will destroy the lot of us. We must destroy her first." He gestured to Rowan. "Go on."

Rowan hesitated. "Ealdor Salal? I'm afraid I haven't been appointed as executioner. This task is beyond my expertise—"

"I am appointing you," Salal said impatiently.

Rowan stared at the knife in his hands.

"Now, sentry!" Salal said.

Rowan seemed to jolt awake. He spoke to me then, his voice low and urgent. "Tell me the truth, lass. Do you love my brother?"

My eyes met Alder's from across the room. A small, tremulous smile formed on my lips. He responded with a look of worry, then confusion, then a slow smile. I answered Rowan without even having to consider. "I think I'm getting there."

"Then to move against you would be to move against him." Rowan faced the ealdors. He held up his knife, and with a flick of his wrist, he tossed it across the room. "I refuse to comply," he said. "Alder is my brother. His blood is my blood. He has wounded me deeply, but I'll not destroy him. Or the lass he loves."

Several outraged cries echoed across the council chambers. Alder gazed at his brother in outright disbelief. Underneath the grime and stubble, Rowan's features still betrayed a boyishness he hadn't yet outgrown. He was still human, still Alder's brother. Maybe there was hope for restoration between them after all.

Salal looked like a storm cloud preparing to unleash its fury. He began shouting orders. Other sentries moved in to seize Rowan. Soon, Rowan had his limbs pinned and a knife at his throat. Alder threw off the sentry pinning him and scrambled to his feet. He lifted his arms like he was ready to command a hurricane.

"Enough!" Alder shouted.

The council chambers went still. Oil-black clouds gathered outside. The ealdors who were standing huddled close behind Salal.

"Stand down, Wind Shaper!" Salal urged. "This Outlander has bewitched you, lad. She has begun to turn you against your people and our way of life."

The room grew darker. A gust of wind exploded the windows. Glass shards scattered across the floor. The wind began to lash and tear at the ealdors' robes. Just for a moment, I caught a glimpse of the terrifying true nature of Alder's gift, and so did Briar. She looked on, gripping the back of an ealdor's chair protectively—I could only assume the ealdor was her father.

"No one has bewitched me," Alder said firmly. "I am acting on behalf of the Elder Tree and of the ones I love. You have neither the power nor the right to order executions without a unanimous vote from the council."

Salal glowered at Alder. "An exception may be made in emergencies."

Briar's father stood and addressed the ealdors still holding their seats. "Then we must call a vote, starting with our leader. What say you, Head Ealdor Valerian?"

Valerian stirred and seemed at last to recover from his shock. There was a slight tremor in his hand as he passed it over his face. Finally, he pushed himself up out of his chair. "Forgive me." He stepped down from the dais like a man half dazed. "I will refrain from this vote. I find I am not well."

Valerian avoided my eyes and hurried past like the coward he was. Alder watched him go with a look of disgust. The light in the room went still dimmer. Oddly, I wasn't angry at Valerian's decision. I was hopeless. My chest felt like caving in. Valerian's inability to face his own demons meant that someone else had to.

"Now, for the Outlander." Salal strode forward.

Someone grabbed me and shook me. I felt my hair yanked back followed by the cold press of a knife against my throat.

"Your execution will commence forthwith. A fitting end for the half-breed whose very existence is a blight upon the Sylvaen way of life."

"Salal, no!" Lupine grabbed Salal's arm, but he shook her off.

Valerian paused in the act of walking out the door. Alder looked like someone had kicked him in the chest. The wind continued to stir the air, whipping his dark hair into a frenzy. My own insides turned and writhed like a seedling searching for light.

"Sentries," Salal said. "Take your positions. As of this moment, I am promoting all of you to executioners. Anyone siding with the Outlander from this moment onward will be subject to immediate death."

A hollow feeling filled me as the sentries bound me with a shape-cast chain and carried it to the far corners of the room. Alder stared at me, his pulse jumping in his neck. Outside, all was dark. Even the Elder Tree stood still like it was holding its breath. This was it. The end.

Salal raised his fist and held it aloft, ready to give the signal. "I take no pleasure in ending a life, but rebellion, it seems, spreads like blight. Trees must be hewn down and burned before their sickness infects the whole forest."

"Please," I choked out, "there has to be a better way."

Salal turned to Alder with cold eyes. "For defying the ealdor council and for harboring the half-breed traitor bent on destroying our ways—"

Alder gave a desperate shout and thrust both hands outward. A bright flash issued from his hands as a sentry collided with him. Alder's shape-cast lightning went wild, crashing into the woven tree limbs and shape-cast gems hanging from the ceiling. Shards of silver and broken twigs rained down on the startled ealdors. Salal gave a yell and let his fist drop. As he did, the hiss of arrows filled the air.

I closed my eyes, waiting for the arrows to hit their mark. But even in the dark, an image remained. The Elder Tree was stamped like a tattoo on my retinas.

CHAPTER 29
DAUGHTER OF THE FOREST

I EXPECTED MIND-NUMBING PAIN, but death was surprisingly gentle. I felt myself go weightless as my feet lifted off the ground. The soft folds of a silver chrysalis bundled me in its blanket-like embrace. I was safe. Completely.

I took a calming breath, then another. I stopped. If I was dead, why was I still breathing? Why was my heart hammering my insides the way it was?

The chrysalis holding me was translucent like a dragonfly's wing, but the shape of it was more like the bud of some giant flower. If I looked down, I could see the crowd still gathered on the dais. The archers were still firing their weapons up at me. Alder was still on the ground, wrestling with the sentry who had attacked him. I had seen his shape go awry and explode the crystals on the ceiling, so I knew he wasn't the one who saved me. So, who had?

"Do *not*—harm her." Valerian's labored words filled up the council chambers and made everything fall silent. Everyone looked at him. He was visibly under strain, his trembling hand stretched out toward me.

"Head Ealdor Valerian!" Lupine dashed to his side. "Your gift—"

"Stand down, Lupine," Valerian interrupted.

Lupine blinked in surprise but stayed back as instructed. Valerian looked and sounded weary. His veins were visible beneath his pale skin, protruding in his neck and forehead. I remembered that his gift was not strong. Even with plants, his signature magic type, he could only expend a little energy at a time, or he would face failure and exhaustion. The shape he'd cast to protect me had to be taxing his body to its very limits.

"I've—been a fool and a coward," Valerian panted.

He sank to his knees. His whole body was starting to shake, but he managed to keep the shape intact. Barely. I called up my gift and pressed a hand to the side of the chrysalis to lend Valerian some of my energy. Valerian relaxed a little, but it wasn't enough. His nose started to bleed. "Wren speaks the truth. She is no Outlander," he said through a grimace. "But her father is not dead as she says he is."

The strain was too much. Valerian gave a gasp and collapsed. Several attendants rushed to his aid as the light cocoon faded around me. My feet hit the floor with a gentle thud. Quick as a blink, Alder pinned the sentry through his sleeve with an arrow and made his way to my side.

"I am he." Valerian pushed himself to his feet and faced the gathered crowd. "I am Wren's father."

The silence that followed was eerie after the tumult of the last several minutes. Salal moved his lips, but no sound came out. The other ealdors shifted and seemed unable to look each other in the eye.

Finally, Salal found his voice. "You—you are head ealdor. Yet you have kept this matter concealed?"

"I've done many things I am ashamed of," Valerian said. He shook his head like he was trying to clear the spots from his eyes. "Were I to recount them, I suppose we'd be in these chambers a very long time."

Another of the ealdors who hadn't spoken before made an indignant sound. "You, Valerian? *You* were intimate with a traitor and an oath-breaker?"

"Laurel was no traitor. Breaking her oath was an act of survival—one which I, her mother, and Sylvaen laws drove her to. The real traitor was myself. I exercised violence and cowardice where I should have acted with compassion and humility. I insulated myself from pain and allowed others to shield me from difficulties. I lied when I claimed to uphold truth and order and moral uprightness."

Valerian was still shaking when he pulled up a stool and sat before the dais. The ealdors looked on in amazement as he recounted how he had abandoned my mother and me in favor of retaining his position on the council. Several council members shifted uncomfortably during his narrative. Two of them got up and walked out. It made me wonder how many had unclaimed children. How many of them had people like me—people they wanted to keep invisible?

As Valerian spoke, the dark-haired boy in my dreams flashed across my mind, but he was faceless no longer. He had a name. A story. A future twisted by shame and lies and by the hurt of not knowing his own father. As angry as I was with Valerian for all the pain he had inflicted on Mom and me, I also ached for him. So many years had been wasted on trying to escape his past when he could have simply asked for help.

"As Wren was speaking the truth about her parentage," Valerian continued. "I suggest we heed her when she says there is a rift. The lass has been far wiser than me."

Alder grabbed my hand and gave it a gentle squeeze. Valerian looked at me then. He didn't quite smile, but there was a look of pride in his eyes.

"You are a thief and a liar, Valerian," Salal said in a venomous tone. "You ought to be stripped of your rank and thrashed."

"Aye, I am all that you say and more. All that I am is laid bare. And although I cannot undo my wrongs, I will do what I can to mend my part in this rift."

He unclasped the tree-shaped brooch at his throat. He then drew out his ealdor's knife and laid at the ealdor's feet. Finally, he bowed, placing his forehead against the cold floor of the council chambers.

"I hereby relinquish my role as head of this council, and I give up my claim to all the benefits that accompany it. I accept whatever punishment the council deems fit, whether that be death, banishment, imprisonment, surrendering of all my possessions. My only request is that you spare Wren"—he raised his eyes to mine—"my daughter."

The council chambers filled up with the ealdors' silence. No one seemed to know what to do in the face of the head ealdor resigning his position. The ealdors did not adapt well to change. Their inability to be flexible or alter their course was shown in the policies they enforced throughout Síorghlas. Operating without their head ealdor would be a new kind of challenge.

One of the ealdors, a woman with vines and wildflowers woven into her braid, spoke up. "Valerian, the crimes you've admitted to are grievous, but you have also served on the council faithfully. You have worked for the betterment of all Síorghlas for many years. I think we can eliminate death as a necessary sentence."

"Aye," said Briar's father. "And as you know, we are not in the habit of keeping prisoners long-term. That leaves us with two options."

"We might strip him of his gift and banish him to the Outlands," suggested another. "Or confiscate his home and possessions."

Lupine tapped her chin. "Nay. Depriving one of the necessities of life is not our way, even for criminals. As Sylvaen, are we not in favor of restoration above all? Perhaps the laying aside of his power has been punishment enough, and we can now move toward healing."

A handful of ealdors muttered their assent, but others were visibly dissatisfied. A murmur went up about the need for order. Salal tapped his fingers impatiently on his polished armrest, and when his turn came, he stood.

"Valerian is a lawbreaker, and we cannot allow him to obstruct justice. We will deal with him later. Right now, we have an Outlander in our midst who has thus far evaded punishment. She should not be spared."

"Why?" Lupine demanded. "What evil has she done?"

"She is guilty of criminal insurrection," Salal said.

Alder stiffened beside me. A few of the ealdors rose up from their seats then and began to argue. The fact that Valerian had claimed me as his child apparently made it harder for them to justify killing me simply for existing. But the fact that I had teamed up with Alder to confront them still made some of the ealdors think I was a dangerous rebel.

"The solution is simple," the ealdor with flowers in her hair said. "The lass must lay aside her gift and return to the Outlands."

An ealdor with a long face and about a dozen rings on his fingers dismissed me with a gesture. "Send her away, then."

"But what about the rift?" asked another.

"The rift will be mended in time," said Briar's father. "We will see to that ourselves."

Lupine brought her fist down on the armrest of her chair. "What nonsense. The lass is the very one who called our attention to the rift. She was appointed by the Elder Tree. We would do better to honor her."

"The Elder Tree does not appoint messengers apart from the Wind Shaper," another ealdor said. "The lass must be returned to the Outlands where she was born to prevent her from infecting us with more lies."

"Aye. I second that. Send her away!"

"The lass does not belong among us."

Several of the other ealdors chimed in in favor of my banishment. My heart hammered wildly. Even though I'd only spent a short time there, Síorghlas was a vital part of me. One day, it might even feel like home. It was the one place where I felt connected to the part of me I'd never known. Before coming here, my surroundings had always been too small, too cramped, too rigid to fit my form. When I was in the Outlands, I was a ghost. But even in Síorghlas I didn't quite fit. I'd been born at the wrong time and in the wrong way. I grew up separated from my heritage and my people. I didn't know their laws or customs. Like Mom, I was caught between worlds.

Alder faced the ealdors with me and gripped my hand tighter. "They're wrong."

"Does it matter if they're wrong? They still hold all the power."

"Not all of it." He turned to look at me, his eyes reflecting the light of the Elder Tree. "You are a daughter of the forest, Wren. You have a shape-gift. The blood of ealdors runs in your veins. That's why the Elder Tree called you, because you belong here as much as any of us."

My tempestuous thoughts calmed. Alder was right. The forest was my home, my heritage, my heartbeat. The Elder Tree spoke to me again, and when it did, I felt it all the way to my core.

This is your home, Wren. This is where you belong.

I faced the ealdors again, my hands filling with the warm tingle of my shape-gift. As if from a dream, I recalled the words hung above the entrance to the history wing in Síorghlas's library. Some instinct drove me to one knee. I pulled my hand out of Alder's and placed my fist over my heart. I knew what the Elder Tree wanted me to do, and I was ready.

"Here do I pledge myself, body, mind, and spirit, to Síorghlas; to the Sylvaen people; and to the Elder Tree which sustains the forest and keeps all things dwelling together in harmony. I promise to uphold the values of the Elder Covenant; to submit my will to the good guidance of the ealdor council; to dedicate my energy to the care and cultivation of all living things; to extend justice, mercy, and hospitality to all within my power; and to forsake all other paths until the ending of my days."

The ealdors heard the words and froze. A shimmer pulsed underground and in the air. It crawled up my legs and twisted up my spine. The feeling washed over my skin and passed on, spreading like roots and sweeping me up in a current of magic. I shut my eyes. Soon, individual shape-gifts appeared in my consciousness. The gifts of each person present were like stars in the night sky, like strings of melody that resonated in their own unique ways.

Then, Alder touched my shoulder. A new light appeared. Alder's shape-gift roared like a hurricane, filling me with a sun-like energy. By comparison, all the other shape-gifts were mere blips in the expanse. The loyalty oath was doing its work. It was tying me to the Elder Tree, the forest, and the Sylvaen people—*my* people. I opened my eyes.

The whole chamber was full of light, but that wasn't what made me stand up. Mom was there, edged in silver and standing before the whole council. Her hair blew like ribbons of flame. When her eyes fell on me, it felt like coming home.

"Mom," I whispered.

Smiling serenely, she reached out and touched my face. "I love you, Wren. I've loved you every moment."

I blinked through my tears and reached to grab her hand. She was solid, but not quite warm. Not quite there. And then, she was gone. A bright flash tore through the council chambers, and then all was still. Alder's storm vanished. All the broken glass and splintered crystals had been swept clean and restored. The ealdors stirred and shook themselves, looking dazed. Outside, the sky was a perfect crystal blue. The Elder Tree gleamed brighter than I'd ever seen it. And for the last time, I heard Mom's voice fading like the stars at sunrise, echoing the words of the Elder Tree.

This is where you belong.

CHAPTER 30
ALASKAN SUNSET

I T WAS A MILD day for early spring—mild enough for Leslie and
Peter to suggest eating on the patio. The shadows across the lawn
weren't as long as they had been when I left Síorghlas. They would be
even shorter on my next visit.

"Hang on a minute," Emery said. "The ealdors let you walk out of the
council chambers after that?"

Emery wasn't the only one who wanted answers. Matt sat on the edge
of his seat, his plate of pizza momentarily forgotten. Even Leslie paused
in the act of tending her blueberry bushes. She knew about the Sylvaen
ealdors and my arrangement with them, but she didn't mind hearing the
story again.

"Well, yeah," I said, picking up my pizza crust. "There wasn't a lot they
could do after my mom showed up."

Matt tasted his pizza finally. His eyes instantly took on a possessive
glint, and he drew his plate closer. Alder finished his pizza slice and
reached for another. The pizza, which involved a lot of bacon, was another of Peter's wizardly creations. Peter might have been an Outlander,
but his gift for combining flavors was every bit as magical as anything the
Sylvaen could do.

A lot had happened since I returned to Ketchikan. Peter and Leslie
helped me sort things out with the police and with my school, which
were a lot less simple than they sounded. Alder returned to Ketchikan
and reclaimed his sport bike. I had to get used to him wearing Outlander

clothes again. The shirt he had on that afternoon was a red-orange plaid, exactly the right shade to make his eyes stand out. His perpetually windswept hair had been trimmed and styled, but he still kept in the most careless state possible. I couldn't imagine him looking any other way. While he and I were gone, Matt started playing guitar to impress girls and got a job working for Peter. Leslie had put up some colorful artwork in her house, Peter adopted a houseplant, and Emery dyed her hair blonde—which was only surprising because it was a natural color.

"So, you're full-fledged Sylvaen now," Matt said, struggling to compete with the noise of bird chatter returning to the forest. "I'm curious—why aren't you living in Síorghlas?"

Matt's question was harder to answer than Emery's. The Sylvaen had no choice but to honor my oath, but it was clear they weren't all happy about it. Some of the ealdors thought I should assimilate fully and live in Síorghlas. Others were willing to let me roam between Ketchikan and Síorghlas while I adapted to the Sylvaen lifestyle over time. And still others begrudgingly admitted I couldn't be barred from entering the forest, but they thought I should be restricted from spending time in Síorghlas.

The ealdor's resistance to change was frustrating, but things had improved with the mending of the rift. The Sylvaen had seen their errors. They were better equipped to make good decisions for themselves and future generations. They could choose to welcome outsiders instead of shunning them. Síorghlas was finally becoming what it always should have been: a city of refuge for the people who needed it, a beacon of peace nestled in the evergreens, a place of beauty filling the world with its gentle light.

"The ealdor council couldn't decide what to do with me," I said finally. "For now, they've agreed to treat me as if I were on my Becoming." I took another bite of pizza and picked up my drawing pencil. "I have to report back to Síorghlas like Alder does, but I'll be here for all the normal teenage stuff: prom, graduation, driving, getting hounded for not having a job yet—"

Leslie looked up from her pruning and made a face at me. Smiling, I bent over my sketchbook to shade in some of the details. Leslie wasn't worried about me being jobless; she had other concerns. I had an official curfew now. I also had to report to her when I made plans. She and Peter accepted my identity as Sylvaen and my need to return to the forest, but they wanted to know when I was going and that my life wouldn't be in danger because of it.

"Being jobless might not be an issue much longer." Alder pushed his plate aside and leaned back in his chair. "Thanks to Aster."

Matt and Emery looked confused, so I set down my drawing pencil to explain. "The ealdors want someone on staff at the school to help Sylvaen students navigate the Outlands. Aster thought I would be a good fit. I've lived as an Outlander, and I understand some of the more subtle details, so I can help people with that."

"And you're on track to graduate with us?" Matt asked.

"Almost."

Alder and I had worked like mad to catch up on all the schoolwork we missed over winter break. It made the rainy days go by fast, and it also gave us an excuse to spend time together. Not that we needed a reason.

"So, you'll be like a guidance counselor for Sylvaen students," Emery said.

"Something like that."

Emery nodded like the idea of me helping kids from an isolated community of magic-wielders blend in at school made perfect sense to her. The Sylvaen had been working to repair and reinforce the third barrier, so Emery technically shouldn't have been able to talk about the forest. Fortunately, I figured out a way to override the distracting effects of the forest barriers using my shape-gift. And because Alder was in the habit of letting me bend the rules, he conveniently looked the other way when I did it.

"Would have been nice to have a guidance counselor three years ago," Alder grumbled.

"You needed one," Matt agreed. "Figuring out the lunch line was a problem for you. And you also had that strange obsession with Velcro."

Emery was ready to change the subject from Velcro. "How are things with your dad?"

I took a moment to decide before answering. The boy in my dreams was so different from the man who gave up everything he'd fought for to save my life. And yet, he was the same. Valerian still liked messing with plants. He still had weird ideas about Outlanders, and he was still formal and stand-offish with me. It was beyond disorienting to think of him as my father. There were so many lost years between us, so many missed moments. I didn't know if we'd ever have any kind of normal parent-child relationship.

"They're fine," I said at last. "We don't talk a lot, but he did show me his plant experiment garden that almost killed me. And he even gave me a mushroom knife last time I saw him."

"Mushroom knife. That's what every girl wants." Emery raised her root beer mug like it was a toast. "That might be worse than my dad getting me a tire pressure gauge for my last birthday."

"Both of those things can be surprisingly useful," Matt said.

Emery snorted. "For you, maybe."

I laughed. The wind whipped up the scents of evergreens and ocean. It smelled like home, which meant that it smelled a little like Ketchikan and a little like Síorghlas.

"By the way, Alder," Emery said, setting her root beer aside. "What's the deal with you and Briar? Are you still bound?"

"Well—" Alder met my eyes and looked away. "I married her."

Matt and Emery stared at Alder in open bafflement. He stared back at them, the expression on his face giving nothing away.

The last time Alder had seen Briar, she had been in the process of confronting her father and the rest of the ealdor council. She didn't want to be bound to that disgraceful-dolt-with-unkempt-hair-and-an-idiotic-smile a moment longer. Also, she had another guy she was into. Afterward, Alder smiled like he'd never been happier to be called a "disgraceful-dolt-with-unkempt-hair-and-an-idiotic-smile" in his life.

"I'm joking," Alder said finally, chuckling. "She dumped me. The ealdors granted her request to annul our binding a while back. Wren's verbal assault really did her in. So, I married Wren instead."

I flicked an olive at his face. "Liar."

"What?" He twitched his fingers, tossing the olive aside with a gust of wind before it hit him. Sometimes, it was incredibly inconvenient having a boyfriend who could manipulate wind.

Emery's eyes bounced between us like she was watching plays at a tennis match. She nudged Matt and grinned. Matt ignored her, but Leslie switched on the lights she had strung across the patio. Emery and Leslie knew Alder and I were dating, but that didn't stop them from practicing their strange matchmaking rituals on us from time to time. Privately, I thought they were conspiring to get us to go to prom together. Like we needed encouragement.

We talked a little longer about our plans for after graduation while the wind made the patio lights dance. Emery didn't know what to do and was planning to stay in Ketchikan. Matt had been accepted at a university in California but hadn't decided about going. Alder planned to keep bouncing back and forth between Ketchikan and Síorghlas as long as the Sylvaen would let him, and I had enrolled in an online art program. None of us, it seemed, really wanted to leave Ketchikan.

Finally, Matt checked his phone and said he needed to go. He bumped Alder's fist and then mine, saying he had family stuff going on and didn't want to miss it. A few minutes later, Leslie put away her yard tools and went inside to watch a movie with Peter. Finally, Emery pushed her chair back from the table and started gathering plates to take inside.

"This was fun," she said. "We should do it again sometime."

"I guess we have a lot of time to make up for. And a lot of snickerdoodles."

"So many snickerdoodles," she laughed. "I'm glad you're back. I'm glad you found your mom too; you'll have to tell me about it when you get the chance."

"I will." I walked her to the sliding glass door and paused. "Hey, thanks for helping me look for her before I went to Síorghlas. I didn't say anything at the time, but your support meant a lot."

"Good, because I was ready to go to jail for you."

"And I'd pay bail."

She set her stack of plates down and gave me a rib-splintering hug. "We're getting sandwiches on Friday. Tell Alder he can bug off if he wants to join. Girls only."

"Girls only," I agreed.

She picked up her dirty plate stack and let herself back into the house. Alder came to stand beside me.

"Ready to go back tomorrow?" Alder asked, reassuring me of his presence with the warm press of his arm against mine.

Alder was planning to accompany me back to Síorghlas. This time, I was supposed to have dinner with his family. As if that wasn't enough to be anxious about, Aster had plans to give me more lessons in magic, plant lore, and yes, dancing. But at least I would get to spend some time doing archery with Alder and Camas.

"I think so," I said.

I looked forward to returning to Síorghlas, but in many ways, Ketchikan was also my home. My heart was always in two places, and now that I knew that about myself, I didn't know how I could ever be content. I didn't know how to make it all last. The world never stopped turning for a minute. I'd lost Mom suddenly, and it still hurt. I was scared of finding myself in that dark place again. Alder seemed to understand some of what I was thinking without even hearing me speak. He picked up my hand, filling the gaps between my fingers with his.

"Come here a minute," he said. "I want to show you this sunset."

I let Alder pull me to the edge of the patio. I even let him squish my cheeks to point my gaze in the right direction. Like I didn't know where to look to find the giant blazing fireball hovering in the sky.

"I bet you don't have sunsets like this where you come from," Alder said, putting his arm around me.

Deep purple clouds clustered over the horizon. The mountains were lit with alpenglow. I could feel the tree roots beating out their heartbeat melody as they churned and stretched beneath my feet. I greeted the forest like an old friend, thinking of how Mom must have done the same.

"I came from here, weirdo," I reminded him.

"I mean after that. When you lived in Cali."

"Right. The place I lived for eight months." I snuggled up closer, enjoying his warmth. "Ever heard of Huntington Beach? Santa Monica Pier?"

"But this is an Alaskan sunset. That makes it better."

I laughed at his logic. "How is it better? More trees and mountains to block the view?"

"I'll show you."

He cupped my chin and tilted it upwards. I stretched up to meet him halfway. The zing of his shape-gift was like a small fire on my lips, making them tingle. I locked my arms around his neck and pulled him still closer. He might have had a point to prove about sunsets, but I wasn't done kissing him yet.

"Now you understand?" Alder chin-pointed toward the sunset. "It's better because it's ours—the one we're experiencing right now."

I stared at Alder, trying to understand. His eyes were almost yellow in the glow of the patio lights, a shade between sunset gold and chlorophyll. Mom's parting words came back to me, both filling me up and making me ache.

This is where you belong.

All the people around me enriched my life and made it full, but nobody could replace Mom. Losing her meant that there were still places inside me where shadows crawled. I hoped that one day, spring would come back for me. Moss would creep along the walls I'd constructed to protect myself from hurt, and slowly, it would break them down. Where death and hurt had ravaged my mind, ferns and wildflowers would grow. Light would fill the void. For now, I would try to live enjoying every moment with the people I cared about: the ones in Ketchikan, the ones in Síorghlas, and the ones caught somewhere in between.

Smiling, I reached for Alder's hand and clasped it even tighter than before. *Thanks, Mom. For everything.*

The wind brushed our skin like the deepening of a kiss. It made a longing sound as it swirled in the treetops and traced its paths over the mountains. Brilliant streaks of red and gold shot across the sky, bathing the trees in the last remnants of daylight. The spring air was brisk, but with Alder's warm hand in mine, it was better than a dream. It was the sort of day that made me want to keep on living. No matter how dark the days became, there was hope.

I wasn't alone.

ACKNOWLEDGEMENTS

When I first started writing the story that would one day become *Betwixt*, I was still in high school. I put the unfinished manuscript aside for a few years before completing my first draft in 2016. At that point, writing felt like a solitary experience. But as I look back, I'm astounded by the kindness and support I've received along the way.

To Lauren, thank you for being one of the first people to read that thing I wrote in high school that later became this story. I'm sorry Emery doesn't have throw pillows in her car anymore. I didn't realize that it wasn't a thing people did, and now I do.

Ariella, you read multiple early drafts of *Betwixt* and still stayed friends with me. I am barely resisting the urge to apologize yet again for subjecting you to the horrors. I'm wildly thankful for your friendship!

Thanks to my friend and critique partner, A.J. Wilcox, for celebrating with me, encouraging me, and for sharing your own beautiful stories. I'm so glad you came up and talked to me at SWWC, even though I was lurking in a corner and probably hunched over a sandwich.

Madame Publisher, AJ Skelly, thank you for believing in *Betwixt* and for this incredible opportunity to get it into the hands of readers. And thank you for your patience as I asked my 75,000,000 questions. I'm blessed beyond words.

Huge thanks to my editors, Brittany Eden and Stephany Araujo, for the time and toil you spent getting my book up to snuff. You took my words and made them shine!

To my Q&F fam. I'm not as big a fan of Oreos as the rest of you, but I'm 100% with you on the matter of pickles. Thanks for always making me cackle.

EmaLee, your gorgeous artwork is everything! Thank you for bringing Wren and Alder to life and for giving them so many beautiful details inspired by Southeast Alaska.

To my family: Mom, for your love and support, and for teaching me to always eat my vegetables. Kyle, for the work you did on creating my crazy-beautiful author website! To my little girl Chloe, for loving Mommy in the way that only you can and for my first ever glowing book review.

These acknowledgements wouldn't be complete without thanking Nick, my cute husband and partner in crime—and innocence. I'm not sorry for ignoring your suggestion to kill off Alder, but the rest of your suggestions helped make *Betwixt* what it is. I'm so glad that we're in this life thing together.

Lastly, to Jesus, the greatest storyteller of all. Thank you for life, for beauty, and for the words to express it all. Even when the days are dark, you are my hope.

AUTHOR'S NOTE

When I first started writing about the Sylvaen, I took inspiration from J.R.R. Tolkien's description of the Rangers of Ithilien in *The Two Towers*. Tolkien portrays the men as cloaked in green and brown, armed with bows, and having bright eyes.

As I wrote, however, the Sylvaen took on an identity of their own. Their language and cultural symbols became heavily inspired by Irish culture. Some of their customs are like what you might see among the Amish communities of North America. And their magic, which began as very plant-centric, evolved into a broader, element-based system.

But as I worked on this story and spent time studying Ketchikan, I became increasingly aware of the diverse array of real people living in the region. The Tlingit, Haida, and Tsimshian people have called Southeast Alaska home since time immemorial. So, it became a goal of mine not just to acknowledge Indigenous presence but also to honor it.

In *Betwixt*, Alder briefly describes a history of peaceful interactions between the Sylvaen and the Indigenous people of the region. He goes on to speak of Indigenous influence on Sylvaen culture as well as the continued allyship between people groups. This, of course, contrasts with the way Sylvaen struggle to accept Outlanders, and particularly those of mixed heritage.

Like most people groups, the Sylvaen have noble ideals but struggle to live up to them. They get some things right and others wrong. Their struggle is symbolic of the way that we, as humans, tend to accept some and push others outside the realm of belonging.

At the end of the day, *Betwixt* is about hospitality. It's about our human need to belong. It's about the ways that we have the capacity for kindness and for hate. It is my attempt to imagine what should have been, what is, and what we can work toward to make a better future.

ABOUT THE AUTHOR

Kimberly writes stories about dark forests, elemental magic, and sandwiches. She was a finalist in the 2023 Aurora Contest by Realm Makers for *Betwixt*, and she has had a short story featured in the *Seasons of Romantasy: Summer* anthology.

Kimberly writes a quarterly newsletter about books, forest plants, and whatever else strikes her fancy. You can sign up at kdunham.substack.com.

Currently, she lives in the rainy Pacific Northwest with her husband and daughter and has turned into a coffee snob because of it. The coffee is necessary as she balances writing with homeschooling her daughter and working on a creative writing degree at Central Washington University. When she has a little downtime, which is never, she enjoys forest hikes, fawning over houseplants, trying to decorate cakes, archery, camping, and playing guitar. Betwixt is her debut novel.